Faster Horses

Faster Horses

JUDITH CLAYTON VAN

atmosphere press

© 2022 Judith Clayton Van

Published by Atmosphere Press

Cover design by Kevin Stone

Faster Horses is a work of fiction, and any resemblances to persons living or dead are unintended. Names, characters, places, events, and incidents either are the product of the authors imagination or are used fictitiously. Best stated by Thomas Wolfe in the reader's notes of *Look Homeward Angel*. He wrote . . . "this book is a fiction, and that he [Wolfe] meditated no man's [or woman's] portrait here."

atmospherepress.com

To Andrea and Barbara

Nothing gold can stay . . .
    - Robert Frost

Table of Contents

CHAPTER 1 3
In 1999 Annie Hunts for Missing Pieces While in 1948 she is Stuck at the House on the Hill When Her Mother Becomes a Rodeo Star

CHAPTER 2 24
What Befalls Annie on the Day of Her Uncle Jack's 21st Birthday Party

CHAPTER 3 39
How Annie Recovers and Finds True Love Rodeoing with Linda

CHAPTER 4 52
What Annie Finds at the Ranch and How It Solves Almost All Her Problems

CHAPTER 5 59
Annie's Alarming Adventures at the 1951 Emerald City Chamber of Commerce Rodeo and What Happens When She Meets a Man Who Will Change Her Life

CHAPTER 6 83
How Annie's Search for Money and Dresses Lead to Her Biggest Adventure Yet

CHAPTER 7 100
In 1999 Jim is Delayed, While in 1953 Annie Flies to New York City to Meet Her Father and Arrange for Bud to Marry Linda, Star of the Madison Square Garden Rodeo

CHAPTER 8 121

In a New World Linda has a Fall, While Annie Ventures Underground, then Discovers Alfredo Sauce but Begins to Fear the World May Not Follow Her Plans

CHAPTER 9 132

With Aching Feet Annie Sails to the Statue of Liberty Where She Loses Margo, Befriends a White Russian, and Learns Mam is a Possible Dictator

CHAPTER 10 146

In the Search for Bud, Annie's Dancing Shoes Lead her Underground Once More

CHAPTER 11 160

The Roy and Dale Episode and What Happens to Annie

CHAPTER 12 165

The Party Where Annie Meets her East Coast Family and Inflames Linda's Passions

CHAPTER 13 178

How Annie Learns There is no Place Like Home

CHAPTER 14 183

In 1999, Jim has a Drama in Texas, While in 1954, Annie has a Chance

CHAPTER 15 214

Annie's Encounter with the Real World: 1954

CHAPTER 16 218

What Happens to Annie When Linda Abdicates her Rodeo Throne?

CHAPTER 17 226
About Margie: 1957

CHAPTER 18 237
Annie Goes Underground for Good

CHAPTER 19 253
What the White Diary Reveals

CHAPTER 20 268
How the White Diary Ends, and
What Annie Learns About Ron and Margie

CHAPTER 21 287
In 1999 Annie Makes Linda an Offer,
While in 1958 She Meets Gabe

CHAPTER 22 318
What's Wrong Now?

CHAPTER 23 336
Big Red Makes a Mistake and Annie Escapes with Billy

CHAPTER 24 348
Annie Attends the Ancestral Reunion
in the Dappled Shade

CHAPTER 25 367
Annie and Billy Call on a Natural Beauty

CHAPTER 26 374
In 1959, a Consequence of Annie's Misconduct
Brings Uncle Jack to the Rescue, While in 1999,
Annie Makes a Fateful Decision

Chapter 1

IN 1999 ANNIE HUNTS FOR MISSING PIECES WHILE IN 1948 SHE IS STUCK AT THE HOUSE ON THE HILL WHEN HER MOTHER BECOMES A RODEO STAR

THE ARMITAGE HOUSE, EMERALD CITY, OREGON, MAY, 1999

The first time I wondered who assigned people to their particular places on earth I was three years old. It was soon apparent that unlike all previous generations of babies, I was the one who did not like to try new food without first seeing if the dog would eat it, did not believe what I was told without looking into it for myself, refused to wear proper clothes unless I found them comfy. I insisted on questioning everything. According to Uncle Jack, I was a once in a blue moon freak, a black sheep, the cracked pot in the family scheme. At four, my tentative theory was that someone somewhere gave out parents and houses to each new being, and when it was my turn, they'd had their minds on other things.

Over fifty years later, looking out my bedroom window at the big walnut tree and line of hills beyond the ranch house, I still wondered. How had I come to this place, to these people? They were so full of certainty and I, of doubt. I felt a total alien.

Mam, my grandmother, had always affirmed this and more. She said I was bound to be bad because of some sin of my father's. A sin she would never reveal.

A small red cedar box sat on the dresser under the window at Armitage House. While it is in our bodies that we store our histories, I had also tried to save moments in little boxes. At six years old, I had arrived at the ranch carrying a suitcase holding all my clothes and three matchboxes I had retrieved from Uncle Jack's wastebasket. Seeing these items and having them near I could reexperience the luxury of purple as I had when I'd placed dried pansy faces and a leaf in one, a gleaming penny and dirt from behind the house on the hill in another and filled the third with tiny blue flowers from the hilltop, their fragrance gentle as my mother's breath. I had stacked the boxes in a corner of my dresser drawer and unpacked my clothes around them. When I was nine, I had placed the cedar box beside them. Coiled inside it is a wave of bright chestnut mane tied with blue ribbon and a folded ten-dollar bill.

Turning from the window, I encountered a cubist design, a welter of packing boxes choking the doorway. Their sharp angles made me consider the choices that had brought me to this time and place. Jim, my husband, kept to his "your mother has a secret" theory. He was sure we could not understand the puzzle because we didn't all see the same picture, and even if we did, key pieces were missing. As for my mother, whose actions I was attempting to understand, there may have been no one secret that altered her life, maybe only moments that I could never know, none carefully stored in any container, just lost in the black hole of her mind. Trying to puzzle it out, I found not clarity but a feeling, a tremendous, sucking force concealing truth that overrode my power to understand. Soon, I had to put aside the mystery of *why* and decide *what* to do with the boxes holding a lifetime of accumulated possessions.

FASTER HORSES

*

THE HOUSE ON THE HILL, EMERALD CITY, OREGON, 1948

Molecules, alive since the moment of creation, reside in our blood and bones, exist in the shining eye of the swift horse running beneath the moon. Still, we cannot penetrate the miracle of attraction that creates new spirits in a dying world.

Each of us carry within our genes the seeds of all life: stretch us on the harp of the universe to the highest, coldest note, and there remains, waiting on its trembling edge, the alchemical magic from which a child is thrown through time to land in a north country valley ripe to accept her. Yet, the seed of her destruction is also buried, waiting to blossom from the hills overlooking that valley. Her life is haunted by English and Irish who were born and died on another northern shore in another time, caring not for the child, yet living within her, passing freely through time, her blood their window on her morning world.

My name is Antonia Rose Butler. I was born during the final hours of the Second World War in a wide Oregon valley laced with green rivers. From the first, I seemed to sense the presence of my pioneering ancestors. Forever there, looking down on me from a somehow exalted past with a tut-tut of regret, as if I had arrived at their party inappropriately outfitted, braids coming undone, with scuffed cowboy boots, and without invitation. Worse, I had apparently appeared without regard for my mother's plans, and certainly not my grandparents' plan for their only daughter.

Nine months after their wedding, while my father was in an Italian hospital recovering from a battle wound, I had invaded my grandparents' house at 22 Sunrise Drive, Emerald City, Oregon. Set high on the hill behind the university and grounded on a steep bank among tall fir and pine, its sparkling, leaded windows looked out on the town and valley. I valued each gray-green shingle of the Tudor cottage, cherished all nooks and crannies, and formed affections for each step and stone of its paths. The flowering bushes under the windows and in the side yard often held me spellbound, but the grand swaying trees, many of which I named, were my real loves.

A family portrait, an image of what I think of as the "before time," would show me at the house on the hill with Mam and Granddad; my mother, Linda; Linda's brother, Uncle Jack; two bird dogs, Spike and Buddy; and a yellow canary my grandmother named Tweety. We'd be standing in front of the big Emerald City map in Grandad's office. It would show the house on the hill at the top of the map, with a red line heading south indicating the road Granddad drove twice a day to feed the small herd of horses we kept at the fairgrounds on the edge of town.

A blown-up picture of the fairgrounds would show the glassed-in Hunt Club meeting room perched above the indoor arena, the scene of my many riding lessons. When I wasn't riding, I often stood at the big windows watching people work their horses, and on Monday nights I'd go with Grandad and watch him gallop around the circle with the mounted posse drill team to the Stars and Stripes march. Most thrilling were the spring shows where my mother made star performances in the dressy English classes accompanied by beautiful organ music.

Inside the clubhouse, you'd see Mam, always in a nice dress and high heels, with bright red lipstick, red hair rolled high, wearing her new pointy glasses, ruling not only the Emerald Valley Fairgrounds office but the clubhouse kitchen, the refreshment sign-up sheet, and almost anything else that crossed her path. A dark corner of the picture would show the basement of the house on the hill where my grouchy Uncle

Jack had a bunkroom for his high bouncing buddies by the sawdust-burning furnace that caused the whole house to smell of wood.

*

The story begins with a racket, a commotion which should have warned that my impending journey might not be graceful. I was just four years old that morning, but according to my grandmother I was far too old for my age, and way too big for my britches. It was early spring, and so bright outside that I thought the pansies had caused the light. If Granddad had not planted quite so many, their faces shining along the front walk, it wouldn't have been so bright that the morning hurt my eyes. I was running across the sunny carpet toward the front door that was closing as my mother left the house. If I could run fast enough, I could catch her and convince her to stay.

"Mommy, please, please, don't go," I'd cried.

For days, I had suspected my mother was leaving because I knew the signs. The first was when she stored the black Singer in the closet. Then, I had to be very quiet while she sat for hours beading gauzy sleeves designed to billow in the wind as she raced her horse around the rodeo arena. Listening to the whoosh of Mam's iron steaming the purple body of the new costume, an interior voice, shrill as the rodeo announcers, had shouted: *She's going to take Lady and leave.* I had ignored the voice because I didn't want it to be true.

At my renewed sobbing, my grandmother had practically pushed my mother through the door.

"Just don't pay any attention to her, Linda. It'll only make her worse." Mam looked back, shot me the snake stare and slammed the door.

"Let me say good-bye," I howled, darting between Mam's

legs yelling, "Please, please! Mommy, don't leave me with her." Mam's hand flashed off her hip in a powerful swipe at the top of my head.

I bolted for the sofa in front of the window and leapt to its back. My foot had nearly connected with the glass when Mam lunged from behind and tore me from the frantic child reflected in the window.

I fell, screaming, "Mommy, Mommy, come back," thumping my head on the arm of the sofa.

"Get away from there—now! Why would she ever want to come back to this?" Leaning over me, red lip raised high, Mam sneered, "Look at you, screaming like a banshee. Just shut right up, or I'll give you a reason to howl, by God." She glared me down and pinned my arm behind me, her large bosom seeming to rise and fall like waves with her efforts. I tried jerking away, but I was as battered by the skirmish as she and no longer screaming, but sobbing, and teeth bared, glaring back. Our eyes locked when we heard the Chevy shift into gear and start down the driveway. When the car disappeared, she let go of my arms.

Now, my mother was gone, and I had to face Mam. Alone. I couldn't stand to be under her thumb; I hated it, and in that moment, watching her little high heels stomp into her office, I hated her. Accompanied by the racket of Mam's typewriter then the ringing of the telephone, I trailed up the wide stairs to the bedroom that my mother and I shared. *Had shared.* She wouldn't be there to tuck me in or protect me from Uncle Jack who, from the time of my first memories, had been out to get me any way he could. She wouldn't be there for prayers or to keep Mam from force-feeding me liver or rhubarb, which always made me gag and started a fight. *No more rides together along the leafy creek. There was no one for me now, only the dogs and my trees.*

I crawled on the bed and reached inside my pillowcase for the hankie I had snuck from her purse that morning. Inhaling her smell, crying myself into silence, I lay staring out the window at the tree I'd named Walter. It's whispering presence calmed me, and I gazed at the branches swaying against the spring sky until the light moved slowly off the trunk and fresh rain bounced onto the leaves.

I finally stuffed the wet hankie back in the pillowcase, rose and wandered into the kitchen to find Mam at the stove, enveloped in steam, stirring something in a large pot. Spike, Uncle Jack's brown and white spaniel, sat at the door with his tongue hanging out.

"Why don't you take Spike out, Annie? It'll do you both good."

That morning, Granddad had let Buddy go with him in the green truck but not me and Spike. They would go to the fairgrounds to feed the horses, then into town and the bank by way of the donut shop, and I always wanted to go too. Mam wiped her hands on her apron and handed me my yellow raincoat. Her small hand reached for the doorknob and with the other she scooted me out. "Stay off the top of the hill," she said.

On the porch, I stuffed my feet into my new rubber boots and went off with Spike. Under a mist of rain, we worked our way up steep banks of gold grass and bare branches: me trudging up the hill, getting used to my new boots which according to Mam were big enough to grow into, he bounding after rabbits, sniffing every hole.

At the crest of the muddy trail to the river, I sat crying in the thin sunshine. I was alone but for the dog sitting beside me watching the birds flit about, occasionally swooping earthward to peck at tiny seeds. Bare legs splayed in the wet dirt, I made mud pies for my mother, and even though she wasn't there to enjoy them, I decorated the pies with tiny blue flowers that grew in round patches on the hilltop. Looking out over the town, its foggy outlines receding into the mountains, time seemed to stretch into a gray forever, a dark loneliness punctuated with black torments that I did not want to imagine. *Why did she go off like that and leave me alone again? Didn't she know how mean Mam was? She knew Uncle Jack kicked me because she saw him. Didn't she care?* Through tears I looked up to see Spike, head cocked, long eyelashes shading his eyes. I was so full of dreadful feelings, I reached out and yanked his ear. At his yelp, the astonished hurt in his eyes, I threw my arms around his wet neck and sobbed.

Several days later, days during which steady rain had kept me hiding under the bed with the phone, listening on the party line for hours, Mam saw promise of sunshine and sent me outside.

"I can't watch you! I have too much to do to get ready for this shindig to watch you too!" Then, she added that not only was I a mess, but given my wicked reputation as a liar and a troublemaker, she couldn't find a single soul willing to keep me—even for money! Worse, Spike still wouldn't play with me but hung in the corner and tried to be invisible when he saw me coming.

The rain had finally stopped and again that morning Granddad had let Buddy go to town but not me and Spike. When I complained, Mam said it was a big day for Granddad and she didn't want me pestering him. "Your grandad's an important man in this town, Miss," she said, hanging the broom on its hook. "He's a State Commissioner now. They're going to get this town back on track and plan all the new roads in the state! That's a big, big job. You better steer clear and quit being a nuisance. I mean it," she said, eyes narrowing. "You steer clear."

No horses. No maple bars. Just Mam. After the green truck had disappeared down the hill and I was sure he wouldn't come back for me, I dressed in my yellow raincoat and new rain boots and left the house by the basement door. Under a lowering sky, the stiff spring breeze blowing hair in my eyes, I slogged to the top of the hill where large machines had been digging the foundation for a new house. A house that Mam claimed would ruin the neighborhood.

"C'mon, Spike!" I yelled as he bounced down the hill. Remembering the look in his eyes when I'd yanked his ear, I felt like crying again. I was deeply ashamed of my meanness but seeing no immediate remedy shook my head and continued toward the silver sky over the hilltop.

Pushing my boots through short yellow grass that finally turned to mud, I arrived at the rim of an enormous mud-filled pit, water glittering thinly on its surface. Intending to see why Mam had predicted ruin, and why they had to dig such a wide, deep hole, I was stepping closer when my boot slipped. With a sucking thump, I slid into the muck on my behind. I tried jacking my heels into the slick wall but only lurched forward and deeper. With slimy hands, I struck out for something to hold onto but as the mud swallowed my boots, I sank along with them. Wildly testing for hard places, my splayed hands descended further, legs treading into the mire oozing over my belly.

I closed my eyes, took a breath, then raised my head and opened them. Above me, dark clouds thickened, their underbellies blue-black, their tops gray feathers across the silver sky. The mysterious beauty of the skies made me forget my predicament for a moment. Bone-splitting cold snapped me back. "Spike! Help!" I shouted, flailing through the sea of mud for the edge but only sinking deeper, to the middle of my chest. After redoubling my yelling, I was so worn out the air left my lungs and strength left my arms. "Please save me. Please," I begged Great Aunt Elsie's God who, according to her, was my real father and saw everything I did. With all my strength, I screamed "Please!" at the darkening sky.

It seemed to happen instantly. With a clash of brush, then a booming "Hallow?" the neighbor boy burst from the brambles at the foot of the hill. Tony, one of the big kids, was Doc Barton and Jo's oldest. Handsome and brown-haired with freckles and bright white teeth, he was always drawing cartoons of people with huge heads and tiny bodies that made me laugh. When I realized he was there to save me, I held back tears of relief, and hid my complete adoration and gratitude.

Instead, I'd squawked, "C'mon! Let's get me outa here," then hooted with laughter.

Throwing off his jacket, he wrestled a branch from a small tree then with much grunting and effort held it out and hauled me up.

I heard myself pop from the mud when Tony grabbed the neck of my coat then tortured sucking sounds as he hauled me onto solid ground. My boots and pants were history, the yellow raincoat not only slimed but pierced by the rocky soil. I had one sock on, which was covered in mud. The other foot was bare—except for the mud, which clung to my body and dripped from my hair. Rubbing my filthy hands together to warm up, I couldn't feel them. They were numb with cold, covered with sludge and spotted with blood from clutching the branch.

Thick clots of mud scalloped Tony's pants and shoes and splashed our legs as we made our way to the edge of the road.

"Don't tell your mom, Tony." Even as I said it, wiping my eyes with a dripping arm, I knew I didn't have to warn him. He already knew what would happen if Mam found out.

Above us on the hilltop, wind soughed along the ground and raindrops began to fall. Shaking, slimed, blue-lipped, I raced home hoping to arrive before my grandmother missed me. And, although I knew I must not talk about what had happened, I wished very much that I could tell someone about being saved. *Was it really Aunt Elsie's God who saved me? I had definitely asked, but who had answered?*

No one but Spike was at the house to see me run barefoot down the basement steps, leaving muddy footprints on the cold stones. I was so happy to see him that I reached out.

He leaned away, pulling his head from my hand. Spike and I had become best friends when we were both babies. We recognized early that both of us had to stay alert to Uncle Jack and Mam's moods, and that we both needed someone to play with. The loss of his friendship would be unbearable.

"Spikey, I am sooo sorry. I am so sorry, boy," I whispered, consoling him and myself until he finally let me pet his head. He followed me to the basement door but still wouldn't come inside. Throwing my filthy clothes into the iron sink, I climbed in on top of them, and turned on the icy water. After scrubbing my body with the clothes brush then rinsing myself until I couldn't see dirt, I turned off the water and climbed out of the sink. Too cold even to shake, I hid my wet clothes under Uncle Jack's work pants then dressed from the dirty clothes basket and hurried upstairs without being caught. Mam never did miss my rubber boots, or if she did, she didn't say.

*

That night at bedtime, I was still trying to warm up. Surveying me with covers clutched to my chin, Mam handed me the hot water bottle and stood over me, small hands clenched on her hips asking why I was so cold. "That's all we need," she said, pulling up another blanket and stabbing it around me. "You'd better not be getting sick. We don't have time." She left the room and turned off the upstairs lights.

Finally, warm in my covers, my toes on the hot water bottle, I listened to her hurry down the stairs but soon became aware of a change in the usual goings on. Most nights the tall radio in the living room played softly, quiet talk and good smells drifted upwards making it feel nice to be in bed. That night, despite being saved, and considering Aunt Elsie's God— who I now suspected may have been my helper—there was something wrong. I could hear the rise and fall of voices through the hallway vent but couldn't make out the words. They hardly ever went into the kitchen after supper, but it seemed to be coming from there.

If Uncle Jack caught me on the landing that was our perpetual battleground, I would be in serious danger, but I tiptoed to my door and looked through the keyhole anyway. Seeing no light under his door, I dashed across the landing and crept down the stairs. Straining to hear Granddad's muffled words, I crossed the hall and placed my ear against the kitchen door. Inside, Mam was walking back and forth, hard heels smacking the tile. Granddad mumbled something and Uncle Jack replied, "It's probably just broken bones." From his tone, I could tell he was not unhappy about the situation. "They said they'd call back if she was bad." His words trailed off as if he had something in his mouth.

"I don't care, Jack!" Mam said in a voice that could sear meat. "You're going with Daddy. You'll drive her rig and bring the horse back. If you leave now, you'll be there before morning." Then sounds like pan lids being put away; "We can get her to Holy Heart and have Doc admit her by noon. Get whatever you're taking *now* because when this food's packed, you're on the road."

Mam using her mad voice with Uncle Jack or Granddad was not right. She usually saved that voice for the dogs and me. *What was going on?* When heavy footsteps approached the door, I ran for the stairs and slid under my covers before Uncle Jack arrived on the landing.

At my door, he said softly so only I could hear, "You're gonna git it now, brat. She's gonna run out on you but good." He rattled my doorknob. "She's cracked open and she's never coming back. Hear? Now, you'll quit your sneaking and lying, and *I'll* be the one to make sure of it." He turned the knob hard.

Body rigid, eyes on the band of light under the door where two foot-like shadows smudged the glow, I lay still as one of

Mam's roasted chickens. *A dead chicken, like Uncle Jack would like me to be.* He often threatened to kill me and leave me out for the wild dogs to eat, so when my mother was gone, I had to be very careful to stay clear of him. I did sass him occasionally, but I never knew what terrible things I'd done, things apparently so bad that he was required by someone or something to catch me and punish me. Later, I'd try to remember to look by the door and make sure he hadn't left anything. He would bring cookies and sometimes money from downstairs and push it under my door. When Mam came up to go to bed and found it, he'd say, "Annie just keeps dragging this stuff up here." *But I didn't. I didn't do it so why did he say it?* I always wanted to be out of his way because if I was in his way, and no one was looking, he might kick me. But, worse even than the kicking was the whispering voice on the stairs.

Turning to the dark tree shapes outside my window, I inhaled, then again, holding each breath until the ache grew too big and I had to let go. I remained motionless and breathing deeply for what seemed a long time, trying to imagine what I'd do if the door opened. The floor creaked. I heard him on the steps, and then no more. Finally, reassured that he wasn't coming, I stood on the mattress and turned the latch on the long window. Outside, the moon silvered my tree, and inside set gray limbs and leaves across the blanket. The cold scent of camellias drifted in the silence enclosing the yard where the orange cat sat, cream-colored, in the moonlight. His head flashed up at the hoot of an owl sailing into the neighbor's tree. Wrapped in covers, head resting on the windowsill, I gazed through Walter's branches at the stars.

My body seemed to float out into the night, and away, beyond the river and town. With no company but the winking stars, I sailed over mountains and fields. Abruptly, I saw daylight; the light exploding into brilliant sunshine beating down on a gold field, that I somehow knew would be hard and dry as bone. The thumping of horses' hooves on the ground; a group of ceremonially dressed Indians riding black and brown spotted ponies through a circle of tents. I recognized Crawfordsville, Oregon, and the famous rodeo grounds where I had seen my mother ride. Floating above the tepees, I smelled smoke, and looked through an opening. Below, a group of women in white and cream buckskins, all beaded and fringed, ornamented each other's hair. I could somehow see the women's thoughts and knew they were preparing for a dance. The smell of smoke was stronger as I drifted toward a wooden pen where shouting cowboys were branding calves. The choking scents of burning hair and flesh hurt my nose and my ears rang with the harsh calls and grunts of the cowboys as they threw the calves to earth. I was alone looking through a fence and the cows were crying. Everyone was busy and no one noticed me. Vaguely sorry that I couldn't help the calves, I moved back toward the tepee with the smoke rising from the top.

A terrified, ululating scream tore across the campground, and I knew it was my mother. As if in reply, a big whoosh of the audience releasing its breath rose from the sun-washed bleachers, and I was floating over the arena where the horse was running away with her. Wearing the new purple costume with sleeves like silver wings, her foot was caught in the stirrup, the horse was dragging her around the track striking her arms and head with flying iron-shod feet, and the Indians were preparing to dance, and my mother was still in the dirt, and the horse was stepping on her red hair. My grandmother appeared, mouth stretched in a scream, but no sound came. She was running toward a small white hospital house when I heard my mother's body hit the dirt. Somehow, and with certainty, I knew by the sound that the fall had not, and would not, kill her. I thought, *If you'd stayed home, it wouldn't have happened.* But she wasn't dead.

I must have fallen asleep because there the vision ends, and I have no further memory of the events on the hard gold rodeo ground. Did I close the window? Maybe my grandmother closed it because when I woke, it was bright sunshine outside, the window was shut, and the house was very quiet. I scrambled from bed and rushed downstairs.

My grandmother stood at the kitchen sink peeling apples, her whole body jiggling with effort. When I approached, she shoved a wet apple slice at me. "Eat this. I'll fix something in a minute."

"She didn't die and she's not going to," I said.

My grandmother swung around with a face I'd not yet seen. Towering over me, it was like a "mad" face, but the eyebrows tented upwards in a questioning arc that didn't fit her mouth, which was drawn up like a bad cherry.

"Well," I said, "I already know she didn't die." At that age, I simply accepted what I knew and didn't worry about how the knowing came.

Mam bent at the waist, cupped an apple-cold hand under my chin, and yanked my face up. "You'd better be very nice to her when she does come home, or she will die."

"She won't die."

"The doctor says it's bad. And they don't know when she's coming home. And you don't know as much as you think!" She sniffed and wiped her other hand across a powdered cheek. "You better be very, *very* nice to her, or she won't want to get better."

"That's not true."

She let go of my chin and slapped me, the sound exploding in the quiet kitchen. The blow didn't quite knock me down but caused my eyes to water and my head to go dark.

"I'm gonna tell Granddad. I'm gonna tell my mom," I screamed, reeling backward.

She scrambled for the pancake turner. I ran. Right into

Spike. Squatting to back away, his toenails lost purchase on the slick linoleum, sending us falling together, a squirming, squealing knot, at her feet.

Mam grabbed my arm and jerked me off the floor, slashing the slotted metal across my legs. I was kicking frantically, landing some pretty solid blows too, but she was stronger than me and even more furious. I fought her with all the muscle I had, but it wasn't enough. After the whipping, and screaming, the dog peeing in fear, me sobbing and slapping back, she heaved Spike out the door, dropped unsteadily on a kitchen chair, and hauled me onto her lap. I suspected that if I said what I wanted, she might hit me over the head and throw me out with the dog. *She could even kill me.*

She gathered my arms and legs as she did yarn to knit, tying me to her until my shrieking and thrashing subsided. Exhausted, I decided to yield for the moment and let her think she had won. I tried to relax against her, but the plump softness of her body made me want to tear into her as she had done to my legs with the pancake turner's metal edge. At four, I may still have wanted to lean against her in love but what I felt was rage, rage so overpowering that only by reining it in could I survive her. I couldn't lean against her in love, so I leaned against her in secret and terrible rebellion, rebellion and withdrawal which seemed instinctive.

That morning in the warm kitchen imprisoned on her lap, not trying to stifle my sobs, she began. "I'll tell you a story. I'll tell you what it was like in the mountains when *I* was a little girl."

These were stories of pioneers and Indians, forests and loggers, horses and hunting dogs, the legends of the Woodwards, her famous pioneer family. I always begged to hear them, but even at four knew it was unfair of her to offer a bribe while holding me prisoner. That morning, her offer only made me more convinced and furious. She had a strangling grip on my arms and legs making it impossible to move or wipe my nose, so I gave a grudging nod. She settled against the chair, causing my outside arm to dangle from the vice of her clutch and begin to grow numb.

"Do you remember me telling you about Snooks, my school horse?"

Eyes fixed on the tree outside the kitchen window, I tried to wiggle away. I did remember Snooks but liked to hear about the dogs too, especially Music, her dad's best cougar hunting dog, and Silly, the pet deer. Her stories were about her family who owned whole mountains of trees they hunted in and logged with horses and big machines they called donkeys. Mam always boasted that through the family logging camps and the mill business, they knew everyone in the state. At least everyone worth knowing, Uncle Jack had added.

"That's influence," she had said with a lift of her chin.

That morning, with all the power and intent of a draft horse pulling a plow she surged onward with her story, describing the high mountains of her childhood, how she had risen on splendid mornings, breakfasted on cold cornbread with warm milk fresh from the cow then jumped on her horse. She said not only had she ridden Snooks to school, but unlike some worthless people she could name, she had had a paying job delivering the mail.

"I was only a few years older than you are now. That job took some doin' too. It was wilderness then. No stores or gas stations on every corner, that's for sure. Riding those trails, I could imagine critters—cougars mainly, but bears too—sneaking up and pouncing, and Snooks could too." She lowered her voice. "He'd be sniffing the breeze, his ears twitching back and forth." She lifted her head, hazel eyes moving back and forth like she was peering about the forest. "But times were too good, and mornings too dear to let anything scare us for long."

Dipping her head in emphasis, a gold earring shifted, revealing an angry mark on her earlobe. "Snooks was black as night, with a white star on his forehead." Her fingertip touched between my eyes then she reached up, removed her earring, and slipped it into her pocket. "And small, like he'd meant to be a bigger horse and hadn't quite made it. He had trim, tidy legs, and tiny feet hard as flint. Oh, I loved him," she said.

On hearing her say she loved her horse, my resolve against her softened--a little.

"That morning, we'd just entered a green clearing. We were going along quietly under tall trees, when Snooks stopped in his tracks. In an instant, a doe broke cover and leapt across the trail, headed for the river. The pony quivered, but stood motionless, his ears sharply forward when a big wolf came silently into view, running hard. As it reached the trail it saw us and stopped dead not more than twenty feet away."

I looked up at her then. As if reading my thoughts, she said, "About as far as the front door to the driveway."

Pretty close for a wolf, I had thought, impressed. I made a sour face and turned my gaze to the driveway where there was neither a wolf nor my mother's car.

"It sent chills up the back of my neck and caused me to forget the emergency gun Daddy made me holster under my knee. The lord of the mountain, he just curled his lip and was gone, still on the track of that doe. Not a sound was made, and we sat there frozen for a couple of minutes waiting to see if he was a lone hunter or if there were more wolves behind him. On the ride home, I thought what a good horse Snooks was." She shifted in the chair and twisted around, trying again to make me look at her. "What would have happened to me, do you suppose, if Snooks had thrown a fit? What if he'd spooked and bucked me off or tore off through the trees?"

I shook my head.

"Well, that's why I loved that old horse; I was always safe on him."

When she finally let me down, I hurried to the bathroom, hauled my tooth-brushing stool to the sink, and climbed up. I splashed water on my hand-printed face and all over the floor. Considering my welting cheek, mauled legs, and Mam's story, I thought I'd better get a horse like Snooks, so I'd have someone to look out for me.

*

While my mom was in the place they called Holy Heart, each day had seemed an eternity, but I learned later it was only ten days. The morning after Mam's story, I had run downstairs to see if there was news about my mother. Mam had immediately reminded me of the importance of being nice to my mother when she came home. Her line, "You have to be very good, and very nice to your mother. She's had a rough time. If you're not nice to her . . . she won't get better. It could kill her."

Kill her? I could kill her? With my words? By being naughty? Killing people?

When Mam said this, I felt sorry for my mother and mad at her at the same time. I thought the same thing every day: *If she hadn't gone off like that—if she'd stayed home with me—well, then she'd be okay, wouldn't she?* I had worried a lot, wept through breakfasts, lunches, and dinners, and chewed my lip raw because Mam had come up with even more proof of my sins. Selfishly stealing cookies, causing trouble with Uncle Jack, letting the dogs in, getting dirty, getting the whole damn house dirty, lying, being mouthy, eating too much, and looking like a hair-raising mess, these were only a few of my iniquities. The next day and the next, according to Mam, I failed to be nice enough to make my mother well. "You'd best toe the line tomorrow," she'd say, "because today you have let your poor mother down." All of her pronouncements made me mad—then made me cry.

Every night I said a prayer, *Now I Lay Me Down to Sleep*, the only one my mother had taught me, adding a special ending begging Aunt Elsie's God to let me be good enough so that my mother would get well and come home. I stayed awake in the cold nights listening for her to come, fearing she would not, trying to sleep but thinking instead . . . *I should have sunk beneath the mud and died, then I couldn't have failed her and she wouldn't be dying. Even if she does come back, she'll leave again. I'll have to stay here alone. No father to help me. I am no one's best girl, so what am I good for?*

My mother came home from Holy Heart not long after the marks of Mam's pancake turner attack had faded. The day was cold, and her red hair flared in the wind as she hurried up the walk wearing high heels, a dress, and a navy-blue coat that swung around her knees. My grandfather had driven her, and when Mam opened the front door, the whole family, her cousins and some of the neighbors were downstairs waiting to welcome her. Everyone but me.

I was watching from Uncle Jack's upstairs bedroom, where I was never supposed to be. In spite of my constant badness, there she was. Alive . . . moving up the walk, laughing, hair shining, a bright scarf draped over the sling holding her arm. *Had Mam been wrong? According to her I had been very bad. So bad I'd nearly caused my mother to die.*

But she hadn't died, so had the invisible God answered my prayers or did he have reasons of his own for deciding this wasn't her time to die? Since I was now quite sure it must have been Aunt Elsie's God who let me know that she wouldn't die, why had I still worried so? Cried so much? *Why had God, who was supposed to be a good one, made me do all that begging, and on top of it, allowed Mam to get away with lying so forcefully? Being so mean.*

Thinking of what Mam had said about my wickedness, of my many prayers, and Aunt Elsie's God who was supposed to be attending to them, I stood listening to the sounds of greetings, of coats being stored, and such goings on below. I turned from the window and raced down the stairs, right into my mother who was standing at the bottom landing. As my mother's uninjured arm reached for me, Mam stooped to pull me back. I'm still not sure of the exact goad that made me do it because all I had been able to think of for days was having my mother back, of being in her arms.

When she reached out, I hauled off and kicked her in the shin with every ounce of four-year-old strength that I possessed.

Chapter 2

WHAT BEFALLS ANNIE ON THE DAY OF HER UNCLE JACK'S 21ST BIRTHDAY PARTY

THE HOUSE ON THE HILL, EMERALD CITY, FALL 1949

A November morning nearly a year later; I would soon be five. From the kitchen doorframe, I peered into the darkness of the hall behind me and listened. I was hoping to find food before my grandmother took over the kitchen for the day. Instead, I saw my grandparents already standing in the coffee smells, in the buttery sunlight just beyond the open door. I caught Granddad's eye and smiled.

Still in her pretty nightclothes, her back to me, Mam had said, "Take the dogs with you, Daddy. I can't have those mudslingers lounging around making mess after mess. Maude's coming to clean, and I've got the cake to do." One red-tipped hand curled her hip. "Bad enough to have Annie underfoot. She's worse than the dogs."

"You wait, Jessie," he said, winking at me. "This will be just the ticket. The way the town's going, that land will be worth a fortune one day. We all agreed with the Federal plan, and I got it straight from Dan McNaughton at the legislature that we have the votes. It might take a while longer for the whole project to be approved, but they're all talking about it in town—Tom and old man Baker at the bank, the bunch at the Country Club. Federal money. Can't fight it. It's going to mean a lot for the town, the whole valley." He finished his coffee and placed his mug in the sink. "We'll make our money back five times over as soon as they start buying right of way for this new highway—the feds are calling it an interstate, and the fellows in Salem are calling it a freeway." At the back door, he took his hat from the hook and stood holding it. "It's the biggest engineering project the country has seen—except maybe for the dams. They think the whole thing will go on for about fifteen years. Then there will be gas rights, and electric, all on long leases and we can still use the land for pasture and hay. We'll never go wrong with land," he said, grinning. "They aren't making any more of it."

"Well, Daddy," she said as I eased out of the door and watched it swing shut, "if your mind is made up, then that's what we'll do. All that space so close to town suits me." She paused. "Old Lady Tyler will be higher than a kite. She won't have anything to complain about when we're gone. Annie and Spike won't be at her flowers every minute, and she won't be able to beat us up about Jack's truck. What will she do without us?"

Old Lady Tyler and the whole college hill neighborhood had been upset with us recently. This time it wasn't because Spike and I were in her flowers, it was because of my mother's brother, Uncle Jack. According to Mam, the problem was that Uncle Jack had never been a town kid. My mother said he liked to hell around Uncle Blue's ranch with his logger cousins, riding horses, bear hunting and dancing with women in low down dives. I knew that for work, he went into the woods, climbed tall trees and cut off the tops, then other men chopped them down, which killed them dead. Finally, a crew loaded the logs on Jack's truck, and he hauled them to the mill and the mill spit out the boards which were made into people's houses and fences. He did this three times a day, six days a week because he was a gyppo. I heard Great Aunt Maggie say that he was a hardhead, an idealist, too darn independent to work for anyone, especially family. He'd make it on his own or sink. No sucking off the big family tit for him! Just recently, Granddad had bought him a gigantic diesel log truck with huge side horns that sounded like an explosion when it started. He parked it in front of 22 Sunrise Drive every evening. Granddad said it was to give him a start. Uncle Jack started it exactly at 4:00 a.m. each weekday.

Later, that afternoon, after complaining of starvation then having to eat my tuna fish sandwich outside on the porch step, I pushed back inside. Finding the kitchen empty, I had climbed on the chair and stirred up a big cloud of flour left from the cake making. As a fine white layer settled evenly on the clean floor, I apprehended that this could be seen as another criminal act and jumped off the chair to find Mam directly in front of me. She grabbed me by the arms, and squeezing hard, hissed, "Annie. That. Is. Enough."

Avoiding her eyes, I looked at the little crack at the edge of her mouth where bright red lipstick lumped. I could smell Black Jack gum on her hot breath, and she was chewing fast, which meant anything might happen.

"I want to help. I'll be good," I said, trying to squirm away. "I will. I'll just watch."

My grandmother finished the cake frosting with a swirl and handed me the spatula. I licked it clean, not bothering about the chocolate on my hands and face and decided I didn't like birthday parties. *Except maybe my own.*

When I handed back the spatula, she squeezed my arm again as if to plant her resolve in me and turned to the biscuits, punching out biscuit dough with a glass, leaving puffy moon scraps across the board that I immediately stuffed in my mouth.

"GIT!" she hollered and struck out with her hand. She yelled after me, "If I were you, Miss, I would get wise and get up those stairs, and wash those hands."

After crawling lizard-like up the stairs, I slithered into the bathroom and pulled out my red stool, then climbed up to the sink and turned on the faucet. Waiting for warm water, I gazed sideways and into the toilet bowl.

"Toilet," I said. "Toilet," I said louder, accentuating the "let." Then, "toi-let, toi-let," then, "too-let, tou-let," leaning forward to sing in a whisper, "toilet." On a higher, louder note, I bellowed "TOILET." Standing over the bowl singing as loud as I could, I sensed a presence.

Eyes blazing deadly fire, red crown of braids canted haphazardly to one side, Mam's small hand reached for me, but the hand was wet and slipped off, empty. The hard hiss of the pancake turner sliced the air, but I was down the stairs and out the door before she could catch me.

Outside, I crouched behind the white camellia below the dining room window, eyes closed to the stinging sweat, hot cheek against the green shingles, listening with all my being for the sound of pursuit.

Why should I care if I spoil his stupid birthday party? Last night he did it again. He won't quit either. He lies and says he doesn't do it. But it's his voice.

The front door flew open and banged against the house. "Annie," Mam screamed, "ANNIE!" I opened my eyes and tried to make myself smaller. *Okay, who was that? The one who could get smaller? Jack in the Beanstalk? Who became invisible?* I had forgotten. "Be back by dark," Mam hollered. I heard the door slam and peering through the bushes spotted my red sweater on the porch.

As I hurried up the hill shrugging into my sweater, the sun

was almost down, and the late November evening was clear and cold enough that my breath clouded the air. *Everybody will be eating, Everybody but me. When it's time for my birthday dinner I'll just have cakes. Five. When I'm big I'll do what I want all the time, like they do . . . If anybody's mean I won't talk to them anymore. . . at all. Forever!*

I decided to go up the road and see if Marsha could play. I was happier playing with Spike and Buddy, but they had both been invited to go with Granddad that morning. "Bad enough to have Annie underfoot," I heard her say again.

"It's all right, Mother," Granddad had answered. "After lunch, I'm meeting with the real estate fellow at the ranch. We'll sign the papers. The dogs will think they're in heaven. Won't you, Spike?" As I pushed up the hill, I wondered what the dogs would find so wonderful about some papers. Marsha's house was higher on the hill, bigger and fancier than ours but Mam said ours was more genuine. "Better to have the perfect bungalow than an outlandish, made-up castle," was her comment, but Marsha's house did look like the castles in my picture books with tall roofs sticking into the sky. It seemed huge in the failing light but inside it was as boring as Marsha. The house was bare of dogs or even a cat.

At the door, I knocked, then more loudly with the palm of my hand. The three rectangles of glass filled with light, then hurrying footsteps, and Mrs. Solberg opened the door. Enveloped in the smell of warm berry pies, I stared up at Marsha's mother. She was moist and harried looking, a dishtowel slung over one plump shoulder, a parade of dark purple stains crossing her aproned belly.

"Can Marsha play?"

"Oh, no, Annie, it's too late. It's almost time for us to sit down." I liked the way Mrs. Solberg said things. She made everything sound like a question. Mam said that was because she had a Swedish accent. "Does your grandma know you're out?" she asked.

"She told me to come. Can't I just come in and play until dinner?" I leaned through the doorway, trying see up the stairs. "Where's Marsha?"

"Marsha's getting over a cold, so you shouldn't be around her. Now, you best get home," she said. "Come back tomorrow, Annie." Cutting off my protests, she shooed me backward and closed the door. I felt a definite loss as the door shut on the warm pie smells.

Instead of turning toward home, I continued up the hill. I wasn't going home until Mam forgot being mad or Granddad came so she wouldn't start in on me again. Peering up the deeply shadowed lane, I hurried past the ivy-covered bank where the foxes lived to the spot where stone steps cut into the hillside. From a landing at the top, I could see over the neighborhood and spot Granddad's truck when he turned onto our street. Standing before the steps, looking up into the dark trees, I heard the voice echo in my ear:

NOW I'M ON THE FIRST STEP, it said. When I was very little, I had thought it was an alligator coming up the broad carpeted steps of the house. I'd seen a picture of an alligator and was convinced it had to be that . . . that or a scaly-mouthed, people-eating crocodile.

NOW I'M ON THE FOURTH STEP. That's why I could never see anyone at the door of my room, because an alligator would push the door open with its long teethy nose, then slither darkly across the floor and wait under the bed.

NOW I'M ON THE NINTH STEP. I knew Uncle Jack was the alligator. There were twelve broad steps in my house, but nobody ever heard the alligator with Uncle Jack's voice climb them but me. NOW I'M ON THE LAST STEP . . . NOW I'M COMING. Crreeeak . . . the door would make that crying sound then swing the rest of the way silently.

Those first times waiting in the dark for it to get me, I screamed my guts into jagged red blasts that Mam had called bloody murder. Mam and Grandad said it was a bad dream. Poking his burred head around the door, Uncle Jack said I was just a bad girl who was screaming to get attention. He did not tell the truth, which was that my stupid uncle was trying to scare me crazy, then to death, to make me appear even more stupid than he was.

Walking up the hillside steps in the failing light, gawking into the swaying trees at every rustling noise, a page from Aunt Elsie's picture Bible presented itself to me in living color. As Moses stretched his rod over the sea, a kid was herding a bunch of younger children and some sheep through the valley made as the ocean swirled up and parted. Standing among the trees, peering into the dusk, I imagined the Bible scene, pretending to be the kid from the tribe of Israel, the very last person in line. When Great Aunt Elsie told me the story, she had stopped there to make sure I understood that the boy had stood fast to protect his family until they all crossed safely. According to her, the water washed the Egyptians away, but because of the boy's courage, he and the rest of the tribe were saved. He was holy because he had helped God save the family.

Making my way under the oceans of tree branches, gaining the landing and winning my game with myself, my whole body was shivering with excitement and cold. Just down the hill from Old Lady Tyler's, all the lights from my house poured gold on the ground, lighting the vacant drive where Granddad parked his truck. Blowing on my hands, I tried to match lights with the houses of our friends. In the darkness across the river was a pillar of fire, the blazing cross of what Mam called the Born Aginner's church, and further west a net of lights over the town. Ears sunk in my collar, I stood watching the cold rind of light ride the gray band below the tree line when a sound caused me to turn.

"Oh, hi, Barbara." Coming out of the twilight, I recognized Marsha's big sister who was visiting home from Catholic boarding school. "I thought you were supposed to be eating. Did you already have pie?"

"What are you doing so far away from home, Annie?" she asked.

"I'm not far away. See?" I stabbed my finger toward the window where our dining room light shone. Maybe she would be more fun than Marsha.

"Oh, my! You are lost," Barbara said. "That's not your house."

"What are you doing here then? Your house is by my house."

"Annie, you shouldn't be out here all alone. Do you want to play a game with me?"

"What?"

"Let's go to the hospital." Clutching my sleeve, Barbara started down the hill.

"Did we get wounded?" I thought of a spear leaping the frothing Red Sea and stabbing the boy in the back.

"Yes, you did."

I glanced back at the empty driveway. The party wouldn't start until Granddad came home. "But, I'm supposed to be home by dark."

"I'll take you home in time," the older girl replied. "You couldn't find it without me anyway."

I was about to tell her that I could find my way very well without any help from her, and then wondered if this might be part of the game. We hurried toward the house outlined against the sky, then entered through the back gate and followed a stone path that ended at doors mounted in the deep foundation. Barbara opened the big door and held it for me.

Inside, the huge basement smelled of raw, hot sawdust. Illuminating the space, a thin bar of light gleamed from the threshold of the door leading upstairs, and one high, dirty window reflected an orange square flickering around the furnace door.

"I'm hungry," I said, eyeing the light under the door. If I could get upstairs, there would be pie. I thought I could smell it. "This is your house, Barbara."

"No, it isn't." Her face formed a pattern of triangles in the slate light. "This is a hospital where sick people have operations."

"Let's turn on the lights."

"There aren't any." Her back to me, she rummaged on the far wall and moved toward me carrying a pan containing a jumble of rusty spades and garden tools.

"This is Sunrise Drive, you're Professor Solberg's daughter and you lived here, and my house is right down the hill." When I scowled at her and moved toward the light shining under the door, she grabbed my shoulder.

"I'm going home," I said.

"Not without an operation. You are a sick, sick little girl."

"I don't feel sick."

"That's how you know when you're really sick," Barbara said, "when you don't feel sick. Now I have to examine you."

"I'm going home," I said, hollering, trying to pull away.

Her hand tightened painfully on my arm. "Shut up right now," she whispered, "or you'll never go home, little girl. Ever." She grabbed my other arm.

"I will," I said, raising my voice.

"But, after your operation." She unfastened the top button of my sweater, her fingers digging into my arm where it was still sore from Mam's grip. When I felt Barbara's hand move between my legs, I pulled harder. "Why are you doing that?"

"Your examination," Barbara croaked, jerking me against her. Barbara's fingers worked under my clothes and over my body, like energetic white worms. Her breath came louder, and she yanked me closer.

"Stop that!" I screamed.

She snaked an arm around my head and clamped a hand

over my mouth. Gripping my knees with her other hand, she sat on a stool, hauled my rigid body over her lap, and in the dim light bent to her task. As the cold steel slid inside me, my consciousness seemed to rise above the basement and I was somehow looking down on the struggle while my real eyes sought, found, and grimly attached themselves to the frail line of light under the stairway door. With an eruption of force, I freed my mouth, then shrieking for all I was worth, tried to move toward the pale bar of light, and the tentative voice calling "Barbara, Barbara?"

Barbara jumped to her feet.

Still screaming, I fell through the blackness, sprawled on the cold cement and crawled toward the light.

The basement door swung open, illuminating me on the floor and the older girl desperately scrambling at the outside doors. A dark figure framed in light descended the stairs.

"Why, it's Annie Butler," Mrs. Solberg said, crossing the floor, her shadow covering me.

"She wanted to play down here. She wouldn't go home," Barbara shouted. "I was trying to take her home."

"The child has no clothes on," Mrs. Solberg said. Turning, she called up the stairs, "Father! Father, call the Chapmans. Have them come." Then to Barbara who was still struggling with the outside door latch, "You stay right here."

I ran to the stairway and began climbing after the man. Then it seemed that everyone started talking at once. It sounded as though I were in the middle of two radios turned up full blast but to different stations. At the head of the stairs, I scurried past Marsha and her brother who gaped at me with their mouths wide open. *Don't they look stupid,* I thought and then felt bad I'd thought it. In the living room, blinking in the lamplight, I winced as I eased myself onto a stool by the fireplace. My bottom was on fire. Examining my scraped knees, I could hear the father talking on the phone.

"Oh, she's fine. Fine," he said.

Mrs. Solberg came through the doorway holding my dress and sweater. "Put these on," she said.

I rose and snatched them from her outstretched arm then slumped back to the footstool. Wishing the burning in my behind would stop, I sat gazing into the empty fireplace, tugging absently at damp socks that had wrinkled into my shoes. When I heard Marsha's voice in the kitchen, I began to wiggle into my dress.

I had my arms in a tent over my head with the dress turned backwards and the cold coming in all around when the doorbell rang.

Striding into the room, Mrs. Solberg smoothed her dress and turned to her husband. "Stay with Barbara," she said.

Framed in the light through the door-glass, I saw my mother and grandfather on the porch. While I was still struggling with my dress, my mother stepped into the living room.

In the hall, Granddad said, "Evening, Professor."

I looked up at my mother with relief, but her pretty face was rumpled and grumpy. She moved swiftly to me and began tugging the dress around my stomach. "You shouldn't have stayed out. How often have we told you not to go off like that?" She knelt down, unbuttoned the top button of the damp and mud-spotted dress, roughly pulled it into place, then tied the sash with a hard little jerk.

"She put that thing up my behind, and it hurt."

"Oh, Annie," she said, soft brown eyes welling with a disconcerting mix of disappointment and anger, "why can't you stay out of trouble? Just for once?"

Her red fingernails patted around, tidying me, then she rose and took my hand. As we entered the hall, Mr. Solberg said to Granddad, "They were playing dress-up in the basement. A child's game. Annie just got scared."

"No," I said, looking up at him. "No, Sir. She told me I was lost and I had to come with her and play hospital and she took off my clothes and stuck that cold thing up my fanny."

"So, you do it again," Barbara's mother whispered in a voice that hurt my skin. "We allow you home, and you . . ."

I saw Barbara's arm strike out and connect with the side of Mrs. Solberg's head, a dull thumping, then a snapshot of the circle of faces watching as Mrs. Solberg's body lifted slightly, crashed against the wall, and slumped there as everyone began moving and talking at once.

*

The voices of my mother and grandfather traded back and forth down the hill, through the chill and starry November night.

At our front door, my mother leaned over, enveloping me in her cold flower smell, whispering. "I do not want to hear one word of your wild stories at dinner tonight, Annie. It'll spoil Jack's party."

"That'll do Linda," my grandfather said. "It's over now, isn't it, Punkin'?" He swung me into his arms, and opened the door. "You did just fine, kiddo," he said, giving me a hug before he put me down.

Inside the warm house, redolent with the smells of her afternoon labor, Mam's eyes, pupils like meat prongs, pierced mine. They were implacable and held a silent message just for me. Sizing us up and seeing we were all present and in one piece, she turned, and clucking like a Banty hen, shooed my mother and me up the stairs. Directing Granddad to his chair, she called up the stairs in a fake-polite yell, "You hurry up now. Granddad has some news," then volume fading as she hurried toward the dining room, "I can't hold this dinner forever while you're off gallivanting around the countryside."

In our bedroom, in front of the dresser mirror, I watched with resignation as my mother jerked my chestnut hair into fanlike sections, tightly braided them and wrapped the ends in rubber bands. I already had a little white scar where she had dug the comb into my head and made it bleed, and that night in honor of Uncle Jack's party I had to endure further tugging and pulling as she tied stiff blue ribbons on the ends of my braids. My white cotton dress had small pink and red rosebuds embroidered on the collar, but I thought my scuffed Buster Browns looked cloddish with the party dress. I had begged for patent leather Mary Janes so I could look pretty, but my mother said they were too expensive, and Mam said they weren't any use for a tomboy like me.

Examining myself in the big mirror, my gaze drifted to a new picture stuck in the lip of the frame. A tall, slender man wearing a white shirt, jeans, and a cowboy hat stood in front of a wood fence, a rodeo arena in the background. I looked at it until I was sure I didn't know him and then looked back at my image.

"Let's hurry," Linda said, pretending she hadn't seen me studying the picture. "They've been waiting all this time. Jack will be starving, and with it his birthday, and well. . . you know how he. . ."

What I knew was that Uncle Jack was mean to me at every chance, and seemed to particularly dislike my mother, but he was Mam's honey-boy, and she never seemed to get mad at him no matter what he did. "Twenty-one is a very special birthday," my mother said, running the comb through her shiny red hair, fluffing the ends with her fingertips. Still smiling into the mirror, she touched the corner of her scarlet lip with a fingertip and drew her mouth into a pout. Lifting the glass perfume bottle over our heads, she sprayed us both, the smell of heartless gardenias filling the room. "You be nice to Jack. Let's make things special for him. Try not to spoil things any more than you already have." She set the perfume on the dresser. "Come on," she said, "or I'll be here all night."

Watching my mother leave the room, I wondered if "spoiling things" meant I wouldn't be having any birthday cake. Thinking about the cake, it occurred to me that if my mother and I had our own house things might be better. I loved the house on the hill, but if the two of us had our very own home, maybe I wouldn't be spoiling it, and no one could come in and tell lies or take people away—or threaten to kill them. If I had my own place, I would be safe.

I lingered before the mirror, looking at the girl in the white dress, examining the little face framed by braids, stiff blue ribbons poking up like defiance. I stared into river green eyes looking for myself in the darkness at their center. In that space of darkness, I was completely alone and adrift yet somehow sensed myself speeding toward the edge of . . . something . . .

"Annie! Right now," my mother called from the stairs.

Still captured by my eyes, I smiled experimentally at my reflection and headed for the door. At the top of the stairs, I froze at the sound of laughter and the clinking of dishes, my heart pounding so loud I knew everyone could hear. I pictured Uncle Jack waiting at the table with a smooth smile on his face scheming to tell some tale on me. And after that, there would be Mam. They were a pair. My friend was Granddad but if it came down to a choice, he had to be on Mam's side too. At any signs of unpleasantness, my mother would cry. And according to Mam, I could forget about my father because he didn't want to see me at all. She said I was the last thing in the world he wanted.

I thought of the pictures in Great Aunt Elsie's Bible of lions and warriors and mad old men trudging shoeless through the sand. The dogs, home from their day with Granddad, sat at the bottom of the steps still dirty and wet, wiggling from suppressed excitement, smiling up at me with pink, snaky tongues. Passing like a vision, I saw myself run out the door and keep on running as the Israelites had run from the Egyptians. Surely, if I ran far enough, I could find a promised land too. A land where everyone could be bigger or smaller and you could be invisible whenever you wanted, then change back at will.

Chapter 3

HOW ANNIE RECOVERS AND FINDS TRUE LOVE
RODEOING WITH LINDA

CALIFORNIA, 1951

In the summer of 1951 when I was six, we moved from the house on the hill to the ranch on Armitage Road. This was also about the time my grandparents fell wildly in love with Dwight D. Eisenhower—or at least the first I had heard of it. According to Mam, he was the only hope we had to beat the devil Adlai Stevenson. She had taken him up as her new cause and was busy making sure the whole state knew it. After the governor appointed Granddad to head the Oregon State Highway Commission, Mam had announced to the family that politics was now her duty too, and if she didn't take a hand in fixing things, who would?

I had learned that big changes were in store the previous November night of Uncle Jack's birthday party, when hunger and the wonderful smell of quick fried venison finally drew me down the stairs to the festive dining room. After the dinner and before the presents, Granddad had risen from his place at the head of the cake-bearing table.

"I have news," he had said, looking around at each of us and then down at his big hand holding a white napkin. "Mam and I have been talking it over for a while now. Today, we bought a place north of town. It's two hundred acres. We'll be all moved in by the end of June." His silver hair shone like another light in the room. "We won't have to keep the horses at the fairgrounds anymore—but we'll still go to the Hunt Club," he said, looking at me from under black eyebrows. "We'll walk right out our back door, Annie, and there the horses will be." Turning toward Uncle Jack, he said, "Now, Jack, won't you open your card?"

Uncle Jack, his fleshy cheeks hanging above the envelope, worked it open with a thumb and read the card quickly. When he looked up, his usually grim face was all smiles. "Oh, Dad," he said, "Property! That's just the best . . ."

"No! No!" I shrieked, surprising myself at least as much as them, "I won't leave!" I jumped from my chair, tore into the dark living room, and hid in the shadow under the piano. Though I had wondered about my mother and I needing our own home, at the thought of actually leaving the house on the hill, I knew I could not leave the comfort of my trees. *I couldn't leave my trees. And where would I sleep? Where would I eat? Who could I visit? Where could I ever find another camellia bush as white and beautiful as the one under the dining room window? If I were moved, I would somehow lose myself. What was wrong with them?*

"I don't care if we're closer to the horses," I hollered from the piano shadow. "I don't care about the daawgs," I sobbed, kicking wildly as Mam and my mother hauled me from beneath the baby grand. "I don't care, I don't care, I don't care. I won't go!" They ignored my panicked refusals to budge. Mam said I was acting like a baby, and a spoiled, bratty one at that. From then on, whenever the new ranch was mentioned, I would stop whatever I was doing, plant my feet and scream,

"You can't make me go."

Perhaps, it was to cushion the blow of the move, that my grandparents sent me on the road with my mother that summer. The previous spring, as Linda had packed her suitcases and trunks, I had dogged her through the packing clutter, taking out the items she put in the cases, sometimes hiding them, all the while offering reasons I should go too. "I can help you with the horses," I'd wheedled. "I can feed them every night. I'll read comics to you in the car—so you won't get lonesome. We could learn songs together." If my mother and I could be together, away from Mam, I knew we could go back to the good time before she became a rodeo star.

Pushing newly hennaed hair from her face, she had looked at me, then wrapped another of her beaded costumes and placed it in the trunk. I had made my eyes sad as they could get. "I won't be so lonesome here without you and Lady." When she bent over the trunk, I had removed the colorful western hats from the tall hatbox and carefully returned them to the shelf.

"Mommy, if you take me, I'll never be bad again. I'll never whine, and I'll do everything you say. I will . . . I promise."

As the time drew near and I was sure she would be leaving, I became by escalating degrees more morose and furious. Just before she left, I had hit my mother on the arm because she wouldn't quit packing and listen to me. This, of course, lost me big points with Mam. My grandmother had torn into me with the broom, chasing me down the stairs to the basement, hollering, "That'll be the last time I ever see that!" Narrowly missing Buddy, who happened to be sleeping in the doorway, she clattered after me crying, "Look at what you've done to your poor mother. Yewwww brat! You're just like your crazy father. Neither one of you could find your ass with both hands and a coon dog."

That time, I had escaped through the sawdust door in the

basement and my crime was added to the long list of my offenses, then finally ignored except for Mam's lingering nasty looks and meanness.

Then in the late spring of 1951, suddenly and without giving any reasons, they let me win the fight, and I was packing too. It didn't dawn on me that I'd been duped, that I was to go with Linda only because it would be less trouble for Mam. I just figured my time had come. The sunny morning we finally set off, Mam had leaned into the car window, "Well, you're higher than a kite," she said. I noticed that she was too. I was so excited that I wasn't even sad as I said good-bye to Granddad, who was telling my mother how to write down gas mileage in a special book for the tax man.

That summer may have hit records because there was no escape from the heat and dust. My legs were sweaty and sticking to both my jeans and the seat of the car, and my bangs sometimes dripped with sweat. We drove endless millions of miles in Linda's new green Chevy, pulling Lady in the silver trailer. To the accompaniment of country radio stations, we headed north to Ellensburg, Washington, then south over mountains and through stretches of blooming artichoke fields to Salinas, California, then back to Red Bluff, and finally to the Cow Palace in San Francisco.

Stopping for roadwork on boiling afternoon highways, Eddy Arnold singing "Kentucky Waltz," me wandering away from the car, once following a dog down an embankment to an icy creek where I couldn't hear her call, forcing her to pull out of her place in line—and with the horse trailer. Having to pee just when we were rolling good, begging for food, talking incessantly, singing over the roar of wind through the windows—those thousands of miles with Linda didn't make us closer. Every hot and sun-dusted mile seemed to separate us further. But it was in Red Bluff where an incident occurred which caused her to lose all faith that I could ever amount to anything and to proclaim that I would never, ever, come with her again.

That evening, we had arrived at the Red Bluff fairgrounds and parked in the shade of a long-whitewashed barn. "Finally," she groaned, stretching her arms and removing the keys from the ignition. Outside, she bent down to stretch her back, then locked her leather purse in the trunk, and handed me the keys. "Now, I'm trusting you, Annie," she said.

I stuck the wad of keys in the front pocket of my jeans and patted them tight into the corner. Then Linda shoved her hand in my pocket and pushed on them too.

That day's drive took us longer than Linda planned, so we had arrived just before showtime. Linda changed in the trailer and when one of the cowboys led Lady from the barn calling Linda's name, she adjusted the black glittery flower in her hair, looped a rope over her shoulder, stepped from the trailer and started after them.

A few minutes later, I stood in the warm-up pen, knee deep in fresh wood shavings watching her performance through the fence. Under the blazing night lights, Linda, wearing her chartreuse satin and black lace costume, hung by one ankle from the side of the charging black and white mare, scarlet hair streaming in the dirt as Lady careened around the arena at a dead run. Linda called the trick the Suicide Drag and claimed to have invented it. On the final lap, Linda and Lady hurtled from the ring, skidding to a stop at the back gate in a rising cloud of dust. Accompanied by loud cheering and yahoos, Linda vaulted off Lady and turned toward the barns.

Linda and Lady were the warm-up act for the Valkyries at the Red Bluff show, and if Linda was dramatic with all her red hair and dancer's body, the Valkyries were heart-stoppingly magnificent. Dropping to my knees in the shavings, I had craned my neck through the fence to get the best view when the arena lights went out, plunging us into darkness and deep silence. The clashing notes of the "Saber Dance" blared over the loudspeakers and the big gates flew open.

Teams of twelve white horses yoked four across burst from the gates at a run—forty-eight hooves pounding with the drums. Riders in scanty flesh-colored garments stood, seeming to float naked atop the horses' backs, figures blazing out of the night, feathered war bonnets casting them upward as wings, their screams riding the music. A second team flew on the tails of the first, the horses' legs passing inches from my nose where I gawked through the fence. Clowns ran to the center of the area carrying twenty-foot hoops, secured them, set them ablaze then sprinted for cover so as not to destroy the illusion. With more bloody screams, the riders jumped the thundering teams through towering rings of orange and blue flame. And, I had a perfect view for by then I was reclining in the bed of shavings, head propped at just the right angle to see horses and humans illuminated by fire, racing gloriously past me as they circled the wide arena. I inhaled the close, thick odor as the horses' hooves threw chunks of sawdust and manure toward the dark sky, seeming to fly on the current of wild, clashing music.

My mother must have been jealous because later, at the barn, I heard her telling another trick-rider that the Valkyries thought they were something—really something, but any no-talent could be really something if all they had to do was stand up and take off their clothes. No talent in that. But they were the best, and she knew it as well as I did. I was raving their praises when she came to find me.

"Oh, Annie, for crying out loud, will you just stop!" she muttered.

Later, I was in the barn filling Lady's water bucket when Linda walked up the aisle and stooped to pick up her saddle. "Keys," she said, hoisting the saddle onto her hip, and holding out her hand.

We rummaged through the sawdust and shavings, the dirt, and manure, searching like chickens hunting dinner for the bunch of keys, but the blazing lights over the warm-up pen hissed off, and we couldn't see. Finally, Linda reared back, satin haunches in the shavings, and cast me a look I couldn't then read. By the time we had given up the search, it was late, everyone had left the fairgrounds, there was no one to give us a ride, and no money to pay a cab or to use the pay phone. And so, bruised (my feelings), and disgusted (her), we walked the several miles to the motel up on the highway, she marching ahead, hair coming undone from the net, me plodding behind, eyeing her furious back. She quit talking to me for three days.

But that was hardly the worst of it. Soon, I compounded my crimes. After the key incident and having to get a whole new expensive set made, we had to get back in the car together and although it had been nearly a week, she was still barely speaking to me. Only "yeses" or "no's" and an occasional "shut up." We were on the way to San Francisco, our last stop where she was to headline for ten days at the Grand National Livestock Exposition at the Cow Palace. On the broiling drive from Red Bluff to San Francisco, over my mother's repeated threats and objections, I'd taken care to learn every word to Lefty's newest and my most favorite song, "If You've Got the Money" from the car radio. Over and over, to accompaniment of the radio and wind through my window, I warbled about honkey tonkin' and good times, imagining myself grown up and making the nightspots and dancing to the music fine.

We had just unloaded Lady at the fairgrounds and found her barn. I was forking clean straw into the stall, singing my new song for her, when a cowboy walked up to the open door and squinted in.

I was perfecting the last verse, singing about someone having no more MUNEE, and concluding on a loud and lengthy note that I had no more TIME.

Tall and slender, he looked down on me from under his Stetson and grinned. His shirt was bright white, legs long and solid in his jeans, and his gold and silver championship buckle was bigger than both my hands. It was the cowboy who had looked out at me from the picture tucked into the bedroom mirror frame at home.

Bud was laughing and warm, smelling of sweat and soap and leather. He was the RCA World Champion that year, but though he was famous, and people followed him around with cameras, he took time to teach me to twirl a rope, tie knots, and cuss. That first day in the stall, I didn't guess at any of what was to come. I only knew I liked him. His voice was low and quiet, and he looked at me when we talked. He listened to what I said, and when he teased me, his eyes lit up. They were warm dark blue with black eyelashes that turned golden on the ends. His hair was black and shiny too, and I wanted to be with him. That day, when he turned to leave, I followed him from the barn and was still shadowing him when he met my mother that evening at feeding time.

I followed him everywhere he'd let me. I'd sit and talk to him while he mended his saddles and he taught me to work the stopwatch and write down his times while he practiced calf roping on Toots, his pretty pink roan. On a quiet afternoon soon after we arrived, Bud had led Toots into the empty practice arena and stood adjusting her saddle.

"What's your best event?" I was trying to read his big silver and gold buckle.

"I do just about all of it, except bulldogging. Got over forty thousand points right now, and I'm goin' fer top money again." He rapped his knuckles lightly on the top of my head and pointed to the raised gold writing on the buckle. "I was All-Around Champ last year. Fixin' to do it again."

He swung into the saddle, patted Toots on the rump, and eased her into one side of a spring-loaded chute where a door banged shut behind her. Her ears snapped to attention as another cowboy herded a calf into the other side of the partition where it stood rolling its eyes and bawling. When Bud called for the calf, the operator pulled a lever. When the barrier dropped, the calf bolted into the arena and Toots busted from the enclosure on its heels. Bud's rope flicked out, looping the calf's neck and signaling Toots, who slid to an abrupt stop, haunches folded beneath her, plowing dirt. The rope cleaved to the saddle-horn with a slap that echoed like a shot in the high arena. Bud vaulted from the saddle and ran down the taunt rope while Toots, still on her haunches, backed like a train, pulling slack. Bud threw the calf to the ground, snapped the piggin' string from his teeth, tied the hocks, then threw his arms overhead.

"Seven seconds," I said, stopping the watch. After Bud released the calf, Toots trotted back toward me, Bud coiling up the hard rope. Still bawling, the calf ran toward the gates at the end of the arena.

"If I can do that tonight, honey, we'll be eating high for a week." Looking over and flashing his dimples, he said, "It's all about payin' attention."

I carefully wrote down the time in his little book like the real timekeepers who sat in the announcer's stand did. Later when I asked my mother what "All-Around World Champion" meant, she said it meant that he was the best . . . the best ever.

"He made more points—more money—last year than any other cowboy *ever* made. He's the best there is."

It was me, not Linda, who knew that he liked butter on his sandwiches instead of mayonnaise. And I could tell before anyone else when his old broken leg was hurting. Bud hardly ever let Linda leave me in the hotel room by myself at night. He'd always say, "Let the kid come too," and we'd go to fancy restaurants that had dark, cool bars in the back. He'd play "Hey, Good Looking" on the jukebox and order me Pink Ladies every time they had a drink. I ate the cherries and oranges from my drinks and my mother's, collecting a stack of colored swords that I saved in a special box in my suitcase. Sometimes I'd fall asleep in the pillowy booths with my head on Bud's leg. On those nights, he would gather me up, hold me close, and carry me back to the motel room. I always woke up, but I'd pretend I was still asleep because he felt so warm and good.

*

It was October, we were road weary, and the California shows had ended. I stood outside the livestock pens full of dozing Brahmas while Linda went to the barn to collect Lady. We were leaving the Cow Palace, and I was trying not to cry. Bud was in the rodeo office collecting his prize money. He came out and stood on the porch of the whitewashed office looking toward the barns. Tucking an envelope into his shirt pocket, he pulled himself up, straightened his belt, and looked around the way you do in a motel room that you're ready to leave. Flipping his cigarette into the hot gravel, he crossed the parking lot heading my way. I didn't want to look at him because that morning, eating eggs in the quiet hotel bar, I'd tried my best to talk him into driving home with us, but he'd said no.

When he reached the car, he stopped in front of me, took off his hat, put it on my head, and lifted me onto the warm fender of the Chevy. He pulled a ten-dollar bill from the envelope and handed it to me. I looked up from under the hat brim.

"I'm high-point man right now. Manuel and I need to be in El Paso tomorrow night. Gotta keep winnin' so I can come see you. Get yourself a dress. When I come north this winter, we'll dress up and paint the whole place red."

He didn't kiss me or anything, just took his hat from my

head and bowed a little when he put it on. His friend Manuel drove the Cadillac pulling a double horse trailer around the lot and stopped in front of us. They slammed their saddles into the trunk, threw themselves in the car making the tires whoosh, and fishtailed for Texas.

Right after Bud and Manuel drove off, Linda settled Lady in the trailer, and we started on a fast trip home over sizzling roads so I wouldn't be later for first grade than I was already. This was the last thing I wanted. I had more important and exciting things to do than attend some boring school named for an ancient pioneer friend of Mam's who at ninety-two years of age still rode at the head of all the town parades. But there was no help for me. The hotel switchboard lady had left a message from Mam saying that they'd moved the last of the furniture from the house on the hill to the ranch and were expecting us. Not only had Mam and Granddad moved to the new ranch, but my mother said Uncle Jack had a new house trailer he would park on his own part of the place. *A house trailer? In the summer, lots of rodeo families travelled in small trailers—but to live in one all the time? Like gypsies?*

Linda was jumpy and quiet as she drove north through California with her red hair down and her elbow stuck out the window. Her shirtsleeve fluttered against the blazing green door and the car smelled of the Sea and Ski she slathered on her arms. Although I was enchanted by what I could see of the huge trees, we didn't stop at Trees of Mystery because she said it was a tourist trap and too expensive. I wanted to play more word games. She didn't. She gave me gum to chew, then hollered at me because she couldn't stand mouth sounds. She said I sounded like Lady when I chewed. I stopped trying to talk to her and thought about Bud. He was now my special person, and he loved me. It also cheered me to think that with Bud, Linda's taste in men had taken a sharp turn for the better. So much better than the town guys or ranch hands she went dancing with when she was home for the winter rodeo break. If I could make sure Linda married Bud, my troubles would be over. Then, I would have my own house and my own family. And I wouldn't have to worry about Mam because she didn't care who my mother went around with as long as it wasn't my father—and there was no danger of that because, according to Mam, he was long gone. But also, according to Mam, long gone wasn't far enough. She also said that just because he had trouble in the war didn't mean he could use it as an excuse forever. *Trouble?*

I closed my *Best of the West* comic book. During the seemingly endless drive when I was tired of reading the same comics, and had temporarily exhausted my dreams of Bud immediately moving to the ranch with us, I'd look out at the countryside and dream of the way the new ranch would look. Though Linda and I were both well aware of our destination, we had avoided the topic of the ranch for the entire trip. Now, after meeting Bud and cheering up considerably, I imagined a glorious spread like the ones in *Best of the West* comics. I glanced at the cover where a title read: "Tim Holt, aka Redmask Faces the Female Villain Black Rider and her Riverboat of Death." Bud would be a hero like Tim Holt. Tim Holt aka Bud would be a secret partner in the ranch and would rescue all the wild horses from bad men, and he would love and protect me from everything bad too. He would not only be half-owner of the ranch with Grandad, but he'd be married to Linda and also be my father, and we would all live in a beautiful ranch house behind wide-open gates under flags flying our brand like the big ranches we'd seen in California. I imagined each square on the comic book page: The new place would have huge trees lining a lane through perfect green pastures with bright white fences, and beautiful long barns for the horses. In another square, Bud and Linda would be married and so happy taking care of all the horses that they rode and danced and had fun all the time—with me. In another square there was me, happy in the barn with Granddad and the horses. And Mam—well, Mam could live . . . in another square. It would all be perfect. I knew it.

On the last leg of our trip, Lady, bored from standing, threw herself from side to side against the trailer walls making the car rock, her dainty iron shoes pounding thunder as my mother tore down the winding mountain road into the Emerald Valley. I wasn't bored like Lady. In my excitement to get back and see the new place, I jumped up and down on the front seat, polishing my version of "Jambalaya," braids flying in the wind.

Chapter 4

WHAT ANNIE FINDS AT THE RANCH
AND HOW IT SOLVES ALMOST ALL HER PROBLEMS

Given my dreams of the perfect ranch, resulting somehow in the perfect family and perfect life, imagine the misery I felt that evening when we drove up the dusty little road to the ranch for the first time. The ranch on Armitage Road was nothing like those in California or my comic books, and nothing at all like our beautiful old house on college hill. The land wasn't hilly and green but flat and gold-colored. There weren't many big trees. After negotiating a country two lane with wide-ranging fields on either side, we pulled into the long, graveled drive. Linda sat bent; hands clasped over the wheel looking at the place. Heaving a huge sigh, she turned off the engine. "It's seven miles to town. There's nothing out here," she said, looking over at me.

The ranch house, its fading paint the color of dirty bones, seemed like a collection of large bunkhouses strung together with pointed roofs at each end, a lean-to stuck to either side. The front of it looked like a fighter leading with his nose—just a blade of nose stuck right out there, pointed at the cornfield across the county road. Not a tree in the yard.

Yet, despite what seemed its obvious drawbacks, and even if Linda and Mam didn't like it much, I knew Granddad was all for the place. As we piled out of the car, Mam came hurrying down the front steps, all smiles, and the place did seem a tiny bit more welcoming when I noticed Granddad's chair through the big front window. Mam seemed almost happy to see me and kept hugging me too tight, as though her hugs might prevent me from commenting. This wasn't home. There wasn't even a bedroom for us. We were to sleep on sofas, like hobos, in the enormous, carpeted living room where they'd also placed the piano.

After a quick dinner, we lay down on the sofas and must have slept, but there was certainly no sleeping in even after all those months of driving and living in motels. Early the next morning, my mother was up, dressed, and anxious to get on the road. White tennis shoes planted firmly on the cement floor of the garage that was to be our new bedroom, Linda gave Mam and Granddad hurried decorating instructions. To begin, a new kind of drawers Linda called built-ins were to be fashioned and installed. They were to be painted flat black, the new chic color in New York. Linda paused in front of the wallpaper samples and pointed to an all-over pattern of gray rocks featuring loud scarlet and gold cactus flowers and handed it to Mam. The woodwork was also to be *all* flat black. The carpet, cherry red shag.

Moving to the doorway, Linda looked around the room, the former garage that she now called "the suite." The large main room had been an oversized garage and shop. It had a concrete floor and shoulder-high windows all around. At the far end of the space, another door led to a pleasant sitting room with thick pine paneling and a fireplace. That room had a private door to the outside and good screens on all the windows. Looking carefully at the brown tile floor, Linda finally said she was sure the place could be fixed up so it would look "nice." When she turned away, my grandmother and grandfather looked at each other and my grandmother lifted her shoulders. Before I was even awake, my mother had loaded Lady in the trailer. Now she kissed us all, hurried to the car, and headed for Texas. Watching her drive off through the flat gold fields, I didn't say anything, but knew I'd never be happy there.

That morning, Mam made my favorite breakfast of waffles with little pig sausages and eggs. Sitting at the table she told me all about the move and how they almost lost one of the horses, but then they found her running loose by the river, and how Spike and Buddy had gotten sopping wet chasing her, then come back through the orchard and jumped all over the new sofa. After breakfast, I followed Grandad into the sunshine and across the graveled drive. Spike and Buddy came trotting from the field, and we walked slowly along the wide driveway which ended in a turnaround in front of the barns.

I had to admit that the barns and outbuildings looked good. They ranged behind the ranch house in a wide circle, roofs of cedar soaking up the sun. The main barn, in line with the back of the ranch house, was a huge three-story, peaked roof affair, more impressive than the ranch house, in my opinion. It had six box stalls each with its own paddock, a tack room, an aisle on one side to groom and tack the horses, and on the other side, a place to park horse trailers. The whole upstairs was full of hay stacked to the ceiling. Next to the main barn arrayed around the circular drive were the foaling barns, double gates to the pastures by the river, a machine shop with a tractor and other machines inside, next a pump house, and finally a long glass greenhouse close to the garden behind the house. Granddad pointed to an empty space alongside the kitchen garden where he planned to build a new chicken house. Jutting into the pattern of cedar shingles and sky behind the machine shop was a white gas tank for the farm machines. Everything looked shipshape, square, and tight.

"We'll grow our own hay," he said, raising a suntanned

hand, indicating a stretch of gold grass north of the barn, then gesturing east where the tree line fluttered against blue hills. "And those little trees are filberts, not very big yet, but they'll grow."

"We need trees like that one." I pointed to an immense tree in the field south of the ranch house. Drooping branches traced black and green against the sky and though it towered over the countryside, the giant tree seemed to kneel in the morning sunshine, arms wrapped around itself, head bowed.

"That's a big old black walnut," he said. "It goes with the Armitage place down the road." He nodded toward a small, tilled field. Just beyond the field, the only other trees in sight partially concealed a two-story white farmhouse. "We don't have any that big, kiddo." He smiled, and I could tell he loved it all. "Besides," he said, "we can plant as many trees as we want, anywhere we want to put 'em. This land is river bottom. It'll grow anything, and it'll be good!"

That evening after dinner, I hurried outside and through the barns to see if the horses were happy in the big pasture. Missy's colt turned his head and watched me start across the field toward the giant tree.

I stood beneath the black walnut in the hay-smelling evening peering into its arching branches, tracing shapes against the sky. The big tree reassured me, and as I gazed upward, I had a hint of hope for the future. I felt the warm trunk under my hand and thought things here might just work out after all. When the sun started to slant off behind the dusty yellow field, I turned and followed a faint path toward the neighboring Armitage House set among the maples.

The Armitage House was old even then, two-storied, huge and white, with long green porches. The setting sun reflected off five gleaming pillars that stood down the porch like soldiers at attention. Staying close to the flowering hedge, I hesitated and peered into a waxy pink and gold blossom before continuing up the drive. The pure green transparency of clean air carried the scent of warm tarred road and cut hay, the heavy sweet smell of fading roses. That evening, the breeze blowing off the mountain and across the river also carried fragrant pollen dust from the orchards and ruffled the leaves on the maples. I seemed to float up the steps in the warm wind sighing across the field.

Careful not to let the heels of my cowboy boots make noise, I crept up the porch toward a glass-paned front door. The door stood open; screen door unlatched. Shading my eyes, I peered through the screen. It was silent except for a clock ticking somewhere in the shadowed interior.

It seemed perfectly right; I opened the screen and slipped inside.

Hardly breathing, I peered into the living room on the right. The furniture was old, like the house, but it shone in the golden light slanting across the field into the big front window. At the opposite end of the room, tall glass doors opened to a shady back porch, long lace curtains stirring in the warm wind from the field.

As I stepped into the living room, sudden voices caused me to dive into a corner between the wall and a piano. My hand clutched the snarling head of a carved lion with spread wings, surprising me as surely as he appeared surprised by me. About an inch from where my nose came to rest, a clawed foot clutched the wood supporting the piano. It was wonderful: the flaming dark wood gilded with honeyed light from the evening fields. The carving was so fine that the teeth of the lion, his roaring tongue, even the hair of his mane, stood out perfectly in a halo of sunset gold.

A finger lingering on the lion's head, I took a quiet breath then tiptoed toward the glass doors and gentle voices. An old man, holding a newspaper in front of him, sat on the porch facing a long yard where a vine-covered gazebo threw blue shadows on the grass. He made a comment to someone I couldn't see, and there came a murmured reply. Further back, at the end of the yard under some old fruit trees, a forest of red roses spilled over the horse fence.

Maybe it was the warmth of the light as it moved across the field and lit the room or the ticking of the clock and the smell of the roses. It might have been the way the polished furniture smelled. Maybe sneaking inside and making it mine for a moment. Or just a little girl who missed her old house. Whatever it was, I decided at that moment that this house was the best of all the houses in the world, and that I had to live there. It was home.

I slipped out of the front door and hurried around back, yoo-hoo-ing. Standing before them (likely in their flower bed), I introduced myself to Mr. and Mrs. Armitage, who sat side by side in rocking chairs. Thin and white-haired, both inclined to be kindly, they listened attentively as I gave them a detailed description of our family, the name and special characteristics of each of our horses and both dogs, then continued at length about how much I admired their beautiful house and tree and then I may have paused for breath. Later, when the sky had turned a dark, transparent blue, I walked back toward the ranch trying out names for my new tree. I wondered if it already had a name. I turned in the middle of the soft, tarred road, and drifted backward looking at the Armitage House and tree from a broadened perspective. The smell of warm blackberry vines, mixed with the first cool of evening and a hint of promise, followed me back to the ranch house.

I found Granddad in the big living room reading the paper, white head illuminated in the glow of his lamp, cigarette smoke curling his head. I told him where I'd been, and that I *had* to have that house. "Buy it, could you, and let us move there?" I said, moving his ashtray from the arm of his chair to the table. He smiled, folded the newspaper, and patted his knee.

"There are some things, kiddo, that just aren't for sale." He laid the newspaper on the footstool and stubbed out his cigarette.

As I was quite a pouter, I am sure my chin began to crumple as I sat there in the cradle of his lap. He made the face so fierce it always caused me to laugh and begin to sing the bear song—a song that also made me laugh but puzzled me too. It was about a bear going over a mountain to see what it could see. Then, when the bear got there all it could see was the other side of the mountain.

Why did he sing that song?

Thirteen years later, after Mister Armitage died and his wife went to live with their daughter, my grandfather did buy the Armitage place along with some of the furniture and the lion-legged piano. On an Indian summer afternoon in 1964, the day I moved into the Armitage house, I stood with him on the back porch looking past the roses at the mature filbert orchard. He took off his hat and ran a hand over his head, smoothing his hair.

"Well now, Annie, you and the girls will always have a home," he had said.

Now that I'm older, I've wondered if it might not be a sin or at least an aberration to love a house. But that's like wondering about anything you love that seems inappropriate, man or house; it has nothing to do with shoulds or decisions. Some things just *are*.

Chapter 5

ANNIE'S ALARMING ADVENTURES AT THE 1951 EMERALD CITY CHAMBER OF COMMERCE RODEO AND WHAT HAPPENS WHEN SHE MEETS A MAN WHO WILL CHANGE HER LIFE

ARMITAGE HOUSE, MAY 5, 1999

The early morning living room was a wash of green and gold shadows from mock-orange blossoms floating against the windows. By noon it would be hot, and I had drawn the curtains to keep the morning chill. Though sure my mother and I would finally work something out despite her despicable husband and slimy lawyer, I had slowly began packing the downstairs—one cupboard in the hall closet. But even though I had made a start, I had still been sure it was a mistake, an epic blunder. I had been waiting but I didn't know what for, so how could I know what to watch for? Would she or her dreadful husband come and say something? Apologize?

I wasn't crying quite so often but drifted above the world as though disconnected from it, an unmooring that reminded me of my childhood. I knelt in the hallway and pulled out the bottom drawer of the big linen cabinet which revealed another collection of boxes and magazines. As a kid, I was much too busy to faithfully keep a diary, but I was a religious keeper of souvenir boxes—all sizes and shapes. One of the small matchboxes still contained dirt from the house on the hill and dried blue flowers from the hilltop. I removed a larger box which held horse show and rodeo programs, colorful hotel and restaurant matchbooks, shiny plastic cocktail swords, hanks of horsehair, and my golden braids that one morning in an angry fit, Mam had cut off with the horse clippers. I'd kept this particular collection in an old wooden box with a brass lock. The Emerald City Chamber of Commerce Rodeo program, September of 1951, was on top, a spotted bucking horse drawn in pen and ink sunfishing across the cover. I turned the page, revealing splotches made by my root beer snow cone and the checks my grandmother had placed next to the names of the winning cowboys as we sat together in the glaring hot grandstands watching the rodeo.

*

CHAPMAN RANCH, ARMITAGE ROAD, EMERALD VALLEY, OREGON AUGUST 1951

That morning, before we left for the rodeo grounds, the fields behind the ranch house had been still and cool, a slight haze drifting over the river. Across the water, blue mountains rolled north into lilac lines that smudged a pink edged sky. As I had hurried through the back pasture, the sun approached the eastern bank of the river where a fish jumped, leaving a rainbow circle that trembled in the sunshine. I was lost in plans for my first step toward rodeo stardom. Carrying Lady's halter, I moved through the vast golden field where beneath dusty hedgerows field foxes drowsed in cool dens, and possum rested pink-rimmed eyes waiting for night. A red-tailed hawk floated above the river hunting field mice, snakes, anything that moved, but unearthed nothing to carry away on that quiet morning. The silence was broken by the looping hum of a bee and a nearby jay, shrieking, get off, get off.

I see myself as I was then, a small girl, six years old, soft dandelion fuzz around my face, long golden braids flying. I was hurrying through the tall grass carrying a red halter and lead rope, my yellow shirt shining like a second sun. Playing in my excited imagination were the results of my task, to be my mother's helper at the rodeo. I was sure that my new position would significantly improve my status both at the new school and with the kids at the fairgrounds, but even more important, catch the attention of my rodeo friends. At the edge of a grove of wide-leafed maples, I hollered, "Lady, Lay-deeee."

A sleek black and white head emerged from the tall grass by the river. She was smart and if she knew I wanted her for something important she might play with me and make me chase her. After boasting over breakfast to Mam and Granddad that I needed *no* help to catch any horse on the place and certainly not Lady, I was determined. Even before we moved to the ranch, people had started saying I was a natural with the horses, and there hadn't been a horse I couldn't catch, make friends with, and ride. My only worry was that she might spook and take off across the river like she did when Uncle Jack went to catch her; but she wouldn't do that to me. Lady was my favorite and had been with us since I was born. We had spent a lot of time together and I loved her almost as much as my mother. And even though she was a star rodeo horse, with me she was sweet, gentle, and always minded. Working with the horses was the one thing I was good at, and everyone would see this now! In my excitement, I was full of plans for this most important day. A day I had marked to initiate my new self-advancement strategy. Advancement I needed so I could make Linda listen to me and help her get us a husband and father.

I turned and trotted up the path toward the collapsing homestead house hidden in the old orchard. Lady watched, not me, as there was likely nothing visible except the top of a golden head merging with the gold of the grass, only ripples in the tall grass marking my passage. The original Armitage homestead cabin, then merely boards rotting in the dry grass and a tall column of river rock that Grandad said was a chimney eighty years before, sat amid high grass in a grove of gnarled fruit trees. I moved through the arched shade of the abandoned orchard, braids swinging, placing deadfalls in the yellow T-shirt basket I held before me, revealing a white belly shining like another species of ripe fruit.

The black and white mare stepped toward the gate, eyes on me, curious nose in the wind.

*

There was no greater feeling than riding Lady over the ranch, surveying my new realm from her warm back, seeing it intimately but from a broadened perspective. That morning the fields, layered with tansy, fresh Timothy grass, and the rich stink of alfalfa, pricked my nose and made my eyes stream, but I had already grown to associate the scents with home and took pleasure in the tickle of my nose. Looking at the colored pictures in Granddad's plant book, I had learned that the pretty yellow flowers that grew everywhere were called monkey plants and knew the difference between the many types of sunflowers and daisies that grew wild in the fields. I was also learning which insects were attracted to the plants. I had memorized the Latin names of all the trees not only on our place but in the whole northern part of the valley and rode along naming them, often stopping to collect their leaves. I had been surprised to learn that my tree at the

Armitage house, which I called Walter, was officially named Juglans nigra, which meant black nut of Jupiter. On reading this, I had immediately looked up beautiful Jupiter in the encyclopedia and had imagined the tree's branches brushing the glowing planet, connecting earth and sky. On horseback I felt more myself than anywhere in the world and whenever I had a chance, I'd bridle one of the horses and ride bareback for hours, stopping to investigate trees, crannies, ditches, and creeks, whatever I fancied, unless the horse spooked and refused. Now, Lady walked along swishing her tail, then we turned onto the lane and stood waiting.

"Lady, Lady," I murmured, leaning over her and patting both sides of her neck.

A dusty, once green pickup loaded with hay wallowed down the lane and stopped.

My grandfather, silver headed, unshaven, smiling, wearing an undershirt and hay-flecked jeans instead of his town white shirt and dark slacks, stretched across the cab and opened the door.

"Git in, kiddo. Did you get the gate chained good and tight?"

I slid to the ground and nodded, "Good and tight, Granddad."

In the truck, my behind sunk in the rump sprung seat, an arm sticking out the window holding Lady's lead, the mare standing patiently beside the truck, I smelled my grandfather's good smoky smell mixed with the sweet fragrance of grass hay. The smell of the fields, the river, the man and horse, the color of the morning, my small success catching Lady, all of it, made me turn to my grandfather and smile. He smiled back.

Our smiles, that moment, created a place in my mind and imagination that is a touchstone still.

On the drive back, the light flickering among tree shadows highlighted dust drifting in sunlight, reflected on gold fields, settled over warm blackberries, and shot haloes at the sun as it rose higher into a wild blue sky. At first, I'd thought the ranch could never make me happy, yet somehow it had become the only place in the world I wanted. And, although I suspected that my mother was leaving again, I was becoming resigned to her absence, and aware that I was on my own, making it even more urgent to make a name for myself.

Yet, that day and the next, Linda would be performing in Emerald City! As the truck bumped across the dusty field, I thought how proud I was that she had finally come home to star in our town's rodeo, and that afternoon everyone would see I had an important part in her act. Now the kids would know. I could prove to the doubters (Myra and Janice) at school that I didn't make up my famous mother, and they could see her for themselves in her second skin, a magnificent, beaded costume, riding her beautiful black and white horse at a dead run, performing death-defying tricks. A star! Even Uncle Jack called her, not Linda, but "the big star." I had no misgivings about shining in her reflected glory.

That afternoon at the Emerald City rodeo grounds, my grandmother and I sat in the blazing wooden stands waiting for my mother's performance, rooting for our favorite cowboys with folded newspaper hats perched on our heads, my grandmother's like an upside-down boat about to sail off her crown of red braids. As the last roper chased his calf down the dusty arena, I looked over the crowd trying to see kids from my school, but there were too many people sitting too close together in the high grandstands to tell them apart.

We held our breath as the gates flew open and the three trick riders swirled into the arena, horses at a dead run, my mother in the lead. The announcer's voice boomed over the fairgrounds, echoing above the crowd, over the barns, and bouncing against the distant hills.

"First up, this beautiful little red-headed star is a hometown girl. She and her black and white mare have entertained all over the country, and this winter she'll wow the folks in New York City! Give a big hand for Miss Liiiiinda Chapman."

Lady burst down the track, gleaming black legs stretching high, hooves churning the dirt into clouds that smoked the arena. My mother, the famous Linda Chapman, was spectacular. Sheathed in red satin with long black fringe and flashing rhinestones, she stood atop Lady like a neon sign, hands thrown over her head, scarlet hair flying behind her as the horse thundered past. As the mare leaned into the curve, my mother's body seemed to fly through space, silhouetted against the hot sky.

My grandmother stood on her toes, her hand grasping the newspaper, shading eyes that followed my mother's every movement. Mam always worried when my mother performed but she never wanted me to know. She was also mad at me because I never worried. I didn't know how to tell Mam I'd used up all my worry after Crawfordsville when the strap broke, and the horse kicked her in the head and smashed her bones. And then she had vanished. Vanished into the hospital where I was not allowed to visit and had never been good enough to save her. When I began thinking of her as Linda instead of Mom—or Mommy.

Back at the gate after her first lap, Linda dismounted and stood in the dust close to Lady. She tested the cinch, then jerked the saddle horn to test the saddle. She had to be extra sure everything was right because her next trick, The Suicide Drag, was the showstopper. The same scary trick where her body hung upside down, arched from the side of the running horse, one leg pointing at the sky, the other thrown over the saddle, a tiny strap around one ankle connecting her to the white saddle. Linda vaulted onto the saddle and secured the tiny strap as Lady danced in place, waiting for the signal.

When Linda dropped the reins on the mare's neck and

flung herself off her side, Lady bolted down the track as if wolves were at her heels. Linda's head bounced inches above the arena floor, red hair and pale hands trailing the dirt under Lady's flying feet. It was a ballerina's stance, only upside down and flying thirty miles an hour. Our eyes locked on my mother's ankle where the thin strap linked her to Lady. When Lady slid to her final stop, Linda arched her body into the saddle and the audience rose, still yahooing, clapping, and stomping their feet on the boards for more.

Mam jumped up with a grimace of relief. "C'mon, let's get out of here, before we're stuck," she growled in my ear, smiling at the people next to us. She grabbed me by the arm and over the sound of the booming announcer barked, "S'cuse us. S'cuse. She can't wait."

"Mam, I don't have . . ."

She pushed me in front of her, navigating around the slower onlookers, through the racket of popcorn, flying programs, and spilled snow cones to the barn looking for Granddad.

It was time to make my big debut, to do my job, which Grandad had said was especially important. I was to care for Lady who had to be walked, cooled down, and fed before the evening show. I was ready. I'd been rehearsing as I sat in the grandstands. On the way to the barn, I kept hoping to see some of the kids from school in the streams of people leaving the grandstands but didn't see one of them. No rodeo officials or cowboys to see me either because it was time for their break before the evening show. When we arrived in the barn alley Mam looked at me, took a swipe at pushing my bangs out of my eyes, then bustled off in search of the rodeo photographer to make sure he had the perfect shot of Linda Chapman starring in her hometown rodeo for the Sunday paper. I drank from the hose, peed in the corner of the stall, then ran to find Granddad and Lady.

Out in the dusty arena, Granddad picked me up and placed me on top of Lady, on the slick white seat of my mother's trick-saddle. Following a sprinkling water truck, the machine that smoothed the track had just come by, bricks bouncing on top of the metal grate as it turned, trailing bright dust, and clattered through the gate. Eyeing the tractor, Lady danced, first on one foot, then the other.

"Just walk her," Granddad said, adjusting her chinstrap. "Cool her out. Fifteen or twenty minutes. Don't get her excited."

She kept dancing and I knew she wanted to run, but I wasn't to let her. She always minded me, so I didn't shorten the reins.

"Walk now, Lady," I said, leaning down, sliding my hand along her soft neck.

In one smooth motion, she gathered under me and sprang forward, legs stretching full out, her jaw wrenched hard against the bit. Clamping my legs to her side, I grabbed the tall saddle horn and hauled on the reins, trying to pull her up, but she was already lunging down the track.

"Lady! Whoa!" I screamed, dragging harder on the reins.

"NO!" Granddad yelled, "Hang on . . ."

As she ran full out on the stretch, wind and dirt flew in my face, blinding me. Coming into the first curve, she leaned so far over, I knew her shoulder would touch ground. I crouched over her neck, afraid we were falling, one fist welded to the horn, the other gripping the white hide reins, praying to the god of horses, my second true prayer.

"Lady," I screamed, now past commanding.

As we tore by him, coming full circle, Granddad hollered, but the words were lost as we cut into the wind falling from the dark and faceless grandstands. Again, she gathered speed then laid into the next curve not slowing but dropping her inside shoulder and galloping even faster, jolting my teeth and pummeling my whole body. My imagination split between staying with Lady and falling under her iron-nailed, flying feet.

Pounding into the stretch, coming to Granddad again, she was still pouring it on, her breath harsh and loud. One hand gripping the horn, I held out the other arm readying to jump and have him catch me. With a bone-stunning jolt, she snapped her legs out in front of her and slid to a stop, almost sitting down in front of Granddad.

"I hate you, Lady," I screamed, holding out both arms, choking on tears, thin snot running from my nose. He reached out and swung me to the ground.

"Shoulda thrown the reins on her neck. Let her go. You might have pulled her down hauling on her like that, kiddo. Gotta go with it."

"I hate her," I shrieked, my heartbeats sounding like a hurtling train in my head.

"Can't hate her for doing her job. You just got to be one up on her."

Sobbing, I threw my arms around his leg. He reached down and shook my shoulder gently. Lady's hot breath was falling over me, light green foaming her bottom lip, nostrils wide, hot, red.

When I held up my arms, Granddad's eyes widened, and he smiled—a smile that dimpled his usually solemn face, changing it entirely. "That's right, Sis. Get on up."

I heaved back but he caught me by both hands. "I'm not getting on her." Planting my feet, I struggled to pull away. "I won't."

He circled my hands in his. "Now, Sis, you've got to. You can't ever let man nor animal buffalo you. If they do it once, it'll be all over. If you ever get throwed, 'specially if you ever get scared, well, you've got to climb right back up there and show 'em what for." I reared against his hands, shaking my head at his betrayal. "Never let anyone see you're scared. Can't let being scared stop you."

He began reeling me forward, talking softly. "If you don't get back up on Lady right now, you'll never ride another horse on the place."

I sobbed louder.

"You scare her, and she'll run off with ya' again. I can't be proud of you crying like a baby. It's just Lady, now. You've rode her a hundred times. She's all wore out. She's not going to run off with you again. Come on," he said, lifting me up.

I felt like kicking him, kicking Lady in the nose, and running off myself, but Granddad was the nicest of them all, so I didn't. He stood by the fence, his hat shading his eyes, and made me walk her around the scorching arena five times before he let me off. One hand clamped to the saddle horn, the other tight on the reins, I wasn't trusting her for one minute but her every step was perfect, her manners so good that it seemed she knew . . . well, she must have known I was prepared to do my worst! On five, Granddad threw his cigarette on the ground and swung me from the saddle.

"There now, that wasn't so bad, huh, Punkin'? Besides," he said, a hand on my shoulder, "you'll ride faster horses. No doubt about it."

Walking Lady up the lane to the barn, we passed my mother who was in her car sitting with one of the saddle bronc riders. Her red head was bent, forehead on the steering wheel, and he was rubbing her neck because she had a headache. While Granddad fed Lady, I stood at the open car window and gave them a detailed account of Lady's crime.

"The kid does pretty good for a six-year-old," my mother said, smiling, squinting her eyes at the cowboy.

*

That evening, after I'd changed clothes and trudged behind Mam to the Fairgrounds dance hall, I was still mad at Lady, deeply ashamed of my failure, and while earlier I'd wanted all the kids and rodeo people to see me, now I didn't want to see anyone. Inside the large hall, I was crawling under the tables to find a cool, dark place to hide because the overhead lights hurt my eyes and the fiddles were going too fast. I parked under the table where Bud's brother, Sherman, sat with some of the bareback riders, their jean-clad legs bouncing up and down in time to the music, boot heels clacking.

Most of the cowboys still wore their taped-up and dusty riding boots, but one of the men sported shiny sharp-toed boots that even in the dim light under the table gleamed like black mirrors. In our family we called them dude boots, and dudes were not to be admired but laughed at. According to Mam's rules, a man who was more concerned with his appearance than his work was no man at all. All hat and no cattle. But those boots sure were shiny. Sherman laughed, then with a thunk and a crash, beer came spilling over the side of the table like a sour waterfall, and all the boots pulled back to cusses and laughter.

One of the cowboys said, "We gonna have to git you a nipple fer that beer, boy?"

"Not unless it fills out a shirt like those on that one there."

I thought this was from shiny boots because the voice, coming from directly above me, sounded mumbly, and the black boots didn't back straight away from the puddling beer like the other boots. The shiny boots rather stuttered backwards, the legs in the boots swaying.

I peered from under the tablecloth to see who filled out the shirt in time to see my mother's red suede boots two-stepping, her purple bellbottoms fluttering, dancing with the cowboy who'd been rubbing her neck that evening. I heard her laughing and stuck my head out farther to see her whirl away, big yellow earrings swinging into her scarlet hair.

"Annie, git out from there, and git back to where you

belong. You're gettin' beer all over ya'." A big hand covered with freckles and orange hair reached down and grabbed me by the braid.

Uncle Jack's round face came down close to mine. The mole on his cheek had turned a hot color that matched his red suspenders, and his beery breath blew in my nose, little hard puffs as he spoke. He was always telling me that I wasn't acting right and even more upsetting, tattling on me to Mam and Granddad. Just lately, he and I were doing worse than ever because since we'd moved to the ranch, he couldn't sneaky-pete around at night anymore, scaring the daylights out of me and causing me to make a fool of myself. This made him even more determined to make me look bad at every chance.

"Oww," I hollered. "I don't have to," I said as I brought my bootheel down on his toe but not nearly as hard as I could have.

"She's leaving again. She's not gonna be here to spoil you rotten, brat." His face in mine, a triumphant snarl on his fleshy lips, he said, "You wait 'til she takes off. You're damn sure gonna straighten up this time."

Our heads swung around looking for Mam and Granddad, his guiltily because my mother said he wasn't to touch me, and me desperately because he always tried to boss me and scare the tar out of me with new threats. One delivered with fierce intensity was that he'd hit me so hard I'd "disappear into next week and be gone forever." That particular threat didn't bother me much because I figured that if he hit me into next week, then when next week came around, maybe Wednesday or something, they'd surely find me.

But so much for next week, now when I needed them, my grandparents were nowhere in sight. And Linda *was* leaving again! *Damn, Damn, Damn,* I thought, copying the curses my grandfather used when the cows tromped down the new fence. I jerked from my uncle's grasp, bolted to the other end of the table, flung my arms around the shiny boots, and held on.

"Whoa, Sally," shiny boots said, lurching backward.

Sherman's dusty brown boots moved behind shiny boots and stopped their backward reel. With a grunt, shiny boots dropped to his knees and stuck his yellow head under the dripping table. He squatted there, peering at me, then plunged his arm under the table like a bear digging for honey. Before I knew what he was up to, he'd swung me onto his shoulders, causing my dancing dress to fly up when he plopped me around his neck.

"Ride this bronco, girlie," he sang, half dancing, half bucking, pulling hard on my feet, so the inside of my bare legs scraped against his bristly cheeks.

Just then the music stopped. The dancers stood clapping and hooting at the music makers, and though shiny boots had come to a stop, he swayed like loose hay bales when they're stacked too high.

Uncle Jack came up behind us. "Pup," he said, glowering, trying to haul me from my perch. "Let me have her." Then to me, "You c'mon now or you're gonna be in for it."

"I'm not getting down. I'm riding," I said, kicking my boot heels against the chest of my steed.

Shiny boots, whose name it seemed was Pup, which I thought was a very peculiar thing to name a person, went into uneven action as the musicians started up again, leaving Uncle Jack standing on the dance floor with a mean expression on his round face. As Pup lurched forward, I almost came off. He couldn't run as fast as Lady and I couldn't fall quite as far, but the seat wasn't as good and there was no horn to hang onto. I grabbed his ear with one hand, the slick yellow hair with the other.

"Hey, kid," he said, trying to untangle me, "easy on the hair." Swinging me from his shoulders, he clasped me to him, and holding me against his bright white shirt, waltzed in wide looping steps around the slick floor, hot whiskey breath searing the side of my face.

"Let me down," I bellowed, trying to wriggle out of his arms. Usually I'd have loved the attention, but it was too hot, too loud, too bright. He was pressing me too hard, and it made my head hurt. "I want to find my mom."

As Pup waltzed in front of the band, Uncle Jack made another grab and we almost wrecked. Pup clutched me even tighter, until I squealed. "Stop it!" I was taking a breath to holler, even if it meant losing my dignity and having to let my uncle rescue me, when Pup turned, still clutching me under the arms.

"Catch!" Pup hollered and threw me at Uncle Jack's head. I liked the feeling of flight, the intense pressure of being hurled into the air, as though if I tried, I could keep right on sailing—but my flight came to an end when Sherman stepped forward and caught me in his arms.

"That was a jackass thing to do, Pup," he said, lowering me to the floor. "You'd better catch some slack."

"Ah, she was havin' fun. Weren't you, cutie? C'mon then," he said, reaching for my hand with his sweaty fist. Then to Jack and Sherman, "I'll take her to Linda."

Sherman looked around the long room, then at me. "You okay, kid?" He shifted his hat and smoothed his dark hair back.

"I'm going to find my mom."

"Let's do 'er, little honey," Pup pressed. "Let's find her right now."

I wasn't about to go with him. I smiled at Sherman, then whirled and darted off through the forest of legs and boots.

Along the back of the dance hall, stretched like a long wooden horse trough, was a makeshift bar where my grandparents were sitting with another couple at a small table. Granddad was easy to spot in his dark green Mounted Deputy Sherriff's outfit, which he and Uncle Jack wore to all the rodeos and sporting events in the county. He had told me that if something bad were ever to happen, he and all the men in the mounted posse would get their horses, put on their green uniforms with the gold piping, pin a silver star over their hearts, and go help the police keep us safe. He waved when he saw me tramp off the dance floor. Light gleaming from her new diamond cat glasses, Mam, looking very nice in a summer dress and high heels, was leaning toward the other lady at the table, apparently very interested because her eyes danced like they did when she was on the telephone hearing something really juicy. She looked up but didn't see me. I turned my face away and strained to remain invisible. I didn't want her to swoop down on me.

My mom stood at the bar with her back to the dance floor, talking and laughing with her girlfriend, Mae. I pivoted in their direction. I liked Mae, my mother's all-time best friend. She was always nice and not bossy, but she didn't miss anything either. Short, and sweet-faced but a hard-tongued woman, she was forever talking and laughing, usually moving her beautiful, red-nailed hands in time with her fast red mouth. Just then, her red-tipped hand held a drink. She turned, saw me first, and elbowed my mother, who also turned to see me coming, trailing Pup like a tail. Mae made her "Oh, boy, what now" face, and my mother didn't look happy.

"Well, now, hee hee," Pup laughed, falling up to the bar between Mae and Linda. "Ain't I got all the prettiest girls in the room in one place? Look at you, look at you," he said, looking at my mother. "Bartender, git these ladies whatever they're drinkin'. Gimme a whiskey, straight."

"I have a drink," Mae said. "I don't need another."

My mother giggled at Mae. "Why, Mae, you just said . . ."

"Linda," Mae said, volume rising, "we told Dan we'd only be a minute."

"C'mon," Pup said, butting in on Mae. "It's early yet, ain't it, girl?" Looking at my mother like she was a big dessert, his hand rose and almost touched her shining hair.

I could tell she was liking the way he looked at her. "Thanks for finding Annie, but we're taking off."

"Ahh," he said, grinning, resting his hand on her shoulder, "I got to dance just once with the Queen of the Rodeo." He slid his arm around her waist and started dancing her around.

"Pup," Mae said, "that'd better be about the end of it. Put money on it. She's going with me and Dan."

Whirling my mother onto the dance floor, holding her way down, past her fancy tooled belt, I heard Pup say, "I've got something for you that money won't buy, darlin'."

They moved off and he was still talking but their voices were taken over by the music. Mae was glaring, dark eyes shooting harpoons at my mother, who ducked her head. Linda's lips moved and she smiled, but he must have said something wrong because she pulled away, finally jerking her hand from his and came toward the bar stiff legged, her face seeming to swell, casting visible streams of fury. She snatched the unfinished drink from Mae's hand.

"He's damned hard to get rid of." She took a cigarette from Mae's package. "I didn't want to have to do that."

"Do what? It's good you gave him the score instead of Bud hearing about it from someone else."

"Oh, Mae, Bud's not. . . He won't . . ."

"Look, you're gonna be with Bud in Cheyenne next week. He's the real article, not like some of these other yahoos nosing around." Linda looked at the floor then raised her head and opened her mouth to speak, but Mae jumped in again. "It doesn't matter what anyone says about what happened in Walla Walla. If Bud could ignore that, you sure don't want someone to see you here and tell Bud you're goin' around with another one of these dumbasses."

Left standing on the dance floor, Pup held himself very straight and marched off toward the big outside doors, passing Uncle Jack who stood by the doorway, fists clenched, watching him.

My mother finished Mae's drink then looked at me and looked again. "Isn't it about time for you to go to the car?"

"I'm staying with you," I said, feeling grumpy and wanting her for myself. "Why didn't you tell me you're leaving?"

"Oh, Annie. Who told you that?" Her face was in shadow, but her startled voice told me it was true. "We'll talk about it in the morning. We're going to a big party this new stock outfit is throwing. It's business; you know you can't go."

I knew, but I figured that if I hollered and made her feel bad enough, she'd take some time with me before she locked me in the car. Besides, with all the noise and people, with Lady's scaring me out of myself earlier, I felt the light was an attack, the noise a beast, all the world mean, and no place for me but the damn car. Tears came to my eyes before I could work up to hollering.

*

Outside the dance hall, the night was still warm, but there was a cool breeze and the stars were quiet. The steel guitar that had been like an assault inside the hall now seemed to embroider the stars and trees with silver ribbons of sound. My mother was walking through the grassy parking lot without talking, holding onto my hand. With the other hand, I wiped tears from my face.

"Stop that crying now, Annie," she said. "It's not going to do any good." We had arrived in front of the little outhouse. After listening at the door for the sound of other occupants, she cautiously pulled it open and pushed me inside. "Go now," she said. "You can't get out of the car."

"I can't see the hole. It stinks! You have to hold onto me," I howled, and started crying again. Just then, Virginia, my Uncle Jack's curly-headed girlfriend, came down the path toward us. I liked Virginia because she talked to me like I was a real person, not just some haywire kid. My grandmother didn't like her much though. She said Virginia was a hick and that no amount of training would ever make her into a lady. When I had said I thought Virginia was pretty, my mother had replied, "Pretty? With all that makeup caked on her?" After a moment she had flared, "I wear thee-at-rical make-up for my shows . . . it's different. I'm not cheap!" I had been embarrassed for my mother but wasn't sure why.

Standing in front of the outhouse, Virginia shuffled in her purse and brought out her Zippo, then held the flame over the doorway of the dark outhouse while my mother positioned me over the stinky, steaming hole.

Later, in the car, distracted by the ritual of bedtime, I'd quit crying and was snuffling, digging my fists into itching eyes.

"Puhleezz, pleeeze stay," I wheedled, knowing it wouldn't do any good but hoping. "You can sleep right here." I patted the wide back seat of the Packard where I lay with my riding clothes rolled under my head.

She had pulled off my boots and was banging them against the running board. "Look at that dirt. Hardly room in there for your feet."

Watching her, I wondered why she would rather be with her friends or riding in some rodeo than be with me.

"Good night, Anniekins," she said, placing my boots on the floor. Cranking up the car windows, her pretty head outlined against the silver glass, she peered toward the dancehall.

"Don't put the windows up," I howled. I didn't like to be

shut in, but also hoped to gain more of her time through my objections.

"Annie," she said, "stop. They're waiting. You don't want me to get Mam out here, do you?"

She knew that was exactly what I did not want. Mam would hit if I didn't do what she said, but the hitting was better than her words. "What do you mean spoiling your poor mother's fun," she'd say through gritted teeth. "You are one selfish brat, and that's the truth." I wondered if she might be right about me. I must surely be the *very* worst child in the world to put us through such tortures.

My mother kissed me on the forehead and left, closing the heavy door, but didn't roll up the windows all the way. I wanted to say, 'You know how mean she is,' but I knew my mother was determined to go with her friends, and if I said any of this tonight, I would be met with a furious Mam.

Curled against the roll of my riding clothes, I looked out the window trying to see the stars, but the tree's dark arms stretched over the car. It was quiet except for the sound from the fiddles and steel guitar, an occasional laugh or a few muffled words from people walking to the outhouse or horse barns. I put my hands to my wet face. *I was just a scaredy-cat, bad girl with wild hair that nobody wanted. Even Lady was bad to me.* At the thought of Lady's betrayal, new tears rolled down my cheeks, then came even faster until I was sobbing, my nose so choked that I couldn't breathe. I finally stopped because I couldn't get air.

In the silver darkness of the car and the deeper darkness inside me—darkness I felt as a hot, wet animal in my chest—I was the one human being in a mean and lonely world. My thoughts were as convulsive as my sobs and cries had been. Teeth gritted, new tears scalding my eyes, I chanted between wails. *I have to be big! Big like them. I have to be big now. They won't take care of me. Maybe,* I thought, wiping tears and snot from my nose and face, searching for something of light among my black thoughts, *maybe Granddad will help. He still loves me.* But as soon as I thought it, I knew that he was Mam's, my mother's, and even before me, Uncle Jack's, not mine. *There's no one for me. Nooo one . . . even my own father left and didn't care what happened to me.* Mam had beaten me with this fact since I could remember, and no one said different, so I guessed it must be true. He didn't even want to meet me. Didn't want to know me at all. *None of them want me. Why do I care about them?* The effort of crying numbed me, and I sat in the dark, patting it around me like love.

I was staring out the window, my desperate thoughts finally trailing into resolution and silence. From somewhere in my desensitized mind, like a mouse scurrying through a rapidly closing door, I heard a soft voice . . . *If you're bad anyway, and they don't care . . . why then, it doesn't matter what you do, does it? What else can they do to you?* This fleeting voice caused my spirits to prick up the way Lady's ears had that morning. It caused my somehow resurrected feelings to race. *What could Mam really do to me? Beat on me some more? Leave me? Kill me?*

Let her! Maybe then, somebody would be sorry. Very sorry. My mother would sob over my coffin. I'd be lying there in my dancing dress with tears on my face. Her tears. She'd throw herself down and weep and moan like I'd done tonight. She'd wish she'd spent time with me while I was alive. Mam would be stricken, like a dead person herself. She'd be broken, and never lift a hand to strike anyone again. Uncle Jack would be glad to get rid of me, but I didn't care about him. He was ruined already. Only Granddad would be sad. The thought of his sadness tempted me to recant and forgive, but I hardened myself. *It would be best this way.*

And just at that thought a vision overtook me, coming in full daylight color. There was Bud in his gray hat and white shirt, standing on the porch of the pay booth at the Cow Palace. He was flicking a cigarette into the hot gravel and walking toward me. He had said he was coming. I still had the ten dollars he'd given me to buy a new dress. I'd folded it carefully and hidden it in my Nancy Drew book because if Mam knew, she'd have hounded me to save it for a rainy day. *If I tell Sherman about the money, maybe he'd help me buy a dress before he leaves for California, then I'll be ready when Bud comes.*

I felt in the dark for my boots, stuffed my feet inside, and struggled to lift the tight button on the door lock. *When Bud saw me in the dress, he'd think I was so nice and beautiful—and good—that he'd marry Linda, and then he'd make her stay home and we could move to the beautiful old house by my big tree and be a family all of our own. I'd still see Granddad and the horses, but Mam couldn't get to me anymore. Bud would protect me.*

He would.

I stood in the warm darkness looking up at the sky, surging with hope and feeling happier just to be outside. Trying to rid myself of the dark feelings that had overwhelmed me in the car, I shook myself all over then stood still, watching the trees behind the barn make curly patterns against the moon-bright sky.

Wondering how to find Sherman, I noticed a faint track that headed toward the sound of singing and guitars. The path ended in a clearing where a campfire glowed, red sparks shooting upward into a glittering sky. Lazing around a circle, a few cowboys and their girls sat before the fire, their backs mostly to me, some lifting paper sacks to their mouths, some singing.

I heard a bang and peering behind me saw a woman's dark figure leave the outhouse headed my way. *If a man found me, I probably wouldn't get in trouble, but if a woman was involved, she'd get all in a tizzy and have to go tell someone—like Mam—that I was on the loose.* I squeezed myself off the path into some dusty brush, lay on my stomach, and held my breath. Suddenly afraid that she would see me, I lay my forehead on my hands and closed my eyes. As the rustle of her skirt through the grass came almost even with me, I heard heavy steps hurrying up the path behind her.

"Hold up there, sweetie," a voice said, thick with breath, yet soft. It was a voice I knew.

"What's a beauty like you doing out here all by your lonesome?" All the feet stopped moving, and the woman giggled.

"I'm not alone, honey. Jack's down at the fire." Then there were some heavy sounds, and some touching sounds, and Virginia said, "Pup!"

Taking a chance, I looked up. At first, I couldn't see anything, then I saw a shiny-toed boot planted in front of my face, the hem of Virginia's skirt swaying in front of it.

"God, you're so beautiful, darlin'. I just can't help it. Just touch him, honey. Touch him."

The shiny boots backed up and almost touched my cheek. Not caring if they did see me, I rolled on my back and stared straight up. Virginia was pulling back, and Pup had hold of her hand, dragging on it.

"Oh, get away," she kind of screamed in a very quiet, squeaky way. "You're drunk."

I felt the night collapse around me and a roar over the top of my head. Pup turned, trying to stuff his dangling white worm in his pants. Then Virginia screamed, and a demon flew into Pup, knocking him on top of me, taking my wind. I tried to crawl away, but something grabbed my leg. I heard grunts and thumps, then a crack, a pause, then more grunts honking through the night as the demon lifted Pup's head and banged it in the dirt. I was kicking for all I was worth, trying to get loose.

"Jack, Jack, Jack," Virginia screamed, over and over.

Pup lurched to his hands and knees, freeing me to scramble from the dusty path and run right into Virginia, who was still screaming into the night, one hand to her curly head, the other stabbing the air in Pup's direction.

Uncle Jack had Pup in a headlock, standing there with flat gray eyes like he couldn't see anything, his breath starting to wheeze with the asthma.

Sherman and a couple of cowboys came tearing toward us when Jack shoved Pup headlong. Sherman caught him in a bear hug and held on, while the other cowboy, his face cracked in an ugly frown, moved up behind them.

"P-pperverted- son- of- a- bitch," Uncle Jack said, straining to say each word.

"She wanted it. Just like your sister wanted it when she got it, Jackie boy." Pup's words were slow and nasty, and before he finished saying "boy," Jack jumped right into him, hitting him smack in the middle. Pup howled and fell on the ground where he lay in a ball; a slug curled around salt.

That moment seemed to last the night. All I heard was Uncle Jack's wheezing breath, then he deliberately turned his gaze from Pup. His bulging eyes moved slowly, slowly, past Virginia and finally fastened on me. Now, somehow, this was my fault too.

Chapter 6

HOW ANNIE'S SEARCH FOR MONEY AND DRESSES LEAD TO HER BIGGEST ADVENTURE YET

EMERALD CITY, OREGON, FALL 1951

Like the aftermath of any blast, the incidents that night at the rodeo grounds set in motion waves that continued to roll over me, enforcing the resolution I'd come to in the dark car—I had to be a grown-up like the rest of them, and *fast!* I was determined to either find a husband for Linda and a father for me, or if Linda couldn't do it, find my own husband and create my own family. But while still hopeful, I had made no progress in either direction. How to go about it? That was my problem. Though I couldn't see how, I was sure it was up to me alone to solve; if left to others someone would surely mess it up. Everything in me was straining to bring about my ideal immediately but it wasn't happening, so there was nothing to do but wait for my moment and try to develop a new plan.

I never did talk to Sherman the night of the rodeo dance, never bought a dress, and didn't see Bud again for almost a year. After all the commotion that night at the fairgrounds, Virginia had walked me back to the car wiping tears from her face. Patting me on the back, blowing her nose, she had said, "Don't tell about this, Annie." She turned her wet hankie over and blew again. "And please don't tell Mam."

"I won't tell, Virginia." I had felt sorry for her. We both knew that if Mam found out she'd blame everything on Virginia—or me—no matter who started it. Black streaks dripped down her face, her pink mouth was wiped away, and her curly hair was a mess. "You better fix up if you don't want them to know."

"I will, honey . . . Oh, my purse!" she said, turning and looking out the window. "I left it in Jack's truck."

Virginia was next to me on the backseat where my mother had sat earlier, looking toward the dance hall the way my mother had. I didn't think Virginia looked as pretty, especially because of all the crying, but I remember thinking that even though Mam didn't think much of her, she might be nicer than my mother. Then I felt like a skunk for thinking such a thing.

In spite of Mam's reservations about her, a few weeks later, on a September afternoon, Jack and Virginia were married. They stood side by side on the parklike lawn of Great Uncle Ed and Aunt Fern's big, fancy house that Mam called a monstrosity. Squinting her eyes as we walked up the drive, Mam said, "Well, after all, who but a timber camp cook would paint that huge place pink? Money can't buy taste, Annie." As we drew closer, she looked over at me. "But Fern just loves color. She always did love color."

It was my opinion that she was jealous because her brother made more money being a timber baron than Granddad made at the bank. But Mam didn't have to be jealous. Everyone knew that Granddad was the best catch in the whole family. He was the handsomest, the one who had been to the best college, and had been a track star, then coach at the university. He acted in the Little Theatre plays and could recite "The Cremation of Sam McGee," and he knew all about gardens and horses and he was even giving Virginia away because her father was dead. He was everyone's favorite—and mine.

When Jack saw me standing with the small wedding party, he headed for me, a look in his eyes that told me what he had to say wouldn't be welcome. *What have I done now?* I ducked around Mam, aiming to hide in her wake when she firmly detached me and walked down the aisle to her seat, leaving me exposed. Happily, for me, the music started, and Jack stepped back to stand beside his bear hunting buddy and best man.

We trailed solemnly behind Grandad and Virginia down the long lawn toward the minister, Georgiana in apricot silk, me in tight, scratchy blue. Virgie wore a white summer dress with red flowers on it and a red hat with net flouncing off the back. Uncle Jack did not dress up, but he did wear a clean white shirt with his best red suspenders. Standing behind them during the ceremony, I was feeling a little happier too. Now Uncle Jack would finally be moving out of the ranch house and into his own place. And about high time, Great Aunt Maggie had said. I looked over at Georgiana, who was gazing at the ceremony with big eyes, thinking, *Now he'll have you to torment.*

After the wedding, waiters from the country club wearing short jackets and bow ties served dinner. After dinner and a big, delicious cake, Uncle Jack took Virginia, Georgiana, and Penny, their new puppy, around to all the white-draped tables introducing them to every single person there. Georgiana was Virginia's daughter from a former—and in Mam's opinion, disastrously common—marriage. Georgiana was pretty with blond curls, big brown eyes, and had some kind of heart murmur or something. Everyone at the wedding made a big fuss over her, even Granddad. I hated her guts.

※

Not long after the wedding, the torture of third grade in full swing, my mother left again. Several days before, when Linda had gone with Granddad to pick up Monte, her new trick horse, Mam had cornered me on my way to the barn. She stood by the back door with a rag, kind of washing at the woodwork, pretending she wasn't waiting for me.

She said there was to be a little party to celebrate my mother's big contract and that she would be leaving soon. The smell of cleaner going up my nose, she said, "You'll have to get used to it!"

She set a hand on my shoulder as I was trying to edge out the door. In my view, she never told me anything unless she had some reason—usually to make me do something I didn't want to do. I didn't want to hear it. *Parties—boo.* I always had to dress up, could never do what I wanted, and no one would let me talk. I looked up at her.

Oh, yeah. I'd be having a real good time. I'd be happy to see my mother go and not say a word to make her feel bad about leaving. No other specific directions, just an open-ended threat. I had to wear my tight flower-girl dress to the party. I had to listen to noisy congratulations on her big East Coast contract, the talk of her new horse, what a runner he was, her arrangements to leave, and pretend I wasn't dying inside. Maybe that was the last time I thought of her as Mommy: *Oh, no, Mommy. Don't go.*

It was around then I noticed I couldn't sit still and was tuned to a new and higher pitch of alertness. I'd find myself investigating whatever space I occupied, my eyes searching bookcases, following the lines and angles of ceiling and walls, taking detailed inventories of dark closets, questioning each object sharing my space, even exploring the thoughts crowding my mind. Mam said I was either acting like I had ants in my pants or lying around like a lazy slug. But I was thinking.

*

WINTER 1952

I didn't like much of anything that winter. Except Lady. She was my friend again, but after the big rains, the flat fields to the west became beautiful marshes, too soggy to ride in. Just after another downpour that had lasted two days, Lady and I were looking over her stall door watching the ducks swimming in the new lakes spreading like silver over the ranch pastures. I was supposed to be in school, but instead of catching the bus, I was hiding in the barn, brushing Lady and thinking about our problems.

Lady, now retired from her job as trick horse, had to stand in her stall. I was supposed to go to school every weekday. I was also supposed to take the rural school bus but usually missed it. My mother was gone, and Mam was mad all the time. For one thing, just as I thought, she didn't like the ranch house. She said it wasn't shaped right, the kitchen was cramped, and none of the furniture from the house on the hill fit. She wanted to rip it up and remodel it all. Apparently, Granddad said she had to wait until they made money off some kind of highway leases. She was furious but instead of getting mad at Granddad for saying no, she took it out on me—for being me.

When the teachers at Elijah Bristow Elementary began sticking pictures of hearts above the blackboards, Mam and I had had another big fight. Even though I envisioned myself as a girl out of a Wild West show, a rough rider, and the scourge of any bad guys, the girls at my school had other models. They also had pretty dresses. I thought I should have some dresses, so I'd fit in. I also thought my new clothes required the flair to suit my status—heiress to the World Champion Trick Rider's throne. After looking myself over in the floor length mirror, I had figured the girls made fun of me because of the way I dressed and the way Mam braided my hair. My dresses came from Great Aunt Maggie's tall granddaughters and were always too tight around my stomach with hems drooping to my ankles. My school shoes were tennis shoes, run over cowboy boots, or the same kind of high-top Buster Browns I'd been wearing for good since I could remember. The kids at school called them baby shoes, and to make things worse, my socks were always knitted with different colored yarn ends from Mam's famous argyles. Mam said they were original. Her attitude was, "Why would you want to fit in?" She said the country kids were hicks, and when she saw them, she was kind of too nice and creepy to them.

I had insisted, "I want *new* clothes for school, Mam."

She had stood in the kitchen slicing potatoes into the new electrified frying pan. Granddad sat at the kitchen booth thumbing through a seed catalogue. He looked at his watch, then stood, and walked into the living room where he switched on the T.V. In the kitchen, I heard the music for the news program. Mam had watched him go and didn't look at me. In the other room the announcer was saying, "Sit back, light up a Camel and be a witness to the history that's taken place in the last twenty-four hours. This story begins with the revelation and the admission that senator Richard Nixon was receiving what amounted to a private salary . . ."Mam, who had her ear trained on the T.V., let out a sigh and adjusted the heat on the frying pan.

"Mam," I'd said, moving closer and standing next to her at the counter. "I *need* new clothes for school. I look like a baby, and all the other girls' mothers sew pretty dresses for them."

"Clothes? You've got clothes. Plenty," she said, ear cocked

at the T.V. in the other room. Now that she had become even more political, always working for "the party," she listened to the news every morning and every night and read all the newspapers trying to figure out how to get her Republicans elected. She removed a round tub of shortening from the cupboard, scooped out a glob with the spatula, and zapped it into the pan. Fat jumped up and stung me on the forehead.

"Oww," I howled, jumping back feeling injured as if she'd burned me on purpose. "I want clothes," I hollered.

"And just where do you think the money for those clothes is going to come from?"

She had me there. Aside from having someone give me money, like Bud or Granddad, I'd never before thought about where money came from. "Well, where does it come from?"

She moved to the sink, rinsed her hands, then turned and placed her wet hand on my forehead. "Where does money come from?" She lifted her hand, looked, and clamped it down again. "That's a good one. It seems like some people around here think it grows on trees."

"C'mon Mam, tell me." If I knew, I could get some, and buy my own clothes.

"Don't be silly."

I pulled away, suddenly furious. "Tell me! Tell me right now!" I screamed.

"I'll tell you this," she said, turning on me with the look I knew meant that she might whack me if I said anything more, "You bother Granddad with your bellyaching, and you'll be sorry."

"You have money," I said, backing from the kitchen and disappearing out the mudroom door. I had moped past Granddad's garden and across the drive to the barn. Of course, I still had the money Bud had given me, but that was for a special dress. Not an everyday school dress. Lady, on seeing me, had come trotting to her stall. Brushing her and updating her on Mam's latest treacheries, when I came to the main problem with the dresses, I had changed to the stiffer brush and began to work on her mane. She put her head down and pushed hard on the brush, wanting me to scratch her more. During the further recitation of my woes, I had been brushing like mad, had finished picking her mane and tail, and had scrubbed her feet until the light part of her hooves was white as bone, and she was gleaming all over. I put her feed in the manger, stored the brushes, and walked toward the ranch house hoping that Mam was busy with one of her projects so she wouldn't start in on me again.

That night, arms full of my clean T-shirts and jeans, Mam had marched down into the red and black room as I was getting in bed.

"Your faaather is supposed to send money to feed you and keep you in clothes." She had said *father* in that mean way, dragging out the A sound, like she always did when she had to talk about him. She dumped the clothes on Linda's empty bed and began to put them away. "It's called support money. Haw! That's good. He doesn't send enough, and I will *not* have you saying anything about it in front of Granddad." She shoved my socks in the shirt drawer and shut it with a thud.

I was about to ask why, but the look in her eyes and the way her mouth tightened down had warned I'd better not or she'd launch into orbit like the devastating dark star she could become. *Money . . . For me?* Here was a clue to . . . something. I lay in bed and thought about support money until I slept.

About two weeks after Mam got so mad about the clothes, she brought me one pink plaid, pleated wool skirt and a white blouse that was too tight around the arms. I wore the skirt to school almost every day, until I stained it with the orange Kool-Aid I kept in my desk and licked out of my hand during class. Then the kids made fun of the pink plaid skirt with the orange Kool-Aid stains. Soon, I couldn't wear it even if Mam had sent it to the cleaners, because it was too tight around the stomach. Then Mam started telling me I was fat and no one had any use for fatties. That winter in the cold barn talking everything over with Lady and thinking on what Mam had said caused a move further into myself, and away from my family. Especially Mam.

*

ARMITAGE ROAD SPRING AND SUMMER 1953

"I like the way your hair's wrapped up like that." Margie smiled down on me from atop a little red horse standing in the ranch driveway.

That morning in an agony of pulled hair and commands not to move an inch, Mam had wrapped my braids in round circles and pinned them tight to my head, so I had hair muffs covering both ears. "The Indian children in Arizona where your mom is wear their hair this way," she said. "Don't you want to try it?"

I'd shrugged and attempted to pull away. After Margie's compliment, I thought maybe it didn't look so bad after all.

Margie's hair was shiny black, cut in a grown-up pixie, and her laughing black eyes tilted up over high, round cheekbones. She sat easily on her little mare, softly bouncing moccasined feet against the horse's belly. "Saw you all moving in," she said. "You've sure got a horse or two. I've only got Gypsy here. I'm going down to ride with Vena." She gestured to the big turn in the road toward a tiny white house across the western cornfield that I later learned belonged to the Andersens. "I'll wait for you to get your horse if you wanta' come. You sure do have a bunch."

Me, go with her? I was thrilled that she paid any attention to me at all, as I was younger, and a newcomer. I ran to get

Lady, jumped on bareback and hurried to join her. This was a whole new and exciting area of investigation.

As the weather warmed and the daffodils came up in the ditches, I lost myself exploring the countryside, walking and riding in the valley fields, and spent hours up the road at Margie's. The Delaunay's small house sat north of the ranch, in a hollow of their walnut orchard. It looked like Snow White's cottage with a peaked roof, rounded wood doors, and pink roses climbing the rock pillars in front. Gypsy, Margie's little horse, lived in a small red barn behind the house. When I asked how they got such a beautiful house, her dad, Edward, held up his hands, "Well, I made it myself. That's how."

Now, not only did I have Margie's whole place to discover, but across the road from Margie's, on the same side of the road as the ranch, Margie's grandmother (her grandfather had died before I came along) lived in a big old farmhouse with two tall maples shading the house and barn. I thought the place was perfect, but when I told Mam about it, she told Linda that the Armitage and Delaunay houses were the two oldest farmhouses in the county and belonged in a museum.

Though Margie was six years older, our birthdays were the same month, which I thought was somehow significant. From the first day we rode together, I adored Margie, and thought she was the most beautiful girl—almost a teenager—I'd ever seen. I think she liked being the object of my adoration, and since we were both only children, we confided in each other during long rides.

We talked about everything. I would tell her things I noticed about my family, and she'd laugh and say, "Annie, only you'd think of saying something like that."

When I asked what she meant she wouldn't meet my eyes, but a little later she said, "Well, you're certainly not afraid to say whatever you think."

All through the hottest months of summer and into

October, we rode our horses miles over the gold and violet countryside. We climbed to the top of the mountains overlooking the river where we sat on our horses in the sunshine watching the red-tailed hawks glide across the valley toward the west. We pulled the still ripe berries from the vines, eating them until we were full and then feeding them to the horses, their noses slathering berries all over our hands, leaving the horses with blue stains around their soft mouths. Riding bareback, we would set out in the mornings, and sometimes not return until dark. Our eyes on a distant goal—a mountaintop, a small neighboring community, once the library in town—we saw no problem in riding straight for our landmark. In their time, our pioneer ancestors had gone much further than the next range of mountains and we had heard the stories all our lives. Why not us? Mam never seemed to mind, so I stayed out more and more.

Later, that fall, on purple evenings, we bundled up in sweaters and rain gear, and rode along the river's edge, through golden dripping branches in a mist of rain. Margie had been riding the valley floor all of her life, and knew every kid on the surrounding farms, the cutest boys, and all the shortcuts to the wide meadows where we could run the horses, the ferny thickets where in the heat of summer we could climb down, lie in the tall grass while the horses ate beside us, and lazily dream our futures.

One Indian Summer evening, after a long day of riding alone, I had turned Missy out and walked barefoot down the center of the road to Margie's, popping warm tar bubbles with my toes and inhaling the farm smell of blackberries and hayfields. To get to Margie's, I had to pass Jack and Virginia's new trailer plunked down at the edge of the far horse pasture. Uncle Jack, pipe clamped in his jaw, eyes like silver dollars behind his glasses, seemed to always be sitting in his chair, scowling out the window, never seeming to miss anything. I figured if anyone wondered where I was, they could find out from him. At least I didn't have to be in the same house with him anymore.

When I had turned Missy into the pasture earlier, she had trotted off in search of the other mares like a middle-aged auntie with news, and they still huddled together in the middle pasture, swishing their tails. Ambling up the road to Margie's, I was a little stiff from riding all day and felt the pinkness of sunburn on my nose, arms and top of my legs, dirt, grit and leaves in my hair, dust sticking to my tacky skin. I had found a new friend, I loved the ranch, and felt happy. Linda would come home and marry Bud, and then it would all be perfect. Almost at the end of our fence line, I crossed to the other side of the road so I wouldn't have to walk right in front of Uncle Jack's window.

Approaching the cottage set in the shady walnut grove, I could smell apple pies. LaVetta, Margie's mom, stood at the kitchen sink looking through the window at me, hair in pin curls, a bright scarf tied around her head, the ends tucked behind her ears. Tall, slender, and black haired like Margie, she was pretty, with black eyes and high cheekbones like a movie star, and she wore wire-rimmed glasses. She was the first person I'd known who wore glasses and was also beautiful. She was a beauty operator too and had said she'd cut my bangs anytime they needed it. At first, when I started to show up and hang around, LaVetta had made me call and tell Mam I was staying for supper, but now she just smiled and waved as I pushed the iron latch on the back door, skirted a basket of apples, and walked in. Sometime that summer, I'd stopped knocking. That evening, the Delaunay's house was full of pie smells, and somewhere in the background, meaty aromas made me want to open the oven and look inside.

"How are you today, Annie? I saw you coming home on Missy. Margie was upset she wasn't out there with you, but we had to get the ironing done."

I was fascinated that Margie actually knew how to do "house" things, and that LaVetta not only let her but insisted that she do them. She nodded toward the garden.

"She's out back. Tell her dinner's about ready. You staying? That's a ham in the oven."

Passing through the cozy house, I followed an electrical cord through a door opening onto a patio and a long yard and garden surrounded by fruit and nut trees. Margie stood barefoot on the lawn, leaning over the ironing board attacking a shirt. She was singing along with the radio to "Glow Worm," patting her tanned foot on the grass, pink-painted toes winking in the shade. Edward, Margie's dad, was in the barn at the end of the yard sawing and banging on something, and Margie's little red horse was pacing back and forth along the fence waiting for her dinner. Walking into their lives was like walking into a carefree, safe movie with a full-time mom and dad on duty. It all seemed perfect to me. I came to know their family story like it was my own—imperfectly.

*

FALL 1953

I now had the comfort of the ranch, the horses, and Margie—but still, something was missing. Of course, I missed my mother, but it was more than that. There was surely more, but it was vague and intangible. As that fall turned to another winter, I moped around and pretended to be sick so I didn't have to go to school. Alone in the sprawling ranch house all day, I watched the new television—never missing *Queen for a Day*—and ate sugar out of the brown sugar box. Restless and becoming even more unable to sit still, I felt an urgent need to know everything—to know something, to find something—but

I didn't know what.

One winter afternoon, feeling especially restless, I rose from the sofa and without knowing quite why, began rummaging through the drawers and bookcases in the living room. I soon concluded that there was little of promise in the books and magazines stored there. I moved on. After exhausting all their hideouts on the floor of the bedroom closets, I started on the top shelves. Scooting a chair to the door of my bedroom closet, I stacked my red stool on the chair seat and climbed up to reach the shelf above the hanging clothes. There, I hit a modest jackpot. On the highest closet shelf in the black and red bedroom, I found pictures of my mother and father's wedding. I had begged to see pictures of him, but my mother always said she couldn't remember where she'd put them. Well, I had found them for her. They were in a big white book on the top shelf of the closet, under the round box full of Mam's old hats.

Balancing on my stool, the big album propped against the closet doorframe, I turned the book toward the window and considered my father's face. He didn't look like anything special. He didn't look bad or ugly. He didn't look like me. He was about as tall as my mother, smooth, and round, with darker hair than mine combed back from an oval face with eyes that might have been shaped like mine. He was standing very straight in a dark uniform, not smiling. My mother was doing the smiling, standing beside him in a white satin dress that flowed around her in waves covering the steps leading to a church. I thought my mother looked very beautiful, but they were people I didn't know, who seemed to have nothing to do with me. I was glad to have found the pictures, and I thought my mother would be happy they weren't lost, but I still wasn't satisfied. Standing on my swaying stool, gazing out the window at the rain falling sharply on the bare crab apple branches, I realized I hadn't found whatever it was I needed to find.

Every time I stayed home from school, which was more and more often, I'd burrow to the back of the most crowded closets. I wasn't looking for the beaded moccasins in the back of Granddad's closet or the tiny sparkling handbag and lace dresses in Mam's bottom drawer. I wasn't looking for pictures of the horses or Granddad's book of lists and figures, although these items and others sometimes caused me to sit in front of an open drawer puzzling over its contents. Shoving these items back where they belonged, I intently rifled through desk and dresser drawers, under sinks, in suitcases stored in hall closets, and moving outside ransacked each cupboard and crevice on the ranch.

I explored behind the hay in the loft and dug through old dusty boxes stacked in the shop. Finally, on a windy February afternoon, having moved the search out again to the long shop, I stood shivering in the dim building. I pulled the string on the light bulb and moved toward the back wall. There, in a dark recess, behind a partition where my grandfather kept tools and farm things, rickety furniture and loosely framed pictures, I discovered a tall cardboard box, damp on one corner. I felt like my favorite heroine Nancy Drew when I looked inside it and found a heap of sagging shoeboxes, full of letters bundled with string.

The envelopes were of thin, nearly translucent paper, with red and blue stamps all over, little stars of mildew dusting their surface and mouse-chewed along the edges. Dated 1944 and 1945, most sent from Italy, they were addressed to my mother in loopy, cursive writing. The name on the upper left of each envelope read Lt. Jeffrey Butler. Forgetting the cold, I sat on the concrete floor and worked them open with my fingers, careful not to further tear the cracked paper. Inside were places where the writing—one word, sometimes whole sentences—was blacked out. The shop was lit by a single bulb and the cursive was hard to read, but that didn't matter. I was only looking for places where he talked about me. I sat on the cold floor and read, eyes watering and sneezing from the musty, mousey smell, and finally found a place where he wrote about me. He had wanted me to be a boy, and he wanted to name me Spike "Killer" Butler. Cold burned the hand that held me propped on the floor. *Killer? Wasn't that what Mam had said about me? And Spike, after the dog!* With numb fingers, I put all the letters back, and didn't tell anyone I'd found them. In fact, I ignored them. Or maybe only thought I did.

Yet, that didn't stop my search. Idling around on another rainy afternoon soon after I'd found the letters, I was pacing the entry hall and ended up in front of Mam's tall glass-fronted desk beside the gun case. Outside, rain came down in silver sheets that broke onto the porch steps, while inside I pawed through the little slots and pullout drawers, through letters, wrinkled receipts, her notebooks and folded scraps of paper and finally uncovered a white book, *Addresses,* stamped in gold lettering on the front. I opened it and moved closer to the window. On the inside front page, in her distinctive flowing handwriting was the number of the hotel where my mother was staying.

I dialed zero for the operator and recited the number. When the hotel switchboard lady came on, I imitated the way I'd heard Mam say, "Linda Chapman, please."

In a moment she said, "She isn't in. Would you like to leave a message?"

I hesitated, picturing a blond woman with red lipstick who knew it was me, and was considering whether to tell Mam on me. I hung up without answering. Slumping in the chair, I turned the pages of the address book, studying the names. I turned to the Bs. Directly under the big B at the top of the page was the name Jeffrey Butler. Below was my father's address and a phone number in New York. I picked up the phone and dialed the operator. *I'd see if what Mam kept telling me about* him was true. If he was the kind of person who really wanted to name their child "killer," and wasn't at all nice, shouldn't I know? But maybe they were wrong, maybe he was really nice, maybe he was a kidder, and if he saw me, he'd be so excited that he'd hug me and smile and be thrilled to meet me after all this time.

Chapter 7

IN 1999 JIM IS DELAYED, WHILE IN 1953 ANNIE FLIES TO NEW YORK CITY TO MEET HER FATHER AND ARRANGE FOR BUD TO MARRY LINDA, STAR OF THE MADISON SQUARE GARDEN RODEO

SUMMER 1999: MAY 23, ARMITAGE HOUSE

Jim called that morning to say there was a problem on the job, and he would be delayed. His news hardly penetrated yet was so upsetting, my feelings so unfocused and hopeless, I was crying as we hung up. Outside sitting on the porch, staring over the cornfield, I finally wiped my face and determined that delay was good. The sooner he came the sooner "it" (I could not characterize or label the situation) would be over. I also could not imagine "over." Then, I thought perhaps I could imagine it, and my mind shied so violently that I went back to blanking it out.

I rose and went inside to contemplate the downstairs bedroom and the pantry. I could pitch giveaways in the laundry room. Everything within me had fought it, but I had finally forced myself to form the beginnings of a rough plan. I knelt and drew a shoebox from under the bed. Inside, was a small bronze replica of the Statue of Liberty. Feeling the weight of it in my hand, I knew it was probably just a cheap souvenir but, in those days, even cheap, they made things better. At seven, Mel, my travel-loving daughter, had adopted it. When she moved the first time, I had packed it away . . . . And then I was in tears again. Plan or not, to avoid another full-out, lay-down crying episode, I found my purse and left the house.

Driving up the lane, stopping at the crossroads, trying to distract myself from "it," I kept my eye on the road ahead and not on the many changes going on at either side of the intersection. The only change I approved was the new movie theater at the mall where the Crossroads Tavern had stood in what had once been Calef's' cornfield. I parked and crossed the lot toward the theater, smelling not the pungent fields and wildflowers but only the hot reek of gently rolling blacktop.

Inside, I bought a ticket for the show and took a seat. This movie-going wasn't a new solution for me. I'd always loved movies, and like any love affair emerged from them somehow changed, but this particular bout of compulsivity had started about two weeks after I had arrived that summer. I'd go in the afternoons when tickets were still cheap and I was too tired or upset to work anymore, when the cruelty of "it" became overwhelming. Suspending my feelings through an obsession with the stories of others, I often moved from theater to theater, not even seeing a whole feature, but only parts. Somehow, this movie-going returned me to sanity, and I could leave the dark theater, return and face the house, the family mess.

With *The Spy Who Shagged Me*, and a John Travolta murder mystery about a female U.S. soldier being betrayed, tortured, and finally killed re-running in my mind, I drove slowly home. For a period of about three weeks in the spring of 1962, just before I'd met the girls' dad, under the lure of the cool uniforms and the fact that the government would pay for college and travel, I had decided to join the Army where I would surely become a woman of the world. *Where would I be now if I had? Dead? Serving life in prison? Or maybe the discipline would have been the best thing for me?* I never found out. Mam certainly had strong ideas about how I'd end up though. She was so genuinely horrified by my plan that I probably would have enlisted immediately if I hadn't just met Ted.

Back at Armitage House that evening with new resolve, I faced the box again and took up the bronze statue. Holding it to the light reminded me of the Columbia Pictures symbol with torch aloft, of the hours of joy, and exposure to worlds I might never see that the movies had provided me. I wouldn't be giving it away.

I thought of the next part of the story as a movie, a cross between *Dr. Zhivago*, *The Godfather* (in my case it would have to be *The Grandmother*), and *Pulp Fiction*, the point of view omniscient.

*

THE CHAPMAN RANCH, ARMITAGE ROAD, SEPTEMBER 1953

The scene opens on a sunny fall afternoon; an Oregon hayfield in front of the Chapman ranch house.

Eight years old, with long chestnut braids, wearing jeans and tennis shoes, and brandishing a whip, I stood atop two black and white horses with a foot on the back of each. I had lengthened the bridle reins with rope and the long-suffering horses were yoked together at the neck, also with rope. In the background, a long expanse of gold field led to a river and blue mountains in the distance. I threatened the horses with the whip, hollering, "C'mon, get up, you lame-legged hay burners. C'mon, Missy! Get over there, Lady."

FASTER HORSES

The horses, with me standing atop them, bounded forward in a headlong gallop. As the horses reached the road, a shiny orange and white Mercury convertible rounded the deep curve directly in their path. Judging speed and distance, I urged the horses to run faster.

Mam, driving the convertible, was well dressed for an afternoon tea. She hit the brakes, causing the car to skid, as the horses skirted the Mercury's bumper, jumped the ditch at the side of the road, and continued at a dead run across the field toward the mountains.

I looked back to see Mam, scowling, chewing gum furiously, jump from her convertible. She stood at the side of the road, hands on her hips. The car sat with one wheel in the ditch.

Mam hollered, "Annie Butler, you git back here right now. I'll skin you alive! You'll break your neck."

Urging the horses to go faster, high with excitement and fear, braids flying in the wind, I could feel myself grinning wildly. I didn't see Mam, turning back to the car, break a heel and twist her ankle painfully. But even with my back to her, I could feel her glaring after us as the horses ran at top speed across the field.

That evening inside the ranch house, Mam and Granddad sat side by side in easy chairs. Mam looked up from regarding her soaking ankle to say, "She just can't go running around the countryside with her hair all over the place like one of the darn horses, Daddy. Just like a wild Indian. Why, Jack saw her down in the pasture with the horses in the middle of the night. Just standing there in her nightshirt, holding her arms to the sky. I've about had it!"

Granddad, using the newspaper as a gentle shield, rose and turned the new T.V. to the fights. He adjusted the sound and returned to his chair.

Mam continued over the loud T.V. "I can't stay home and

watch her every minute." She raised her voice again, "I just *cannot* do it."

Granddad shifted in his chair and viewed Mam from beneath a worried brow.

"You wait until you get the phone bill. She's been trying to call New York again. I heard her then she lied about it. The only reason Annie's not calling her mother every minute is because the hotel people can't ever find Linda and get her to the phone. Now, Daddy . . ." Mam, more agitated than when she began, leaned toward him to make her point, and almost upset her soak water. She rose, looking daggers over her shoulder, and hobbled into the kitchen. "We can't just leave her running around the hills like a wild Indian. It's dangerous, Daddy."

I sat to the side of the screen door, looking out at the pasture and the horses. When the Gillette Blue Blade song came on, I quietly opened the screen door as Mam disappeared into the kitchen carrying the pan of water. I crept inside and slipped between Grandad's chair and the wall. He raised a knotted finger to his lips.

When Rocky was done beating La Starza for the rematch, I snuck out the back door and hightailed it to the barn. I turned on the barn light and slumped on a bale of straw, talking to Lady, who hung her head over the stall door, seeming to listen to every word.

"Roy and Dale wouldn't treat us this way. They adopt kids and horses. They take very good care of them, and they wouldn't go off and leave them alone, would they, Lady?" I looked up as if expecting an answer. "If I could meet Roy and Dale, we could go with them, and be in their show. They adopt lots of kids, and you could come too. They all have a home together on a big ranch."

*

NEW YORK CITY, OCTOBER 1953

For the next couple of weeks after the car and ankle incident, I would hear Mam talking. She talked to Granddad, Great Aunt Maggie, Aunt Jessie, everyone, even Aunt Elsie. "I just do not know what to do with her," she'd say to anyone who'd listen. Mam tried to make Aunt Virginia take care of me and she would have done it too, but thanks be to whoever's really in charge, Uncle Jack said no.

Then, one morning during breakfast, Mam presented herself at the dining room table and announced that I was going to New York, that I would be staying with Linda at The Belvedere Hotel, and more astonishing, that I would be meeting my father. She told me to hurry up and get into something clean so she could take me shopping. At my look she said, "You have to have clothes to impress the East Coast folks."

By then, I'd been eating handfuls of brown sugar, often having dinner at Margie's, and a second dinner and dessert at the ranch before bed, so I was officially fat. That meant all my clothes would need shortening, which Mam said would cost plenty. While my mother was a champion seamstress, Mam didn't sew—she was more a knitter. So, this meant that we had to find Chubette sizes, which Mam said were darn hard to come by besides being more expensive. Again, I did not volunteer my Bud money. I was saving it, as he'd said, until he came to Oregon.

Finally, after hours of tromping around downtown, Mam dragging me from one hot, stuffy store to the next, we wound up at a stifling beige department store. A tag on one of the dresses said, "She can have a tummy and still look yummy." *Hmmph!* I so remember that suit. Both A-line skirt and fitted jacket were a huge orange and red plaid with thin gold and yellow stripes. A big, loud, orange and red plaid, the skirt uncomfortably tight around the waist and descending almost to my ankles, the jacket tight at the shoulders. Though I'd wanted new clothes, for a person used to wearing T-shirts and jeans on her daily rounds, that suit was some kind of weird symbolic costume—a too tight cross between a dwarf court jester and a rodeo clown. The saleslady came hurrying back carrying a bright turquoise sweater. The only one in my size.

"It's just fine, just fine," Mam said. As I slumped to a sitting position in front of the mirror, she growled, "Now, Annie, get off the floor right this minute."

✻

Aunt Virginia, on hearing of "the suit" from Granddad, offered to make a navy-blue cotton dress. This was working well until she sewed the white collar and cuffs onto the dress. We found that I had outgrown the cuffs and couldn't fit my Chubette-size arms into the sleeves. Virginia sat in the ranch house dining room, curly brown head bent over my mother's sewing machine, fixing the dress. My grandmother stood over us, red lips tight, looking as if she wanted to clean off her table and us with it.

The trip was also the first time I had dress shoes. I mean nice shoes for every day, not just for special occasions. These were black leather Mary Janes with slanted straps—not plain old straight straps. They were so pretty that after whining and pleading for them, embarrassing Mam in the shoe store, causing her to grit her teeth and finally slap the money on the counter, I couldn't tell her the straps cut my instep and hurt everywhere they touched. At home that night when I tried them on with the new orange and green winter socks Mam had knit for me, I was in pain the moment I set my foot on the floor. Helping Mam pack my suitcase, I decided I'd better take my old shoes in spite of it being important to make a good impression on the East Coast people and stuffed them into a corner. I couldn't let Mam know the fancy shoes hurt because after spending all that money on me, I pictured her sawing off my feet at the ankles and inquiring whether we had a fit.

*

I was so excited, and there was so much to do to get me ready that it seemed no time had passed until I was standing outside on a cement balcony at the St. Paul, Minnesota, airport waiting to board the second plane to New York. Shivering in the October wind, I pulled my coat around my ears, wondering who would be crazy enough to want to live in such a bare, cold place.

Soon I was hustling down the aisle to the seat where the stewardess directed me, in a hurry to sit because my feet were warming and with warmth came more pain. As I approached my seat, a woman sitting several rows back, wearing a purple hat shaped like a pot with a big pancake on top, stood and motioned me toward her. With the other hand, she tugged at her husband's sleeve.

"Hank, let her sit in your seat. Hank!"

I slumped into my seat, surprised that they let such a nut on the airplane. Mam had lectured me every day of the previous week about how to behave on an airplane, and for a change, I'd listened closely because I really wanted to go to New York. No one on Rural Rt. 2—not even Mam—had been there, and certainly, no kid in my school had ever been much further than the state capital. So, the trip, besides providing a means to meet my father and help my mother marry Bud, would give a big boost to my standing at school because Mam said I was to have a special meeting with Roy Rogers and Dale Evans, who were the stars of the 1953 Madison Square Garden Rodeo! When I told all the kids at Elijah Bristow Elementary about going to New York and meeting Roy and Dale, they thought I was making it up. But they would see! They would really see when I came back with autographs and signed pictures.

Settling myself, I slipped off the shoes and began to struggle from my coat and the tight suit jacket Mam had insisted I wear. The man next to me said, "lean forward," and helped me out of the coat. I heard a little scream from the hat lady and looked around to see her staring at the man next to me. Her mouth opened in a big O then her eyes shut tight. I looked over to see that the man next to me who was folding my coat and putting it beside me on the seat was a Negro. I thought this was interesting since I'd never been close to a Negro and had only once seen one in person.

"I'm Annie Butler from Oregon," I said. "We don't have any Negro people where I live."

His name was Mr. Jackson. He worked as an accountant for the railroad and he told me all about his children who lived in "the city" and who had never been closer to a horse than to see one in a parade or trotting through the park. He said they were even a little afraid of the wild countryside. He smiled, showing big white teeth with a gold strip on one, and said he couldn't understand it, but he guessed it was because his children had grown up in the city and didn't know how nice it was to live in the country.

After the plane heaved into the air, I ordered a root beer and looked at school pictures of the man's children that he kept in his wallet. I wanted to ask him what it was like being a Negro, but I guessed that since I'd talked with him, I knew. He was just regular. I'd seen pictures in *Life* magazine of people who lived down south and read what they had to say about not wanting to share their bathrooms and water with Negroes, but I always thought they must be pretty stupid. Lady was black and white, and Frenchie was brown, but they were both horses. Why would it be different with people? Who thought one was better or worse just because they were a different color? Color didn't have anything to do with whether they were a good horse.

I handed Mr. Jackson the Madison Square Garden Rodeo program that Linda had sent. Pictures of Dale and Roy were on the front cover, and I explained to him about the adoptions, the big ranch, and why Roy and Dale were really something.

I read to him from the large print, adding that "Roy and Dale are 1953's stars of the Madison Square Garden Rodeo. Mam says I'm having a special meeting with them."

He nodded, black eyes full of light. "That sounds fine," he said. "Fine. I just might have to go along to that rodeo and take a look myself."

Mr. Jackson handed the program back to me and closed his book. He turned and looked out the window but there was nothing to see, only a floor of sunlit clouds. We sat looking at the clouds, me sipping my drink, noticing the changing light.

Finally, to meet my father, and Dale and Roy, was big, but even more thrilling and in line with my grand plan was that Bud would be in New York. Bud and Linda would be married soon, then Bud would be my western father, and I'd have an eastern father too. If I could have Bud for my Oregon father, maybe I could ease up on the search for a husband of my own. And even though my real father had a new wife and two new children, I now felt sure that the moment he saw me he'd take me in his arms and hug me and tell me how much he'd missed me. He'd ask me to please come and visit him all the time. *He'd buy me dresses.* Meeting Roy and Dale, meeting my father for the first time, and being with Bud again made me sure this would be the best time of my life. The answer to the new prayers LaVetta had taught me so I could fit in at the First Christian church. Looking down on the rolling clouds, there ran through my brain like the steady hum of the engines, the words, "my dad, and Bud, my dad and Bud, mydadandBud, mydadandBud," repeating.

Later, I opened the program and showed Mr. Jackson the picture of Bud in his white shirt and best hat.

"He loves me, and he gave me dress money," I said, pointing a sticky finger at Bud's picture. I turned the page and pointed to the picture of my mother. "The one with the big flower in her hair," I said. "She's a rodeo star."

At the New York airport, I stood at the top of the airplane steps looking for my mother's red hair, which would be flying in the wind and easy to spot. At the bottom of the tall steps, the stewardess took my arm.

"You stand by me, honey, until you find your mommy," she said, smiling.

After Mr. Jackson met a lady in a long black and yellow dress, her head wrapped to match, the stewardess had to leave. Standing beside a pillar inside the airport, I noticed two big men in fancy suits looking over at me. One was even taller and bigger than the other with black hair going silver around the edges, his solid body stuffed into a black suit with a very bright gold tie and a diamond pin holding it to his shirt. He wore a nice overcoat, and one gloved hand carried a creased newspaper. The other man, the slightly shorter giant, had curly black hair slicked back and covered by a gray hat, his black suit coat hanging open over a white shirt with no tie. Relaxed and slow moving, he gazed over his shoulder, watching a kid on the other side of the lobby. He looked like Dean Martin's bigger, more substantial brother.

"Ahem," I said to a lady with an umbrella, who was blocking my view, "I'm looking for my mom."

She was old and humped in a big brown coat, and looked just like a bear in winter, even the same square nose. The bear woman turned like she was thinking of replying, but the bigger man stepped toward me, and she kind of melted away.

"You Annie Butler?"

"Who are you . . .?" I glared up at the older looking man wondering how he knew me. I was pretty far from home.

"Hey, Tony," he said, hailing Dean Martin's brother.

"I'm Mr. Gray," he said. "You can call me Leo, and this is Tony." Tony strolled over and smiled, showing big teeth that leaned every which way, like tombstones in the pioneer graveyard.

Leo had come to pick me up because Linda (Mam told me to always call her Linda in New York, so people would think we were sisters) was having publicity pictures taken wearing mink Levi's. "Linda had an appointment this afternoon," he said, "and we had to be over at the gym earlier, so we thought we'd give you a ride to town."

Apparently, the Levi's people couldn't change their shooting schedule, so I drew Leo and Tony. As we waited for the baggage cart, Tony informed me that they were in charge of "The Garden Box Office and Publicity." In the herd of noisy, fast-moving people, the two seemed as big as Brahma bulls among horses, and I had to tilt my head back and look straight up to see their faces. I swayed back and forth, shifting my weight from one aching foot to the other.

"Er," Tony said, looking down at me, "didja get sick on the plane, kid?"

"No," I barked. "Do I look to you like I'm sick?"

Tony jerked his head back, his chin lifted, and he looked down on me from over his nose.

Leo snorted.

Finally, after what seemed like forever, beset by pain from having to stand there in my torturous and beautiful shoes, the airport man slammed my suitcase in front of Tony. He picked it up and we followed him from the building where a long black car waited. Everyone at home had said New York was huge and brilliant, a city where everything happened. I was sure that the important people I'd seen in the magazines, the most famous, the best, the happiest, and richest people lived here. I wanted to see it all.

Earlier, waiting for my suitcase, I had felt especially cranky because my mother hadn't come for me herself. But now, I figured if a person were a star in New York City that must come before everything else. I also recalled Mam's relentless instructions: "You better be on your best behavior, and I'd better not hear otherwise. She'll be working."

"Okay, Mam" I'd said, looking up with my good girl face, but thinking, *When I'm in New York, and away from you, I'll do what I want.*

Riding along in back with Leo, Tony driving, I looked out the window at the scrawny buildings, flat grassland and marshy, watery mudflats leading to a lead-gray river, and wasn't impressed. As if he could read my mind, Leo tapped me on the shoulder with the paper and pointed off to my left. There in the distance, framed in the car window, was what looked like a set in one of Granddad's little theater plays. It was the 1953 New York City skyline shrouded in mist from the river, the lights from the city and bridges shining softly through pinkish light. I moved closer to Leo and craned my neck to see. Tony's smiling eyes shone from the rearview mirror.

"Pretty, ain't it?" he said.

Soon, Leo sunk in his newspaper, Tony pointing out sights; we travelled deeper into the cold shade of tall buildings. I was on my back, lying over the hump in the carpeted floor, looking up through the window, trying to see the tops of the buildings.

"Gad! That's as tall as a damn mountain. I can't see the top. You mean people live in these darn things?" I squirmed lower on the floor, scooting Leo's big feet away so I could see the tops of the towers. While trying to position myself to see even higher, I happened to look up Leo's pants leg. There, nested outside his leg, appeared to be a leather case with a snap. I reached up and shook it. It was heavy, with straps holding it tightly in place. The edge of his paper came down on my ear with a hard slap. "Keep yer' hands to yerself, kid."

"What the heck you got on your leg, then?" I asked. "Why'd you thump me? You better not thump me!" I jumped to my knees, my face even with his yellow tie. "Jack can't thump me, and you can't thump me either—my mom said." I was close to hollering.

From the front seat, Tony's voice cracked out, "Siddown, kid. You're makin' me lose my concentration. Sit on the seat." Then to Leo, "Never heard that before. Ha, ha," and he laughed in his throat, "'Oh, no. Don't do it! My mother said.' Ha, ha."

I wouldn't look at Leo, but instead glared into the rearview mirror, hitting Tony with Mam's snake stare, the black, skinny one she gave people who had crossed one of the big lines in her cupboard of crimes.

※

Soon we were deep in the city. The landscape colors of the city—black, gray, bronze—punctuated by chrome and the bright slash of signs framed by jostling coats and jackets of those much taller, busier and darker than myself, formed my images of New York. This view was topped by a leaden sky carrying wisps of darker gray clouds, a bit of dirty sun occasionally peering down on the honking of taxis and the howling of the stampeding people.

The city that had looked so elegant and ethereal from a distance, inside and up close was full of sound and dirty air. I was used to vast stretches of quiet green and gold fields broken by blue mountains, green rivers and swaying trees. Here, were not so vast stretches of concrete and asphalt, encircled with foggy dirt, rivers of bellowing automobiles, and buildings whose tops I could not see from the sidewalk. There was one bright spot: travelling through Central Park, I had seen real trees, horses and a lake. As we were leaving the park, Tony had pointed out a stable, about seven stories high, where they kept police horses. "They wear rubber shoes. Whatdaya think a that?"

"I think we better get where we're going because I have to go to the bathroom."

*

The face, framed against the moving elevator dial, towered over me. It had a mashed nose, a dirty bandage over one eyebrow, and big black marks under bright blue eyes. The body, enveloped in some kind of uniform, was enormous, almost covering both elevator doors. Under one arm, he carried what looked to be a cage for a medium-sized animal, and the other hand held a big stick that he leaned on like a cane. Instead of turning and watching the doors as I had, he stood looking down at me as the elevator dinged up the floors. He smiled, showing big black holes where teeth should have been.

"I'm Annie. I'm from Oregon. Who are you?"

"Victor. Rangers."

"What's Rangers?" I asked, not stopping to let him answer. "I'm looking for my mother. Do you know where the rodeo is? Do you know where the bathrooms are?"

His lively blue eyes looked me over, and he grinned. "Hockey," he said, looking down at the word Rangers, spelled across his shirt. "The bathrooms are right outside the elevator door when we get to the top. I don't know about the rodeo. I think the animals are in the basement. Your folks in the rodeo?"

Just then, the elevator lurched and came to a sudden stop. The door opened, revealing a whole herd of guys as big as Victor.

"Hey, Vic, ya missed the group shot," the first onto the elevator said. "Where'd you get off to? The photographer's gonna quit in about two minutes. Get your skinny butt in there, we've got a meeting with Mac at 1:00. He's gonna chew yer ass. Tell you to stay home at night, pretty boy."

"Publicity hound," said one of the men cuffing Vic on the arm.

The men piling onto the elevator, all laughing and joking, smelled of sweat and something sharp and dry. They were huge, with big towels around their necks, and looked even bigger because of giant pads covering their shoulders and chests. I scuttled through the tangle of legs and smells to the hallway. Vic's hand rose above the men's heads and pointed. I rushed down the hallway. In the elevator on the way back to the lobby, I rode with the biting odor of the men who had earlier crowded the elevator.

Tony waited in the busy lobby holding his hat in his hand. "Well, you got off like a shot. You was supposed to wait for me. We got awhile before your mother's done." He placed his hat on his head, matching it exactly to the red crease across his forehead. Peering up at him, I was engulfed in the stench of tobacco. I wondered if he kept it in a bottle and slathered it on like perfume. "That, over there is publicity, and the box office," he said, gesturing toward the front of the lobby. "Me and Leo run the place."

On either side of glass entrance doors were windowed stalls like movie theater ticket booths, and beside it, on a big red padded door, a sign read, "Box Office." I was thrilled to see a towering color poster of Roy and Dale to the left of the door, in a large glass case. To the right and bigger than Dale and Roy's was a poster of Bud astride "Snowball," the Brahma bull he rode to win the All-Around Cowboy Championship of 1951. Snowball hung in the air, about four feet off the ground. His gigantic head and brutal horns swept back toward his shoulder, eyes rolling, froth flying from his bawling mouth. Bud had lost his hat but otherwise looked perfect. He sat erect, straddling the flying bull, shirt tucked in, long legs hugging Snowball's shoulders, one fist glued to the rigging, the other raised over his head. Taken the summer when I'd first met him at the Cow Palace, it brought him back like a dart in my middle. I had to find him.

"Can we go see where they keep the stock?" Bud was never very far from Toots, his roping horse.

Tony looked at the box office door like he was expecting someone to appear.

"Whaddya want ta go see that for? I don't think kids can go down there. And lookit you, you're all dressed up. Wouldn't want to wear that red suit in front of any bull, would you? Ha, ha, ha."

I started toward the elevator. New York was to be my biggest investigation yet. "I want to see Monte."

"Aww, kid, I don't know. Linda's due back . . . who's Monte?" he said, checking his watch.

"My mom's new trick horse, that's who," I said, continuing toward the service elevator I'd ridden with Vic. "Anyway, I thought today was mink Levi's day."

"That was after lunch."

As we stepped off the elevator, we found ourselves in another world, a dark, low world lit by single light bulbs along steel rafters, the concrete floor covered with shavings, dirt, and straw. I could tell from the cowish smell that cattle were to the left. I turned right and started down a narrow alley. Other than the animals I sensed in the gloom, there didn't seem to be anyone around.

"Kid, err, I don't think . . ." Tony was looking down at his shiny shoes.

"We'll just go down here a ways and see if Monte's there. You like horses, right?"

A cowboy wheeling a barrow of hay passed, the wheel squeaking with each turn. He was hunched over the thing and didn't raise his head.

"Trick horses this way?"

"Keep going," he said.

Imagine a whole rodeo, several hundred cows and calves, hundreds of horses, two strings of Brahma bulls, various donkeys and jackasses, tack shops, veterinary stalls, dogs and monkeys used in the clown acts, and tons of manure, straw, and bales of hay—all this in a huge, steaming, enclosed basement under the streets of New York City. Imagine the smell.

That was when I began to sneeze. About three times a minute. Choo, ahchoo, and so on. As usual my eyes then turned scarlet (to match my loud red suit), and my hair slithered from its braids, electric strands standing at attention with each sneeze, acting somewhat like lightning rods to attract more dust particles and floating debris.

"You'll scare the horses," Tony said.

I poked my head into the first stall we came to. It wasn't Monte, and I continued down the row of dark cubicles. Finally, in a dim corner stall, we found him. He was so slim and black that he seemed a shadow in the dreary space. I only know the horse sent me a strong impression. I felt him say that he was bored, it was dark, he was cramped, and that he wasn't having much fun. I reached up and ran my hand down his long silky face. He nosed my hand for treats.

"Pet him, Tony! He won't hurt you."

Tony stood about two feet from the stall door, hands behind his back.

"I don't think so, kid." Trying again to scrape the manure from his shoe, he cocked his head at me. At my look, he said,

"I ain't worried," and held a hand out to Monte, who snorted and nipped Tony's sleeve just as I sneezed loudly.

"Jeez, he wanted to bite my arm off." Tony, unbitten, lurched away and backed down the aisle.

I giggled. "Monte likes tobacco. I forgot." Walking back, I looked into every stall but didn't see Toots. There had to be more stalls somewhere close, and I would find them—as soon as I could get away.

Upstairs, Leo stood by the box office door adjusting the hankie in his suit pocket. Before him stood a very tall woman with long, curly, almost white hair. She wore a tight red dress with pleats over the bust, a fur coat thrown over her shoulders, and extra tall open-toed high heels made of clear plastic so you could see her feet and red-painted toes. I thought the toe cutouts were a great idea. No hurt feet for her.

She seemed about to leave, but as she turned, Tony walked toward them and boomed out. "Maizie, hold up. Say hello."

She turned back, smiling like Marilyn Monroe. She was just beautiful with big green eyes, a bright red mouth full of white gleaming teeth, and an angelic face framed by cloudlike white curls.

"Why, Tony honey, how are you doin'?" Her voice was warm, thick with sweetness. Not waiting for him to answer, her eyes held mine. "Now tell me who your friend is."

She leaned down, took my hand, and shook it with a soft hand. Her fingers were long and silky with a big sparkling ring on one finger, her nails were red—maybe Cherries in the Snow. Her hands were like those in the Swan Lake ballerina picture that had hung over my bed at the house on the hill: curved, beautiful, and suggestive of things I didn't understand but wanted to.

"This is Annie. She's come all the way from Oregon to see her mother ride in the rodeo. Haven't you, kid?"

"I'm Maizie, honey. Welcome to New York. I'm just so

pleased to meet you."

I gawked up at her. Why would she care about seeing me? She brought her face closer to mine. Her smell was pink and sweet, but not too sweet. Not like my mother's sneeze-making gardenia smell. Brilliant diamonds flashed from her ears as she rose and plumped her glossy fur coat around her neck. She looked just like a movie star.

"See ya at the club tonight," Tony said. "After the second show."

Still looking at me, she nodded. "An Oregon girl, are you? I was there once when I was a kid. It was real pretty. You're all dressed up. Are you going somewhere special tonight?"

"I'm going to meet my mother when she's done with the photographers, and then we're going to have dinner with our boyfriend."

"Well," she smiled, showing deep dimples, "I know you'll have a good time." Then, looking over her shoulder at Tony and rising to her real height, she asked, "Is she staying at the hotel?"

"My mom's staying at the Belvedere," I offered.

"Me too, Miss Annie. Maybe I'll see you again."

"Wow!" I said to Tony as we watched her walk off. "She's really dressed up nice, isn't she?" My estimation of New York had risen. Maizie looked just as I hoped to when I grew up, and now we lived in the same hotel.

Tony's eye focused on Maizie's swaying walk. "She's the star of the chorus at the Copacabana."

"What's the name of it? That's where I want to go!"

This surely wonderful place was exactly where I wanted to go next, but first I had to find Bud and make a plan to get him to propose to Linda. The spot had to be like the places we used to go in California, somewhere nice and dim with a bar and lots of good food. I already knew how I would bring up my plan, and what I would say to convince Bud that it would be perfect for all of us. Now I just had to find him and get us all together for dinner.

Chapter 8

IN A NEW WORLD LINDA HAS A FALL, WHILE ANNIE VENTURES UNDERGROUND, THEN DISCOVERS ALFREDO SAUCE BUT BEGINS TO FEAR THE WORLD MAY NOT FOLLOW HER PLANS

After taking leave of Leo, Tony picked up my suitcase and we headed for the hotel. Outside, the streetlamps had blinked on and the wind blew people's raincoats, sending them flapping around their legs. I was cold and limped heavily along beside Tony.

"What's wrong with your leg? Didn't hurt yourself, did ya?"

"New shoes."

He stepped to the curb and raised a hand over his head, causing a taxi to slice to a halt directly beside me. After a very short ride, we pulled in front of a brightly lit entrance with a big sign reading The Belvedere, where a man in what looked to be a blue circus costume opened the cab door.

Handing the driver money, Tony nodded to the man in the loud outfit. "Annie, this is George. He takes care of us."

George, thin and neat in his loud uniform, peered down on me in my brilliant suit. Between the two of us, it would be a toss-up as to who would win the loudest outfit prize. "You must be the young lady that's come all the way from Oregon by herself. I've heard all about you." I immediately wondered if he was a spy for Linda or a friend to me. Then I wondered at myself for thinking such a thing.

I followed Tony through an immense lobby where pinkish-gold lightshades made everything look friendly and dim. Ringing the lobby, we passed a shoeshine stand, a tiny dress store, a jewelry store, and a place selling newspapers that smelled of candy and cigars. Rich, heavy smells of tobacco and sweets drifted over mellow brass fixtures, tan marble floors, and palms in tall urns. To the right a sign over scarlet-draped glass doors announced, The Belvedere Dining Room and Lounge. As we passed, I could see a desk, a shadow from a lamp, and a lady in a short skirt taking people's coats. Piano music billowed into the lobby when the door opened. That looked like the most interesting spot in the hotel and the right place to meet Bud for dinner. It was the perfect place to get him to ask her—but after I changed into my old shoes.

Lines of rain-coated regular people, alongside big-hatted cowboys and cowgirls, crowded the lobby, some retrieving keys, others talking on special desk telephones, still others giving money to the people behind a counter. To one side of the lobby a group of men sporting fancy cream-colored western suits with snappy red piping and matching western hats stood together, some leaning on their instrument cases and joking with each other. Looking up at all the people moving through the place, I was amazed by the number of cowboys I didn't know. It hadn't occurred to me that there could be cowboys or rodeos that I didn't know a thing about.

"Is Bud here?" I asked.

At a rustling commotion behind us, I turned to see a pale-faced woman, bright hair awry, limping into the lobby supported between two large men. It was my mother wearing her patient saint look, smiling weakly but gamely. Her jockey silks of green and blue were scuffed and torn, a big slide of dirt marking one leg. Tony bolted across the space between them and practically knocked one of the men out of the way.

"Get those photographers out of here, Frankie," he said to one of the doormen, gesturing to several people standing at the end of the lobby pointing cameras at us. Then to Linda, "Sweetie, what in hell happened to you?"

He slid his arm around her. At this, her eyes misted up.

Oh, boy, I thought. *What now?*

Then, catching sight of me, she held out an arm and motioned me to her. "Annie, now don't worry. It was just a little spill."

Linda smiled, seeming really happy to see me. Jeannie, a slender blonde and my mother's friend, followed her, then several more trick riders also wearing racing silks entered, making a tired-looking but bright line through the lobby. Jeannie and my mom were friends because my mother wasn't too jealous of her and could feel some pity for her over her choice of men. Jeannie was in love with Mac Ross, a bullfighting clown, and as Mam had proclaimed, everybody knew what that got you.

"Tony," Jeannie said, "she's got to get in the tub and start soaking, or she won't be doing a show tomorrow."

My mother frowned. "I'll be just fine. This doesn't amount to a thing." Then she turned to me. "This is my Annie," she said as introduction. "So, how'd you like flying?"

We moved in a jabbering wave toward the elevator. I limped along with her, hauling my suitcase beside me.

In the high beige hotel room, I stood at the window looking out on the flowing lights below, while my mother sat in the bathtub running hot water. I was shoeless and relieved for the moment. I shoved my suitcase under the cot next to my mother's bed and hung my loud suit jacket over the chair because there was no room in the closet. Costumes and clothes were stuffed everywhere, with fancy-colored boots lined two rows deep on the closet floor, the tall aluminum hatbox serving as a table, and a long phone cord snaking through the jumble on the floor.

"When are we meeting Bud?" I asked, moving to the bathroom doorway. She lay back in the white tub, eyes closed. Thinking she hadn't heard, I walked to the edge of the tub and sat on the rim watching her. "When are we meeting Bud?" No answer.

Her eyes opened just a slit, glittered out at me briefly, then her eyelids dropped shut again. I went to the sink, ran water, scooped it up, and washed my face and eyes. In the mirror I witnessed a wild-looking creature with hair escaping every which way from its braids, eyes pink as wallpaper roses. Thinking I'd made a mistake in asking about Bud first, I said, "Well, I want to meet my father too. Are we seeing him first?"

A thin little voice from the tub said: "We'll meet your father and your other grandmother for lunch on Saturday."

She turned on the water again, then sat back and sighed as the steam rose around her. Saturday was five days away.

"So, we're seeing Bud for dinner? Let's call and have him come get us."

"Bud has lots of work to do for this show, Annie. We all do."

"But he's gotta eat. I'm hungry. Aren't you hungry? Where is he?" The buzzing telephone interrupted my interrogation. I swooped on it, thinking it must be Bud calling to welcome me to New York. It was Tony. I took the phone to Linda and sat on the toilet lid waiting for her to hang up.

"I can't come now," she said. Then eyeing me, "maybe around nine. Annie's hungry." She paused, listening, the steam causing her curls to slip from the pins on top of her head. "Oh, that's great. She'll like that."

Glaring at her, I knew that whatever it was I probably would not like it.

"Oh, no. That will be perfect, and could you bring some ice? Yes. Yes, I do. Bye ,Tone."

Oh, worse, and worse, I thought. "What now?" I said. "I want to see BUD!"

"Don't raise your voice to me. You're tired. Tony's sending something from the dining room, and we'll eat right here."

"I'm not tired. I want us to go down and eat in the dining room with Bud."

She pulled the plug in the tub and water sounds covered my words. Linda, now encased in big white towels, stood at the sink running cold water over a hand towel, her back draped with damp curls. She put the chilled hand towel on her bruised leg, wrapped a big towel around it, and limped to the bed, shrugging into her robe. Easing under the covers, she asked for her brush, and then her alligator makeup case.

She patted the side of the bed. "Sit here. You can tell me about your trip." She started brushing her eyebrows, and I told her about Mr. Jackson. When she applied foundation, I told her about Leo, him smacking me. If I expected sympathy from her, I shouldn't have. She sighed and fixed me with big brown eyes. "You watch what you say to him. Leo is a very important person at the Garden. He takes care of all the money for the fights, hockey—and the rodeo. Tony works with him and between them they decide what happens at the Garden, with the program, publicity, all the appointments for radio, and T.V., and public appearances. The girls and I get paid extra when we do public appearances, so you be nice to him."

I just stared at her. Then came the mascara, then more mascara, then she curled her eyelashes and I told her about going to see Monte, but thought better of mentioning my meeting with Maizie. She wiped the fresh lipstick off, leaving her mouth pale pink, slicked Vaseline over lips and eyebrows, fluffed her fancy red hair, and closed the makeup case just about the time there was a knock at the door.

It was Tony with a big tray of food, two yellow roses, and a bucket of ice. "And, for you, I got a Coke," he said, setting it on the hatbox. "You know you were lucky, doll," he said to Linda. "A whatchamacallit strap breakin' like that, you coulda been killed, insteada just roughed up. Be sure I'll talk to them."

"I should have checked it," she said.

The chicken smelled wonderful, reminding me that I hadn't eaten since morning. Tony set a glass of wine on the table for my mother. "What you want on this pasta here, Annie? Little of everything? You want this red sauce, or white?"

"Is the white kind cheese?"

My mom nodded.

While I ate and looked out the window at the tiny car lights below, they talked quietly. I was lost in the food but more particularly, in my scheme to find Bud and get him to the dining room with Linda. I pricked up my ears when I heard him say, "Have you told him?" But my mother didn't answer. She asked Tony to pour more wine, and said she needed to get the ice on her leg. He stood.

"Good cheese stuff," I said.

"It better be, kid." He moved to the end of the bed, like he was going to lean over it, then thought better of it. "See ya later, dolly," he said.

My mother's head was turned but I could see her lips moving. She waved as he backed out the door then let her head fall against the headboard when we heard him walk down the hall. "Turn on the radio, will you?"

The radio voice announced *Your Hit Parade*, a program we listened to at home. Les Paul and Mary Ford commenced singing "Vaya Con Dios."

I set the tray outside like Linda said, left the roses on her table, then crawled on the cot and spread my funny books around me. I opened the *Archie* and began to read.

*

I woke in the semi dark to the click of the door and sat up in bed. The bathroom light was on, the door cracked open casting a rod of yellow onto the rug.

"Mommy?" I croaked, sleepy and a little scared, thinking someone was trying to come in the room. There was no answer. I rose and tiptoed to her bed, but she wasn't there. I rushed around to the bathroom and looked inside. Bare and empty, with only a pile of white towels in the middle of the floor. "Damn, damn, damn," I whispered. *Here I am all this way across the country and she's out running around without me.*

I tried the door to the hall, but the knob wouldn't turn. *Damn!* I slumped on the end of her bed, angry tears in my eyes. *Damn, damn, damn—her!*

In the dim light, I could see hairpins scattered on the dressing table by the overflowing ashtray in front of her open makeup case. A big fake red rose sat in the top tray, a glittery, tattered bloom. Tears began to roll down my face as I gathered the pins and started making jumbo curls in my bangs, cramming the pins tightly to hold my slick hair. *She was hurt, wasn't she? Shouldn't she take care of her leg? And this is the first night of my trip. Wouldn't she want to be with me?* By the time I'd pinned up my bangs, I'd quit crying. I flopped on the cot and began to cry again when I thought about how far away from home I was. Thinking of home, I imagined not the ranch but the beautiful Armitage house set among the maples where I would live with Bud. Picturing myself walking down the long lawn toward the horse fence, I finally fell asleep.

*

"You better not lock me in again. If you do, I'm leaving." I was standing over her bed looking down on her. I'd flung the curtains back to gray morning light and was dressed and ready to find Bud. My eyes were swollen from crying and my bangs were standing at odd angles across the top of my head, some strands curly as corkscrews, others like bent nails. I had debated wetting it down, but thought not, as I was hungry and wanted to get going. I would find Bud and that was the end of it. Linda groaned and dragged her hand over her eyes. "Did the alarm go off?"

I didn't answer her. "Did you hear?"

"MMMhhh, Annie, go lay down." She opened a murky eye to the clock beside her bed. It said 6:30, which was a little later than wake-up time at home and I'd been asleep long enough. "Annie, go lay down. I don't get up until 8:30. It's too early."

"If you hadn't been out all night, you could get up." I was still staring down at her. She hadn't washed off her makeup, and her face was smeary and black stained beneath her eyes.

Without opening her eyes, she croaked, "Annie, I promise. You'll have a big day today. I've got a surprise for you. Just let me sleep. I have a show this afternoon."

I stood, glaring down on her closed, drowsy face.

She turned from the light and pulled the covers over her eyes. The hotel was silent except for an occasional muffled sound from the hallway, the distant hiss of water running in pipes somewhere. I closed the curtains and went into the bathroom searching for the duffle bag that Linda took when she rode. Sometimes she kept an apple for the horse or a candy bar for her lunch. I found it in the hallway by the door but there was no apple, nothing to eat, only a glass jar of pills, orange heart-shaped pills, a whole bunch of them, each one scored with a cross. I screwed the cap back on and rummaged deeper. A pair of dirty Ace bandages, her wrist brace from when she broke her arm, an extra pair of white tennis shoes, a cake of rosin, an extra silver bit for the white bridle, a green plaid shirt, and a bottle of aspirin. No food. I slumped to the floor, my back against the wall, bare feet sticking straight out.

In the silence, I studied my feet for some time, counting blisters (six) and thinking about how I could find Bud. When I found him, Linda would quit the nonsense and we'd get back to normal. I figured that she'd be out cold until the alarm went off then she'd run around trying to get ready, and finally she would dress, and we'd go out to eat. I didn't like eating breakfast out. I rose from the floor, tiptoed to the cot, scooped up my comics and took them to the table. I slid beneath the curtain, trying to read "The Three Musketeers" in the pale light from the window, but mostly thinking about Bud. *Where was he?*

I was right. She had to drag herself around, spend an hour in the bathroom, then gulp down some of those orange pills, and we didn't get to the breakfast place until about 9:30. I was hungry as hell and exceedingly angry because when I'd gone to get my old shoes from the suitcase, they weren't there. I dug around, ripped everything out, burrowed in all the pockets, but all I had were the new killers. I had put my old shoes in the corner of my suitcase myself. I couldn't think of spending another day wearing the new ones. I watched Linda shrug into her jacket and didn't tell her because Mam had immediately reported "the fit" I'd thrown to get the shoes.

Finally, on our way, we crossed the street dodging lines of honking traffic. We passed a big store with red signs on the windows that said "Fall Sale," and proceeded to a small, glass-fronted restaurant with limp lace at the windows and door. Seated in the hot restaurant we waited for my food, Linda drinking coffee and complaining about the cost of everything.

"Is Bud staying at the hotel? What room?"

"Annie, don't you dare bother him. He's very famous now, and ahh, well, everyone's after him. So, *we* won't bother. . ."

Everyone? What does that mean? Just then, the bell over the door rang and Jeannie hurried toward the table trailing a dark, lanky woman.

"Hope we're not late." Jeannie, blond hair shining, looked fresh and raring to go in turquoise sweatshirt and clean jeans. "I have to get down there and give Penny her medicine."

"Annie, this is your surprise." My mother nodded to the tall woman. The woman they introduced me to—Margo—was not as old as Mam, and she didn't look like anyone's mother that I knew of, much less bright Jeannie's. She was a tall bone rack, wrapped in a brown dress coat, wearing shiny black high heels. Her hair, also blackish, was slicked straight back from her head like someone had surprised her. Huge chunks of silver pulled at her earlobes, making them seem unnaturally long, like African women in *National Geographic*. Her face was white as the bathroom towels. She wore black sunglasses that covered the whole upper part of her face, and the bottom half was all red lips, like a bunch of dead flowers spray-painted glossy red. Hoisting a black bag off her shoulder, she settled uncertainly onto the chair across from me then lowered her head to look at me over the tops of her glasses. Her eyes were hooded with what appeared to be exhaustion.

"We don't have much time, Linda," Jeannie said, and then looking over at me, she winked. "Oh, well, just some coffee then. Are you eating, Mom?"

Margo propped her chin on the heel of her hand. Her hands were huge, fingers dark yellow—from holding cigarettes, I guessed.

My mom's face lit up in her picture-posing smile. "Annie, you and Margo are going to the Statue of Liberty! You'll ride the ferry and see the whole harbor and eat lunch on the boat. Won't that be great?"

I looked over at Margo. I think she was looking back at me, but I only saw my face and my weirdly twisted bangs reflected in her glasses.

"Whole damn day," she muttered. Then to me, "Ever been on a boat?" I nodded, no. "That'll make two of us then."

"Lots of the people who move to America see that statue first of all," Jeannie said. She'll love it, won't she, Mother?" Jeannie still had the bright smile, now pasted over an anxious look.

No one asked me what I thought. My mother knew that given a choice, I would not be going to the Statue of Liberty, or anywhere but the rodeo. I wanted to be at the Garden watching the trick-riders practice and looking for Bud. I wouldn't look at her. She rummaged in her purse and handed me a five-dollar bill.

At the curb, Margo barked, "Hudson Street Pier," and slumped into the opposite corner of the cab, snatching the coat around her. Linda and Jeannie, both wearing tight jeans and flat-soled tennis shoes, started down the broad sidewalk toward the Garden. Linda was limping a little. Watching her move down the long sidewalk, I hoped it wasn't a long walk from the cab to the boat because the blisters I'd only contemplated that morning now demanded attention; the slightest pressure was like the continual stinging of a bee. The pain did not let up.

Chapter 9

WITH ACHING FEET ANNIE SAILS TO THE STATUE OF LIBERTY WHERE SHE LOSES MARGO, BEFRIENDS A WHITE RUSSIAN, AND LEARNS MAM IS A POSSIBLE DICTATOR

The morning wind blew in cold bursts as we walked up the ramp onto the green and white boat that was to take us around the island and to the Statue of Liberty. Margo offered her sleeve. "You can hold on if you want, so I don't lose you."

I didn't want to hold onto her. I had my hand in my pocket gripping the five-dollar bill that Linda had given me. Through her pointy black glasses, Margo surveyed the crowd of people swarming ahead of us onto the boat ramp. Apparently, Margo was what Mam called a social type, because as soon as she saw all the people, she perked up. At the top of the ramp were signs that said "Lounge" and "Dining," bright green letters outlined in white waves, and the doors had green velvet chains across them. Margo bent over to read a small sign. She sighed, fiddled a cigarette pack from her bag, stuck a smoke between her weird lips, then went digging in the bag.

"Can't get inside for ten minutes," she said, coming up with a lighter. She turned out of the wind and held the lighter to her cigarette but it sputtered and went out. She ran a thumb over the roller again. I thought Margo was smiling at me when she turned. Then a gray-coated arm jutted over my head, and a polite voice asked, "May I help?"

A man, graying hair combed to the side, wearing a tan raincoat over a dark blue suit, held out a lighter. She smiled—dazzlingly for her—and leaned toward the flame.

"Damned wind," she growled, as a puff of cold wind blew the flame sideways and almost whisked it out. Her cigarette finally lit; she took a long drag. In her black glasses, his reflection made his nose look bigger than it really was.

"Gustav Melnyk," he said. Then looking at me, "So, you've come to see the statue?"

Margo broke in. "A friend's kid. I've brought her for the day. First time in New York."

"I've brought my father. He likes to come often." The man nodded. "He's on the bench, there. I try and get him to come inside. It's chilly but he wants to sit right there."

On the bench a thin old man, stooped and mostly bald-headed, sat peering out at the water like a pointer looking for ducks. He wore a thick gray overcoat, a black scarf wrapping his neck and held a black hat, resting it on his knee. "He'd come out here every day if he could."

"Not me," Margo said. "I'm not a water lover. I'll take my tour from the lounge."

"May I join you?" He moved closer to her, like he'd found an old friend. "We'll have a nip before lunch?"

At this Margo lit up like New York at night. She bit her big red lips and cocked her head toward him, "Why, how lovely," she said.

Inside the smoky lounge, Margo and Mr. Melnyk were talking and drinking up a storm, keeping the waiter busy coming back to deliver more drinks. I had been drinking root beer, and resting my feet, but now I was bored with the roomful of loud people and anxious to get out.

"Margo, let's go outside," I said in my most reasonable

voice. I was on to Margo. She didn't care what I did, as long as I didn't interfere with her. She wanted to be right where she was, inside with Mr. Melnyk slurping brandy.

Mr. Melnyk looked up from his drink. "Why don't you go out and see how Dad's doing? His name is Mr. Melnyk too. Tell him we'll eat shortly."

Up close, the senior Mr. Melnyk looked really old. He was a little bald-headed bundle of sticks. His only noticeable hair was long eyebrows that jutted like sails over his weeping eyes and thinnish wisps of hair draping each side of his head. His top was shiny bald. As I stood in front of him, a stout lady who had been sitting on the end of the bench rose and moved to the rail.

"Hi, I'm Annie."

His eyes turned from the water to me. "Oh, an Annie, ees it? And vass an Annie, doing on my boat?" He didn't smile. His eyes reflected the color of the sky. Gray.

"I came from Oregon. I'm being babysat, and she brought me to see the Statue of Liberty. She's in there with your son having brandies." I nodded toward the lounge, and then sat beside him on the bench. "How come you're out here? They're going to eat pretty soon."

He returned his eyes to their former occupation and continued to stare across the water at the slim statue in the distance. The wind was cold, but every so often the clouds would sail apart, and the sun would shine down briefly, transforming the water from gray to shimmering turquoise.

The old man's hands were long and fine, heavy blue veins rippling down their backs like worms in Granddad's garden. They lay on his knees, fingers curled loosely inward, his fingernails long and pale as a woman's. "Your son said you come here all the time. That statue must be pretty good."

"She's beootiful. A beeoootiful woman. Goddess." He continued to stare as if looking beyond it. All I could see was the long thin slice of haloed statue. We weren't close enough to see her every feature. Tears slipped from his eyes, and he pulled a white hankie from his vest pocket and dabbed under his glasses. As he replaced it, he glanced down at me. "Remember this, as important day in your life. No one sees her and remains the same. Where ees home?"

"My house?"

He nodded and turned back to the statue.

"Emerald City, Oregon."

"Tell me of Emerald City, Oregon."

"It's far. It's by the other ocean, it's by rivers, and mountains, with a big green tree, and pastures for the horses, and my granddad has some new fruit trees, and he planted roses for Mam."

Old man Melnyk nodded and looked down again, his pale eyes still watering. Suddenly I wanted him to see it as I did.

"We have three houses; one's the ranch where we live now. Mam says we have to remodel it. The other one is across the little field. The Armitages live there now, but someday Granddad is going to buy it for me, and I'll live there. And there's a very old falling down house by the river where nobody lives anymore, but it has lots of old fruit trees, and flowering bushes, and the whole place has lots of horses. It's very, very nice there."

"Sounds veddy gut."

"Where's your accent from?"

He smiled then. "What accent?"

All his Ws sounded like Vs. "Tell me where you come from."

"Am Ukrainian. What was Russia. Also beeootiful country, like your Oregon, maybe."

"Why did you move here? New York's too loud."

"You go to skool?"

I nodded.

He raised a hand and pointed at the statue, now coming into closer view, still not close enough to see details. "They don't teach you historee yet?"

"George Washington and Abraham Lincoln. I'm in third grade."

"You will learn, Annushka. You have no soldier in your home?"

"My father was a soldier, but he doesn't live with us."

"Where I come from, have been many wars. Many wars. But now, I'm done with war. I am here, and this is my home. I knew that when I saw her." He was gazing at the statue in the distance.

"But why did you come? Did your whole family come? I wouldn't leave Oregon."

He turned and looked down on me again, I thought more closely. "Annushka, you sound like girl from Ukraine. Never left, now vill never leave. She grew up there in wild country. She love riding horses with her father and brothers."

He continued to stare down at me, his face very white in the pearly light reflecting off the water. One piece of snowy hair had fallen over the side of his head, over the gold earpiece of his round glasses. He looked old, but his eyes now almost blue in a moment of sunshine, were not. "She was my wife."

"What do you mean she won't leave?"

"In Russia, before first war, was revolution. You know what revolution is?"

"A war?"

"That's very good. It is a very bad war, like your civil var. You know of that?"

"Abraham Lincoln freed the slaves, and people in the South got mad."

"We had da Tzar." He shook his head slowly, rolled his lips inward and I thought he was expecting me to say something. After a moment, he volunteered, "The Tzar was like King." I was about to ask if he ever went back to visit Russia, but he didn't pause. "I was officer in his Army. White Army, dey call it after . . . I was thirty, just married Katya. She was young voman of eighteen, and dey kill the Tzar. Then we fight. We ride across the plains, then back fighting and starving, nothing to eat that spring. Was very bad. Later that year, I come close to our home in Ukraine and go there at night. I tell Katya come with me, we leave Russia, go to China until war is over."

I was able to understand the words now that I was used to the way he talked. When he said "war," it sometimes sounded like "for."

He slowly rose from the bench, and I thought he had finished his story, but he just stood, still looking at the statue, coming closer now. He stomped a foot, and then the other. "Legs sleeping. I am old. Like old dog now." Lowering his eyebrows like a bad dog, he looked around at me. "Katya wouldn't leave pretty home, and I went back to army, then Red's prison."

He turned his head down and peered at me. "You want to walk to rail?" He tilted up the hat he'd been holding in his hand and settled it carefully on his head. Thinking my feet were up to a short walk, I rose.

"What happened to you? What was prison like?"

"Prison was like nothing you know." His voice sounded choppy as the waves in the bay.

"First, prison makes one wonder why one is alive, then made me think only of home. That was winter, 1918. In summer, White Army capture prison, and I went back to work. Very sick, and weak. Reds took forty people when they took me, and when we were released only six of us. Typhoid very bad in dat prison."

I was looking up at him with what I imagine he took to be an expression of disbelief because he shook his head strongly. "Yes, yes, dat was all." Now at the cold rail, he breathed in deeply then took a gold watch from his inside vest pocket. He tapped it with his finger, held it to his ear, and slipped it back in his coat. "We be there in seven minutes."

"Then what happened?"

He smiled down at me, like Granddad sometimes smiled when we talked. Also, like Granddad, in Mr. Melnyk there was nothing hidden, no meanness, only kindness. It was a secret, silent something that flowed from him, and I wondered how he got that way. Right then, looking up at his thin old head framed against the pearl sky, I had the feeling that he might know everything—all the things I wanted to know. Yet, I also felt that he would not simply gift me the answers. I must ask the right questions. Then as now, I wasn't sure of the question, so I just keep questioning everything.

"And then what happened?

"That world changed, and everything changed, and it will never again be da shining wide skied world where I learnt . . . about love, Miss Annushka. My vive Katya was a brave, strong woman, raised on big wheat fields her father owned. She rode like Cossack and could shoot better than me. Katya joined the partisans when I vas in prison, and she died out there somewhere during the civil var. Never did I see her again. She wouldn't leave her home, and now she never will. She vas only twenty. It's been long . . . without her."

Cossack? I'd have to look it up. I hoped that we would soon sit again, as the blisters on my feet were throbbing nonstop, but I wanted to hear the rest of his story. "But how did you get your son?"

"Oh, yas. Sascha . . ." Mr. Melnyk glanced quickly back at the lounge as if just recalling that he had a son. "Friends helped me get to China, then I come by luck to America. My son born in dis country, later, after that war was over. His mother is dead now, too." He was still staring off across the water past the green statue that was now quite near.

"It's much bigger and stronger looking up close, isn't it?" I was looking up at her arm. She was huge!

He nodded and smiled without taking his eyes from the Statue. "She was friendly woman I met here after var. She come from Belarus, was without family too, and we married. She was not strong woman like Katya. She died when da boy was in school. Before that, we used to come on this ferry many times together. We would remember the first time we saw her." He nodded toward the statue, checked the time again, then tapped the glass face. "See da time." He held it down for me to read. "Always is right time," he said. "Sometimes when we are young, we think the days will not be remembered. But little Annie, we find when we are old that we remember even smallest things. A rock by the river where Katya and I met. A big black, stout fellow of a rock, where I sit in da sun waiting for her to come. I bring fruit from orchard, and she brings bread, and we sit in sun by river and eat our first meal together. I remember da way little rocks look under da water, grass waving in sunshine and the sound of her big horse, up to the belly in grass, big jaws working. Sometimes now I remember every day."

For the first time, the thought came over me that someday I, too, might be old. If I didn't get polio and die first. I hoped it wouldn't hurt, but other than that, I didn't care much. If there was a God, like LaVetta and Great Aunt Alice and Elsie said, then everything would be fine—unless I went to hell.

"What do you think about hell?"

Mr. Melnyk glanced down at me, then lowered his head and looked over the rims of his glasses. "What do I think of hell? What do *you* think of hell is better question?"

"Mam said it's where I'm going if I'm not nice. She said I'd burn in fire forever, and that there was no way to get out, and the Devil comes and pokes at you with a pitchfork every day when it's time to eat."

Mr. Melnyk turned to me, his glasses fogged in the shifting light. "This Mam, your mother?"

"No. Grandmother."

"Ahhh. Well," he regarded me for a moment, his eyebrows glinting like raised sails in the sunlight. "I think hell is right here." He raised a long index finger and tapped himself twice, hard and harder, between the eyes. "We make our own hell, and we make our own heaven." Then he said it again, louder.

This was confusing. Mam had not even hinted at such a thing. "How?"

"By da way we think about it. You think you going to hell to burn, maybe you go. You think you go to heaven to see dead friends, then you go there—maybe. That's what I think. And I think this Mam of yours, she tell lies about hell to make you do what she say. She is criminal. Dictator."

I was astonished. I had never heard adults (except Mam and Linda) say anything bad about another adult. "Mam's not a criminal, Mr. Melnyk. She's never been in jail." I stopped, hoping he didn't think I was calling him a criminal. I fumbled for something to say and was relieved that he seemed to understand.

"It's good you come to Statue. Look! There she is. Telling peoples that they don't have to live with dictators. People come to America to be free people, not like old country where they slaves. Where they put you in prison for having own thoughts." Here, he tapped his finger to his head again. "You must know this. You free person, not have to think like anybody else. This Mam, not know she criminal, maybe. But remember this, anyone try to tell you what you have to think is criminals."

I was about to ask if that meant teachers too, but somehow, I knew what he meant. The idea that Mam was a criminal . . . sounded possible. I looked up at the huge green statue now right off our side of the boat. Mr. Melnyk patted me on the shoulder. "Now we go see this fine lady. Come."

My shoes were causing slicing pains in my feet, but I limped along beside him. As the ferry pulled to the dock, Mr. Melnyk the younger came hurrying from the restaurant wearing a lopsided smile, hazel eyes all jolly.

"Margo is not feeling up to going," he said. "We had a bite, and the boat, the motion, got to her. She must rest. Will you take Annie with you, Dad? Watch out for her, and send her back in a cab?" He handed his father a five-dollar bill. "Annie can spend this, but she needs to keep three dollars for the taxi to the hotel."

Mr. Melnyk glanced sharply at his son, then took my hand. "I will show her, if . . ." He bent his head down to my level, "you want to come with me, Annushka?"

"Sure." Mr. Melnyk was by a long leap more interesting than Margo.

"But," young Mr. Melnyk said to me, "you wait for Margo when you get back to the hotel. Take the two forty-five ferry and you'll be back at the hotel by four. Wait in the lobby and Margo will come for you. Can you remember that?"

"I'll remember," I said, looking up at him, turning on my good girl face.

"Here, Dad," he hauled a lumpy, napkin-wrapped bundle from his coat pocket. "Rolls and cheese from the buffet. I didn't think you'd be hungry after this morning, but she might be." He nodded at me, still smiling hugely. "Don't worry about Margo, Annie. She'll be all right as soon as she gets her feet on land. Just a landlubber, I guess."

Yeah, I bet, I thought, but kept it to myself. I looked up at the elder Melnyk and found his eyes on mine. I was sure we were thinking the same thing. I smiled, and he smiled back.

We didn't wave good-bye to Margo and Mr. Melnyk the young as the ferry left. By then we were already heading for the entrance to the Statue. Mr. Melnyk showed me his favorite bench by the museum entrance where he would sit and watch the crowd. He stopped and watched a man and two boys, all eating ice cream cones, walk off, the man fussing over the front of a boy's coat; Mr. Melnyk smiled.

"When I first come here, was on boat from China with many refugees, many children. We stood at rail of boat and cried we were so full of feelings. The sky was not cloudy like today, but was beootiful blue, and sunny." He craned his neck to look at lofty green arm holding the torch. "You better be going, to make back on time. I be here. Go along."

As I started up the steps behind a group of schoolchildren, he called out, "Looking down too much makes you feel . . ." He whooshed his long index finger in fast little circles.

"Dizzy!" I hollered and started toward the entrance.

The group of children I was following turned into the dim museum. The elevator was full so I started up the stairs, looking down and out at the water. After struggling up several flights, I slumped onto a steel step, rubbing my feet. I couldn't go on. The beautiful shoes came off my swollen feet with a pop. I set them on the step, wondering how they could be so unaffected by the pain they caused. Scooting against the railing, letting others pass, I peeled the socks from my oozing blisters. The blisters had broken, and the socks, driven by the straps of my beautiful shoes, now rubbed raw meat. I needed Band-Aids, and those lacking dress socks rather than the heavy woolens Mam had knitted for me. Damn, damn, damn! I hadn't come all this way to sit on a step and cry about my feet. I wanted to be at the top, looking out over the water, taking in the whole scene.

Hoping something might happen to resolve my dilemma, I decided there was nothing to do but go on. I removed a sock to reveal a ragged pink blister blazing from the top of my big toe, another from the bone of my instep, and a nasty one, the size of a raw quarter, where the buckle rubbed. I shook the sock out then rolled it down and very carefully pushed my foot back inside. Not bad without the pressure of the strap. The other foot was worse but by holding my breath and concentrating, I was able to slip the sock on without too much pain. I stood! I walked! I left my beautiful shoes on the steps!

On my way up the steps, I had immediately wondered why they made them so steep. I had to hold the rail and help myself up each step. It was slow going, but the stairs were mostly without people, and for that I was glad. I rested finally, shoeless, at the top level of the Statue of Liberty looking out at the water and the distant city, trying not to think of how high I was. I leaned out, feet hooked to the inner rail, trying to see Mr. Melnyk, but I was so high, so far away, that people below appeared like skittering, colorful sow bugs. I peered between the rails, and over the green water at the city, its outline pearl green in the distance. Finally, I moved from the rail and lumbered around the Lady's hat. I might have stayed longer but my feet, while not throbbing any longer, were stiff and aching, and my stomach had begun growling loudly.

Turning slowly to take in the whole view, I had no hint that my visit to the statue was momentous, but I was aware, thanks to Mr. Melnyk, that the statue was very important, apparently to many people, and not because it was a huge green woman towering in the midst of what appeared to be ocean. For many of the people Mr. Melnyk had talked about, the statue was about being lost, without family, without a place or home. For them, the statue was about finding a new home, new hope. For me, the statue was not only about home, but about Mr. Melnyk and Katya. It was independence and romance. Somehow, in those minutes alone, standing in the shifting wind, green waterscape sparkling, the world going on forever, I translated the liberty concept into a ticket to do as I pleased. Damn the torpedoes, full speed ahead, I'm drivin' the boat, etc.

My growling stomach drew me back to myself. I took another long look at the wandering people, the milky sky and choppy bay, the glimmering cityscape across the water. When I had firmly transcribed the whole picture in my mind's eye, I turned from the rail and began the climb down, which was even harder than the climb up. Near the level where I remembered leaving them, I looked for my shoes. Later, I could at least say—I looked.

By the time I gained solid ground, I'd created a whole story about giving the shoes to a girl who was barefoot, a homeless orphan too poor to own shoes. But Mr. Melnyk didn't ask about my shoes. He was looking at his watch as I walked toward him. When he looked up, I could see by the lift of his eyebrows and smiling mouth that he was relieved and happy to see me. Not like Mam, relieved and nasty. He was glad to see me, even though I'd been gone awhile and worried him. *Nice.*

He hadn't eaten all the cheese and bread, so on the ferry ride to the dock we shared what was left. As we sat eating thick sandwiches of yellow cheese and brown rolls, talking about what I'd seen from the top of the statue, I noticed him looking at my bedraggled sock feet sticking out in front of me, but he didn't say a word.

At the dock, we walked down the ramp together. On the sidewalk, he gave me a frail hug and a small copper-colored replica of the Statue of Liberty, which he placed in my hand.

Smiling, he murmured, "You write da name, M E L N Y K, vhen you get to da hotel, so you remember." I shoved the statue in my coat pocket. "Maybe I see you again, Annushka. Dis was gut day to meet." Then in a voice more stern, "You remember what I tell you about Grandmutter." He held up his long finger and wagged it gently in front of my nose, then we were at the taxi stand. He pulled his watch from his pocket. "You will be just in time to meet da woman." He searched another pocket and handed me a square of folded bills.

"Do you think you can come to the rodeo, Mr. Melnyk? I'll be right down where the horses come into the arena. Watch for me, okay?" He opened the taxi door. "The Belvedere," I said as though I rode in taxis every day. Mr. Melnyk stood on the curb, holding his dark hat in one hand, waving with the other.

Chapter 10

IN THE SEARCH FOR BUD, ANNIE'S DANCING SHOES LEAD HER UNDERGROUND ONCE MORE

When Mr. Melnyk disappeared, I turned forward. In the cab, wondering if I'd see him at the rodeo, my disreputable socks again the objects of my contemplation, I had an idea.

"Mister," I said to the cabdriver, "drop me off at that big store down the street."

"Same fare," he growled.

I stood in the warm entrance of the store displaying the big red sale banners that we'd passed that morning. Just off the entrance, a woman wearing an orange scarf shuffled through a rack of coats, one by one, taking her time. I headed into the belly of the store.

The shoe department was so big I couldn't see it all at once. On a tangle of walls, shoeboxes were stacked to the ceiling. Fierce-eyed salespeople crawled tall ladders to find shoes for chattering sock-footed pedestrians. I headed for the sign that read, "Children's Shoes—CLOSE-OUT" and stood pondering them. First were brown ones with lots of thin, pinchy-looking leather straps, then a shelf of brightly-colored canvas sneakers. I liked their looks but wondered how they'd look with my strange suit. The longer I stood in the hot basement brooding over the shoes, none of which seemed right, the more discouraged I became. Even the thought of the slightest pressure on my feet was unacceptable.

"What ya lookin' for, missy?" I glanced up to see a smiling round face, cheerful brown eyes beaming down on me. The man wore a pink shirt, gray pants, and a thin gray tie. My eyes held to the little pin in the middle of his tie, a gold poodle, glittering blue stones for eyes, a dainty collar of shiny pink stones, a white enamel bow on its tail. The man's dark hair was longish and combed off his forehead to the side. His nametag read, "Donny."

"That's quite an outfit there. Looking for shoes to go with?" He was smiling and looking too friendly to think that he was making fun of my hideous suit. I gazed up at him but didn't reply. "We've got lots of shoes just now. What you wantin', honey bun?"

I leaned over, peeled the sock from my worst foot, and thrust it forward for his inspection. "Something that won't hurt."

"Oh, my goodness! Honey, your feet look just like those gypsies from the alley. My dancers, my dancers, my beeootiful dancers," he sang, skipping in a tight circle. I looked around expecting someone to stop him, but no one was paying any attention.

"A shoe for milady, a shoe for milady. . . I have just the item." He dropped to his knees to rummage in a cupboard. "Let's see, you're about a three, about a three, umm, here's a suede, and a smooth leather."

Talking non-stop, he burrowed into the cupboard, his behind wiggling like a dog wagging a stub tail. Drawing forth a box, he sat back on his heels, and brushed at his shirt.

"Now you just sit in that chair, miss dancing lady, and let's see." With a primish smile, he raised an eyebrow, and ever so slowly, holding the box before my face, opened the lid by half inches. Only then did I begin to smile. Inside was a pair of black suede dancing slippers. I reached for them.

"Allow me." He lifted one slipper from the box, raised it high, and turned it this way and that.

"Yes, Mr. Donny," I said, jumping in the game with him. "They're good."

The slippers, Donny called them jazz shoes, were soft as socks. No heels, a sole that appeared to be of slightly harder leather than the tops, and only a flat elastic ribbon to hold them snug.

"Ahh, miss dancing lady. Let us proceed." From his pocket he produced nylon knee socks and two Band-Aids. "We usually keep more in the drawer, but this is all we have right now, milady. I'll throw the nylons in with the shoes" he said and winked. "Now, off with the tainted footwear."

I winced as he tossed my dirtied, and in some spots bloodied, wool socks into the wastebasket next to the chair where I perched with my foot stuck out.

"They aren't fit for milady," he said, noting my grimace. Peeling the paper from the Band-Aid, he raised the same questioning eyebrow, waited until I nodded, then placed the Band-Aids. Smoothly and painlessly, he eased the nylons over my feet and snapped them in place above my knees. "So, they roll down a bit. Not to worry, they'll do better than those nasty knitted golf club covers."

I wanted to tell Donny that if not for the nasty socks I'd have been worse off than ever but knew there was no sense arguing with him or trying to retrieve Mam's famous knit socks from Macy's wastebasket. And I didn't want to anyway.

But I did want to give Donny something besides the $1.99 for the dancing shoes. "I'm not really a dancer," I volunteered. "I'm with the rodeo. My mother's the star, and Bud—he's the All-Around World Champion—is our boyfriend, and if you come to the rodeo, you'll really like it. If you look at the stands by the bucking horses, you'll probably see me."

"Oh, my dear. You're with the rodeo! The rodeo? Oh, those cowboys are so big, aren't they? Oh, they're tough too, honey. Ahh," he said, with a big inhalation, "no, Donny can't go to the rodeo, honey. All those animals and little me?"

He was pretending to be afraid, but he really wasn't. He was laughing, and a curly-haired saleslady was smiling with him.

"Donny's quite the clown," she said and hurried off with boxes clutched under her arm. I paid, and at the elevator, turned to wave, but Donny was lost among the shoes.

On the wide sidewalk the streetlights blinked on over the hurrying crowds, giving the street a merry look.

"Hey, lady," I said, touching the coat sleeve of a chubby-faced young woman wearing a red knit hat with a yarn ball on the top. "Which way to Madison Square Garden?"

Without answering, she swung around and pointed up the block.

The relative lack of pain after so many hours of torture was like a numbing shot at the dentist. Heading down the busy street, I felt I could have walked over mountains and rivers, walked clear home to Oregon if I'd had to. My dancing shoes had made all the difference to my quest and checking to make sure I still had the little statue in my pocket, I took off in the direction the woman pointed.

At the blazing Garden entrance, I hunched my shoulders and hurried through the heavy doors, hoping to avoid recognition or outright capture. In the lobby, face turned from the entrance, I punched the elevator down button. If any rodeo people stepped off the elevator, I'd hurry away like I was only passing by.

In the basement, I rushed toward the stalls where they kept the cowboys' horses. Like all the contestants and show people, Bud always fed his horse at this time of evening. I started down the dark, strawed alley, stepping gingerly around wet spots and occasional bags of grain, careful of my new shoes. With no trouble from my feet, now my belly was hollow and quaking not only with hunger but excitement. The rest of me—legs, arms, etc.—could have belonged to someone else. I had only one aim in mind.

To my right, a tall bay stood looking over a stall door, red coat gleaming out of the darkness like rust satin in candlelight. To the left were dull metal tack rooms with padlocked doors securing saddles and horse gear.

Toots was a red roan with a silver mane and tail, and Bud always said she was the real champion, not him. When I found her stall, two doors from the bay, she was standing near the door, rosy head down, silver mane brushing the straw, munching grain. The warm smells of feed and the horse made me feel at home for a moment. But damn! I'd missed him. From the looks of her hay, still over half a flake, I figured Bud had been there only minutes before. At that moment, the overhead lights snapped off, leaving only a single dim bulb burning at the end of each aisle. In the distance, a door slammed, then a hollow bang echoed through the space, maybe from the top being slammed onto a grain barrel.

"Night, kids," boomed a voice in the dusk.

Crouching in front of the stall door, I held my breath. *Had everyone gone? Maybe they locked the doors at night when there was no evening show.* I turned to run back the way I'd come, barreled into a gunnysack full of grain, and fell on my butt with a thump. Not pausing to see if I was injured or manured, I scrambled to my feet and tore down the alley, gasping for breath as I stumbled up the wide steps to the elevator doors. The down arrow was green, the letter B flashing. I twirled and ran down the steps into the dark.

At the bottom of the steps on the other side of a short wall was what looked to be a huge box with a wide, deep platform, and double doors with buttons to one side. Led by the faint warm smell of animals and feed, I entered the box and without hesitating, pushed the top button on the panel. The closing doors shook the box, floor, walls, and me as they ground together. I lurched into darkness, hands suction cupped to the crusty metal wall.

Now, I had to go to the bathroom. Contemplating this sudden need, a loud beeping erupted, so blaring and shrill it almost frightened me into letting go right there. The beep, more a piercing shriek, shrilled, stopped for a moment and started again, seeming to go faster and faster. The box pitched, and the top sprang open with a metal squeal. Thinking the sky had finally fallen, I crouched in the corner, arms bracing the walls, breath sucked to my backbone. My mouth must have been open, my eyes bugged wide in the dark. I was slammed to the sidewalk on the busy New York street, a yellow cloudy sky above me, coated, muffled people hurrying around the wide box resting on the pavement. My legs were shaky, and, oh, did I ever have to find a bathroom, bad.

*

I had learned from observing Mam and Linda that when grown-ups were busy, if a kid pretended to know what she was doing, and didn't get in their way, adults wouldn't pay much attention. I made my way down the street to the hotel, ran around back, and snuck through the hotel kitchen entrance. After relieving myself in the workers' bathroom, I hid in the toilet stall, planning the strategy and tactics of my mission to find Bud. My planning session was short because I didn't have much to go on, but though I wasn't sure where to start, that wasn't stopping me. I'd figure out what to do as I went. If I didn't find him soon, I would ask for him at the front desk.

Soon, my dancing shoes advanced softly on the carpeted

second floor hallway of The Belvedere, a hunter tracking a wolf through a thick, needle-padded forest. And there were tracks, dirty, wedge-toed and square-heeled boot marks on the carpet, but too many to isolate one lone wolf. Approaching the fire stairs to the fourth floor, my feet didn't hurt that much, but I was hungry, tired, and from the look of the window at the end of the corridor, it was now full night. Dinnertime. My mother would be having what Mam called a hissy.

Hoping to find some sign of Bud, I sailed onto the fourth floor, walking with purpose, glancing at the trays on the floor, checking to see if any doors were open. The frosted wall lights threw beams at the ceiling, giving the hallways a friendly, comforting glow.

Three doors from the exit, I stooped to examine a tray with a mashed red and white cigarette package, the kind Bud smoked, crumpled beside the plate. As I bent over to retrieve it, I felt a cold, wet nudge on the back of my leg and swung around to see a little white dog. It seemed as surprised by our confrontation as I was. It barked, rather a yelp, and we both jumped back, me right into the tray with a crash. This seemed to excite the little puffball further because it barked again and kept springing up and down like it was on a trampoline. Down the hall, a door opened.

"Lucy, Lucy, come!" a soft voice called. The dog cocked its ear toward the voice, but being much too interested in me to obey, it barked again, another high yapping blast. From the door, a blonde head popped, spied me, and popped back. The door shut. Now I had coffee on the hem of my suit, and God knew what on my butt. The dog watched me crawl off the tray and stand up. It approached me and sniffed. No bigger than a red squirrel, a short-tailed red squirrel wearing sheep's wool.

The door opened again, and the blonde woman, barefoot, clutching a white robe around her, looked up and down the hallway then hurried toward us. It was Maizie! If anything, she looked even prettier in her robe with her hair brushed out long than she had when I'd met her in the Garden lobby. Lucy turned and scampered down the hallway as fast as she could go, her little tail sticking up like a parade flag.

"Oh, look at that darn dog, honey. She just does this to get me to run after her. Now, what's your name, honey? Annie, isn't it? Will you just look at that?" She stood in the middle of the hallway smiling after the dog, shaking her head. "Late as usual, and she wants to play."

"I'll get her," I volunteered.

"Oh, honey, that'd be swell. We're just down here in 452. Gotta be quick though." She looked around, finger to her mouth, "No pets allowed."

Armed with a piece of greasy meat from the nearest tray, I set after the miniature hound.

Half an hour later, while Maizie was in the bathroom dressing for her date, Lucy and I were jumping on the bed, the pink spread rippling around us. My small hands, thrown high, made long plump shadows dance over the walls and ceiling and across the lacey beige lingerie hanging over the door. Lucy's tiny ears flapped up and down with each bounce, revealing pink interiors then wooly white fuzz. If I'd thrown a ruffled collar around her neck, she would have looked just like a circus dog. Maizie's roommates, both tall, one a skinny redhead named Johnnie, the other darker with long, shiny black hair, were also preparing to go out. The redhead, wearing a satiny green robe, was curled in a chair sewing a dress hem. Patty, the other girl, wearing only a melon-colored slip, rummaged through the bottom drawer of a tall dresser.

I grabbed for a towel crumpled beside the bed, intent on ornamenting Lucy's neck. Just then, there was a soft knock on the door. Maizie's eyes went big, and the other girls snapped to face the door as if it might open by itself. The action stopped only for a moment then resumed with the other girls grabbing their dresses and crowding into the bathroom, leaving me to make a three-point landing, and bounce to the floor. The inside of the bathroom produced a flurry of dress noises, then Maizie came hopping through the doorway, one shoe on, missing the other. Her long diamond earrings bounced lights onto the ceiling as she patted the silver dress over her hips. She stooped and pulled up the edge of the bedspread.

"Honey, can you see my silver shoe? Scoot under there and see if you can find it for me," she said. Then laughing, she called, "Just a minute, honey. I'll be right there."

I grabbed the silver shoe from under the bed and held it out to Maizie, who slipped it on her red-toed foot. "Annie, can you get that door?"

I scrambled to the door, yanked the doorknob, and when it wouldn't open, pulled hard.

Bud stood in the doorway. He wore his good suit, holding his best gray hat in one hand, a bouquet of red roses in the other.

"Oh," I hollered, happier than anything. "You found me. You found me!" and threw my arms around his legs.

"Whoa there," he barked.

I looked up at him, not releasing the soft material of his pant leg. He stood blinking at me with half a smile, his gaze the same as at the Cow Palace when we'd gone to inspect a bull he'd drawn for his next ride. His eyes had that identical quiet stare.

"Heard downstairs, you was lost." His voice was like always, nice, low, and growly. Lucy commenced jumping up and down, yapping her head off.

"So you came to find me! I've been looking all over for you ever since I got here. What happened to you?" I let go and backed up so I could get a better look at . . . the suit, the flowers. . .

He looked down at me then, the same blue, blue eyes, same

beautiful black hair.

"Well, of course you know each other, don't you?" Maizie scooped Lucy out of the way, shifted the struggling dog to a headlock, and reached out to pat Bud on the arm that held the roses.

"Don't you look handsome, sir." She laughed, a tinkling, merry sound in the warm room. "Look, honey, he brought such beautiful flowers." She took the dark roses from his wilting hand and led him into the room.

The room seemed crowded, the scent of roses overwhelming.

Bud said, "Err, I believe Linda and them Garden boys called the police here a little while back. You best be on the fly, kiddo."

"But I found you. Aren't we going out to eat? I'm sooo hungry."

"Annie, you'll be gettin' me in Dutch." His eyes crinkled and then the smile came to his mouth. He hunkered down, level with me, holding his hat with both hands. "Better not tell 'em you was up here either."

Maizie finished primping the roses, set them on the dresser, and rustled off to the bathroom again. Trailing deadly perfume, Johnnie and Patty fetched short, fancy coats from the closet.

"Bye, Bud. You all have a good evening. We'll see your picture in the paper in the mornin' again—we're takin' bets." Patty, still laughing, leaning into the hall mirror talking to Bud's reflection, smoothed a finger over her eyebrow then took her tiny purse from the table. "See ya there, Maizie. We're meeting them in the bar."

Bud placed a warm hand on my shoulder then rose. "Errr, uhh, Annie, you better hightail it with them. Hold up, Pat."

I reached out and took his hand.

Patty stood in the doorway, long hair perfect, looking like

a picture in the magazines Linda mooned over. Johnnie, also looking very splendid in her green dress and long flashy emerald earrings, scooted me forward on her way to the door.

"Make sure she gets to the bar. Her mother and some people are there in the lobby. Can't miss the commotion." Still holding Bud's hand, we walked to the door. He stood before me dressed up and handsome, looking down on me, chin sunk to his collar. He smiled then raised his hand. I lifted mine then our hands dropped to our sides, and I was propelled away from Bud, away from the person I most wanted. Helpless, as though encased in thick glass, I floated toward the door, unable to speak up, not knowing how to appeal to him, and knowing that if I did, it wouldn't matter anyway. At the door, I turned to look back and saw Maizie, her cloud of white hair glowing above the silver dress, walking toward the door, holding out one long red rose. It was right for Bud to be with her. She was much nicer than Linda, and prettier too. The All-Around World Champion deserved Maizie.

"Bye, honey," she called and handed me the rose.

Bud disappeared behind the closing door.

*

Leaning into the corner of the elevator, the rose drooping from my hand, I hadn't even the energy for tears. Now what was I going to do? Bud was my person. The only one I wanted. I had to get him back together with Linda for the proposal. Soon! Yet there was no time to brood over him just then. As we stepped from the elevator into the lobby, we immediately came upon Margo sprawled in a big chair outside the lounge, her purse lying on top of her reclining form, but no police, and no Linda.

"Should we take her into the bar?" Johnnie asked, scanning the crowded lobby. "I don't want Vic to think I stood him up."

We walked past the gently snoring Margo, her sunglasses cocked at a precarious angle, then through the tall doors into the dim lounge. Inside, looming at the bar like a massive friendly bull with muscles ballooning from a dark suit, was Vic with some of his gigantic buddies. Behind him, strung down the bar like babbling big-headed birds, were Linda and Jeannie in colorful Western dress hats, tailored suits, and loud five-hundred-dollar custom boots.

Tony and Leo stood facing the group, their backs to the door. Ed Ross, the clown everybody called Mac who Jeannie was in love with, was leaning against the bar taking it all in. He lifted his hand as I walked up behind the group. He was very good-looking in his everyday clothes, clean shaven and nice smelling. Tonight, he didn't look at all like the crazed character with the curly red wig and white face who tore around the arena, jumping from the fence, waving a red bandana, giving the Bronx cheer to save cowboys from the monstrous charging bulls.

On this, the rodeo's night off, the bar was crowded with smoke and cowboys, their presence, soft voices and laughter, their big hats, turning the plush city bar into an approximation of a fairgrounds dance hall. Two men stood at the bar talking to Linda and Jeannie, one in a suit, the other, a police uniform.

"Well, hello, miss Oregon." Vic grinned down at me, now with teeth, where before he'd had black gaps. He also had a new addition—a snakelike gash across his swollen nose that ran onto his cheek. There was a black stitch at each end of the cut, neat as one of Grandma Delaunay's cross stitches.

"You know Annie?" Patty looked at Vic with a sweep and flutter of dark eyelashes. Her gold earrings swayed, and her blue dress was shot full of golden threads that glittered in the bar lights.

Holding the rose out, I walked toward my mother.

Just then, Linda looked up.

"What were yeww thinking?" she yowled. "What in the world do you think you were doing taking off—running off like that? I was just about to have a fit. I had to have a drink to calm down. I thought you were kidnapped."

Scouring my face with a rough paper towel, she said, "Oh!" and sounding insulted, "Look at this skirt! My Gawwd. What have you been into? Tony is supposed to take us somewhere very nice for dinner. Mama Leoni's is a very, very nice place. It's real New York, and just look at yewww!" she howled, her voice rising and trembling at the end.

She grasped my chin in her hand and jerked it toward the pinkish ceiling of the lounge bathroom. "Look at me. Look at me right now," she snarled, moving over me so I would have to see her.

I kept looking at the ceiling, thinking that if I didn't look at her or talk, she'd quit.

"I'll send you home." This was more a proposal, like she was trying it for a fit. Then harder, "I'll send you home in the morning, and that'll be the end of it!"

I doubted she'd send me home without seeing my father after Mam had paid all that airplane money and I'd come this far, so I still wouldn't look at her. Now, the sad ploy, the tears. Big, fat, and glossy, I knew they would be gushing into her eyes and oozing down her cheeks, but it was pretty hard to feel bad for her when she was gripping my chin with the same intention and pressure she'd use to break a wild horse. Anyway, I'd seen these emotional showers many times before and they didn't work as well on me as on Mam and Granddad.

At that moment, mention of food at a good restaurant was most interesting to me. To avert a time-wasting, full-blown crying fit, I thought I might as well let her off the hook. "Well, don't go off and leave me, and don't leave me with babysitters, then."

"And where did you meet those . . . people? My Gawwd, they're . . . hockey players." Her voice accelerated to a screech on hockey players. "And those women are no better than, than—OH!" The last a harsh, frustrated cry.

"Well?" I said, not moving.

"All right," she ground out through big, white teeth. "I won't." She was looking in the mirror, fussing at her collar and pushing her hair behind her ears.

"Won't what?" I waited, but she didn't answer. "No! You have to say it." I waited again, looking straight at her eyes in the mirror. "Say it! No more babysitters. Swear!"

Chapter 11

THE ROY AND DALE EPISODE AND WHAT HAPPENS TO ANNIE

MADISON SQUARE GARDEN, 8TH AVE AND 49TH STREET NYC

After eating in the loud glassed-in restaurant on top of the Garden, we rode the elevator to the basement. It had been two days since the horrible trauma my mother had suffered while I was missing, days during which Linda had forced me to track her everywhere. But now she had to leave me alone during a special Friday night show with two performances.

"And don't get any ideas of running off again," she said as we entered the elevator. "I've talked to the contractors, vendors, and everyone else. You better mind your p's and q's this time because everyone who belongs to the rodeo is watching you." She stopped and smiled, "And, you do look nice tonight," she said, fluffing my bangs.

"Humphh."

In the basement, we groomed Monte, washing his white stockings and slipping oil over his face to make him sparkle. We changed clothes, then all three of us, Monte clean and shining, Linda in tight chartreuse satin and black lace, and me in my awful outfit, stood before a huge American flag at the entrance to the Garden arena and had our pictures taken by

DeVere, the famous rodeo photographer. Captured for eternity in my red and orange plaid suit and turquoise sweater, I was freshly mad at Mam because she hadn't let me bring my riding clothes. I wanted everyone to know, and the picture to record, that I was no regular city-kid. I was pure rodeo.

I had especially wanted everyone to know this tonight, because it was the night I would be meeting Roy and Dale. The evening program listed a special performance time for the featured attractions, and Linda and Mam had promised I would meet them. Since no one had mentioned it again, and it hadn't happened, I figured that I'd see to it myself. After threatening instant death if I ran off, Linda had left me on the bench near the announcers stand and walked off to saddle Monte, chartreuse satin legs striding down the alley. But there was no need of her threats, as I had no thought of leaving the Garden.

Ten minutes later, I was planted solidly behind the bucking horse chutes waiting to see Roy and Dale ride into the arena. Just like every other act, no matter how famous they were, Roy and Dale would wait in the warm-up pen just outside the chutes until their act was announced. They would have plenty of time to talk to me. I climbed onto the whitewashed fence and balanced there, one hand gripping the top board, the other clenching the program Roy and Dale would sign. From my roost, I could see the entrance, most of the arena, and the back of the bull pens where the Brahmas stood twitching their tails, huge horned heads drooping lower and lower waiting for the last, most deadly, event of the night. A rodeo always ended with the bull riding because it was most dangerous. According to Mam they planned it that way so people wouldn't leave early.

From inside the arena, the announcer's voice boomed, "...and from Stillwater, Oklahoma, Bud Hartmann on Moonlight." The rump of a speckled white horse sprung twisting from the gate, tail straight up, farting at every jump. Bud, astride the spinning crazy-eyed horse, reared backward, clenching the rope with one fist, knees raised high. He raked the horse's flanks with hissing spurs, an arm flung over his head in exactly the right position. Floating over the horse, barely touching its back, he used his legs to balance. The horse and man became one flying beast, their legs like flashing wings.

The horn blared, and the pick-up men astride matching palominos, their red chaps flying, thundered after the bucking horse. They hoisted Bud off Moonlight onto the rump of the closest pick-up horse, then swung him gently to the ground before tearing off to corral Moonlight. Out in the arena, Bud scooped his hat from the dirt, slapped it against his chaps, then settled it on his head and sauntered toward the gate as the announcer boomed out his score. "Only a 98, folks. First place so far!" Accompanied by the clapping of the crowd, the announcer thundered, "And what does a cowboy get when he's got a winner by the tail, folks?"

Just then Jeannie's boyfriend, Mac, orange wig wired with dirt, white grease paint smeared, and without his big red nose, loped toward me.

"Annie-O. How's it go?" Grinning up at me, white-framed eyes blue and bloodshot, he fumbled at the latch, and opened the gate. His eyes moved to focus behind me. I twisted around.

They rode up the sawdust alley as if parading up a lane in one of my story books, in a halo of brilliant light, and for a moment in the silence of imaginary worlds. Dale rode after Roy, her face a bland blank, the red stab of lipstick a period at the end of her face, blond curls swelling from her white hat. As befit their legendary status, they rode tall palominos with white manes and tails, Roy on handsome and famous Trigger, Dale atop the darker blonde, Buttermilk, who twitched her long white tail with each step. The couple's sparkling suits were white satin, gold fringed, studded with diamonds, the horses' saddles blazing with silver. Roy was smiling slightly; lips lifted gently, eyes fixed on the distance. I straightened on my perch, reached to tug my skirt down, and dropped my program in the sawdust at Trigger's feet.

Not pausing to miss an opportunity, I shimmied down the fence, landing in front of Trigger who, unlike his screen character, did not look either amused or interested. He snorted and braked, causing Buttermilk to run up his tail. I sank on hands and knees in the thick manured loam, head down, trying to jerk the program from under Trigger's white, glitter-encrusted hoof.

"Roy!!" A hollering yodel from Dale. "Rooooyyy! There's not supposed to be any kids back here. Now you tell that contractor that's what we agreed on. You make sure!"

I yanked the program from under Trigger's manicured toe and jumped back to avoid his nervous legs. Reminding myself that even the famous Trigger was still just a horse, I straightened to my full four feet, stepped close to Roy's white-booted foot balanced in the stirrup, and held the program up to him.

"I'm Annie. I came all the way from Oregon to see you."

He glanced down, shook his head, and without a word, raised his hand from the saddle horn and motioned me toward the fence. There passed several long moments of complete silence as I stared up at him and he stared back. Then he looked away.

"But I'm not one of the regular kids. My mother's a rodeo star. . . She had her picture taken in mink . . ."

The Sons of the Pioneers' music blared into the arena, the announcer bellowed "and now . . . Roy Rogers and Daaale Evans, the King and Queen of the West, and the Madison Square Garden Rodeo."

Without responding or even looking down at me, the King and Queen kicked their horses, who sprang forward, missing me by inches. The horses tore through the gate into the blazing arena, their famous riders waving and grinning as the music expanded to fill the high places. Picked up by blue spots, escorted by fiddles, slide guitars, the thump of a stand-up bass, by kids screaming their names and clapping, Roy and Dale raced their horses around the arena under the glittering mirrored ball suspended high in the center of the Garden arena. They brought the prancing horses to a halt in front of the announcer's stand just as the Sons of the Pioneers finished their song. Accompanied only by the reeking Brahma bulls, I stood in the sawdust clutching the dirty program, and bawled.

Chapter 12

THE PARTY WHERE ANNIE MEETS HER EAST COAST FAMILY AND INFLAMES LINDA'S PASSIONS

MIDTOWN MANHATTAN

Black and white rooms, punctuated by rectangular highly polished wooden tables, everything sleek, straight and quiet, the hotel was nothing like The Belvedere. I had decided on the navy-blue dress with white collar and cuffs even though they pinched my arms and had brushed my hair out instead of letting Linda braid it. After the loss of Bud, the spurning by my heroes, incidents Linda immediately found excuses for and I had resolved to ignore, I was hoping my father would be the savior, the long odds winner. We were walking through the lobby of the midtown hotel where we were to have lunch with my father and his mother.

"Now, Annie, don't ask any questions. Just be polite. Tell them about you. They'll want to hear about you."

"But why doesn't he talk to his mother?"

"Annie! I told you not to talk about that. Just SHUT up. . ."

"But what happened?" We were nearing the door where the skinny desk man had directed us.

Linda jerked at my hand, and swung down to face me, her big blue Stetson almost knocking me in the forehead. "We won't talk about it *now,*" she whispered roughly. "I'll tell you about it later, but," then hissing, "Not. One. Word." She slid a hand beneath the band of her dress pants and adjusted the tooled belt so the name LINDA, encircled by big red flowers, appeared between the belt loops. Flexing her shoulders, she straightened her blue suede jacket, then shook out the long fringe trailing from the sleeves, and walked slowly ahead, ignoring me.

"Well, aren't they coming here together? They'd have to talk on the way—wouldn't they?"

At the entry, my mother practiced her photo smile. She glanced down at me, gave me the once-over, and pulled the brass door handle.

Inside, at a long table, a round older couple huddled together, catty-corner to a lone man seated at the head. The woman was round everywhere with bright blue eyes, wearing navy blue with white collar and cuffs—almost like mine—with a little blue veiled hat and white gloves. She seemed timid and displayed no expression, but her moist bright eyes seemed to see everything. The man with her, tall and skinny, round of stomach, slicked back graying hair, and big worked hands, looked uneasy in a gray suit. When I came near, he smiled, causing his rough face to crack into deep creases around a pale bluish mouth.

The man at the head of the table stood. He was short, and round, with gleaming smooth hair wearing a soft black suit, ditto the shoes, a white tie with thin black stripes, and a bright white shirt with gold cuff links. *Looks like a penguin*, I thought, wondering who he was. He extended an immaculate, warm, gold-ringed hand. From behind, my mother pushed my elbow so that my hand connected with his. He grasped my hand and shook it. His eyes were penetrating, large and deeply set under a high round brow, but their expression revealed nothing to me of his character. Staring up at him, realizing slowly that he must be my father though he didn't look at all like the slender young man in my mother's album, this containment, this not doing, told me all I needed to know about him. Had the look in his eyes been more vulnerable, the expression on his impassive face more friendly, in my state, I could easily have thrown my arms around him and hugged him. As it was, I merely looked up, studying him, but did not remove my hand from his.

"How *do* you *do*, Antonia?" His voice was dry and polite. Not even a penguin; this was a still odder bird. One I hadn't seen in any book.

Incoherently mumbling some pleasantry or other, Linda pushed me around the table to meet my other grandmother. I let go of his hand. Beatrice was lively eyed and sweet appearing, her features formed of pink fat lumps, moist, trembling, powdered, reminding me of the plump older women Mam clucked over at Red Cross meetings. All decked out in their good clothes, sitting properly, ankles crossed over orthopedic dress shoes. *Mam could eat her in one chomp,* I thought. The big man, maybe the most interesting, and certainly the most rumpled of the group, was my grandmother's husband but not—and Linda had made this very clear in an earlier briefing—my grandfather.

"Well, it's so wonderful to finally meet you," she said, smiling kindly and taking my hand between her white gloves. "Are you enjoying New York?" My mother hugged her and shook hands with her husband, Ernie.

We sat stiffly around the long white-clothed table, Beatrice and Ernie across from me and my mother, me sitting next to my father, passing awkward comments, pausing as the male waiter asked what we wanted to eat and filled our sparkling glasses. I had root beer, Beatrice and Ernie ordered coffee,

Mother and Father (hah! me saying Mother and Father) had wine. My mother simpered and fumbled over ordering. Fidgeting and mumbling, smoking like a movie star, laughing her phony laugh at the ceiling, she maintained a progressive, idiotically disconnected stream of chat. I looked on wondering why she was acting so dopey. I glanced up from the menu and snuck a look at the others, but they didn't appear to notice anything unusual. I observed that my father's hand holding the wine glass was plump, well formed, and much cleaner than mine.

"What do you think of the city, Annie?" Beatrice smiled across at me, glancing shyly at my father, almost as if she was asking permission to speak. Ernie patted her on the hand.

"It's a hellhole," I said, using Uncle Jack's favorite expression for cities. "How can anyone live here?"

My father cleared his throat, reached for his water glass, and took a swallow. Ernie laughed. "But, from on top of the Statue of Liberty, it looks pretty. From across the water it's nice with the lights and everything. There's lots to do. I like Madison Square Garden. They've got lots going on, and the hotel where we live is fun. I've met loads of friends while Linda's working. I went to the Statue of Liberty, and Margo got, err . . . sick, and I met Mr. Melnyk from Russia. He told me about his wives and where they lived before the war. Margo and his son were having brandies, so I went with Mr. Melnyk and then I walked up in her hat and looked all around . . ."

"Annie," my mother broke in, "why don't you tell everyone . . ."

"The Garden is really fun. Do you go there a lot?" I was asking my father, hoping he'd say he did and then I was going to ask him to come to the rodeo with us.

"Occasionally. I take clients to the boxing matches."

"I go for the hockey," Ernie submitted, setting his cup in

the saucer, resting his arm on the table. Beatrice smiled across the table at me then patted him on the arm. He glanced from me to her then slowly moved his arm to his lap. "Maple Leafs are doing good this year. I been there a couple a times and it's a h-heck of a good game they put on."

"Do you know Vic? He's a Ranger."

"Vic?"

"OOH, hah!" my mother half laughed, grinning broadly. "Someone Annie met by accident at the Garden."

"He showed me where the bathroom was."

"Now, is he a player? Would that be Big Vic Parelli?" Ernie had leaned forward, turning his ear a little toward me.

I glanced up at my mother, who was boring down on me with her eyes.

"I don't know his name. Sometimes he doesn't have a tooth, but when he dresses up and goes to the bar, he does. He's bigger than a Brahma, bigger than Tony and Leo put together. You should see him when he has his head thing on and the pads and everything. But, then he doesn't smell very good."

"Oh, well, now that sounds like it could be Parelli, doesn't it, honey?" He adjusted the glasses he had taken from his pocket to read the menu.

My father, smiling slightly and watching me closely with his big gray eyes had waited until I paused.

"Annie, I'm interested in hearing about you and your school. What subjects do you like?"

My mother slid her hand under the table and snapped me on the leg. It didn't hurt that much, but I glared back at her. Why didn't she just speak up if she had something to say?

"My school?" I flailed back at her under the table, but she had moved her hand, and was sitting calmly, smiling over at my father. "It's down the road, across the field." What could I say about school? It was nothing to me but torture and according to Linda I wasn't supposed to talk about "unpleasant" things. "Sometimes Mam drives me, sometimes I ride a bus. But I like to ride Lady. I tie her up on the post behind the baseball field."

"You must be in third grade?"

I nodded.

"And what subjects do you study?"

"I like art day and reading. I sang 'The Battle Hymn of the Republic' in the school assembly." I didn't tell him that I forgot the words to the second verse and had to sing the first one over. Ms. Price had said not to worry, that it was courageous even to attempt that song in front of the whole school, but I knew she was just being nice. Everyone had laughed at me.

"Oh, your great-grandmother Callahan was a fine singer," Beatrice oohed.

"Annie does *like* to sing . . . and she does have a pretty voice, but her art teacher says her real talent is drawing."

"And how about other subjects—arithmetic?" This from my father in his quiet, pleasant voice.

My total, complete, and hideous downfall were story problems, so I was not talking about it. "I met the singer at the Copacabana. She's famous. She lives down on the fourth floor. She has a poodle in her room, but it's not supposed to be there."

Beatrice laughed, and then complimented Linda on her outfit, then Linda had to tell all about how she had to always appear in western wear during the entire run of the rodeo because it was in her CON-tract. And how her CON-tract was such a monster, how her CON-tract . . .

I tried to sit still and studied my father. I had thought maybe he'd look at my mother a lot and fall in love with her all over again, but it didn't appear to be happening. And now that I'd met him, I wondered if that was such a good idea after all. Bud was the one for me.

The waiter entered with a cart, which he placed against the wall. I had learned that the cheesy noodle sauce Tony brought me my first night in New York was called Alfredo, and I asked for it everywhere. This place had a special kind with chicken, so I embarked on lunch with delight—also delighted to escape more quizzing about school. I was not a bad student, certainly not a stupid one, although my extremely selective application often made it appear so. It was a secret known only to Ms. Price, my second-grade teacher, and myself, that I was the smartest kid in the class—maybe the school—except for numbers. Linda had already warned me not to talk about my attendance and attitude marks—they were also on the unpleasant list.

After we finished lunch, the waiter took our plates and asked if we wanted to see the dessert cart.

Over the top of Linda's spluttering, "No," I barked, "Yes!" I had to have more time to bring up my problem.

"Well, I guess we have time." Linda turned to my father. "I have to be back in time to dress for the show and get my horse ready."

"Quite an interesting career." My father took a sip of his wine and placed his napkin on the table. He stood as his mother rose.

"Excuse me," she said. "Ladies."

"Oh," my mother squeaked, pushing back her chair and rising, "yes." She placed her hand on my shoulder. "Annie, come with us."

"Where are you going now? Let's have dessert."

"To the restroom. *Now*, Annie." Her voice had the 'I mean it' tone.

"I don't have to." I wondered what she would do when she realized I wouldn't budge. In the presence of any but the family, any hint of what she called "unpleasantness" usually made her back down immediately.

"Annie!"

"I don't have to GO." At the threat of my raised voice, Linda took a deep breath and pushed her chair in. She looked up, smiled at the two men, then staring back at me, she walked to the door and left the room.

I hitched my chair closer to my father, who was lighting a cigarette. Ernie was smoking a cigar and had asked the waiter to bring him his own pot of coffee that he had placed in front of him.

"I hear that you send money for me."

My father, who had been inhaling, gazing up at a picture on the wall, looked directly at me. He raised his dark eyebrows and put the cigarette in the ashtray.

"And who told you this?"

"Mam. She said it's not enough, and she won't give me any to buy dresses. I want you to send it to me from now on."

"So you can buy dresses?" Hearing my indrawn breath, he raised a finger letting me know that he had more to say. "Do you have a savings account?"

"Savings account? No! I don't even have any dresses. You should see the other ones she makes me wear. They're bad. Worse than this! What about your other children?"

"Er. . . Donna, and James. They're a little younger, so they aren't quite so concerned yet . . . with dressing. But *they* have savings accounts. You could start one."

"What do you mean 'save'? I don't have any . . . just my penny box. Grandad gives them to me."

My father seemed very calm, his eyes steadily observing me, apparently considering what I'd said. Ernie was hunched forward, looking into his coffee cup, bouncing his cigar gently into the ashtray.

"Saving is when you *get* money, but you don't *spend* it. You save it until you have a lot of it, and then you buy something . . . er, more expensive. You've saved for something . . .dear."

"Oh!" I immediately knew what was dear. "My house on Armitage Road. Okay, I'll save it and buy my house. It's the best house in the whole world. It's next door to Mam and Grandad, and it has a big tree, and it's beautiful. I want to move there so Linda and Bud and I can have our own house and be right next door to Mam and Granddad. You'd think it was perfect."

"I'm . . . sure it's lovely. But a house costs a lot of money, Annie. Why do you need a house? Don't you have one?"

"You know I live with Mam? Do you know Mam?"

"Jessie. . . Yessss . . ."

"So, will you send it to me from now on? Will you?"

The door opened and Beatrice entered followed by my mother, her nose held high, sniffing the air to pick up on our conversation.

I looked at my father and shook my head, hoping he'd get it. It would be bad if he answered in front of Linda. He leaned closer.

"Let me . . . ahh, think over what you've said."

"What's she up to now?" Linda asked, sliding into her seat, looking from me to my father, then to Ernie.

"We were discussing savings accounts," my father said, looking at Linda, his round face rather straight and not smiling. Linda's ears pricked up like a hound on scent, her forehead knitting into a maze of concern.

Linda wanted to share my chocolate cake with cherry sauce, but I wanted my own, so she drank more coffee and swiped the maraschino cherry on top. My other grandmother ate ice cream. My father and Ernie smoked and drank more coffee. Quiet now, the small room was blurred with smoke. My father looked at his watch and said how nice it was to meet me, but that he had to get back to his office.

"Will you write me a letter? I'll write you back."

"I will write you a letter, Annie. I will certainly write you.

And you tell me how your studies are progressing, will you?" I nodded. "School must be of uppermost importance to you, I should think. One has to be educated to take care of oneself."

He reached out and patted me on the shoulder, then stretched down for my hand and shook it again. He stood and moved to my mother, and they talked quietly for a moment, but only saying, "Yes, yes, nice to see you again too" (him). "She's a fine-looking girl" (him). "Yes, yes, she is quite a corker, all right" (her). During all this head shaking and chattering Ernie was helping Beatrice into her coat but he glanced over at me and motioned. I moved toward him while Beatrice said good-bye to her son, who I noticed did not smile at her or anything, only nodded after carefully positioning his black hat on his head. When she hugged my mother, Ernie reached down, placed a piece of folded paper in my hand, and closed my fingers over it. When I looked up, he winked, raising a finger to his lips.

"You have a good time in New York, Annie. If you see Vic Parelli, you tell him Ernie McCully is a big fan. He's got a lot of guys in Philly think he makes that team." Then patting my back, "We'll give a call to see how you're doin'."

I stuck the money in my pocket, but not quick enough because Linda was up on her toes, watching. Beatrice bustled around the table and gave me a big, hard hug. She held me away—then hugged me to her again, the smell of warm soap coming off her like steam from a hot bubble bath. "Oh, I wish you weren't so far away from us, dear. We'd like to see more of you, wouldn't we, Ernie?"

I had to wiggle away from her big coat button digging into my forehead. She kissed me on both cheeks, then we all crowded out the door. In the lobby they were saying good-bye, and we'll call, and let's write more, and I invited them all to the rodeo. They couldn't come because they had to go back to Westchester, so they walked down the loud, busy sidewalk,

Ernie and Beatrice together, my father dashing ahead. My mother rushed to the curb to find a taxi.

Inside the taxi, Linda took off her big blue hat, sat back, and sighed hugely. "Well, what did you think?"

"He's okay. He talks like . . . I don't know. All stiff and boring. Kind of snooty."

"Why, Annie Butler! He was wonderful. That's just the way they are in the East. It's called formal. *They* have manners. Real, honest to God, good manners." She paused, sniffed. "They don't tell secrets in public or disobey their parents. What do you have in your pocket?"

"What do you mean?" I turned to look out the window, trying to think of a way to turn her attention. Maybe throw up?

"What's in your pocket, over there?" She looked pointedly at me, and then at my hand in my jacket pocket. "I know you have something. Did they give you something?" She reached toward me. I scooted away but she came after me. "Let me see, Annie."

"I don't have anything," I yelled at the window. "Okay?"

"You're lying," she hissed, "and you had better stop right now, and think about what you're saying to me, miss. I mean right this minute! . . . Or else . . ."

She didn't wait a beat. She launched herself at me, squashed me against the seat, anchored her knee on my legs and dove her hand into my pocket. I hardly had time to do more damage than scream and take a nip of her arm. Her suede jacket protected her, but I did leave a pretty complete set of teeth marks. Entirely outraged by this pathetic counter move, she grabbed my hair and held me off, clutching the money in her other hand. As she reared back triumphantly, bills aloft, I kicked the money from her hand.

"Shit!" she bellowed.

As I scrambled for my money, I saw the taxi driver peering

back at us. "Leave me alone. It's mine. Ernie said it's *mine*." I was scarlet, blistering, inflamed at her pummeling invasion.

"You . . . asked for money?! I should have known you'd pull something like this. How could you do this to me?" She was puffed up like Mam, her voice shaking, threatening severe emotional weather. "Did you ask for money? Did you ask? Oh no! Yeew begged like one of those damned carnival gypsies..."

By now I was on the floor clenching the money behind my back. "Okay!" I exploded. "I asked him to send it to me, but that's not why he gave it to me. *He* likes me. He wanted me to have a good time."

My mother's expression turned from animated wrath—reddening, fuming, screeching—to petrified shock—color draining, tearing up, whining—in the time it took the cabbie to pull over and kick us out of the cab.

She growled that she wasn't made of money and forced me, grabbed my hand and made me pay the disgusted cab driver with my arduously recovered bill. Then, standing there on the street in her blue suede, foot long fringes ashiver, she commenced to sob, great tearing, hiccoughing slurbs of motherly music and liquid cascading over her contorted, disintegrating mask, menacing the expensive suede.

*

On my last night in New York, my mother left me at the entry gate with tear-threatening instructions not to move until her performance was over.

"Not even to go to the bathroom?"

She turned and walked off without a word or glance. As soon as she was out of sight, I ran down the alley to the rodeo office, asked JoAnne for paper and pencil, and sprinted to the basement.

In front of Toot's stall, madly hoping to see Bud, but not

really expecting he'd come during the show, I paused to catch my breath then sat on a grain sack and wrote this note:

Dear Bud, All-Around Champ of the World, and the best cowboy ever. When you come back to Oregon and aren't so busy I will have a house for us. It has a tree, and it's big, and it has pastures for Toots.

Please come soon. I love you, and want you to please marry us.

Annie—your friend and I wish daughter.

After reading it carefully and deciding it was right, I folded it, stuck it into the stall latch, and wrapped the chain around it. When Bud put Toots in the stall, he'd have to see it.

When Monte and Linda came flying out of the arena at the end of her performance, I was perched on top of the gate watching for them.

At the hotel the next morning, packing my bag, I begged her to call Bud. "Just let me say good-bye. Are you mad at him? Aren't you friends? What's happened?"

"I told you we're too busy. That's all! I don't want to hear another word out of you."

Shoving her face before mine, she ground out each syllable, "Not. Another. Word." She turned back to the suitcase, stuffed the top down and snapped the latches shut.

Not another word about my father, about Bud, about what's happening? My plans to impress the kids at school, for Linda to marry Bud, for my father to be my savior, all failed, and I couldn't talk to her about any of it. What was wrong with her? Mam might be a dictator, possibly a criminal. And I didn't have any say over anything.

Chapter 13

HOW ANNIE LEARNS THERE IS NO PLACE LIKE HOME

ARMITAGE ROAD, EMERALD CITY, OREGON, 1953

At Emerald Valley Airport, I stuck my head from the plane as soon as the cabin door opened and scanned the small crowd on the airstrip, noticing how good the Oregon air smelled. Mam, her new diamond-studded glasses glinting in the weak sun, was waving her hand back and forth. Granddad stood beside her, hat in hand, watching for me. My exact state of mind on my return from New York is difficult to describe—like trying to define the wind, or water. What defines it is change. While earlier scenes are quite clear, this part of the story is out of focus, shadowed with dark thoughts about my father, even darker judgments about Roy and Dale, and morbid suspicions of Linda and her part in driving Bud from my life.

But one thing had not changed. I was most anxious to get back to the ranch, to see Lady, Margie, and the house on Armitage Road. A small but marked fear was that Mam would miss the special shoes she'd spent the fortune on, and this would start an immediate row. Looking back, I think I was very angry. Yet, I wasn't sure exactly who or what should be on the receiving end of my passions. They ran within like wild ponies herded towards a despised corral.

Travelling over the bridge on the way home, Mam pumped me for information about New York. Sitting in the back, arms propped on the top of Mam's seat, a position she normally discouraged, I gave detailed descriptions of Tony and Leo, the gun on Leo's leg, my mother falling off the racehorse (the ice and the wine), my day at the Statue of Liberty with Margo and Mr. Melnyk, and how Linda called the cops. I left out the part about Mam being a criminal, although I briefly weighed the merits of mentioning it. By the time we pulled into the ranch driveway, Mam was in a state of shivering excitement, which I hoped would drive her to the phone with orders that Linda get home, and right now!

Later that night, Mam and I sat in the bright kitchen after dinner. She had finished the dishes and settled at the kitchen table, which was unusual. She usually snapped off the lights and headed to the living room where she'd kick off her high heels and sit reading magazines, tiny feet propped on a fat stool. That night, she had invited me to tell her more about my trip, saying that Granddad was watching a special program, and wouldn't it be good of us to stay in the kitchen and not disturb him?

"Mam, I want to go to Margie's . . . before they eat."

She levered herself from the table and lifted the cookie jar from the high cupboard where it was hidden.

"Not tonight. You can go in the morning," she said, handing me a cookie and laying two more on a plate. "Well, what did you think of him?"

She was leaning toward me, bright hazel eyes squinted as though she could see right into my head if she looked hard enough.

"I liked my other grandmother. She was nice." This was obviously not what Mam wanted to discuss.

"Bea is a fine lady. Very nice." She didn't shift her eyes

from mine. "What about him?"

"Ohhh, . . . He was pretty nice. . . Snooty—kind of. Different . . ."

"Un-hunhh! See? I could have told you that! Oh, he's different all right . . ."

She jerked around when Granddad walked into the kitchen. He took a glass from the cupboard, turned on the faucet and looking over at us, let the water run.

"Now, Mother . . . we said . . ."

"She said it! I didn't." She glared at me, her busy mouth tightening to a defiant pink line.

He filled his glass. "Arthur Godfrey's on. C'mon, Buddy." Buddy, who had been sniffing around the floor, looked up as if caught in a crime, and long ears sagging, wiggled out the door Granddad held open for us.

The next morning, I was up before the sun. It was too early to go Margie's, but I scrounged clothes from the bottom of the closet and jammed my tender feet into dirty sneakers. Yanking my slicker from the hallway hook, I hurried outside. It had rained during the night but on this late November morning the air was cold and clear with strands of mist wreathing the river. A weak pink sun was rising, promising some warmth and lending an ethereal beauty to the ranch. To the east, hills covered with deep green firs poked through the haze floating over the river, leaving the fields veiled in transparent white. Closer to the ranch on our side of the river, the orchard trees were bright yellow and red, their leaves masking the ground in muted heaps of copper, gold, and scarlet. After the putrid smell of New York, the air was pure and cold as high-mountain creek water.

In the shadowy barn, I hurried to Lady's stall. She was lying in the straw, legs curled beneath her, blue blanket snug to her belly. She surged to her feet when she saw me and as I yanked the stall latch, she was already pushing it with her nose. Even though I hadn't thought to bring her a treat, her warm breath filled the air as she curled her head to mine while I told her how happy I was to see her and how I'd missed her. This was my real welcome home.

We walked from the whickering barn into the white morning, down the rain-soaked verge to the drive and so quietly to the road, her in blue, me in yellow. Gaining the lane, I looked back to more fog rolling off the river, enveloping the barn. We stood hushed and clear-eyed before the cornfield, the road blanketed in white to our knees, stark thistles piercing the haze. Nosing the road, Lady leaned to the ditch where clover blossoms were turning gray.

The hedgerow was a weft of blue-green branches woven with bright maple starts, browning wild roses, ochre hips gleaming through the maze, Queen Anne's lace floating gray skeletons over it. Water dripping slowly within the hedge, Lady's rhythmic grazing, all consoling as a heartbeat.

Tugging the mare, her iron feet sounding on the high centered lane, we neared the black walnut. As the sun touched its tips, nuts cascaded from high branches, bouncing and cracking the hush to land spent at our feet. As Lady moved to sniff the thick hulls, a squirrel burst from the ditch then sat still, black eyes intent.

We stopped under the maples and peered across the damp lawn. The Armitage house was dark. No lights, no smoke from the chimneys; nothing gave permission to venture into the early morning yard. I stood beneath the trees, chilled by water dripping on my head from copper-colored leaves the size of paper plates, thinking if we waited, they would surely wake and come for the newspaper under the mailbox. Lady and I gazed at the house as though it might open up, wish us good morning, offer breakfast.

Leaning against Lady's side, admiring the white body and green painted porches, the white climbers draping the chimneys, blue spruce and lilacs over ten feet tall straining at the horse fence—the image took on a new and marvelous layer of reality. I sensed every sound and smell of the river and fields, and the life of the trees creaking in the wind. If I walked closer to the house, I would smell a hint of mock orange that in summer set white blossoms on the rippling window glass. And towering beside us, the ancient black walnut, home to so much life, supported the same white climbers as the chimneys.

The house, framed by maples, the long yard gently sloping toward us, surrounded by miles of wide fields, was wholly right in all aspects, in summer and winter and forever. Looking up at it, I was aware of a new sense of hope. Standing there in the damp grass, I felt connected to the earth like my tree, a part of everything. It was home. It was perfect, and I never again wanted to leave it.

Bud would come. How could he not want to be with us? And when he does, we'll live here together and then everything will be all right. I knew it.

"Let's hope they move soon, Lady."

"Soon."

Chapter 14

IN 1999, JIM HAS A DRAMA IN TEXAS, WHILE IN 1954, ANNIE HAS A CHANCE

ARMITAGE HOUSE, EMERALD CITY, OREGON, MAY 10, 1999

It had rained two nights before, had been sprinkling since, and felt warmer than usual for that time of year. When I'd gone for the mail earlier that morning, the air had smelled so clean and lovely but oh boy, would the grass ever start growing fast. I'd made a note to ask the new fellow who had been mowing the neighbor's hay to come. Still, despite worlds of grass and hours of pruning, the Oregon spring on Armitage Road might be my favorite place and time: yellow daffodils and forsythia dazzling against the blue sky, lilac blooms trailing in the grass, and further east more daffodils formed a yellow sea running to fill the ditch. I had been taking walks through the countryside and not packing, trying to take a break from the drama.

Seems Jim had been having his own drama in Texas. Also seems there was a woman involved. I had guessed his call that night was to tell me before I heard rumors. Apparently, the woman who ran the apartment in Texas where Jim was staying had set her sights on him and gone to the construction site looking for him. That suggested an intimacy that had immediately put me on alert. Why would she go to the jobsite if he lived in the apartment she managed? Since the job was a government contract, she was escorted from the site, but they'd called him out of a meeting to talk to her.

I had breathed into the phone and tried to let the news settle.

"Did you encourage her somehow?" I asked. "What did she want? Why would she just come there if she didn't have some reason to believe she was welcome?"

"No! I didn't encourage her about anything. I only see her when I pay my rent, for god sakes."

"Jim . . ."

"I knew I shouldn't tell you about it." Silence. "Well, I'm tired and have to get something to eat."

"You're just going to get off the phone?"

"How are you doing on the packing?"

"Wish I was there to have dinner with you. I didn't pack much today. I'm taking a break."

"The longer you wait, the harder you're going to make it."

"Okay. I hear you. Tonight's not the night to talk. Right?"

"I've got to eat and get to bed. Unlike you, I have to be up at four."

"Nice. Thanks for the reassurance."

"Night, Annie."

Crying again, I hung up. When he was tired there was no talking, no nothing. After twenty years, I knew. And he was probably disgusted with me for even considering that he might have encouraged her. In all our time together he'd never given me a reason to worry about other women. After Ted (#1), Jess (#2), and Rafe (# 3, #4 & #5), Jim knew how I took any hint of such behavior.

I moved to the window and stood looking at the dark

square shape of the monstrous newspaper complex that had risen in the old cornfield across the road. In fact, I knew Jim prided himself on being a man who was in control of himself, and who lived up to his ideals. In the bathroom I blew my nose and washed my face. I thought he was probably furious with me, but of course would never say so. It would just come out, a barbed comment, when I'd completely quit thinking about it.

In my bedroom, I picked up a sketch pad. Propped against my pillows, and casting within for some reflection that wouldn't produce more tears, the ranch house lights blazing across the little field were unavoidable. I put the pad and pencil down. I had nothing to place on paper anyway, not images or words. I rose from the bed to draw the curtain. The cedar box, container of so much emotion, sat quietly on the dresser. I turned out the lamp and lay down thinking of Jim, probably already asleep in his bed.

*

ARMITAGE ROAD, EMERALD CITY, OREGON, 1954

Looking back on my time in New York I see a small, disheveled girl, feet hot and hurting, emotions just as sore. She is floating against gray sky and water, suspended in space, feet not touching ground. There is no city, nothing tangible, only an after-image of the Statue of Liberty suspended there with her.

My heroes Dale and Roy had spurned me. I'd given up the idea of my father as any kind of hero, but even worse, my mother had let Bud escape. If he didn't come to Oregon that winter, I'd have to wait until summer and hope that I could find him at one of the rodeos.

But then what?

And while I had been so sure my New York City trip would

change everything for me, by my accounting I had received only one gift from my travels. I had the vision of Mr. Melnyk and Katya picnicking by the river under the warm sun of a Russian summer before I was born. Now, that memory was mine, and somehow Katya still lives with me as she did with the old man I met on the ferry. An old man, once a young husband, a man who had remembered one girl, one afternoon, his whole life.

As the weeks passed and deepened into Oregon winter, meadows and mountains drifted with fine threads of feelings, whispered voices, and memories of New York. Often shrouded in a fog thick as the one that had overtaken Lady and me on the road the morning after my return, these feelings seemed to move me, but I couldn't make sense of them. Part of me floated high and away, yet my spirits drifted ever lower. This divided state was becoming normal for me when Mam suddenly struck and hauled me back to earth.

One chilly evening after the New Year, I'd come in from the barn, to find Mam and Granddad sitting in the front room watching the news. The announcer said, "And recapping news this evening, the Senate has voted to condemn Senator Joseph McCarthy for conduct contrary to senatorial traditions. And that's the story, folks. Glad we could get together. This is John Cameron Swayze saying goodnight."

Granddad dropped a section of the paper to the floor by his chair. "About time," he said. Both he and Mam had been unusually upset by pictures on the new television of a bunch of men in a big room asking people questions. It seemed to be a very big deal.

"They're supposed to be looking for traitors," Grandad added.

"What's that?"

"Democrats," Mam said, then as if resuming a previous conversation, "Daddy, it's still expensive to show. Weren't we over that with Linda?"

When he looked up, she shot him her 'don't talk' look, or maybe it was the 'don't talk in front of her' look.

"We might as well, Jessie," Granddad said. "She's a good hand. She's got the makings just like her mom."

Mam was in her comfy upholstered rocking chair, knitting argyle socks. Her specialty. Watching her hook green yarn around the needle, I heard Mr. Donny calling them nasty knitted golf club covers. She looked up at Granddad, then at me. "Well . . . I suppose. It will keep us busy," she said. "And besides, Annie needs her chance. Here's what we'll do . . ."

I learned later that like most good ideas, it had been Granddad's first. He was the one who suggested they find me a show horse to ride in the Five Gaited competition at the Emerald Empire horse show that spring. Shocking me to uncharacteristic silence, Mam had taken up his idea like one of her causes. A cause once adopted had always been her own. Shoes and dresses were too expensive and now I was to have my own show horse? I didn't ask the question, but boy, did I all of a sudden become Miss Charming. They had finally recognized that I was ready to make my mark. *Finally! Now, they would all take notice. When Bud heard I was showing, he would come.* I knew it. *Then he'd see what I could do. We would be the best friends in the world.*

Hauling more yarn from the bag at her side, Mam re-crossed her legs, lifting a small foot and thrusting it forward as if stepping out on a quest. As she outlined her plan, she discussed those with whom I would be competing. "Now Jennifer Caswell-Hooper and Marcia Huntley's horses will be in your class." These were timber-rich high school girls, registered owners of fancy, high-stepping American Saddlebreds who kept their horses in the barn next to us at the fairgrounds. Teenage girls with perfect hair and matching riding outfits whom I admired from afar. Paid trainers rode

Jennifer and Marcia's horses in the shows and when their horses won the high stakes competitions, the girls also won—achievement points at their special clubs, and money. Not one of these older girls ever rode their own horse, much less showed them, so I was pretty sure that this circumstance made my impending adventure even more noteworthy. *The only owner/rider, the only girl, and the only child. I would be the only one!*

Leaning back in her chair, rocking slowly, Mam turned to the difficulties of finding a suit to fit me. Shaking her head so that her crown of braids shifted, she ended any idea on Granddad's part that Linda's old suits would ever do for me. "You'll be competing against highly experienced, bankrolled professionals. The Caswell-Hooper's trainer is from a hot shot show barn in Seattle and Marcia's folks just got a big name out of Chicago to show her stud. They're sharp lookers. They wear beautifully tailored wool suits." She motioned for me to give her my foot then pulled on the bottom of my jeans.

"The pants fit tight to the knee then flare over the boot. We'll have to measure you," she said. Turning me in a circle, she described long fitted coats that floated gracefully from the rider's waist, draping their bottoms and soaring over the animal's backs as the riders drove their horses around the ring. She peered at me over the top of her glasses. "In big shows like Seattle and San Francisco, they wear tuxedos with black high hats and spit-polished English boots." Evaluating me further, Mam flipped the conversation into overdrive by insisting they find me a trainer. At this Granddad dropped his head, and motioned Buddy to come. The newspaper rustled as he rolled it into a long baton and bounced it lightly on Buddy's head.

I knew that the show crowd besides having bossy live-in trainers prized for the dazzling figures they cut and for their signature eccentricities also had beautifully manicured purebred dogs to go with their fancy horses. I had also learned that when Linda was my age, she kept her show horse there with the other expensive horses in the spotless show barns displaying huge potted trees and masses of flowers out front. Inside, colored bunting draped immaculately swept aisles and beside each stall door, rows of satin ribbons hung in glass cases. Buddy was gazing up at Granddad, wiggling his tail, ready to go out. I knew exactly how much rambunctious, rat-chasing Buddy would like getting all brushed and done up for the show set. And, Spike was like me, he couldn't stay clean for a minute. But unlike me, the first thing he'd do after a bath was go roll in the manure. Mam concluded the conversation by gathering her knitting and rising from her chair. She informed me that the show world was full of money . . . not like the rodeo world, which was also full of money, but not, according to her, the best kind of money.

"Gaited people spend outrageous sums to win," Mam said, standing in the doorway, eyes narrowed appraisingly on me. "You're good enough. You might even win with the right horse."

I had often won first place in the western events on Lady, but also according to Mam, those events were not as important as the gaited English classes. If I were ever to show myself as a proper horsewoman and make a name for myself in that world as my mother had when she was my age, I must have a proper horse.

The following Saturday was cold and sunny when right after breakfast Mam shooed Granddad and me out the door. We were to look at three show possibilities she had rounded up, and I was sitting on the edge of the truck's bouncy seat as we headed down the ranch driveway. I imagined hauling a new horse home that afternoon, my mind filled with scenes of show ring success and adulation, and the beautiful dresses I would buy with the prize money. Yet, after a long day of driving to stables tucked far back from main roads, we hadn't discovered one good possibility.

"Ya know," Granddad said as were leaving the last barn on the list, "a good Saddlebred should be shaped like that silver canoe of mine. Bottom line round and full, top line short and straight. We haven't seen that conformation. Let's think about that."

On the drive back to the ranch, I looked out on the brown fields and pastures, reliving my New York defeats, and gloomily reflecting that if we didn't find a new horse, I had nothing to look forward to. Nothing but school and horrible dresses. I'd never have a home and a father. After lighting his cigarette, Granddad glanced my way but said nothing. Finally, at home he turned off the pickup, reached over and patted me on the knee. "We'll find something yet," he said. "Bound to be a horse out there with your name on it."

I hurried to the small pasture, sat in the damp grass with my arm propped on the watering trough and told Lady my troubles. She dropped her head and seemed to be listening intently. Then, I felt like a traitor for wanting another horse because Lady was the best.

On a chilly Saturday morning shortly after my ninth birthday Mam rousted me from my warm bed and stood in the middle of the room picking clothes from the floor and throwing them on the bed.

"Get up now. I have an errand at the fairgrounds. I might need you to deliver some messages."

That would mean I'd get to ride bareback around the fairgrounds delivering messages to horse owners. A chore I liked. "C'mon, get with the program, I'm leaving as soon as I get my coat. There's some toast in my purse. We don't have time to eat." Looking back over her shoulder, "Get your coat."

As we drove to the fairgrounds, I was hardly awake and had no thought of the day holding anything special. When we arrived at the barn, I walked with Mam down the long aisle to a stall door. I expected to see some problem with a horse or a guy asleep in a stall like the last times Mam had to go to the barns on a Saturday and rose on my toes to peer inside. A tall, slim mare with huge brown eyes stood in the stall. She had a beautiful chestnut body with silver mane and tail, and four tall white stockings running up long finely-proportioned legs. Her hooves were those of a show horse, long, black-painted, perfectly shaped and wearing the big, cleated-iron shoes that marked the gaited horses. She stood quietly, maybe snoozing, in the corner of her clean stall. "Oh, she's a wonder, Mam," I said, understanding instantly. "She's just beautiful and I love her."

"Well," Mam said, "she's fully gaited, professionally trained, and already a champ. This is your chance. She's yours. You give her a stable name. Her registered name is LuGeena Dare's Major Sensation."

"Genie," I said unbolting the stall door.

She was tall, about sixteen hands, with a small, neat head and prominent nostrils that were soft as moss. Her pointed ears were slender, expressive, and swiveled toward me as I moved around her. Smoothing my hand along her neck, I followed the graceful arch where head and neck met. Her dark eyes were long lashed, intelligent, and seemed kind as she patiently watched me. I reached into my pocket where I kept Lady's treats and fed her the pellets. She chewed slowly and nosed me for more. *Good natured, and very, very pretty. And she's mine. Not Linda's. Not anyone's hand-me-down. Mine!* I was transported. Not only was she a living, breathing, beautiful friend, she was a sign. With a horse like this, everything was bound to improve. I knew it. My world, which had been very murky, came into sharp focus, and I felt the gloom lift to reveal a thin sliver of light. Here was something I could do. The next moment, I felt a stabbing pang of disloyalty wondering how Lady might feel.

"Now you're not used to a horse like this," Mam said, breaking in on my guilty reflection. "Burt Showalter, the Landinghams' trainer, will give you lessons, and you had better toe his line," she said, stepping forward and rubbing Genie's chin. "You do exactly what he tells you." She paused. "Because this is costing a fortune." She pushed Genie's lips back to reveal strong-looking teeth. "We have a deal with him to get you ready for the spring shows, and it's going take some doin' to bring you up to the mark." She patted Genie on the nose, then walked off through the barn, hiking it in her little spiked heels. "I'm going to check in at the office," she called, the sound brittle in the chill air.

I stood in the stall, going over every inch of Genie's perfect body, becoming familiar with her and allowing her to accept me. According to those who should know, five-gaited horses are the top of the heap in the horseshow world, even higher than jumpers. "No other kids my age ride in the five-gaited stakes classes, Genie, not one. Mam says the prizes aren't just big trophies but money. Lots of money."

I slid to the floor of the stall and, resting against her leg, told Genie what our big win would mean. Not only would we be rich and famous among the barns, I would be as famous as my mother. Bud would be proud of me. I would even win approval from Mam. The kids at school would finally understand that I was somebody and make friends. I would have money to buy my own stuff. I could buy dresses; with dresses I could look nice for Bud. When Bud saw me again, he'd want to marry us. I knew it. I rose and stood beside her, the sweet hay smell enclosing me. Given this chance, I could do it all.

*

The next Monday, and every day after school, Mam, Granddad or whoever they could nab to do it gave me a ride to the fairgrounds. In the corner of Genie's freezing stall, I skinnied into my riding clothes and used the practice arena from four to five-thirty. So, there I was in heaven, but then, there was Burt! It was cold in the arena that winter, and when I think of Burt, I see a steam-breathing dragon stomping around the center of the ring brandishing a long whip, releasing breath in plumes that fogged the air with each exhalation. Also fogging the air was a steady stream of intricate curses that became more creative and mysterious the more furious he became.

How they chose Burt to be my teacher, to be the engine, the crank and soul, of my revision, I never learned. Passionate, filthy-mouthed Burt, oily and slurred, guzzling from the metal flask he kept in his back pocket. Tallish and wire thin, usually whiskered, wands of iron gray hair poking out from his low riding fedora, he seemed always to be holding himself back from committing some type of fruity, explosive violence. A professional. Mam said he also had "a professional woman" to support: Margaret. Mam figured she was so available she should wear a sign. On the subject of Burt, Grandma Thompson, owner of the champion jumpers in Genie's barn, said that professional horse-trainers, especially trainers without their own stables were like gypsies. Exotic, and dangerous to know.

Our everyday practice routine was to move non-stop through the hour and a half training session, then after reviewing the list of the day's faults with Burt, I would groom Genie and catch a ride back to the ranch with Mam. By then, I was spending every Saturday and some Sundays at the fairgrounds too. I was busy from the time I rose in the morning until I crawled into bed in the red-carpeted room each night. Sometimes I had enough energy left to dream of our big win.

It was the last week of February, four in the afternoon and almost dark. Inside the main arena draped with red, white and blue buntings, big lights blazed from high rafters, illuminating the three of us alone in the huge ring. Genie, saddled, breathing columns of steam, was trotting, and I was receiving instruction on proper posting form from Burt.

"Fer Chrissakes! Holy Mother of Gawd . . . collect that horse." Burt paced the center of the arena, fedora jammed on his head, slapping the whip against his tall boot, his words ringing in the high space. He prowled a tight circle, eyes canny slits, stubbly jowls trembling with emotion. "Heels down, damnit. Cain't ya hear? Yer ain't ridin' a camel there, are ya? Keep your damned heels down!!"

A slow trot, weight balanced, heels down, hands down, back straight, elbows tucked to my sides. My form was correct. Genie was going along almost perfectly, legs snapping high, head held straight on her neck, nose tucked at the correct angle. When we did it right it would look to the audience as if we were floating.

"Now, pull her up and give 'er 'er cue. Holy Mother!! Lift up the damned rein." He screamed louder. "Lift 'er! You's deaf as the damned wall." He slammed the whip against his leg, the sound spiraling upward, and came striding toward us—something to avoid. I pressed my legs to Genie's sides. If we kept moving, we were okay. If we let Burt stop us, he could carry the harangue into a medley of fault finding that might last until we froze solid right in front of him. Burt's whip rose, hovered, and when we stopped, forced my hands down two inches. Crop at the ready, he stalked around her and poked at my heel from behind. Genie stood still, not a quiver.

"Fer Crissakes, this is no damned pleasure ride yer going ta. This is ther big time, kid. They's announcin' me as yer trainer. You gotta give the sign. She ain't a mind reader. And keep ther damned rein up!" He reached back into his pocket, brought out the flask, took a gulp, replaced the cap and jammed it in his back pocket. I knew he only wanted us to get it right, but Genie knew her business and after correctly asking for what I wanted, I could trust her to perform faultlessly.

Genie moved off the line and proceeded to slow gait around the ring, rear tucked slightly, neck arched, front feet lifting high in a slow syncopated gait unique in the horse world and designed for the comfort of the rider. Mam said a good five-gaited horse like Genie was the peacock of the show world. I sensed Burt winding up again and tensed.

". . . and rack on!" he screamed, holding up the battered stopwatch. Four distinct beats in syncopated motion, front end in climbing action, back end almost squatting, showing little movement to her topline, we shot around the ring at tremendous speed. Genie snorting, stepping high and fast, me mindful of my conformation, taking care to remember each position so as not to give Burt more ammunition.

". . . and line up, please!" Burt howled mimicking the announcer to make sure Genie's ring manners were perfect. At his shout, I lowered my hands slightly and relaxed the hold of my legs on her sides.

According to Mam, a fast rack and perfect form were the major elements judges considered and whether Burt admitted it or not, I knew Genie performed well. We met Burt in the center of the ring and practiced lining up, Genie's front and back legs stretched out full, head up, ears forward, nose tucked to display her perfect conformation.

"It's about your form. It's all about yer goddammed FORM," Burt bellowed, prowling around us. Then dismissing us with a wave of his whip, he yanked the flask from his back pocket, drank, and drank again while I unsaddled her and walked her to the stall. She gleamed like the bottom of Mam's copper pots, not only owing to her vigorous workout, but to the many hours we spent grooming her.

In the stall, I brushed her and washed her face with a towel, which I noted was also in need of a wash.

"Annie," Mam hollered from the alley, "get on the scoot!" I gave Genie one more swipe, a carrot from my crumpled lunch sack, grabbed my school clothes from the straw, and ran to catch Mam.

This routine continued through February and into March when word of the screaming performances began to draw a crowd of show people and horse owners. Mam said they came as much to watch Burt make an ass of himself as to watch me and Genie. "But ass or not," she said, "he's getting the job done. You'll be ready!"

One afternoon during practice I had noticed a bunch of spectators standing at the rail watching as Burt screamed, "Rack on." Walking Genie past the audience and out of the arena afterwards, I heard Dennis and Grandma Thompson discussing our progress.

"Oh, yeah," Dennis said, leaning on the top rail. "Look at that front action. By the May shows, she'll make it. Big horse, little girl, sure fire with the judges."

Even though our barn neighbors, Grandma Thompson and her son Dennis, were jumping, Thoroughbred people, not gaited, Saddlebred people, they owned prize-winning gray jumpers and knew well the ins and outs of the show world. Dennis and Grandma's stamp of approval was big. I grinned and patted Genie on the neck. I felt that Mam and Granddad's gamble on me was paying off, and I was happy. We passed Marcia Huntley and another of the older girls who had horses in the show barn, and I could tell by their looks that they knew what people were saying and were envious as anything.

Around that time, in my travels about the fairgrounds, when I chanced to meet the other five-gaited competitors from our local Hunt Club, all men, they glanced at me from the corners of their eyes, but soon (a little late, Mam said) they began joining us in the practice ring most afternoons.

*

Then it was the end of April, and we were standing in the alley at the Multnomah Hunt Club show barn in Portland, and Mam was pinning number 121 on my back. Burt was holding Genie and slicking Vaseline around her mouth and Granddad was checking to make sure the tack was perfect and that her fake tailpiece was securely attached. I kept my back turned because I knew if I went near Burt, he would start in on me again not only about my form, but the nasty habits of the professional riders that I had to watch out for. As for my form, I had thoroughly memorized all the positions and most of the time my body did what I told it—my biggest problem was letting my hands creep up, but I almost had that cured. On the drive to the fairgrounds that morning, I had decided that if my form wasn't correct by then it never would be, and that the other riders could hardly be as mean and low-down as Burt painted them. I was ready.

Still, as I reached to settle my new top hat, my stomach was full of darts and flashes because according to Mam my first big show, the Multnomah County Junior League Show, was real quality, where all the horses were more expensive and the riders classier than in Emerald City.

In the tack room earlier, after reading the list of entrants she had dropped the program in the show trunk and gestured to it. "With that crowd, if you could even place in the top six, you'd be doing something."

Humph! Place? Why show unless you rode to win?

Grandad turned me around and looked me over too. "They're lining up," he said, adjusting the pink rose in my buttonhole. "Just do your best, punk."

My eyes cast down, thoughts turning inward trying to remember what Burt had said about how to enter the ring, I did not look up as Granddad helped me mount. Then we were rushing into place as the announcer called our class, horses every which way in the alley, two horses snorting and jigging and everyone jumping out of the way.

A man in a powder blue suit, with tan hat and boots, riding a tall dappled gray stallion gestured to me as he maneuvered into line, "Dropped your crop," he said.

When I looked down to see the crop securely attached to my wrist, the gray stallion swept past us and took our place in line. Burt touched my boot, I saw Mam wave, and then through a pair of erect, tight-clipped ears the long arena full of bright lights, pink and green bunting, and mellow organ music opened before us. It might have been the second-best show in the state but after Madison Square Garden, I didn't think it amounted to all that much.

Out in the arena, Genie behaved perfectly. My form was correct. Genie negotiated the big ring and the other horses like the professional Mam had said she was. Her manners were those of a seasoned matron. She knew the precise right thing to do in any eventuality, even knew to slow gait before I signaled her. She also knew how to keep off the rail and away from the pushy gray stallion—only once displaying bad manners by laying her ears back when the man on the gray tried to crowd us off our position and box us against the rail so the judge couldn't see us. But moments before that, as the gray stallion had come up behind us, I had glanced back, and the judge had been watching. In this case the man's strategy had worked to our advantage and made him look bad. At first, I thought Burt was mean when he'd warned me that the other rider-trainers were, in his words, "right scunners," but now I guessed Burt knew what he was talking about. I managed to keep a distance from the gray, and soon we lined up in the center of the ring. There, I dismounted while Burt and Granddad removed Genie's saddle and wiped her down to show off her conformation. She stood like a beautifully carved rock while the judges walked past smiling.

The announcer's voice soon boomed over the crowd, "Numbers 137, 101, 162, 121 . . ."

One twenty-one was us!

"119, and number 117 please remain in the ring. All others excused for the judging of the Multnomah County Junior League Horse Show Five-Gaited Madeleine Murphy $1,500 stakes class."

During what seemed an enormous music-filled pause while the other riders left the ring and the judges registered their votes, I looked down the row at the other competitors, some sitting quietly, some fidgeting, a horse dance stepping here and there, the man on the gray shooting dark looks our way. Burt stood at the ring entrance twiddling with his hat, stabbing his fingers into his wrecked hair. We waited while the judges bent over their papers, and the longer I sat there the more excited I became. As they announced Sixth or Special Mention Ribbon, I closed my eyes. *This was it! I was going to be a star now, and everyone would know I was somebody!*

But it was not my name they announced. Mam said if I even made it this far, I was really doing something! Really doing something for once. The announcer called out fifth place, fourth and third. *Not me. I guess I showed you, Mr. Burt Showalter! And even better, Uncle Jack can't call me a screwball disaster anymore.* "Second place to Oak Hill's Chief, Angus McNeil of Seattle Pacific Stables, rider and trainer."

I reached down and smoothed my hand along Genie's neck. "You are a good, good, sweet, smart girl and I love you," I said. And then the announcer came back, and the organ stopped playing again.

"The winner of the 1954 Multnomah County Junior League

Spring Show, the Madeleine Murphy Five-Gaited $1,500 stakes class is . . .

"Number 121, Miss Antonia Butler from Emerald City Hunt Club riding her horse, LuGenna Dare's Major Sensation. Trainer, Burt Showalter. Congratulations, young lady," and the crowd started clapping and hollering, just like they did for Linda. I had won a huge gold trophy and money. *Well!*

I nudged Genie and we trotted to the end of the ring where a lady in a beautiful pink suit pinned the blue ribbon on Genie's headstall. The trophy was too big for me to carry on the horse but there was Burt, smiling for once, striding out to accept it. We made our way out of the arena and to the barn, joined by Granddad, Mam, and even Uncle Jack, Aunt Virgie and the kid with her perfect golden curls, who had all come to watch. Everyone praised me and petted me and said how good we'd been.

"It wasn't hard," I said, looking over at Uncle Jack, who had maintained that me riding in the big shows was a knee-slapper. "It was easy."

Now I had really done something, and everyone was going to know about it. I fed Genie an apple and took my big trophy from the tack room shelf intending to walk up to the Hunt Club and show it off. It might have been heavy, but I was so high I felt I could have lifted not only the trophy but Genie too. I strode off toward the Hunt Club clutching my prize. *I was the best! The best! So, this is how Bud felt to be number one. Better than anything!*

※

Five weeks later, weeks during which I had hauled my trophy to the neighbors, to school, and would have taken it to LaVetta's church if Mam had let me, Genie and I easily beat the gray stallion again and won our second first place, this time at the Medford Central Oregon Spring Show. This trophy did not have a horse on the top like the first one but was shaped like a big urn and was almost as tall as me. I knew we had won money too but when I asked Mam for it, she had puffed up like her favorite hen.

"You don't know what it costs to show," Mam said. "We've got gas, tack and entry fees. Burt! That money is spent ten times over, so get it out of your head!"

Emboldened by my new star status, I glared back at her wondering where she had put the money. *Maybe, if I could find it . . .*

"And don't be pestering Granddad about it either, because . . ." she bit off her words as Granddad crowded through the tack room door with the dogs, Burt, and Grandma Thompson behind him.

"Well, kiddo, that was a darn good ride out there," he said. "Nobody can say you only won it for being cute."

"Angus McNeil is sore as a hound after a hunt through the brambles," Grandma Thompson said. "Beat him once, it's a fluke. Beat him twice, everybody can see you're better. You and that horse are great partners. He can't hardly stand it."

I had learned that Angus McNeil was the man on the gray stallion, and Grandma Thompson said he usually won the competition easily. "He can't get himself around it, only taking second again. It's going to bring him down a peg. He rides for the money."

That afternoon, his stallion had not gone smoothly into the rack but had crow-hopped—twice, so he only won a second. *Well, too bad about him. It's my time. And if I can win like this as a kid, there's no telling what I might do when I'm older and a little taller.*

While they were all in the tack room having drinks, I took a carrot to Genie and stood petting her side. "Genie, two weeks to State. We'll win it, girl! Then Tri State. We'll win that too, won't we?"

We might even get to the National Finals in New York. I knew we'd win more trophies, and the State Championship was even more money. Over $2,500, Mam had said. Genie nosed my hand for more carrot. With that much money there was bound to be some left for me. I wasn't worried about anything. Genie was the perfect horse and never made a false move. I was perfect too—for the first time in my life. I made sure Genie had her special show feed, buckled her hoof protectors and headed up the alley to their Hunt Club. If I asked, there would surely be cake for the famous winner.

Two weeks later, on a hot June morning, driving from Emerald City to Salem for the Oregon State championship show, Mam had said it was going to be a record breaker. My wool riding habit, now six months old, was a little short and felt too hot and tight. The hat, which Mam called a bowler, had always been the biggest pain. Earlier, when I was getting into my show clothes Mam had torn out the hairpins I'd put in, and now the hat was clamped to my head painfully, especially where it fit over my braids, which had also been pulled too tight. But no matter, this was the big show, and I was ready. Genie had been unexpectedly grumpy this morning when we loaded her and worse when we unloaded her at the Salem Fairgrounds. She stood in the barn aisle fidgeting from one foot to the other, occasionally turning her head to nip at Burt who was braiding her long mane with blue ribbons.

"Might have figured this would happen," Burt said to Granddad. "She was bound to come into heat but damn bad luck it would be now."

"Annie," Mam barked.

I looked up to see her advancing on me with the clothes brush. Why should Genie be worse in the heat?

After our wins at Portland and Medford, Burt had been less mean but now he was scowling and acting madder than ever.

"Damned worthless females," he growled but not so Mam could hear. But she did and shot him a look that would wither straw.

Granddad emerged from the tack room carrying the saddle and placed it on Genie's back. "She'll calm down once she's in the ring," he said, checking my stirrups.

I turned to place the brushes in the trunk and saw Angus McNeil on the gray stallion clatter into the alley going toward the warm-up area. He'd be trying to cut in line again. He'd try to get ahead of us and then lean in and force us to the inside of the ring where the judges wouldn't notice us, just like last time. I was remembering what Burt said earlier. He had blocked me as I entered the barn. "Now, it's no picnic this time," he said, and I could tell it was important because Burt had paid special attention today. In his suit and vest and clean hat he looked almost as good, as professional, as McNeil and the other trainers. "This is the biggest show in the state, and McNeil has a lot at stake. A lot! He's out for the money but worse, you've hurt his reputation. Keep your distance from him—at all times."

I moved past him to have Grandad help me mount. "At all times!" Burt repeated.

Behind me, I heard a howl.

I whirled around to see Genie taking a big bite out of Burt's shoulder, Burt's fist smashing into the side of her jaw.

The announcer's voice trumpeted over the barns, "Ladies and gentlemen, enter for the Oregon State Championship Five-Gaited Stakes Final Competition."

Before I had time to decide how I'd get back at Burt for hitting her, Grandad took Genie's reins from an enraged Burt, boosted me into the saddle and I was on the way to my biggest win yet. Gathering my reins, I looked down at Genie wondering what Burt could have done to make my sweet girl so mad. Moving down the alley she was hot and a little jittery under me, her skin contracting and releasing like she was trying to unseat invisible flying demons landing on her skin. *Damn Burt! But why did she bite him?*

And then we were in the arena trotting and the music was playing, and I was trying to post smoothly despite Genie's twitchiness. When the announcer asked for a walk, I signaled her, but she did not respond and instead trotted faster until I had to set her down by pulling sharply on her mouth. This was bad ring manners. It meant that I was not able to control my horse and would be a black mark with the judges. *Had they seen me?* I looked over my shoulder to see them all watching Angus McNeil on the gray stallion at the bottom of the circle, moving up fast. Making his move just like Burt had warned. As the gray approached Genie's hindquarters, the announcer called for the slow gait. When I gave her the signal, tightening my legs against her side and lifting the reins, she ducked her butt and almost sat down. I couldn't understand what was happening and looked around again. She was squatting and peeing! That was unbelievably bad manners in a competition. *What the hell?*

As the stallion came even with us, Genie jerked her head up, reached out with her big teeth and took a chomp out of the stallion's neck whereupon he jerked his lips back in what appeared to be a grotesque smile and reared into us. It wouldn't have happened if he hadn't been so close. With no thought but to get the beast away from us, I changed my crop to my outside hand and began slashing the stallion over the butt and kicking out with my leg. My calisthenics caused my hat to fall at the gray's hooves. The stallion shied and reared which unseated Angus MacNeil, who fell with a grimace of horror between the two horses who were bound together in a kicking, squealing frenzy.

"I knew she'd screw it up," Uncle Jack said to Virginia as

they left the show barn later that afternoon.

"It was that crazy mare," Mam said. "I guess now we know why we got a deal."

*

JUNE 1954

My former soaring opinion of myself was now flat as the fields around the ranch but certainly not as pretty or as peaceful. After lengthy discussions with Mam and Grandad, but mostly Mam, I had figured out, in a rough way, the situation with female horses, the meaning of estrus and how it warped female behavior. All female behavior.

"It'll happen to you too," Mam had said.

Looking up at her, I thought, *Maybe it happened to you, but it will sure not be happening to me!* Then she said I couldn't be mad at Genie about it either. It wouldn't be fair because she couldn't help it.

"He'll come back," Mam had said to Granddad. She was talking about Burt, who had stomped from the ring the afternoon of the show and been absent for two weeks.

Setting off to find him, Mam had said, "He won't have a dime left after a spree like this."

And she was right. As she was leading him out of the bar, he hesitated and dragged back. When Mam tugged his arm, he turned and stumbled into the afternoon.

"Well . . . I did put a terrible lot into them two, for it to be a wasted mess," he'd slurred as Mam helped him to the car.

So, after the bitching and the swearing, and finally another bender that Mam had called the Irish Flu, he was back at the barn waiting for me to come for my second practice since the wild uproar in the show ring.

Among themselves, Mam and Grandad with input from

various show friends, had agreed that Burt would keep on with us. No one had asked for my opinion. I would never trust him again. Convinced that planting the roundhouse on Genie's jaw was the biggest part of the disaster in the ring, I didn't care what happened to him. And, although I was still wounded from our humiliating defeat, after the initial crushing tears and self-reproaches, I couldn't let anyone know because our loss had made it doubly important to win again. I couldn't go back to being nothing at all. Therefore, the day before, our desires—Burt's for money; mine for redemption and glory— had drawn us back to the practice ring.

Because of my lack of experience and the fact that Angus McNeil could not manage his stallion, we had been asked to leave the ring that day but had not been banished from further competitions. Mam told me it was Mr. McNeil who was given the severe warning, and that I had the judge's permission to go on to the next show. After extreme embarrassment, tears and lingering outbursts of rage over our failure, shamed by the tittering and laughter I was sure the crowd was directing at me, and beset by Uncle Jack's sneering, "I told you you couldn't do it," I had tried to understand this most horribly painful situation. Thanks to further talks with Grandma Thompson and Mam I now understood more about the mysterious *hormones*. I thought about it for a while, then finally went to see Genie. I stood at the stall door hesitant to enter. She raised her head and took a step toward me with her nose out. She seemed normal again. I guess I couldn't be mad at her. *Could I?* I stepped up and ran my hand down her smooth neck. *No.* I loved her and was sorry for what had happened.

But it was my talk with Granddad that gave me hope I might show and not only show well but even win again. He had waited until I'd quit crying and hiding.

Then, one morning, he'd poked his head around my door.

"Want to go to town?"

At the donut shop he bought two maple bars and two buttermilk donuts and ordered us each a cup of black coffee. After the woman passed the donuts over the counter, we took seats, the ceiling fan blowing the edges of our napkins. He took a bite and then set his donut on the napkin and picking up his coffee, turned to me. "Err, kiddo seems like you've been pretty low with all this, and that's not the way to look at it. See?"

I blew on the coffee and raised the cup to my lips.

"Do you remember when you couldn't tie your shoes? Then sometimes you could?"

I barely remembered.

"Remember? It took a lot of practice and sometimes you needed help, but pretty soon you could do it fast and the knot stayed tied. You remember. Well, you had to keep on practicing and now you can do it without even thinking about it. That's what showing should be, the practice of it, not just about winning or losing. It's the practice that's important." He took a second maple bar and held it in his hand. "And there wouldn't be winning without losing anyway, punk, it goes with it." He was chewing his pastry with his hat pushed back, looking happy.

Although I was still secretly very ashamed of losing, of showing myself incapable of controlling my horse, and was afraid it would happen again, I smiled at him. I almost reminded him that now, I usually wore cowboy boots and didn't need to tie my shoes at all, but I knew he was being nice and telling me to keep trying. *But he thought I could do it! Maybe I had only hit a bump. Maybe I had stumbled—but now I was back, firmly on the fast track. To number one.*

Two days later, Granddad had just dropped me off and I was headed to the arena hoping Burt wouldn't keep on about my posting because my legs still burned from our first practice a day earlier. I wondered what put the burr under Mam's blanket. Before I had taken a step, Mam came barreling down on me and hustled me toward a long black car, prodding me to go home with Jo, Tony's mom. They were my favorite neighbors from the house on the hill, the lovely Jo and her oldest son, Tony. My grandmother who had that summer taken on the "thankless job" of managing the fairgrounds and collecting monthly rent from the "deadbeat" horse owners, had been standing in the open doorway of the fairgrounds office when I had arrived. A clipboard in one hand, her purse clenched in the other, she had hurried to me and was nudging me toward Jo's car with her whole corseted body.

"Jo's invited *you* specially to come and help her make the cake for Tony's birthday," Mam said. "I'll bet there will be something special—for someone. You know you want to go. I'll talk to Burt," she promised. "I'll go to the barn right now and tell him he's got the night off. Just don't you worry about it. Of course, you want to go with Jo. How often do you get a chance?" Certitude oozed from Mam like the scarlet lipstick from the corners of her mouth.

Tony was my favorite, my savior from the mud pit, and I wanted to go but didn't think I should. Still, cake making and Jo, or Burt cussing me into shape during practice, I didn't have to flip a coin. The choice wasn't hard.

The Tri State competition was in three weeks at the Seattle Fairgrounds and according to the audience at the previous practice, I'd done very well in spite of Burt's complaints and our infamous defeat at State. Because of our first two wins, we had enough points to qualify, and I was determined to make the best of it, but what finally tipped my decision to go with Jo were my sore knees from the hour of posting practice the day before. And, after the recent upsets all of us were very tired, and sore in many ways. Without looking back, I scrambled into the big car.

Riding from the fairgrounds to Sunrise Drive in Jo's plush,

walnut-dashed car, passing ivied university buildings set back on long stretches of lawn behind budding trees, the music stopped, and the radio announcer said, "Today, in a landmark decision, the U.S. Supreme Court ruled in Brown v. Board of Education of Topeka that U.S. laws establishing racial segregation in public schools are unconstitutional, even if the segregated schools are otherwise equal in quality."

"That's a mess. Thank God we don't live in the South," Jo said, turning off the radio. She looked over at me, "We'll have such fun. Tony will be here in the morning!"

I wondered why they had to make a special law about schools and thought of asking but didn't. I wanted nothing to do with school or school rules, so instead we chatted about the horses and her sons, me doing most of the talking. Roaring up Sunrise, we passed my old house tucked back onto the hill. The same peaked roof, sparkling leaded windows, my wonderful trees surrounding it, but without my green swing set in the side yard. Directly across the street, Jo's white house was bigger than the hill house and all hedged by laurel except the back veranda where you could look out on the tall-treed town below.

At Jo's, Bumper, her blonde cocker, sped to the rear porch where we entered the hall that Mam had always envied. The hall was windowed on one side with cabinets beneath, fragrant herbs in clay pots parading down the counter in the four o'clock light. The opposite wall was hung with sweaters and sports equipment according to season, littered with shoes, and always with boy smells. That afternoon, the light was lowering, casting shades of gray and ochre through the laurel onto cream-painted walls, shadowing the hall's contents, laying rich tones of brown in the corners, and bronzing the potted plants. The leaf-filtered light added deep layers and mysterious dimension to the space.

Standing in the familiar hall that afternoon was the first

time I recognized differences in the quality of light. The hill light was modulated by the deep green of forests rolling across dark lofty hills, black granite bluffs, bright lawns rolling down and down again to a bottle green river. This light was closer, deeper, cozier. The shadows compact. At the ranch, the light came from far over the mountains to fall on flat coursing rivers, warm gray rocks, and wide gold fields, the deep greens only an occasional punctuation on the land. At the ranch, the light was brighter, pearly, golden, blue and the shadows falling across the fields travelled for miles unbroken. At first, I hadn't liked the openness of the ranch. It was too big, too flat, almost frightening. The curved meeting of golden earth and cerulean sky had seemed too immense to contain such a small person as myself. I had been afraid I would be lost. Walking toward the kitchen, peering through the hall windows that late afternoon, I thought the old hill neighborhood looked a bit cramped and small, darker than I had remembered.

In Jo's beautiful black and white kitchen, she pulled a small stool from a cubbyhole, stepped up, and from a row of bright boxes drew... a cake mix. *Oh boy! Mam would croak. A cake mix for a birthday cake?*

"Annie, why don't you do this? It's easy," she said, passing the box to me.

While the cakes were baking, we sat on the chilly verandah. In the dusk, Jo cut daphne blossoms to place around the cake plate and I told her about the plans for Genie and me, what happened at the State competition, and Burt's cussing.

"I heard about it, but those kinds of things can happen. It may not seem like it, but it was good experience. And Burt, well, just watch out and don't pick up his bad habits."

She stood facing the town, her silhouette trim, her black hair brushing the back of her white collar. It was growing darker and colder now that the sun was moving behind the trees.

"I won't, Jo. Will Tony come see Genie tomorrow? I wish he could see me ride."

She turned and stood gazing down at me. "He'll stop if he goes to the barn, but he's not riding this summer. You know, Annie, horses and showing . . . well, you won't want to do that so much as you get older. You'll find lots of new things to keep your attention."

I shrugged.

"You'll have more friends, and boyfriends when you get older, and then you won't be so interested in the horses."

"Oh, Jo! You still have Queenie." Besides, I already had a boyfriend. I had Bud.

"But I'm an old married lady. I didn't have a horse when I was in college and Doc and I were courting."

Looking up at the petite figure in her smart riding outfit, short black hair framing her pretty face and smiling eyes, noting her perfectly manicured hands clasping the flowers, mistress of her gorgeous, good-smelling kitchen, I hoped I'd be just like her when I grew up. She smiled and patted my shoulder.

"He's only home for the weekend . . . but I'll tell him." She looked at the clock above the counter. "We'd better get going," she said, and called to Bumper.

The cakes were steaming when we took them from the oven and placed them upside down on the racks. I hated to leave the warm cake-smelling kitchen for the cold car. So did Bumper. He came drooping behind us, dragging his ears in the grass, collar tags tinkling in the crisp air. At the driveway, Jo turned toward me in the dusk.

"Of course, you'll all come back tomorrow night for the party." When she spoke again, it was more a sigh. "Annie . . . you, ahh . . ." she looked down and fumbled her keys from her purse. "You're getting to be quite grown up. Before you know it, you'll be going away like the boys."

Suddenly I was in a big hurry. The warm cake smells had made me hungry, and I wanted to get home. I also wanted to tell Mam about the cake making, especially about the mix.

We pulled up to the fairgrounds office as dusk settled behind the barns. Jo glanced toward the empty office, then at her wristwatch. Doc Wheeler's pickup was parked in front of our barn but not much else was going on beyond the regulars who were there to feed their horses, and no sign of Burt. I figured Mam was running down one of the late-paying, deadbeat horse owners, and I'd see her come huffing up the alley with her clipboard in front of her like always, writing a receipt as she walked.

"Well, thanks, Jo. I'm gonna go down and see Genie."

Jo reached across the seat and touched my arm. "Why not wait, Annie? Jessie will be here. It's almost dark."

I put my shoulder to the door. "I'm gonna see what Doc's doin'." I slammed the door and hurried toward the barn. Held in the lights of the big car, my shadow travelled before me.

Mam was walking through the tall barn doors as I approached. Inside, I could see people milling in a swirling knot, barn lights blazing although there was still some light outside. When Mam saw me, her chin jerked up, she glanced over her shoulder and hurried toward me.

"Annie! Done already?" She looked down the alley where Jo's car still idled, white exhaust wavering upward in the gray light.

"How come Doc Wheeler's here?" I brushed past Mam and peered into the barn. When the people inside noticed me, they stepped back, eyes shifting to Genie's stall. Grandma Thompson stood in the aisle holding a bridle in one hand, her jumping saddle clamped under her arm. When she saw me, her seamed face clenched around a down-turned mouth. Her kind eyes held mine.

I began to run. Mam reached out to grab me but not in

time. I barreled into the mass of legs, forcing my way to the stall.

"NO!!" Mam hollered from the door. "Stop right there, Annie. Grab her."

"Genieeee," I screamed. "Genie." Someone did reach out and grab my shirt, but they couldn't hold me.

The stall door gaped open. Doc Wheeler stood, syringe in hand, looking down at Genie. She was stretched out in the bright yellow straw, large golden body still, front feet daintily crossed, her beautiful head lying in a widening pool of scarlet. The brightest red I've ever seen made violent against the brilliant yellow straw.

I stepped forward to cradle her head, and then hands did hold me back. My grandmother's hands.

"I should have been here. And you sent me to make cakes," I screamed. "I could have done something! I could have said good-bye! You knew and you lied. You lied."

And the mist closed over me. Desiccation of the world of sense. Darkness . . .

*

Then glimpses of time through slatted blinds. The long sodden summer, too bright, too harsh, too still for the child sitting alone in the thicket beside the horse pasture. Too still in the red and black bedroom, too still among the screaming schoolchildren, too bright the light of any but the moon. Her only kind companion was Lady, who she felt she had betrayed for another, who was now gone. Where, no one would say.

A disease. A rare bleeding disease. Genie wasn't the only one to die. That was all.

Chapter 15

ANNIE'S ENCOUNTER WITH THE REAL WORLD: 1954

July. I hadn't changed my clothes for days and wouldn't go into their part of the ranch house if Mam was around. Anything that reminded me of Genie made me cry, so I had cried almost constantly and neither Mam nor Grandad could stand it. I looked around the red bedroom where I had remained all summer. I had sprawled on the floor or sat on the bed and brooded. I read all the books that could keep my attention and wrote letters to my mother and my father that I don't think anyone ever sent. I wondered what Linda was doing, and why I'd never heard from him again. After trying hard to write letters to them and finding that I didn't have much to say that would get past Mam, I turned to drawing pictures of faces conjured from my imagination and the Book of the Month Club novels I'd been reading. After weeks of this, Mam finally came and stood in the doorway to my room with the vacuum cleaner, eyeing me.

"This is it! You get up and gather your dirty clothes," she said, looking at the big pile on the floor. "I'm cleaning in here right now. This is a hellish mess and it's gone on long enough."

Without my room to hide in and my books to keep me company and prevent me from thinking about Genie, I couldn't imagine anything. It was as if the world outside had stopped. As she descended the stairs, I flopped back on my bed, crying even louder, and refused to go. She shook the broom at me like she did when she was going after Spike. Her promise of force and a relentless tongue finally drove me outside.

In the garden with Granddad. Squinting in the sun. Sitting on a rock beside the roses watching him dig in the dirt with a long-handled rake then trailing him back to the garden shed. Watching his corded hands wet with liquid work in the shadows, mixing from brown bottles, stirring, pouring. Too harsh in the hot shed. The smell eating at my nose, making my ears ring like a cowbell.

"What's that horrible smelling stuff?"

He, smiling down, eyes lighting up, swimming toward me through his glasses. "Kills the weeds so I don't have to be out there every minute. Did you see those tomatoes? Keeps the bugs off. If it weren't for this stuff"—knotted finger tapping a stinking uncapped brown bottle—"they wouldn't be near that big and healthy."

"Yeech." Wandering out of the shed, skirting the garden. Down the path to find Lady. Sitting in the grass, holding onto her legs, sobbing. Hives that night.

August. A call from Linda.

"Annieee," Mam screams from the backdoor. "It's your mom."

I ignore her. After the big room cleaning, I'd been staying in the barn with Lady and away from the house as much as possible. I don't want to talk on the phone. Lady and I leave the pasture by the back gate. We drift to the top of the hills, around the old cemetery, then stand looking over the snaky green river below and don't go home until dark.

That night, Mam is sitting on my bed, Granddad standing on the steps leading into the red and black room. "Annie . . .Linda called to . . ." Mam turned to Granddad.

He came slowly down the steps, his head glowing in the

hall light, and came to the bed. "Goodnight, Punkin'. Sleep tight," he said, placing his hand on my head. To Mam, "Let's say goodnight, Mother."

"Goodnight, Annie."

"Night."

The next morning, Granddad at coffee, Mam in her robe hustling pots and pans into the cupboard, Granddad looks up as I approach the breakfast bar wearing days old T-shirt and shorts. He smiles, shakes the newspaper, and lays it flat before him. Mam wipes her hands then sits next to him, pushing a strand of hair away from her face.

"Annie. . ." Mam begins.

"Errr, this is the about size of it . . ." Granddad now.

"Bud . . ."

"Bud broke his neck at Cheyenne. And your mother's taking it hard." Mam staring down at me with her 'you better watch it' look.

"Broke his neck! Broke it, how? When?" Erupting from the barstool, springing up and down on the kitchen floor, screaming, "I have to go see him."

Mam, shouting. "Annie, stop! He's dead. He fell. The damned bull stepped on his neck. He didn't come to."

"No! You're a liar. You're lying again."

Running out the back door of the ranch house, tearing across the planted garden, screaming "Bud" clear to the pump house under the Armitage house tree. Sobbing there among the blackberry tendrils invading the pump house window, prone on the dirt floor, tears joining the pool of dark water leaking from the pump.

Later, that evening, I crept onto the back porch of the Armitage house and stretched face down on the warm porch boards. Turning my head, I looked up at my rustling tree, then down the daisy-spotted lawn to the horse fence, but instead of the pasture, I saw Bud in his best suit, on the poster at

Madison Square Garden, in the stall when I first met him. *Pray Mam is lying. This is home. We'll be a family.*

Rousing myself under the moon, walking numbly to the big pasture by the river. Sensing her white spots, drifting across streams of cool river air, finding Lady in the dark, sitting under her belly sobbing, sleeping in the grass, waking to the smell of tansy, drinking from the horse trough. Falling back to sleep under the stars.

There was the next call from Linda. Bud was dead; gored through the stomach by a Brahma—not as Mam had lied, his neck quickly broken.

For me he was still perfect, and huge, and frozen in time. None of them realized my grief was for the loss of my own first love, not Linda's lover.

Chapter 16

WHAT HAPPENS TO ANNIE WHEN LINDA ABDICATES HER RODEO THRONE?

ARMITAGE ROAD, 1956

Later, in the dark winter of 1955, there arrived a one-page note on Stevens & Butler Commodity Brokers letterhead that had only said 'Hello,' and 'I hope you are well.' My father said nothing about support money, nothing about another visit. No further letters. His thin letter seemed only the next step down a dark and horrible path. The loss of my dreams and dearest friends had undone me, but I didn't understand it then. I only realized later that I had quit feeling because it had hurt too much.

A year passed. Almost two. Trouble at school. Teachers were the easy targets of my inarticulate spite. When one morning the home studies teacher chastised me for acting "tipsy" (trying to dodge my cooking experiment), I replied, "Of course I am. Doesn't everyone have champagne for breakfast on Friday mornings?" They called the principal who called Mam who counts me uncontrollable, insane.

An early summer night in 1956, Linda is home for a few

days between shows. Mam asks if I want to stay at Margie's overnight. *Mam is suggesting something she knows I like? Hah! I know Mam now. Know her tricks.* Margie and I ride through the afternoon telling each other stories. When she stops to draw breath, I intervene. "Something's up, Margie. She never wants me to stay at your place unless they leave or are up to something—or something's going on that they don't want me to know about."

At dusk, we turn the horses out, rush down to her place, eat, then at dark, we sneak back to the ranch. Rolling our eyes at each other, we creep along in the shelter of the laurel, slip through the hole in the hedge, duck under the window and stand listening for pursuit. Hearing nothing and not disturbing the dogs who usually burst into fierce barking at the slightest sound, we sneak across the patio, into the red bedroom, then crack the kitchen door to listen.

Linda is there with Mae. They're all made up, wearing bright sheath dresses, and Mam is cooking steaks. Granddad stands at the counter making highballs. Whiskey for Mae, Scotch for Linda.

"I've signed the contract for New York," Linda says. "It's better this year."

"That's nice, isn't it, Daddy?" This is Mam. She's shoveling steaks onto the platter, the dogs gazing at her. Mae's pink silk shoes cross the kitchen floor, her heels like woodpeckers at the holly tree.

Margie and I leave the door open a crack and slump against the red-carpeted steps. They're eating. Margie's gaze drifts around the room, the cactus wallpaper, the gold bedspreads covered with clothes, finally resting on whiskey bottles filled with jewel-colored water alongside my big trophies, all dusty in the evening light. Then she looks at me. I think of her room, and figure she thinks I'm hopeless.

We perk up at Granddad's voice. "Well, now, Linda, we

asked you and Mae to come tonight . . . er . . . How's your drink, Mae?"

"Fine, Marshall. Taking it a little easy. We're going out. Maybe a few drinks there too, so . . . I'm holding."

"Tell them, Mae." This is Linda's voice, but we can only see the back of her head.

"Oh, Linda. I haven't made up my mind when to announce it." She smiles at my mother.

"No, tell them. It's good news."

Mae laughs, a chuckle ending in a drawn out, "Ohh. Frank proposed." She holds a red-tipped hand over the bar; a wide row of gems glitter across her finger. "We'll do it when Linda's home. She can be my matron."

"Why, Mae, that is just wonderful news. Isn't it, Daddy? Just wonderful news." Mam wipes her hands on her green apron and hugs Mae.

Granddad clinks glasses with Mae. "We like him, Mae. Good fellow."

Mam has told me she thinks Frank looks like a girl. She calls him "eyelashes" behind his back. It's quiet at the table. Margie and I shift to un-cramp our legs. I'm thinking of leaving, a victim of paranoid suspicion.

Mam's voice. "Uh, Linda, we need to talk to you . . . uhh . . . about Annie. Don't we, Daddy?"

Silence.

Then, "What's wrong with Annie?"

"Linda . . ."

"NO! What's wrong with her?" She shifts in her chair, crosses her feet.

"Linda, you have to come home." More silence.

"I am home."

"No," Granddad says. "Mother means you have to come home for good."

"Daddy?" This from Linda.

"It's the best thing, Linda. She needs you here."

"Mom! You said she's doing better. You get money from Jeffrey." Linda rises and backs toward us. "Is it the money?"

Mam rises.

Mae pushes her chair from the table and moves toward my mother. "Linda, you've said it's getting rougher."

"But I'm the star of the whole damned show . . . I can't quit now."

"You can finish the contracts you've signed. Then it's over." Granddad moves toward Linda, stands beside her, drink in hand, contemplating the floor.

*

Linda came home. "For you," she says. Soft, sad smile. "I've given up riding for you." I'm ten.

"I'm retiring at the top of my game. That's the way to do it. No downhill run for me."

She no longer has anything to do with the horses, pulls her red hair straight back, wears it in a high bun on the top of her head, always dresses in slinky tight dresses with high, high heels. Lives on coffee and little orange dexies.

Then, with no warning, Linda announces she's engaged to marry a slick-haired man with two younger daughters who Mam immediately names Slick Willy. Linda takes me aside several days after the big announcement. She's quiet on the drive to my favorite cafe. After the girl brings our milkshakes, Linda says, "Don't you think it would be nice if we moved to a house of our own, and didn't have to live with Granddad and Mam anymore?" She said she thought it would be just the ticket, and no, we couldn't take Lady with us.

I don't remember replying. I couldn't wait to get to Mam and tell her. Surely, she wouldn't let Linda do any such thing. I'd been over wanting to move away from the ranch for years.

And now I'd have sisters? Besides having to put up with the fake grandchild?

The next day I got up early and ran to find Mam, who was leaving for one of her meetings, a leather folder and clipboard in her hand. "Mam," I said. She stopped at the door and fished in her purse for the car keys. All in one breath I wailed, "I can't move away from here, go live with people I don't know! I can't leave you and Granddad and Lady and Margie and everybody. I can't leave the ranch. I can't leave the Armitage house."

She told me I'd sure better stand it. "And you'd better not get any wild ideas into your head. If you spoil your poor mother's chances, I'll know the reason why."

The way she looked at me, face all twisted, eyes narrowed to toad slits, I knew she didn't mean she'd know the reason why—what she meant was that I'd surely be sorry because she'd make sure of it.

The next thing I knew, I was meeting Slick's two daughters. They were pretty, and frail, and didn't know one end of a horse from the other. All at once Linda was "miss perfect mother," and I was being crammed into another prickly flower girl dress. Then I had to move in with them. The house wasn't bad. Big old farmhouse about eight miles down the river from the ranch, but lifeless with us in it. Except my portion. It seethed with black and potent wrath. Linda had decided to be the kind of fifties housewife she read about in the *Ladies' Home Journal* and *Redbook*. The kind who bought the exact same striped sheets in three different colors, then assigned each of her "girls" a color. I was green. I became a serious problem at the new school.

※

They weren't any happier than I was. One night after he'd come home late, I heard a loud argument about some money he wanted to borrow from Granddad and wondered why it made Linda cry. I crept into my closet where I could hear better. He was slurring his words, the sound moving around the room.

"All he'd have to do is deed you ten acres now. You're getting land anyway. Jack did. Then there was a pause, then more steps. "He's getting a lot of money from the highway right of way too, so why not help us out? Think of what a subdivision it would make—so close to the new highway." The feet stopped moving and I heard what sounded like the bed springs creak. "He probably doesn't need the money but he's a damned fool if he can't see what a deal this would be for him. For all of us."

"Don't you say that about Daddy," she said.

A door slammed and my mother began to cry again.

Then she had become unusually quiet and busy around the house, and the girls were thankfully with their other grandmother much of the time. As the winter turned to spring, unable to sustain my extravagant wrath, I was like a plant jerked up by the roots: drooping, pale, unwilling to leave my bed for days at a time. I wanted Granddad, Lady and the ranch. I ran away. Well, I walked about three miles, hitchhiked several more with a neighbor, then trudged up the dusty little road to the ranch about nine o'clock one spring night.

"I'm never going back," I said.

Later, after Mam fed me and Granddad made me laugh, Linda came and drove me home. She was bent to the wheel, sobbing, shirt sleeves rolled high, head thrust forward, squinting to see through her tears, her nose dripping furiously. All the way, I gave good, no, excellent, reasons why I should stay at the ranch. Still, she sobbed.

Back at the farmhouse she sobbed some more. After her husband left the next morning, I found her in her room crying again, and on the nights when he didn't come home, after she put the younger girls to bed, I would hear her weeping in the big room next to mine. I thought most of the crying must be about my failures at McKenzie Bridge Elementary and felt sorry for her. I tried to behave better at school and avoid trouble at home by staying in my room and out of their way, but soon realized that her tears weren't only about me. When I asked her where he was all the time, Linda said he had a big deal cooking.

"He's a builder," she said. "He's had his eye on some land for a new subdivision, but he's having trouble."

"What kind of trouble?"

But she just smiled, a sadder version of her photo op smile. "Nothing to keep you from finishing your arithmetic," she said, shooing me back to my book and closing the door. When I told Mam about it her mouth formed into a warning pucker, her eyes slid toward me and from their penetrating glitter, I knew that it wasn't news to her. "What do you know about any of this?" she said. "What else did you hear?"

Back at the farmhouse, I didn't know what to think because her husband was obviously trying to be nice to me. While earlier he had almost ignored me, now when we sat at the dinner table, he was asking how I was and wanting to hear about school. And, he was frequently very happy, his olive skin flushed, dark hair falling over his high forehead, weaving about the place muttering, making phone calls, sloshing drinks on the tables, leaving his stinking overflowing ashtrays everywhere. Then he started coming downstairs for breakfast in his wrinkled pajamas, taking a whiskey bottle back upstairs and staying there sometimes all day. Even though I didn't see him much, I began to understand that he was not like Granddad. Or Bud. I didn't see him getting much done. Granddad was a champion athlete, a banker, a commissioner. A man people looked up to for a plan and who had a say in how things were done. Bud had been a world rodeo champion.

He owned a ranch where he'd bred prized registered quarter horses the cowboys used for roping. Both men were kind. Bud had always given a hand up to young rodeo contenders, and Grandad sought to be a friend to everyone. As far as I was concerned, this was what good men were like. My mother's husband didn't seem to have anything to him, only his good looks which weren't so good in the morning, but nothing else that I could see.

Then, just as I was beginning to think I might have to accept the new arrangement, I woke one night to another big fight. Loud hollering and thuds were coming from the other side of the wall, then he broke a door, and passed out cold, and she left him. The next day after school as I rushed to pack my suitcase and books, I was so excited to get back to the ranch, I didn't even see Slick and his daughters leave. Mostly I remember Linda in the green truck crying. At the farmhouse packing she cried, at the ranch unloading she cried, and everywhere in between she cried some more. Our return didn't make it any better back at the ranch. Mam, who had continually claimed it was my contrariness, my fault that he left, said she'd make me sorry. I should have believed her. The next day when my mother went back to load more boxes, Mam hauled me into the mudroom, her name for the back bathroom, and cut off my long braids with the horse clippers.

"I do not have time to mess with your braids and get you to school with you acting like a hellion," she said, tossing a long braid in the sink. Then she shaved the back of my head.

No one should have heard the commotion Mam and Linda got into over that one.

"If it hadn't been for her," Mam hissed to Linda, "you'd still be there." That was before the screaming.

Still, wrapped around the shrinking pole of my heart was the conviction that if only Linda and I could live together on the beautiful Armitage place life would somehow right itself.

Chapter 17

ABOUT MARGIE: 1957

But it didn't. It was 1957 by then, spring of sixth grade. Dwight D. Eisenhower had been reelected two years before but the next November, he'd had a stroke, which put Mam and Granddad into an uproar. Granddad had rumbled, "My God, if anything happens to him now the damned Democrats will have us at war before summer." He looked over at Mam, "Without him to keep up the pressure for the Interstate, Volpe may not have the support to push it forward and then this place won't be worth anywhere near what I'd hoped." "Well, too late now, Daddy. We're here, and it's just fine the way it is. Why, where would we be without your garden?"

He smiled and kissed her on the cheek.

One morning, I heard them talking about our downhill neighbors from the house on the hill who were building a bomb shelter. Back at Elijah Bristow Elementary, they had a special meeting in the auditorium. The whole school sat together and watched a film showing us how when "the bomb" came, we should get under our desks and put our hands over our eyes. I wasn't worried. I figured the A-bomb was just one more disruption to avoid—like Mam.

My mother had to go to work at the bank like a regular person, and at night I remember her either crying or madly flipping through her fancy clothes and matching shoes, dressing to go out. She often went with Mae to the dark bar in the Banks Hotel in downtown Emerald City which Frank had bought with a vets loan and money he had saved from the $138 a month he'd earned as a Master Sergeant. Mam said that Mae, the hotel manager and hostess, sat at the corner of the bar, chain-smoking, plump legs crossed, welcoming every man who came through the door, and introducing my mother to each one. I already knew all about it because on Wednesdays, I'd ride the activity bus to town, attend modern jazz dance class in Mrs. Pool's big studio above the donut shop, then walk to the hotel to get a ride home with Linda. The bar was dark, fruity smelling, and full of men who I thought should be at work. They were the sales types, slick suited, flashy spenders, always with a joke, fast eyes wreathed in smoke from their endless cigarettes. Waiting in the lobby with the potted ferns and red Turkish rug, I could hear Linda in the bar, laughing. Looking for another husband, I figured. Mam and Granddad seemed to feel sorry for her, so everything she did was okey dokey.

*

That summer, Linda was at work, and the big ranch house was mostly quiet and deserted. Granddad was usually back from the bank by noon, then later I'd see him in the garden or out on the ranch tending to the new special red cows he was so proud of. Mam no longer managed the fairgrounds. She had moved up. She now headed the Oregon Public Affairs Board, and when she wasn't in committee meetings, typing madly or on the phone, she was occupied in town with her good works people. The rambling house was silent, and I stayed at Margie's as much as I could.

I remember that time as the china painting summer. In her tidy kitchen in the shade of cool walnut trees, LaVetta taught me to paint elegant flowers on china. Morning glories and violets were my favorites, and the flowered vines I painted using a special silk cloth to blend colors remain some the freshest images I've ever done. I still have the box she helped me make that summer. It sits on my dresser today, a small rectangular bone china box, green vines sweeping among violet flowers and heart-shaped leaves, the rim edged with gold.

At the Delaunay cottage, the air thick with the scent of roses and walnut trees, I bounded onto the porch and opened the kitchen door which I had quit knocking on years before. In the cool kitchen, LaVetta sat at the booth, her china-painting gear, small dishes, brushes, and glowing bits of silk spread around her. She glanced up.

"Hi, Annie," she murmured, dark head bending intently over a small piece of white china she grasped with one hand. In the other, she held a tiny brush, outlining a flower arrangement in burnt sienna. As she worked on the drawing, she talked about her cousin, Peggy.

"Annie, can you imagine? She sold her farm and moved up to Canada all by herself. She built a cabin all by herself too, but it doesn't have one bit of electricity and no running water. Why do you think she'd do that?" she asked without looking up. "I'll have to write to her. I worry about her up there all on her own. But then wouldn't it be peaceful and quiet?" She smiled, modeled lips relaxing as she lowered her brush into a little dish of chemical stuff. She nodded to a pile of mail on the counter. "There's a letter from Johnny. He and Loreen are coming to see Mom and the rest next weekend."

Her brother Johnny lived at the coast. He and Loreen had recently opened a shop where they sold exotic imported birds from around the world and kept six full-grown husky dogs with them in a 24-foot house trailer. She held the cup high in the light falling through the lace curtains, turning it slowly in her hand, giving it a careful examination.

"Now, I've got four more of these and the saucers for the church sale in September. Think I'll get there?"

She turned and looked up at the red teapot clock above the table. "Time to start supper. You'd better stay. Edward passed his test so we're celebrating. He starts next month."

She didn't seem as happy as I thought she'd be. We'd all been waiting to hear for months, and Edward had been so anxious he was grouchy. He had been a millwright at the cannery. Now he'd be a policeman. He said the way the town was headed there was no future at the cannery, but there damned sure was a good future with the police department. LaVetta didn't like it when Edward cussed but she wouldn't say anything because if she did, he cussed more.

The screen door banged, and Margie came in from helping Grandma Delaunay with the cleaning. "Well, we finished," she said to LaVetta, running a hand over her ponytail. "It wasn't bad at all."

"Can't believe you're done already," LaVetta said. "She can hardly put one and two together anymore." Then she smiled, a rueful down turning of her mouth, and stowing her painting in a box under the counter, turned to start supper. According to Margie, LaVetta and Grandma Delaunay, Edward's mother and the oldest woman for miles around, had a gentle (and sometimes not so gentle) war going on since LaVetta and Edward had built their honeymoon cottage directly across the road from Grandma's big farmhouse under the maples. I liked them both and didn't know why they didn't get along.

I followed Margie through the rounded doors and handmade arches of the cottage to her pink room where she busied herself with a pile of clothes stacked on the bed. She carefully placed fuzzy pastel sweaters in cotton sacks, stacked matching socks in mesh sacks, then nested items according to color.

While she rearranged drawers, I read to her about the lives

of the stars from the movie magazines I'd charged to Mam's account at the Ranch Market. After Margie finished with the drawers and I'd read everything about Kim Novak, she changed clothes. She sat on the bed and removed her shoes one at time, minutely inspecting both for any speck of dirt. She had two pairs of white bucks, so neither of them would show wear! Cleaning them carefully with a little sack of special powder every single time she wore them, she immediately placed them on shoe racks. I felt warm and infected with order in her perfectly clean and pretty room.

Though it was becoming a second home and I was familiar with things, I still investigated everything and mooned over her decorations: soft pink carpet, pink and white striped wallpaper, white eyelet curtains, white linen and lace pillows on the bed. It was simple, and it was pink— yet the effect was of attention, comfort, and beauty. Not like mine with scarlet carpets and cactus flower wallpaper, my side littered with clothes and books, Linda's side empty except for the dust.

To add to the attractions, Margie also had her own 45 record player and a maroon record box with pockets for each record, carefully labeled. After she had dressed for her date in a freshly ironed white blouse and her new turquoise poodle skirt, she swept her hand over the bedspread and surveyed the room, then moved to the record box and took out her current favorite, "Love Me Tender." I liked Little Richard better than Elvis, but she loved Elvis best and had almost all his records. We played our other favorites too, "Party Doll," "Little Darlin'," "Come Go with Me" . . . over and over until LaVetta rapped on the door and told Margie she had to stop because she could hear it in the kitchen, and it was giving her a headache.

That night, after we'd had cake and ice cream to celebrate Edward's new job, Bobby came to pick up Margie. I had an acute crush on Bobby. He was a track star at Harrisburg High and the handsomest boy I'd ever seen, even better looking than Tab Hunter. His hair was golden blonde, he was tall, green-eyed, and tanned from his summer job putting in hay at Thompsons ranch. That night he wore a pink shirt with the collar turned up at the back of his neck where his gold hair curled. I was hanging around in the kitchen, dying to go with them but pretending I didn't care.

LaVetta said, "You be home by eleven. You have her home, Bobby." Margie pulled on the back of Bobby's jean pocket, and they turned to leave.

I sidled toward the door.

"C'mon, then," Bobby said to me. Margie nodded, yes.

As we trooped out the back, LaVetta looked over at Edward as if to say, "See, he's a good boy."

Earlier that summer, after seeing me drive the hay truck for Granddad, Bobby had taught me to drive his Plymouth convertible on the country roads around the ranch, and now he let me drive almost every time they took me with them. It was a hot night, too early yet for the breeze that came up after dark blowing the scent of the orchards over the fields and cooling them. In the driveway, shade dappling his hair, Bobby worked the canvas top back.

"Don't get to do this that often," he said, folding the top into its slot. We took off, laughing.

At the crossroads, he pulled onto the dirt road to the Johnsons' bean field, and we all changed places as the sun was setting across the field. I couldn't see over the wheel, so he fetched a boat cushion from the trunk.

"Here, sit on this," he said, wedging the hard cushion between my bottom and the seat. They piled into the back and began necking. That night I drove clear to Harrisburg Landing, the wind whipping my long hair madly, and they only came up for air when I overtook and passed a car. Bobby gasped something and grabbed the back of the seat.

"Annie, NEVER—NEVER, pull back in the lane until you see the head lights of the other car behind you. NEVER! You'll get us all killed!"

I shrugged and hoped he wouldn't make me stop the car. He should have told me before. Unlike my endless equitation lessons, for driving lessons, Grandad had just showed me how to shift and I drove happily off through the big hayfield behind the barn, "Not too fast, there," his only instruction.

Later, we stopped for Cokes at the drive-in under the bridge where we changed places again, all piling into the front seat, and Bobby drove home. He parked on the dark verge up the road from Margie's and turned off the lights. I was tired but didn't complain because I wanted them to take me again. Margie hit me on the leg to discourage me, but as soon as they went back to the heavy kissing, I watched.

At Margie's, LaVetta and Edward were in the living room, the screen door open, lights off, watching Jack Paar on television. In the yard, the crickets were singing. Margie stopped on the porch and ran a comb through her waist-length black hair.

"Do I look okay?" she asked before we stepped inside.

She looked beautiful, as always. She was seventeen and had grown prettier each year. Boys and men turned to look at her wherever we went. Even Uncle Jack looked. And more than once, because whenever he saw Margie come to the barn with me, he'd make an excuse and come stomping across the pasture to see what we were doing. He'd lean up against the door while we were putting the horses away and watch—not me. Then one night while he was prowling around the ranch, he had seen her parked along the road up from his trailer necking with Bobby. For being so quiet and grouchy, when it came to tattling, he was quite the talker. He told Mam and Granddad that Margie was a tramp, and they shouldn't let me spend time at the Delaunay's, no matter that there were no other kids within a mile of the ranch. Apparently, Mam wasn't as straitlaced about all that as Uncle Jack, and Granddad probably thought all seventeen-year-old girls were virgins. There could be no doubt in the world about an eleven-year-old. I didn't think it would matter to Mam what Margie did. I figured she wanted me at the Delaunay's so I wouldn't be in her hair.

"You girls have fun? We're just about to have ice cream again." LaVetta stepped out the kitchen door into the pantry where they kept the new freezer. "Chocolate, or Peppermint?

"Both for me."

"Chocolate for me," Margie said.

At the counter, LaVetta scooped ice cream for the four of us, the sash of her embroidered apron bobbing as she worked. "We put the cots up out back. It'll be nicer, cooler we thought."

I sat beside Margie in the booth's guest spot, which I had claimed as permanently mine. LaVetta sat closest to the stove and sink in the only chair. Edward sat on the end. Food, camping gear, and cooking utensils waited to be packed into a box by the sink. It was close to eleven-thirty now, becoming cooler, but still very warm and fragrant with the smell of apple pies in the kitchen. I was longing for pie to go with my ice cream. LaVetta smiled over at me as she settled into her chair, "No pies tonight, Annie, they're for tomorrow." *Can she read my mind?*

"Well, I've got to get some sleep. We're taking the cameras and going to the mountains first thing." Edward finished his ice cream and set his bowl on the counter. "We'll be up around Mt. Hood. We're staying over," he said, winking at me, "you'll have to get your own dinner, Annie."

"Edward!" LaVetta rose, trying to keep from laughing and deposited the bowls in the sink.

In Margie's warm room, we changed into our baby dolls. Hers pink and white striped, mine blue and white polka dots.

When I left my jeans on the floor, she snatched them up, folded them expertly, then ran her hands smartly down the legs before placing them on the chair. "Now, they'll look pressed," she said, frowning at me. She was the kind of girl who always stayed clean. We could go out in the morning to ride, both clean. When we got back to the barn, I'd look like Pigpen, hair every which way, caked with dust and generally disheveled, and she would be all tucked in and not a speck of dirt on her. It wasn't fair.

Edward and LaVetta had set up the army cots under the big cherry tree beside the vegetable garden and it was much cooler in the yard. In the green Oregon morning, I'd be freezing, but it always felt delicious to fall asleep outside in the cool bowl of night. Shoving the army cots together, we threw the bedding over them, and crawled on top. We lay in the pleasant old yard, looking up at the stars, surrounded by the wide fields, the mountains across the river keeping watch. Thinking our own thoughts, happy to be together, happy to hear the crickets, the rustlings of birds and animals in the fields, the warm reassuring night sounds; we drifted there watching the constellations above us.

"What does it feel like when he kisses you?"

Margie didn't answer. She stood and searched the grass for her thongs.

"Get a blanket," she said.

I crawled off the cot and grabbed the blanket.

Quick and shadowy as a night creature, she plunged into the filbert orchard, me hurrying after her. We finally lurched out of the dark grove and into the eighty-acre wheat field that ran from Delaunay land north to the river. Moving slowly among the waist-high spears of wheat, passing through currents of warm and cool air, we started as field mice and bats scurried before us. A barn owl screeched from the orchard behind us.

"That's Daddy's owl," Margie said. "It's a good bat hunting night. It's been living in the orchard since he was little."

"How long?"

"Thirty or forty years. Daddy's thirty-nine."

In the half moon light, we stood surrounded by vast stretches of gleaming, unmowed wheat, their spikes whispering in the breeze of our passing. Margie spread the blanket over the plants, making a lumpy tent, and plopped on top of it.

"Lay down," she said patting the blanket. "Look up now."

I lay down, trying to stretch lightly on the wheat spikes piercing the blanket and my legs. In the open expanse of field, the sky was much bigger, blacker, and wilder than it had been in the safe yard. It seemed to me then that the stars were bits of glittering magic playing on a canvas made of time. Margie's face blotted out the stars. Her soft lips came down on mine. So soft, and so very warm, and nothing like the ethereal stars.

"That's what it's like."

"But you're not . . . Do boys kiss the same way?"

She giggled, then an indrawn breath. Her hand enfolded mine and placed it on her breast. "Boys want to do this. Do you like it?"

"It feels . . . nice . . ." I was feeling both interested and uncomfortable now. While I thought being kissed and touching her breast quite fascinating and different, I did not want to carry the investigation further. But I wasn't alarmed as I had been with Barbara at the house on the hill. I dreamed of sex, too much, I thought. I dreamed of being kissed for the first time. I didn't want to hurt Margie's feelings and say that I'd wanted a different first kiss, so I said nothing. We lay together like that for some time, side by side in the dark field, Margie gently holding my hand to her breast. This was a circumstance in which silence held all I could say. Somewhere in the dark silence of the summer wheat field and of our young hearts, we knew that we loved each other, and perhaps she loved me in a way that I could not return. But I loved her too. Besides Granddad, she was the first true human friend I'd ever had.

Chapter 18

ANNIE GOES UNDERGROUND FOR GOOD

ARMITAGE HOUSE, EMERALD CITY, OREGON, MAY 13, 1999

A chilly morning, more like early March, the moisture on the hedges trembled in the weak sun. Looking out the window at the ranch house, wrapped in a robe, not only trying to keep warm but also trying for a normal day, I was preparing to do laundry and clean my room. Any time my interior became too disorganized I could be found cleaning something. Later that morning dusting the tall dresser in the downstairs bedroom, I moved the china box I had painted in the summer of 1957. Inside were three black and white pictures of me; the kind that come in a strip from automatic photo booths at fairs and amusement parks. I had placed the pictures there over forty years ago, and there they had remained.

*

ARMITAGE ROAD, 1957

The next morning, when the Delaunays piled in the station wagon and headed for the mountains, I waved goodbye and walked down the lane contemplating the blooming hedgerow. A sparrow landed on a branch, hopped along inspecting me, then dove into the hedge and hustled to its depths. Judging by the profusion of white hairy flowers on the vines, it promised to be a good summer for blackberries.

By the time I turned into the driveway, I had decided. *A queen for power, and a great beauty for love, a double whammy ought to do it.* At the ranch, I cleaned the red bedroom from top to bottom, and changed my name. After careful consideration, I took Elizabeth as my chosen name, after the Queen of England and Elizabeth Taylor, first the most prominent, and second, the most beautiful woman in the world. Elizabeth Victoria Butler would be my registered name; my everyday name would be Liz. Liz was a strong, sexy name. Not a foolish baby name, like Annie, or a schmancy name like Antonia.

By the middle of summer, I had lost ten pounds, bleached my light brown hair with special heavy duty, blue-white booster powder, and toned it with Clairol 9A, Light Ash Blonde, which I charged to Mam's account at the Villa Pharmacy. At first, my long hair turned a very light golden blonde. When Mam got over her outrage at the cheapness of my new look, I bought more blue-white powder, mixed it into thick goop then fashioned white streaks around my face, the bleach plumping my hair to mane-like proportion, so I'd look even more like a California movie star. Tired of being Annie. Liz would be a woman of the world, would direct her own life, take what she wanted, brook no interference. I renewed my vow. If Linda couldn't find me a father and make us a family— I would. I'd find my own husband!

Staying home more, I rode down the summer days with Margie, and only had dinner at the ranch instead of going to Margie's for dinner number two. I also began staying up late to watch the Starlight movie on Channel 12. For clues on how to find a husband, I paid special attention to how men and women on screen acted and reacted. Only when the test pattern appeared, would I turn off the set and retreat to my springy bed under the open window. There, I turned the radio to the Los Angeles station that played music Mam called jungle jive and said I shouldn't listen to. In the middle of the night, radio from Los Angeles and further south carried all the way to Emerald City, and I'd fall asleep listening to Clarence Frogman Henry, Billy Williams, Jerry Lee Lewis, wishing I could play the piano like Otis Spann.

Lying back on my pillows, I imagined myself cast on the screen of heaven, larger than life, dancing for the musicians as they played. What style of women would draw their attention? My breasts weren't as big as the stars in the movie magazines or Margie's, and I was too short. But I had something. I could see it reflected in the big mirror in my room, where I imagined myself as a sexy, tight-skirted, big-bosomed flirt with hoop earrings like Kim Novak. I'd stand in a dancer's pose, be a Natalie Wood type, cute and smart. I tried imagining myself as Sandra Dee or Elizabeth T. and practiced long passionate kisses inside the crook of my arm. I was hot.

Other nights, I'd take Mam's Book of the Month Club selection from the bookcase in the new family room and read until dawn, then sleep in the hot, heavily draped bedroom until afternoon. On warm, still nights, only Edward's owl awake with me, I'd imagine myself in the character's roles. I tried Lover, Mother, Husband, mentally straining with the effort of envisioning what real people were supposed to know and do. I paid particular attention to my mission: how women recognized and captured the men they were to marry—which at that moment, according to me, were sweet-smelling men, quiet, spiritual men who would love their women more than their own lives.

My favorite book of the summer was *Atlas Shrugged*. I

took it from Mae's after I heard her tell Aunt Virgie that it was full of sex. I didn't care about the railroads and steel mills in the story. I wanted the romance and sex scenes. On passionate examination, I found I could understand the people in the book, people who seemed to hold promise as models for me. The men were brilliant, handsome, and strong. The heroine knew exactly how to get what she wanted and did not compromise. She ignored haters, would not argue but just went ahead with her plans, made herself beautiful and used that beauty to get what she wanted, and she never let anyone boss her around, especially a man. Being I was on a headlong course of developing myself as a woman of the world, it did not occur to me to investigate the results of her efforts.

Taking LaVetta's china painting as a starting point, I begged Mam to buy me oils and brushes. I guessed she would agree because I'd heard her tell Granddad she'd do almost anything to get me to show "a shred of initiative." I arranged my painting materials on a card table in the windowed den off the red and gold bedroom. On hot afternoons after I came in from riding, I sat bent over small canvasses painting women's faces and figures using movie stars from my magazine for models. If I could recreate beautiful women on canvas, I could do it on my own face. I would make myself beautiful—and desirable. That summer I also began to keep my first real diary. As long as I didn't make noise or cause problems, my family seemed pleased at my sudden industry and left me alone. I'd gone underground.

*

That August I was twelve, and we were going to the Oregon State Fair where Mam and Granddad were both to give speeches. Earlier that year Granddad was re-appointed head of Oregon's Transportation Commission, and Mam was running for governor of the state. Like all campaigns, it was hard work. But not for me. For me, there was a major rodeo, the horse show, and the biggest carnival on the West Coast.

As used to these events as I was, the State Fair was a big deal, but I hadn't been back since my humiliating defeat in the show ring three years earlier. A defeat that still made all the cells in my body cringe in unison. It was so painfully bound with the many losses from that time that I had shut them away and still hated to remember any of it. Yet, I was looking forward to the fair that day and without really acknowledging the significance, I was somehow aware of my desire to move away from all that had come before. Reflecting on how I looked, I felt surprisingly good. I had spent a long time getting ready that morning, but nobody paid any attention because they were both going like houses afire loading their papers and gear into the car.

Finally, racing through the house, Mam had hollered to Granddad to get the car, and have it out front because she was sick and tired of us always running her late for everydarnthing. Granddad stopped in the back room; the cabinet door squeaked then he popped the cork on the bottle he kept with the horse medicine. The door clicked shut and he went out the back door toward the barn.

I checked myself in the bathroom mirror on the way out. I wore my tightest black riding pants, proud of the way they fit. After a month-long diet, my stomach was flat and hard, my waist tiny and my butt swelled out like the women I'd seen posing in the movie magazines. I had borrowed a soft yellow sweater from Linda's drawer and wore my black cowboy boots with stitching up the sides. My hair was long, golden and fell to my shoulders in a pageboy. I was proud that I looked way older than my years. I was also developing breasts, and the week before Mam had sent me to town.

"Go to Russell's and have them fit you for a bra. Put it on the account."

"Lightly padded," the fussy lingerie lady had said, holding

it up by the straps. All the other girls at school made a big deal out of going with their mothers and getting bras. In gym they'd giggled and acted goofy, horrified by having saleswomen come in when they had their tops off. "She touched my booobie," they screamed.

Not only did I look older, but I acted older too and didn't have time to waste being silly. I just needed a bra and I had bought one. It was part of my new man-hunting equipment—like a show bridle was part of competitive horse show equipment. I'd also charged makeup and mascara to Mam's account. Walking out of the department store with the pink shopping bag, I carried all the tools to add the final touches to my re-creation. According to the image in the mirror, I'd done a good job.

On the long drive up the valley, Granddad pointed out the window at the cornfield framed by smoking blue hills. "See that stretch of field? The state just finished signing the papers on it. It'll be a different deal than our place."

"What? Expand past four lanes?" Mam looked up from her papers.

"The state will have a right-of-way lease, but the Henricks will be allowed to use the strip until the interstate has to expand again."

"Expand? That looks like a lot of state-owned property to me right now. And from what you said, the owners aren't going to get over it any time soon either. Especially the ones on original land claims. I'd be mad as a hornet too."

I read my new Nancy Drew and, raising my head occasionally to view the green and blue land, thought about the big carnival and what I'd do when we arrived. I loved the carnival lights, the hot mustardy smells, and warm safe livestock barns, the swirl of gypsy tents garlanded with noisy calliope music. Over the years, I'd made friends with the gypsies who ran the carnival games and that afternoon I hoped to see my good friend Madame Rose, the card reader. The summer before my trip to New York she had stood outside her tent smoking with her brother, Yannie. I'd been passing by and stopped. Intrigued by the mystery of her roomy tent and cryptic sign, I'd asked if she could really tell people what was going to happen to them. Squinting up at her, I'd asked what part of her head she used to do it.

She had grinned and invited me inside. From then on, I'd see her three or four times each summer. On seeing me approach and peer around the tent flap, she would rise, sweep the flap back and beckon me to enter. We'd eat bright pink and yellow cookies from a red tin with a picture of Jesus on top that she kept under her chair. I'd drape a fringy old scarf around my head, and sit in the dusty tent, eyes half-closed, while she read the cards, mostly for farm ladies, who paid fifty cents to have their fortunes told. I loved sitting in the dim, glowy tent watching her lay out the cards, dreaming to her whispery voice.

*

It was already hot and dusty at ten in the morning when we arrived at the capital and found our way through the tree-lined streets to the fairgrounds by the river. We had an official sticker on the windshield of the Mercury and drove through the yellowed fields of parked cars to a section near the entrance flagged for VIPs. At the fairground's office, my grandfather scooted his wallet from his pocket, peeled a five from a ruffle of bills and handed it to me. The manager of the fairgrounds, Joe, a skinny little gray man with sour breath who kept jumping up to get things for my grandmother, gave me a book of tickets for the carnival rides.

"You stay out of trouble, now," Mam said. "And don't spend all that money in one place," she added, peering out the window at the flower display building and adjusting her hat. "And don't eat so much you get sick again. Go over to the Creamery Association booth. Don Kesey's boys are putting on their magic show at 1:00. They're fun. You like them, and you'll get ice cream. We have a dinner at 7:30." She looked over at my grandfather, who sat on the edge of a desk holding the event schedule up close, studying it. "When shall we meet her, Dad?"

"Well, Grand Entry's at 1:30. Let's meet at the announcer's stand after that." He smiled at me from under his hat and crushed his cigarette into the ashtray.

*

At 1:30, I was watching Mam and Granddad from the top of the calf pens where I'd climbed to see them finish their ride around the arena in the long, fire-engine red convertible. I finished the dripping ice cream cone that Ken had given me after the magic show and wiped my sticky hands on the gate. The magic show had been fun, and Ken was cute—all that curly red hair and silly paper ice cream hat. He was a showoff, but so nice and funny I didn't mind.

The red convertible pulled up by the announcer's stand, directly in the path of a short dark cowboy wearing a white dress shirt, scuffed Levi's, and beat-up brown boots. The last time I'd seen him was the summer day at the Cow Palace when he and Bud threw their saddles in the trunk and headed for Texas. Now he stood by the steps to the announcer's stand helping another cowboy with his rigging. His name was Manuel, but the cowboys called him "the Basque," and next to Bud, he had been my favorite bull rider.

The summer I was six, I'd seen him get hooked by a bull's horn, but it only tore off his shirt, exposing a thickly matted, hairy back. Watching him limp from the arena that day I remember thinking he looked more animal than man with his wolf-smile, hunched, hairy back exposed, his Stetson mashed like crumpled horns onto his balding head.

I was so unexpectedly glad to see someone from happier times that I jumped down from the calf pen, ran up and threw my arms around him. He reared backward, hat rocking on his shiny head. I kissed his cheek. But he still didn't remember and kept looking at me with sparky black eyes. So, I told him who I was. He reached down, took hold of my behind with both his big, hard hands and jerked me against the front of him, and, laughing, held me tight. I could see his wide teeth, smell his sweat, and the whiskey, and feel the heat of his body. I'd never felt sexual excitement with a man before, but I knew about sex because I'd made it my business to find out. I also knew what it was to have someone's hands on me in a way I didn't like. So, I knew.

This was different. It felt good to be held so tight; I liked his smell and moved easily into his hard warmth. I moved away when he pressed against me, because while I liked it, I knew it shouldn't be happening. When I struggled, he laughed again, and slapped me on the behind.

"You're gonna give Linda a run for her money, kid."

Mam was advancing on the arena gate, a throng of men trailing her, suitcoats slung over their shoulders.

"Manuel," she said, acknowledging him, walking queen-like through the gate, "draw a good bull?" She motioned me up the stairs. "Come on and sit up in the announcer's stand with us."

In the high whitewashed stand where only the announcer and the timekeepers usually sat, I waited for her to finish talking to everyone. As the loud clowns left the arena, she dropped her head and humming under her breath, studied the clipboard. Granddad was standing against the railing talking to a man who had ridden in the red Cadillac with them. Both men were holding cigarettes, dumping the ashes in their cuffs of their pants because they weren't supposed to be smoking in the announcer's booth. The man with Granddad must have been important because Mam had introduced him to me with a great big smile, as Mr. so and so, giving the cocked eyebrow, the 'aren't *we* important' look. The men moved to the bench, where Granddad sat, one hand cupping his cigarette, the other tapping the toe of his boot with the program, occasionally using it to wave away the small, sticky flies. Granddad and the man were still talking about the grand new state road soon to be built.

The man said, "Well, Marshall, I hope I can expect your support for the next stage. It will mean a lot for the town, and that property will be worth a fortune in twenty years."

I leaned over close to Mam and whispered. "I was so happy to see Manuel, I ran up and hugged him, and he put his hands on my rear end and squeezed me up against the front of him."

She looked out from under her cat glasses as if she might say something, but the announcer gestured to her. Rising, she walked to the silver microphone, and as he introduced her, the microphone squealed, and the crowd started to clap and holler. She stood waving, a small cameo against the hot blue sky, then made a short, echoing speech about why she should be the next governor.

"Most of you know us, and we know most of you. You know the family. We've been in Oregon since it became a territory in 1846, and you know what we stand for. I think you also know that I won't let you down. I'll get things done. And we've got a LOT of work to do, friends. Tell your neighbors. A vote for Jessie Woodward Chapman is a vote for Oregon."

Loud hollering and clapping rose from the grandstands. Then, smiling and happy, she sat beside me on the bench.

"Well?" I said.

Fussing with her purse, gathering her clipboard, she

gestured to Granddad. "Well, what?"

"About Manuel."

"Oh," she said, digging in her purse, "Manuel doesn't mean anything by it, any more than any man does. You're getting big now. You're going to have to get used to it. Just don't pay any attention."

I looked at my grandmother. I heard what she said. Holding onto her purse, she gestured to the man sitting with Granddad. "That's the Governor. That's Elmo Smith," she whispered, raising her eyebrows, peering at me as though she expected a response. I watched carefully as she held the gold tube in front of her mouth, screwing up the red lipstick, no longer paying any attention to me.

I left Mam and Granddad outside the roaring arena and went to the carnival arcade where I slipped a dollar's worth of dimes into the flaming juke box. Paul Anka sang "Diana," over and over, while I played the clacking pinballs, hitting the box hard with my hips, flirting with some high school boys from Salem. Later, I went into a bright booth, smiled into the flashing mirror, and took my own picture. I look like I'm about sixteen, golden hair waving to my shoulders, eyelids at half mast, the heavy makeup seeming to weight them, lips full and blatantly provocative.

Toward evening, I left the arcade and wandered through the loud carnival midway heading in the general direction of Màdame Rose's tent. I found myself behind a cool-looking couple wearing matching yellow and white striped shirts, his hand casually around her waist, a ruby-eyed skull glaring from the ring on his finger. Over her shoulder, its all-seeing eyes looking right at me, rested a giant pink panda wearing a baby blue neck ribbon.

To my right rose the loud yellow wall of the Octopus ticket booth. It was my favorite ride, and I handed the tall boy at the gate a couple of tickets. "Pick the car that's the best twirler?"

Smiling, he looked down at me and my book of passes then let a couple enter ahead of me. "Wait," he said. "The fastest one's eleven." Touching my arm, he pointed to a car high on top of the ride.

After fastening the bar over my lap, he patted me on the leg and gave the car a spin. He stood looking up at me as the car circled on its giant arm and took off into the evening sky. High above the carnival in the dark and twirling silence I closed my eyes and felt the warmth and solidness of Manuel's body.

After giving me an extra ride, the boy let me out of the car then walked after me.

"It's dinnertime," he said. "You wanna corndog? I'll buy."

Rudy was tall and copper skinned, with long black hair almost to his shoulders, but his clothes were good for a carnie. His suede jacket was a little rumpled, the black slacks a bit dirty, and his boots, once good, were wearing thin. He had long copper colored eyes, and red, heavy lips that I thought were beautiful. As we walked among the food tents, I wondered what it would be like to have his arms around me, to have his hands on me, like Manuel's.

We ate our corndogs leaning up behind the concessions in the dusty evening shade. He laughed at me when I told him I was still in school, then dropped his arm around my shoulder. We threw our sticks and napkins in the trash.

"Come see my truck," he said, gesturing to the rear of the carnival.

It was already close to seven, but Mam and Granddad would be at the dinner for a long time, and with all the excitement neither one would come looking for me. We started walking past the cries and the wires and the drifts of trash, to the back of the carnival where they parked the generators and trailers.

I already knew I was going to let him kiss me. Since that

afternoon with Manuel, I'd wanted something to happen. I liked the way Manuel had looked at me, and the way Rudy treated me—like I was grown-up.

Rudy's truck was huge. "Give me a boost onto the step?"

Inside I found myself on a wide seat overlooking an expanse of dash covered with rags, assorted papers and hand tools. It was much cleaner than the floor where candy wrappers, crumpled chocolate milk containers, a carton of Pall Malls, rolled socks, and a can of shaving cream were scattered about. His clothes, hanging like skinny bodies in the back window, smelled both fruity and dusty.

Rudy jumped in from the other side and patted the seat next to him. I scooted over as he reached under the seat for a tall bottle. We sat side by side passing it back and forth. Uncle Jack and the other cowboys gave me beer all the time, but this was stronger, and sour. It sat harshly on my tongue, but I didn't want to say anything because I thought if I objected, I'd look young and silly.

He covered my whole mouth with his when he kissed me. It was wet and different than I thought it would be, but I kissed back the best I could, because just the idea of kissing excited me.

I ended up wedged against the truck door with Rudy nuzzling my face with his wet, red mouth, making noises in his throat. He slid his hand under my sweater, his fingers inching along my ribs then nipping at the elastic edge of my bra. I tried to move, mostly because I didn't want him to feel the padding, hardly daring to think of what else he might feel. He kept his mouth over mine until I shifted to right myself.

"Okay, okay," he said, lifting his head, moving his hand.

I tried to sit up, thinking we'd talk, and then maybe kiss some more when his long hands clutched my hips. He dove face-first between my legs, licking me with his hot tongue, and rubbing himself against my leg like a dog. He held me hard and when I struggled, he tightened his grip. When I tried to lunge away, he bit down hard, between my legs. It sent a shock from my core to the top of my head, a sensation that brought me right into the moment, and there was nothing else. I'd been kind of kidding around until then, but when I hollered "quit" and he wouldn't, it didn't scare me. It made me mad.

With my free hand, I felt for the bottle, got a solid hold on the neck, and smacked him over the back of the head. He howled and let go of me with his teeth, but raised his hand to hit me, so I smacked him again, as hard as I could. The bottle broke across his face, and spilled red all down his front. Over he fell, hand to his dripping head. Bracing against the door, I kicked like a wild dog was after me, my flying bootheels connecting with a thunk to his head, then jumped from the truck and ran.

I felt my feet rise from the twirling earth and didn't look back or settle to the ground until I was on the screaming midway. My only thought was that I didn't have time to go to the gypsies because I was already late to meet Mam. I floated with the crowd until I found my breath and made sure he wasn't behind me. In the overflowing arcade bathroom, I tried to arrange my hair and wiped the mascara from under my eyes with a wet bit of toilet paper. Swiping at the dark wine stain on the sleeve of the yellow sweater only dulled it, did not make it disappear. I'd tell Mam my snow cone spilled. On leaving the toilet block, I bought cotton candy from a sweet-smelling wagon and hurried through the rowdy crowd of jostling bodies and heady scents to find Mam and Granddad, shoving the sticky stuff in my mouth to take away the sharp smell of wine.

*

On the ride home in the dark back seat, I dreamed another ending to the episode. I dreamed the red mouth and the long copper eyes fusing with the warmth and smell of Manuel. In the humming dark, head against the cool glass, pressing my hand between my legs, I could still feel the wetness, some from his mouth, some from me and for the first time that I could remember, I felt powerful. The feelings in my body thrilled me. They were all new and all mine.

Tuesday night at dinner, Mam asked Granddad if she should say anything in her final County Fair report about the problem with the carnies. I'd come in from the barn and was washing up in the back bathroom when I caught the tail end of the conversation.

"What's the deal?" I asked, taking my place at the turquoise bar where we ate when there were only the three of us.

"Some carnies got into it the other night at the fair," she said. "One of the guys, Rudy something, was missing from his ride. When they went to look for him, they found him out cold in his truck. He'd been beat up bad enough they had to send him to the hospital with a caved in head; God knows what over." She reached behind her, lifted the clipboard from the counter, and wrote a note on her big yellow pad. It read: Call Gladys about the pig barn. "He's still out colder than a wedge. Can't have the papers making a fuss about this. People will keep their kids away from the fairs."

"Probably one of those damn gypsies," my grandfather said. "The carnie boss said the kid was a troublemaker, anyway."

I stared down at the huge, Texas-sized T-bone on my plate that had once been part of one of Grandad's red cows. I remember feeling that what had happened would show. The suspicion ballooned so large; I knew that if they looked at my face, they would see what happened in the truck. If I wasn't careful to mask my thoughts and do everything as I normally did, they'd know.

I ate the entire steak, slipped the bone to Buddy, excused myself, and went into the living room where I watched an old war movie on Evening Classics Theater. The movie was about this kid who went off to war and left his girl, and then she died, not him. The movie ended with a close-up of him looking into the camera, supposedly at her dead face in her coffin. He was crying. I still remember whole speeches and scenes from that movie.

Later, I wanted to tell someone what had happened in the truck, but I couldn't. Who could I tell? I could not imagine telling Mam or Granddad, and Linda probably wouldn't have believed me anyway. Well, that's not quite true. I had imagined telling Mam and Granddad, but the results of such an interview were finally too disturbing to contemplate—especially the part where I'd try to tell Mam. So, unable to trust them with my secret, I was on my own.

I never did find out what happened to Rudy. The events of that night took on the same mantle as a dead body, and I buried it deep as if it were murder. Then like deaths that are not mourned, and no funeral held to reassure the living, the specters come alive in dreams. When that happened, and it happened too often to suit me, I would reassure myself by recasting the incident as a story, only a story that never really happened. And I've never told anyone, until now.

Chapter 19

WHAT THE WHITE DIARY REVEALS

ARMITAGE HOUSE, MAY 7, 1999

Forcing myself back to packing, I had just popped the lid on a dusty cardboard box that someone, maybe me, shoved under the narrow bed in the downstairs bedroom. It was full of diaries, magazine articles, report cards and programs from 1957 and 1958 when I was twelve and thirteen. On top of the stack was a small lock and key affair, a white pebbly cover with gold script spelling "Diary." It was pliable and grubby—well used. Inside, the loopy handwriting looked neater than my present scrawl. The diary began after the divorce from Slick Willy when Linda bought that damned glass house, made me leave the ranch again and go live with her. Cold glass box. I detested it.

OCTOBER 1957

I'm bored. Linda is out with John, and I have to stay in the new glass box by myself because Mam and Granddad are in—well, they said south of the border. I guess they'll see nice places because they're staying with horse racing people and Mam took her fancy dresses, so there will probably be lots of parties. Mam made sure Granddad took his white coat too even though he said he didn't think he'd need it. This house is freezing, and Linda says I can't turn up the heat because it costs too much. I do it anyway. She says oil is expensive because of the Suez Crisis which is happening somewhere called the Middle East. Tonight, even the dog is shivering, and he has a real fur coat. Everything in this house is bare, and I'm always freezing. She says if it's cold I should put on more clothes because oil is too expensive. I'm already wearing two wool bathrobes (hers and mine) and the big fuzzy red slippers Mam gave me. Any more clothes and I wouldn't be able to move.

I'm supposed to be doing arithmetic tonight, but I can't. I don't know how, and I don't see why I should. Who cares about long division, and when will I ever have to do it anyway? Linda says that I can have a birthday party, but I don't know who would come. It's not for a while yet but I don't know any kids here. The neighbor girls, Karen and Patty, are two years older than me and go to junior high and made fun of me when I walked past Patty's front yard. They were playing tetherball on the lawn, but according to them, I'm too short to play. They don't believe I have a horse. Mam says that as the crow flies, Linda's new house is only five miles from the ranch, but it's too far to walk.

NOVEMBER 10, 1957

Well, now I am in trouble. Linda isn't talking to me, and neither is Mam. After school last Friday I hid in the bathroom until the bus left. I found Mr. Schultz in our room sitting at his desk and told him I'd missed my bus.

"I'm staying at my grandparents, but they won't be back until late, and my mother has a contract starring in a rodeo in South America. Will you give me a ride home? Please?"

Mr. Schultz looked up from his papers and smiled. "Where?"

"Mam says it's three miles. You just go down the road and turn toward the river. It's across Johnsons' cornfield by the big wheat fields."

"I can probably do that." He rose from behind the desk arranging his papers. "How about you finishing the sink and the boards. Have to stop and tell Mrs. Arnold, or we'll be in trouble." When we got to the ranch, I took Mr. Schultz to the barn to see Lady. In the drive, after looking at Granddad's gardens, he turned and looked at the mountains across the river. He shook his head and asked me to please save time to do my arithmetic for Monday.

When he drove off, I slipped Lady's bridle over her head and started off across Johnsons' brown field west of us, guessing that when we finally came to the fence, we'd find a way through. By the time we found the gate it was cold, the sky green-edged where the sun was moving below the dark field. It was shivering cold and smelled of winter, of rushes, hedgerows mulched in musty straw, of dark earth with a crust of frost. The hardest part was going over the highway overpass. Lady didn't like it—AT ALL. Her hooves clanged up the cold pavement like a blacksmith's hammer and cars coming toward us blazed their lights in our eyes, a couple honking like fools. We came down the far side, cut through the empty school playground, jumped another ditch, and rode right past Patty's house but she wasn't outside. Damn!

Almost at the driveway of the glass house, I had realized that Linda would probably have something to say about me riding Lady to her precious new house. What could I say? Lady got loose, they found her on the road, and I had to get her and take her to Linda's? She was almost downtown; we were too tired to go all the way to the ranch and...because...we were hungry?

I lucked out because her car wasn't there. In the driveway, I slid from Lady's steaming back to the cold ground, dragged her rubbernecking through the carport then across the patio to the back corner of the long yard. The new cedar trees that Linda planted when we moved in formed a small dark hedge between her yard and the neighbors. I tied Lady to one of the slim trees. When she took a chomp off the top of one, I untied her and let her loose. Since Linda didn't like to mow it, the grass looked long enough to keep Lady in dinner and breakfast. I went in the house to see if there was anything for me to eat besides toast. It was after six and completely dark, when Linda came home to get ready for her date with big John. She was late already and in such a hurry that she didn't even notice Lady.

"Hurry up and grab your stuff." Linda had changed into her pink sheath and was rushing around gathering my clothes. "And get a nightgown. We need to get there before they eat. There's nothing here."

I was sitting on the couch watching the news. They were talking about the new H-bomb and how it would blow the socks off the A-bomb. I didn't move.

"I'm taking you to Mae's. Now, come on."

"If you do, I'll leave." I picked up the Time magazine on the table, opened it, and stuck my nose to the page. Underneath a gray and black picture, the caption: "Israeli planes invade Egypt." According to Aunt Elsie, another sign of the end.

"Oh, Annie. It will be fun for you. Better than staying here alone."

"It's Rin Tin Tin and Frank Sinatra tonight. I'll eat popcorn. I'm not going over there, and you better call me Liz, or I won't talk to you."

She looked at the ceiling. When John's headlights swept around the circular drive, she hurried out without looking back.

Linda must have been out late because she slept late the

next morning. I woke at seven, jumped into my clothes, and rushed out to find Lady nibbling on the side lawn. I left Linda a note on the kitchen table.

> LaVetta came and got me on her way back from town. I'll be over at Margie's.
>
> Liz

I quietly led Lady from the yard then trotted her across the street where I tied her to Patty's tetherball pole. I climbed the steps and pounded on her front door. Mrs. McGarry opened the door, looked down at me, and then at Lady.

"Will you get Patty? I have to show her something."

"Well, you're the new neighbor girl, aren't you? Now, is your grandfather the Chapman that has the bank?"

"Yes, but my mother's the trick rider." She looked down on me through massive glasses that made her eyeballs appear huge.

"A TRICK rider?"

"You know, they do tricks on the horse . . ." No gleam of understanding in the huge gray eyes . . . "when it's running. At the rodeo? Is Patty awake?"

Patty, hair down, chubby legs stuffed into pedal pushers, her already bosomy top covered by flannel pj's, appeared behind her mother.

"I do have a horse. I brought her so you could see. Can you come out?"

Patty scrambled past her mother and stood on the porch looking at Lady who was more interested in their grass than in them.

"Come down and pet her."

She stood still and stared. "Uhhh, I , I don't . . . it's big."

"Yeah. And her name is Lady, and I don't lie. It's my motto!!"

"Motto?"

"It means it's my saying to go by."

"I KNOW what it means. MY mother is a schoolteacher."

"Oh. Do you like horses?"

"We think animals are dirty... but... this one is... okay."

Lady wrapped her lips around a tall plume of grass and wrenched it from the base of the tetherball pole.

Patty's eyes bugged and she swooped down the steps. "Don't let it pull my pole over." She looked back at her mother who still stood in the open door, her mouth drawn down at one corner, up at the other.

"I have to go anyway. I have to take her back to the ranch. Gimme a boost?"

I showed Patty how to hoist me up.

Standing close at Lady's side, Patty reached out and touched her on the neck. "Oh, kid! She's soft."

Bare feet planted on the path surrounding her tetherball pole, she watched Lady and I prance down the street toward the overpass.

At the ranch, I turned Lady into her paddock. Watching her run to the other horses, kicking and bucking with happiness at being home, I felt relief that we hadn't been found out. I also felt a surge at my center; I'd shown the neighbor kids that I was somebody.

That afternoon, I was sitting at the table with LaVetta and Margie, browsing through snapshots of their last mountain trip. Margie was handing them to LaVetta, who trimmed the pictures into shapes, fit them into her new album, and labeled each one with white ink in a beautiful flowing script that I wish were mine. The phone under the window rang.

"Annie (LaVetta will call me Liz, but she usually forgets), can you answer that?"

And it was you-know-who!! Linda wanted to come get me right then.

"You stay right there." Voice rising, "I'm coming to get you." Growling, "I'm leaving the house right now."

There were two things I hadn't counted on. Uncle Jack—always watching out his damned window—and horse poop. The horse poop gave me away. Without it, Uncle Jack could never have proven where we'd been, only that he'd seen me riding Lady. That afternoon, Jack stood on his porch, a soggy cigar clamped in his jaw, telling Linda that he'd have me arrested if I ever went to Mam and Granddad's again when they weren't home.

Read All About It! My most recent crime was Jack's first news broadcast when Mam and Granddad came home from Mexico.

Linda wailed that I'd ruined her lawn. "Lady left hoof marks all over my grass. What if the neighbors report me for having a horse in a residential neighborhood? No horses allowed, Annie." Sob, Sob, Sob. . .

NOVEMBER 18, 1957

Linda's going to marry Big John at Christmas. I knew it. She's been working hard on him. Better for her to be married than to lay around her bedroom crying all the time. Mam thinks it's a good idea because she says she's sick and tired of paying the bills. There's a big engagement party here next weekend. Big John's nice enough and I like him well enough. He takes me with them sometimes, and he helped me do long division. He's better than Slick Willy. He has a lot of money, and that's good, but Mam says it's not the right kind of money, because he's in sales, and that's trashy. But she guessed everyone had to make a living. Linda said he has two full closets of nice suits and two cars. One is a black work car because he's a division manager, and the other one is a pink Chrysler with long tail fins, and he can turn the wheel with his little finger. He's not that handsome though, and he's a little fat in the stomach, but he's really tall. Six foot four.

Today after school, Karen went to the dentist with her mother, so Patty and I got cigarettes out of John's sample cases and smoked. It was terrible. I almost puked and so did Patty. It's probably because we ate toast with globs of honey on it before we smoked. We'll try again.

DECEMBER 1, 1957

A lot has happened and I'm still sick from it. The engagement party was last Saturday night and everyone was here. Lots of John's friends, the ladies wore furs, and everyone was all dressed up, but they were nice to me. Linda had been tearing around like a demon fixing everything up. As if she could ever fix it up. She'd have to throw out everything and start over. With all this glass, and without curtains, the house is cold, and she has stickery grass mats on the floor, and then Mam and Grandad's old sofa (she says she nursed me on it!!) from the house on the hill—the pinkish one with the blond legs. Anyway, Linda bought a turquoise plastic chair, so we'd have more places for people to sit. She thinks it's really neato. I think it isn't.

The night before the party Mam came over and brought a whole bunch of party stuff. Mam waited in the kitchen, and when Linda and Granddad were outside, she stood in the middle of the doorway and cut me off.

"Don't you think it would be nicer if you called your mother Mom, or Mommy, or something? You can't call her Linda anymore."

"Jeez!! Make up your mind."

She glared at me until I thought she would say something

more, then went stalking off to the car. She's still mad at me for taking Lady out, so she didn't have to go far to be really mad.

Oh, get this! Bobby's brother, Joe, saw me at Margie's and asked me to go to the basketball game at the high school. Margie didn't tell him I'm only in Jr. high. He's in the second year of high school and he has a driver's license! He kind of looks like Ricky Nelson. He's really, really cute, black hair and green eyes!! The game was the same night as the big engagement party, and I thought they'd throw a fit about me going, but they didn't. Granddad told Mam he knew Joe's father and they were good people. Joe was to come pick me up at the party.

At the party, they had already had ordurves, or however you spell it, and were having more drinks. I asked if I could be the bartender, and John's friend, Sally—Mam called her Miss Peroxide Bottle—showed me how. I mixed the drinks and took them to people. Then I quit using the little glass and just poured it in. Every time I fixed a drink for someone, I had to try it. I tried Sally's Tom Collins, John's Scotch (Yechh!), the champagne they toasted with, a screwdriver, a martini (but I didn't make it, and it tasted like gas). The one I liked best was Aunt Virgie's bourbon and Coke. That was good, and I had a whole one for myself. Later, when I went into the bathroom, I saw Uncle Jack in the hallway trying to get the dentist's wife to kiss him. And he saw me too.

When Joe came, I was kind of dizzy, but no one noticed. At the game I was so sleepy I couldn't see the players very well. Then the whole place started to blur, and I thought I was going blind or something. He had to almost carry me down from the bleachers. (I don't think he'll want to take me anywhere again), but I didn't throw up until I got outside.

He took me to Mam and Granddad's because Linda and John were going dancing, and by then I felt worse than I've ever *felt in my life, and the floor was spinning like a record. I don't remember much after that, but Joe called Sunday to see if I made it. Mam answered and said in her snooty, nasty voice, "No one here named Liz."*

He called back right after my quiz show because he knew I'd be in the living room watching, and I answered. He told me what happened when he took me home, but he only hauled me to the door, so he was out of it before the real mess started. He was there long enough for Mam to accuse him of getting me drunk and then she threatened to call his parents!! From the bits I remember, after he left, I puked all over my new black sweater, and cussed Mam out when she was trying to wash me off in the tub. She told Linda I cussed her up one side and down the other. The worst is that I don't know what train my cussing took. I probably used all the cusswords I'd ever heard the cowboys use even if I don't know exactly what they mean, so I guess it was pretty bad. Mam has her feelings hurt "beyond repair," and does not want to talk to me. Granddad is upset too. Later, I woke up in the dark, in the middle of the night, had to drink a gallon of water then I threw up again in the kitchen sink. Puking in the sink in the dark was pretty bad.

BUT! Mam isn't telling, because she does not want to spoil Linda's wedding.

DECEMBER 7, 1957

Today is the anniversary of the day the Japanese bombed Pearl Harbor, and Mam and Granddad have gone to a big party with all their political people. I've been camping out at Linda's because Mam's still furious and won't let me come to the ranch. But Linda is always with Big John, so I can do what I want, I just can't ride or go to Margie's unless Margie comes to get me. She doesn't come much because she and Bobby broke up and she has a new boyfriend. He's older and just came back from the navy. Edward said he'd been in Korea—which I discovered is over by China and Japan. I haven't seen him yet.

Joe keeps calling me. Surprise. . .!! We talk on the phone a lot. I guess he's pretty smart because he tells me about school. He likes school!! Maybe I'll like it when I get to high school, but I doubt it. The other night he read me a poem!! (recited—he was practicing) It was weird, but cool. Stone walls do not a prison make, or something, something a cage. I forgot who wrote it but it's about having freedom in your soul (mind??), and I think it meant that no one can take freedom away from you no matter what they do to you. He read the whole thing then read one called The Highwayman, and that was about a robber back in England, but it was good, with lots of galloping around on horseback. Joe told me that they were learning about something called the Renaissance—and he spelled it for me. He said he'd decided to be a Renaissance Man . . . This sounded weird; "Be serious!" I said.

He said he was serious, and then he told me what a RM was. It means that he would know a lot. He would be good at dancing (I'm good at dancing), learning ideas, and about art (I'm already good at this), sports like fencing and especially riding (good at the riding part), and have really good manners (Mam says I don't have any).

"I want to be one too," I told him.

"A man?" He started laughing.

"No! But I want to be good at all that."

I think I am one anyway, because I can do almost all those things. I don't like school, but I like to know things. I don't know about the manners. They all say you need good manners, but they don't say why.

p.s. Linda joined a church and signed me up. She says I have to go there every Saturday morning until June and learn church rules—yawn, yawn, yawn.

p.p.s. I bet I don't get one single tiny thing for Christmas.

SPRING 1958—AFTER MY BIRTHDAY

"...the white cup shrivels round the golden heart."
Rossetti, "Barren Spring."

Last night, Joe snuck behind the hedge, cut through the laurel and came across the yard into my red bedroom. He was cold from the outside; I was warm from the bed. His cold jacket brushed against me as he leaned over. The outside scent of the cold night fields came with him, the winter ditches, the meadows of flattened grass, and the high cold stars. My nipples hardened as the coldness covered me, and he kissed me and wanted to get in bed but I wouldn't let him. Then he wanted me to sneak out and come with him to the car, but I didn't. He gave me a book of Rossetti's poems. I like some of them, but nothing seems to turn out very well, at least up to Sonnet 83 (when I quit), so I don't get why he gave me the book.

 I don't want him to be the first boy I _____ with. I want to keep him for my boyfriend because he likes me, not because he thinks he can _____. But I am realizing <u>that</u> is what boys want.

APRIL 6, 1958: EASTER

It's still raining. Saturday, I went to the stone church. Now I have to practice with the choir every Wednesday and go to the confirmation classes every Saturday morning. It's a real class, and the minister (he always wears a long black gown) teaches it, and we have to memorize prayers, and the Apostles' Creed. I told him I didn't think regular people had anything much to do with Bible people. He told me to read The Confessions of St. Augustine, *to get it from the church library. I'm reading it now. One of the girls in class told me I should read* 7th *Corinthians* because that's where it talks about the kind of sin I'm interested in. I had been very interested in sin last Saturday when that was the subject of the day, but there hadn't been time to answer all my questions. I wanted all the rules so I would know how to get around them.

Last Sunday after church, I went to the coast with Joe and his folks. When we came to the top of the coast range the sun was silver in the west, hanging above the ocean, and the blue rain stood behind us. We're in a rainbow, I thought. On the way home, sitting in the backseat, I wanted him to kiss me. I pulled his arm so it almost touched my breast and slid my hand onto his knee. I looked up to see his dad staring at me in the rearview mirror. I couldn't remember if you could see the back seat in the rearview. Maybe if you were tall . . .

Yesterday, Joe said that when school starts next year, he's going away to get ready for college. Mam wonders how farmers can afford prep school. I'll miss him. I really like kissing him.

TUESDAY, APRIL 14, 1958

I'm in my red and black bedroom playing Elvis records—I've played "Old Shep" about 20 times and cry every time. In school, I am doing a report on the Jews that died in the concentration camps during the war. Sometimes the Germans made lightshades out of the dead people's skin, and nobody could stop them. At first, I couldn't believe this. But it happened. I saw pictures. No wonder everybody wanted to move to America. Religion class makes me think even more about dying. I don't think I'm afraid. I guess the worst thing ever would be to die. So, now when something bad happens I'll think, well it could be worse, I could be dead. Then things will seem better. What would be worse? To die? Or not face it? I think I'd better face it now and get it over with. I want to always be ready. I don't want to die in a panic. I don't want to die in horror of my death. I don't think it will be like that though. But, okay, being torn to bits, that would be a very bad way to go—eaten by a shark or fish. Then having something fall on you and smother you—you couldn't draw breath. Head explodes. Awful, but what could you do? Should you fight, or relax and let it happen? If you relaxed, would that be cowardly? Then if you died, would that be the end of it? Or what if you had to go to heaven, and then you had to start learning new rules all over again? I think it's important to decide what I think about this. I asked Patty and she says she doesn't think about it, and why would I want to? Margie says she's thought about it, but not much. She thought it would be bad to smother but hates fire worse.

I sort of like church classes because I'm learning a few things about Martin Luther who was a rebel of the church, and about God's ten rules that were written with lightning on stones. (I'm supposed to make flash cards for them!) I wouldn't call it fun, but I don't mind. I notice there are as many kinds of church people as different kinds of dish soap. In the area of my improvement, it's the dance lessons that are fun. On Thursday nights, Granddad drives me to town, to the Knights of Columbus Hall. Seventh grade through high school, twenty of us. Granddad goes to the Elks and drinks bourbon while he waits, but I'm not to tell Mam.

The music is good, and I guessed we might be doing some real dancing because the first record he played was "Money Honey" with the good horn solo. The teacher brings 45s and his girlfriend plays them while he counts off the steps. The boys and girls line up on opposite sides of the basement. That was horrible the first time. I just stood there with all these weird kids I didn't know. Everyone has to dance with the person across from them even if they are less than choice. I've learned the two-step, cha-cha, waltz, and polka so far, and he says we'll *all be doing the swing by the time we go to the dance at the end of the classes. Mam says Linda will make me a twirling skirt. I want it to be white.*

p.s. Jim is my partner for the dance. He's the best dancer in class, and nice too, but he's older, Joe's age. Standing in line when we met, he asked me what I'd done to have to take dance lessons. I should ask him the same.

p.p.s I heard on the news that Mr. Genius from the quiz show Twenty-One *was a big liar and knew all the questions before the show. How could all the television people lie? How could everyone believe them? Mam said it was the eggheads fault, that egghead intellectuals are all liars, like the devil Adlai Stevenson.*

Chapter 20

HOW THE WHITE DIARY ENDS, AND WHAT ANNIE LEARNS ABOUT RON AND MARGIE

EMERALD VALLEY, JUNE 1958

I went out with Margie at dawn yesterday morning. We brought pillowcases full of sandwiches and apples and tied them around our waist. We wore short shorts and sleeveless shirts and went barefoot, so we were chilly in the morning, but I knew that on the way home, riding into the sun, I'd be glad I hadn't worn jeans. School has been out for a while, and we decided to ride the eight miles to Harrisburg Junction and back with a stop at the river. Mam said to stay over with Margie. I figured we'd be home by dinner, but it wouldn't matter if we weren't home by dark. We know the way and so do the horses.

And here the diary entries end with lots of blank pages remaining at the back. But I remember that day in June, and certainly recall all that happened and proceeded from it...

*

That summer morning, we led the horses up to the fence and leapt onto their warm backs. Short-legged, reddish Gypsy and black and white Lady were a good pair of walkers. They kept up with each other, but Lady liked to lead, so Gypsy pushed her, and we had covered a lot of ground by the time the sun came over the rim of McGowan Creek hills. We hadn't talked but as the sun rose higher, we began advancing our aims of the day. I'd been feeling lonely after being in all the trouble and then being banished from the ranch to Linda's. I was finally back at Mam and Granddad's. I had achieved my aim by maintaining steady pressure on Linda (being a pain in the ass in all transactions), to release me from her prison and let me go back to the ranch. So, she had been letting me go. Mam had seemed to relent; Granddad seemed to agree with having me home, and even though I *was* contrite, no one brought it up. I never found the courage to apologize for my lapse, and nothing more was said.

On my first day back, I had stood at the top of the steps leading to the red bedroom holding a duffel bag full of clothes. Everything was just the way I'd left it: my trophies, my good books, Granddad's whiskey decanters filled with jewel-colored water. I didn't want to go back to Linda's at all. My life there had been flat as her humor.

Turning the horses down the tractor road along the river, I thought about my agenda for the ride that day. I planned to talk to Margie about my problems locating a husband and find out what was happening with her and her boyfriend. Margie, my model. Margie with the interesting life. Margie, who seemed to grow prettier every day and had boys around all the time—like ants marching to the ripest thing in Linda's kitchen. And there was the mysterious new boyfriend. I had kept telling her I wanted to meet him, but it hadn't happened. Always before, she had given me the details about her boyfriends and what they did on dates, but since she'd met this new guy, she didn't.

After my enforced exile to Linda's and seeing the wild commotion, the tactics, the clothes, the makeup of a manhunt,

I'd been thinking even more about it. And I wanted to talk to her about it. Hunting a man...

"You'll find another boyfriend," Margie said after I'd told her I thought I'd never have another one now that Joe couldn't come over. "Look how pretty your hair is, and those eyes! You'll have lots of boyfriends. Besides, I'm old enough to have boyfriends. You're too young."

"Too young? You think I'm too young? I'm already smarter about it than Linda."

Margie laughed. She looked at the ground, skimming neon pink toes over the tips of the tall grass. She hunched over; her arms curling the red horse's chest. Margie's shape resembled pictures I'd seen in schoolbooks of a fetus curled in the womb.

"Have you done it yet?"

"Annie!"

"Well... What's wrong with that? I'm gonna do it as soon as I can. I want to know about it."

"We shouldn't talk about this... or I'm gonna have to tell Mom." She kicked Gypsy and they galloped ahead.

Tell her mother? I kicked Lady into a startled run and caught them in two breaths. "Tell meeeee," I hollered at Margie. I figured if practically everybody in the world did it, there was no reason I shouldn't. Was there? She leaned further over Gypsy's shoulder, kicked her in the ribs, and we raced down the side of the ditch.

We pulled the horses up under the stand of trees at the crossroads, then trotted into the dappling shade through the park and over the old railroad bridge that crossed the river. The newly tarred road was long and from the bridge appeared like a lazy black snake making its way between the gold and green fields. In Brownsville, halfway into our trip, riding abreast down the center of the road, we swung down Main Street and turned in at the wood frame store for Cokes. We said hi and waved to everybody even if we didn't know them and hoped the horses didn't let go on the sidewalk. Bobby's mother stood in the parking lot holding a bag of groceries, squinting into the sun at us. Margie yoo-hooed, causing all eyes to turn to the girl astride Gypsy, the beautiful face and figure, the long tanned legs ending in glowing pink toes.

"Tell Bobby hello for me," Margie called. His mom looked at us a minute too long before she answered. I doubted she'd be saying anything to Bobby about seeing Margie.

We circled the watching town and took the cow trail toward the foothills aiming to cross the narrow valley, ride over the McGowan Creek hills where we could see both rivers, drop down to McKenzie View to the meadows along the riverbank, then cross the bridge and go home through Calef's' cornfield.

I urged Lady to walk beside Gypsy. "Where we come out there above the bridge, isn't that where your new boyfriend lives?

"Who told you that?" Margie said, her back to me, not turning around.

"Only your mother. I want to ride by there and see him, Margie. How come he's some big secret?"

"He's no big secret. Okay!?"

"Then tell. What's wrong with him? Did you have a fight or something?"

I couldn't read the look she gave me. I was trying to unlock meaning in her hard penetrating stare, the shake of her head, when a branch hit me in the side of the face. I carried a welt from it for a week. Crossing the meadow, feeling the heat rising around us, I reflected on Margie's moodiness. She wasn't often short-tempered with me, but for the previous year she had been, sometimes for days, much more aloof and unpredictable. Before, she had talked to me about her boyfriends, and everything else, all the time. She was a talker. But, that summer, we'd sometimes go for long periods with her staring off in the distance, not even remembering I was around. My plan wasn't getting me the information I'd hoped for, so I temporarily put aside my quest for the scoop on her love life and just rode along under the hot sun, keeping the river in view. Untying our sacks, we ate as we rode.

Surrounded by the wild scent of the fields, we travelled out of the meadow, up the rocky trail, the afternoon sun beating our faces, the air alive with bird calls and insect buzzing, a thin breeze ruffling the dry grass. Above us, a pair of hawks circled toward us from the west. Moving slowly through the gold grass at the top of the hill, we stopped to take in the river coiling away from us. On the last leg of our ride, we lost sight of the water as we picked our way down the hill, then rode under a grove of dark oaks to the road. I trotted Lady across the pavement then pressed her down the steep graveled bank to the river.

"It's too hot to ride to the bridge," I hollered back at Margie. "I'm swimming across. C'mon." I banged Lady in the ribs with my bare feet and using my knees forced her into the water. The icy water slipping inside me made me gasp. Behind me I heard Margie yell, "Daddy said never . . . Annie, don't!"

But we were already in the river. Lady was swimming hard, her head stretched flat out, nose barely above water, me trailing the surface holding onto her mane. I turned my head to yell back and saw Gypsy slide stiff legged down the embankment into the water. The river was broad and flat, the surface rippling with white water under the bridge, darkly shadowed and quiet along the far edge where trees draped the bank. Lady was riding lower in the water, nose held high, and I was beside her swimming hard, but the river gained strength there and began dragging us toward the bridge. We struggled through the freezing river about halfway across, both of us running out of steam when Lady sank beneath the water, and I went with her.

She bobbed up, hooves thrashing, and I shoved off from her flying feet. The fierce set of her wildly fixed eyes told me she wasn't kidding around. She was heading for home with purpose. As she swam past me, I grabbed her tail and started kicking. Then she was rearing out of the water, climbing a shallow sand bar and slogging up the gravel bank, me tumbling after her. She stood trembling slightly, eyeing me, then shook like a dog and lay down and rolled in the shallows. I turned back to see Margie and Gypsy working their way out of the deep water, stretching for the bank. Gypsy was riding high in the water, eyes bulging with effort when she finally entered the shallows. As Gypsy's hoofs met sand, Margie raised herself from the water gasping like a big fish, long black hair plastered to the front of her. And as I often do when I have been afraid and have been saved, I started laughing.

"You better not say one word about this to Daddy. He knows this river," Margie panted, looking back at the water. "He'll—well, I don't know what he'd do," she said, struggling across the beach, leaving wet footprints on the warm rocks.

"We'll be dry by the time we get home. I won't tell, Margie. Don't be mad," I sputtered, wiping my face, trying to rearrange myself.

Margie looked at me from the side of her eye. A measuring look. "You weren't scared?"

I ignored the question, led Lady to a downed log and climbed back on.

Soon, we trotted past the deeply shaded entrance to the park and turned toward home, riding with the sun on our right where it was setting behind the corn field. A touch of evening chill goose bumped the top of our legs and arms. We could still smell the river and feel it in the air. Margie had to fight Gypsy because she always wanted to run toward home, and we were never to let them. It was a rule.

"Run then," Margie yelled, giving Gypsy her head and

socking her with both bare heels.

At that moment there was a roar behind us that kicked the horses into higher gear. Three explosive bangs, one behind the next caused the horses' nostrils and eyes to flare in fear. A midnight blue '57 Chevy, no chrome, lowered and modified, slid up beside us.

A fast-moving glimpse at the driver: a hook for a nose, dark skin, dark hair, grinning, laughing—henk, henk henk. Whether the henking noise was exclamation or a laugh, I couldn't make the choice given the roar of the car. The car slowed and paced us. Margie and Gypsy stopped by the side of the road, and the rumbling car cozied up to them. I had time to watch him as I rode toward them. He was stretched across the seat, T-shirt pulled tight over his tanned arm, neck craned upward, looking out the passenger window at Margie. Her shiny head was bent close to the open window. Ron looked good, not as handsome as Bobby (nobody was as handsome as Bobby) or Ben, but still okay. He was thin, and he was dark, his skin tan but with marks on his face like he'd once had bad acne. His nose was long, with a diamond-shaped bump on the bridge, skin stretched tight over high, sharp cheekbones and a thin mobile mouth. He had a big smile, and his teeth weren't crooked. His looks, raw and hard, instantly reminded me of pictures I'd seen of dustbowl farmers in *Life* magazine. And he looked older—almost as old as Margie's dad.

As I moved Lady closer to the car, he gunned the engine and growled down the road toward Margie's house.

"Don't worry. You're gonna meet him now. He's going to the house."

She didn't look happy about it, and I didn't get it. "What's wrong with him? He looks . . . nice."

She didn't answer, just a little wrinkle between her pretty black eyebrows. I didn't have time to dig for answers. By then, we were almost to the driveway where Ron stood with arms crossed before the ravishing car. Gazing into that dark blue surface was like looking into a black magician's mirror—deep, mysterious, possibly dangerous.

*

Later that evening, twilight laying dove-colored shadows on the wheat fields, house wrens rustling in the walnut trees, he came back. When he saw us both dressed to go, me in my new blue sundress, and Margie in her poodle skirt and halter top, he just smiled at Edward, then laughing his henk, henk, henkey laugh, crunched across the gravel drive to his exotic vehicle and opened the door. The sharp smell of warm walnut trees permeated the evening as we walked down the path to the car. Before slipping behind the wheel, he leaned against the dark top of the car, promising Edward and LaVetta we'd be back by 11:00.

Margie was quieter than ever while Ron held the door for us. I scooted in next to her. She sighed, half rolled her eyes, closed them and favored me with a tiny Hot Pink Revlon smile.

From my place, riding shotgun, Ron appeared, first a dark arm, then lean khaki leg, big foot encased in wingtips like Granddad's, then he slid in beside Margie and turned the single key that started Stroker. He eased it quietly, almost idling, around the circular drive, past the walnut tree and beneath the soaring fir limbs onto Armitage Road. The sense of power, of hard contact with the earth rose up from the road, through the car, and into me. I sensed an immediate kinship and sense of exaltation at the thought of the speed and freedom I might gain.

I had loved cars and driving since Granddad let me sit on his lap and steer the green truck, but the beauty of this dark blue 1957 Chevrolet, devoid of any chrome, sweeping down the road like it had a destiny of its own, was a revelation. A first. Like the first time I tried to defend myself against Mam, rode a horse, protected myself from Barbara, or took a new name, a change ran through my blood and bones in some inexplicable way that made me think of my life in wider terms. That particular indigo Chevy expanded my consciousness, and the immediate result of this expansion was like a supernatural anointing. It could mean faster progress, development, advancement, to change my rate of motion and get where I was going immediately. A place where rejection and opposition didn't follow. A place of freedom where I could think of something, and make it happen in the flash of an eye. Now!

Riding along savoring the feel of Stroker, and considering my new state, I thought about other cars I'd seen in town. Cars that had wandered up from California, mauve and purple, chopped, channeled and flamed, drooling with chrome, tiny black glass windows in the back and sides. We called them "low-riders" and I associated them with fast boys and faster girls, with Los Angeles and badness. They were modified show cars, Buicks, Lincolns, old Packards. They crawled up from hotter climates like exotic night bugs, and then they must have crawled back again because very few stayed around for long. Once at the drive-in with Ben, we saw a Canary yellow '37 Ford, big chrome pipes spouting from the engine like some kind of raucous kaleidoscopic pipe organ. Those cars were art, not built for a practical purpose. They were like the cowboy with the extra shiny boots, all hat and often no cattle. Ron's Chevrolet was built for speed. It was stripped down to bone, hopped up with hidden purpose—only deft silver pin-striping low on the driver's side front fender identifying "Stroker" as a force of change.

We cruised down Armitage Road, across the green bridge, and onto McKenzie Street, the main drag that runs north south. Downtown, Stroker rumbling at the stop light, I saw the reflection of the blue car in Woolworth's big plate glass window. My gold hair was pretty against the dark blue of the car. Ron saw me looking at myself and laughed, henk, henk, henk. Margie turned on the car radio, the Coasters' song "Searchin'" drifting from the open windows, she sat back, and Ron pulled her closer.

"Get me a cigarette out of my pocket there, honey, and light it for me?"

"I'm not lighting cigarettes." Margie looked straight ahead but didn't move from his arm.

"I will."

Margie glared at me. Ron patted her arm. She grumped and tsked, but reached into his pocket for the cigarette and handed it to me.

"Liz, your clothes'll smell. They'll know."

What Margie didn't know was that I had been practicing smoking a lot. Linda and John said it was okay as long as I smoked his brand, Marlboro, little sample packs of four which he kept stashed in a big box in his office closet. The more cigarettes people bought and smoked, the more money he made. Everywhere we went he passed out the little packs, then lit them for the smokers with a gold lighter with his initials engraved on the back.

I pushed the gleaming lighter on the dash and waited for it to pop. I lit the cigarette, a Pall Mall, and inhaled deeply. It was harsh, stronger than a Marlboro, but I didn't cough.

"Way to go, Liz," Ron said as I leaned over Margie and placed the cigarette in his mouth.

Almost to the end of McKenzie Street, Ron eased the car under the green and pink neon sign that spelled Dine and Dash in big lazy letters and onto the packed back lot. Ron held his hand up to a couple of guys in a turquoise and white '55 Chevy with gleaming chrome pipes running from the front wheels clear to the back. The car was spotless and almost as pretty as Stroker. In the back window I noticed a car club sign: a square silver plate; big, embossed letters spelling The Klan. The driver, a thick-bodied older guy wearing jeans and a white dress shirt, opened the driver side door and galumphed over to Stroker with a big grin.

"Ron, man, how's it hangin'? That beanerwagon showed up across the bridge. Are we goin' out to McGowan Creek tonight?

"Hey, Chuckie," Ron grinned and saluted him. "Cables at 11:30. We can go from there, but we don't want to leave together."

Carrying a tray, a tall waitress with red hair that curled under in a long, fat pageboy, strolled over to the window. The collar of her white shirt was pulled up to frame her face and the rest of her was encased in tight black and white striped shorts.

"Three Cokes." Ron glanced up at her as she started to clip the tray onto the window frame. "You new?"

Her lips were thick, the bottom one positively fat as a little pillow, painted a bright shiny red. "So?"

"Who's miss attitude here, Charlie?" Ron said.

Charlie looked at the waitress, shrugged and dropped his head, as if to say why ask me?

"So, we don't hang trays off Stroker, see?" Ron pointed to the gleaming paint. There wasn't a mark or a speck of dust on it.

I had to crane my neck to see the waitress's expression. Just then she leaned down and looked into the car, right in Ron's face. "What *do* you hang off your Stroker, Daddy?"

His neck bone bobbled, and his dark eyes flashed as they slid toward Margie. A streak of red ran from his neck up onto his dark cheek. I thought he was angry, but then he exploded into his henk, henk, henkey laughter, finally snorting through his nose and rearing his head back on the seat.

"You didn't say that, did you, Shorty?" He dug in his

pocket, dragged out a flurry of crumpled bills and tossed two onto the tray. Lots more money than the Cokes cost. "Got to respect the wheels if you're gonna last around here. Keep it."

Margie had been looking on without much interest. "This car is more important to you than anything," she said, voice flat, as though remarking on unexceptional weather.

I looked at her sitting there, her beautiful long black hair, voluptuous body and breasts, perfectly pink mouth and fantastic nails, and wondered how she could think Ron placed more importance on Stroker than he did on her. That was just ridiculous.

Unaware that we were watching, Ron and Charlie were observing the waitress saunter back toward the order window. She was big, she was tall, soft looking, almost chubby, but not. Ron's black eyes were bright as he gazed intently at her heart-shaped rear end. She turned and looked back at us, tossing her long red hair. Ron turned to Margie with a deeply creased smile, looking more handsome than ever.

"Well, now I've spent a lot of money on Stroker. I take good care of what's mine." He smoothed her skirt back from her knee and squeezed.

Margie sat up straighter, her face, her pursed lips, reminding me of LaVetta. She pulled her skirt down and looking over at me shoved his hand away.

I nudged her. *Why so contrary? She didn't act the same when she was around Ron.*

"I'll see ya later, then," Charlie said, starting for his car, then turning back. "Look for the beaner. Scope it out."

"We have to be home by eleven." Still sounding tired, Margie asked, "What's going on at McGowan Creek?"

"Drags. Midnight Nationals."

I'd been contemplating a possible new scrabble word. "What's a beanwagon, a beaner?"

"Them spic California dragsters, lowered all the way around, can't even go over a piece of gravel, their guts are so low to the road. There's a new guy up here from El Segundo, someplace down there, thinks he can win some pink slip races and clean up on us northern boys. He don't know us boys . . . Yet! Henk, henk, henkity, henk."

Margie closed her eyes.

When the tall redhead brought our Cokes, they were in paper cups that she took from her tray and passed to us. "Can't give ya glass if you won't use a tray."

"No sweat, Shorty. We've got to take off anyways." Ron caught my eye, winked. Now conspirators in some game I didn't understand. "This town's uptight," he said in a voice loud enough for the waitress to hear. Then to Margie, "We'll cruise Springdale, see if we can find Chuckie's beaner."

Stroker growled out of the parking lot, turned east, meandered up the hill then swooped down the back road past the palm reader's sign onto the broad industrial avenue that connected the two towns. The windows were down, the night soft and rich, the familiar daylight land now a mysterious otherworld of darkness and drama, where anything might happen. We passed the Emerald Club emblazoned in green neon, where Mam said no respectable person would ever be seen, and cruised slowly down the wide dark roads toward Tiny's, a drive-in that Ron said was the car club's main Springdale hangout.

"We'll meet up with some of the guys getting ready for the race tonight." Ron looked over at Margie who was sitting up straight staring directly in front of her, as though neither of us were there. "Ah, let's skip Tiny's for now. I'll just stop in at the store, here."

He pulled in under the tall light at M Street market, and parked.

As though he'd hear us if we spoke, we silently watched

him walk into the store.

"Margie," I hesitated. Sometimes when I tried to question her, she'd get so mad she wouldn't utter a solitary word but froze me out completely. I plunged ahead anyway. "You don't act like you're having any fun. What's wrong? Tell me."

She watched Ron walk down the aisle inside the store. Her hand went to her throat, and with her index finger pulled out a heavy ring hidden between her breasts, stretched the chain as far as it would go, and examined it closely. "I'm giving it back. This is all we do. He doesn't think of anything but this damn car and playing bigshot. I'm sick of his dopey laugh too."

"Margie! Be serious. This is the neatest car ever."

Margie's set expression dissolved, heat flooded her face, her whole body, her eyes welling with tears locked on mine. "I just don't love him," she said, and as if I hadn't heard her, she barked, "It doesn't matter what he does, I just don't love him." She was silent for a moment, then, "I tried."

The news drizzled into my unyielding brain. She obviously had the best boyfriend with the best car in town and she wasn't happy? What in the hell was wrong with her? I looked at her severe profile as she patted at her eyes, examining herself in the rearview mirror.

"Don't say anything. He's coming."

Ron exited the market, a six-pack swinging from each hand. I watched him walk toward the car. A rolling thin-hipped walk, a loose-coiled swagger, the cleats on his big shoes ringing against the asphalt.

"Don't you say anything to him, Liz, and no beer. Dad'll know."

❋

The beer was cold and sharp on my tongue, the fizz threatening to come back through my nose. I had opened the bottle on the door lock as I had seen Uncle Jack do often and hoped I wouldn't injure Stroker. Ron and Margie had taken the church key, and the other sixer, as Ron called it, to the river. I was supposed to wait in the car because they'd be right back. I tilted the bottle and drank it quickly, little streams running down the sides of my mouth. If they came back in a hurry, I wouldn't get caught.

Stroker was parked in a small clearing at the end of McGowan Creek Road, a little way from the river. I knew the place well. Margie and I rode here in summer to the good sandy beach where we could slip off the horses, let them drink, and cool our feet in the water. Cathedrals of fir trees rose into the night sky to the left of the car and behind it. To the right, bam and willow trees staggered toward the river creating a deep green path, hedged by nettles and lacy fern thickets. Overhead, the whispering trees formed a tunnel leading to a beach where a large fire circle nested, the wheel of rocks black with summer fires, the sand often so littered with beer and whiskey bottles that we had to climb off the horses and pick them up so the horses didn't step on them.

Margie and Ron were down there together. I peered into the dark trees, listening to the night sounds, the whisper of breeze, the rush of river over flat rocks. *Were they sitting on the beach kissing? Was Ron reaching into her sweater, holding her breast the way she had held mine? Did it feel the same when he did it? Was he as good a kisser as Joe? Hot and hard against her as Manual had been against me? Or like Rudy?* I wanted to know. I put the empty beer back in the sixer, took another, opened it and slid out of the car. If they came back, I'd say I'd had to pee. I took another long guzzle, then holding the beer started down the path and taking care not to trip on the roots crisscrossing the sandy soil, crept silently down the path toward the beach. It was a medium dark night, only faint moonlight glimmering off the water and sand.

I heard them before I saw them. Heard his breathing. I

crouched behind one of the boulders at the side of the beach and as my eyes grew accustomed to the darkness, made out faint, white shapes. Bent sticks high in the air, a henking sound, more a rhythmic growl then a slap, growl slap, unnh, unnnh, growl slap, as his round white buttocks heaved between her prehensile legs.

"Now, now! Ohhh, ohhh," a slippery smack. He drew back on his haunches. A white arm blazed out, her legs folded, the pale bone of her back curving over him.

Gagging, retching.

Lights abruptly flashed through the trees adding muted illumination to the scene. Figures flickered out of the gloom, Margie bent over him, he bucking into her mouth, her gagging. All his weight in front of him, seeming to fall into her.

Electrified, I turned and slipped toward the clearing, circling behind the car so no one would guess I'd been at the river. The turquoise and white '55 had pulled in and was idling beside Stroker, the windows rolled down, the radio blasting, "That'll be the Day."

*

The car seat was hard and tangible. My thoughts were not. We were back in Stroker, Ron driving us home so he could get back to the drags by 11:30. The night, still warm and deep, had taken on a whole new layer of narrative. The summer night now seemed garlanded with full-blown flowers; a dark river laced with exotic blooms. Acts flourished between men and woman that I had never imagined, though Mam continually swore I had an overactive imagination. I had been standing at the passenger side of Charlie's car talking to him and his black-haired buddy when Ron emerged from the dark path brushing his hands together then wiping them on his pants leg. A few minutes later Margie struggled up the path lugging her purse and the six-pack. She didn't come to Charlie's car but slid into the front seat of Stroker, wrenched the mirror down and commenced to fiddle with her hair and apply lipstick. I left the guys and scrambled in beside her.

"Well, did you break up with him?"

She didn't look over, but yanked her hair out of its ponytail, combed it, savagely grabbed it with one hand and with the other re-wrapped the rubber band. She looked better than I had expected her to. I imagined that her face would have been irrevocably changed by her encounter.

"Well, did you?" I didn't think so; when would she have had time? Still, I wondered what she'd say.

"You were drinking beer up here, weren't cha'? I can smell it." She rummaged in her purse. "Here," she said as she lifted a stick of gum from its depths, tore it in half and gave me the big half.

Ron was coming, yelling over his shoulder to Charlie. "Okay, but only a quarter mile."

He burst into the car, grabbed the six-pack, went around back, opened the trunk then slammed it. Back in the car. "You bag the brew, kid?"

I nodded.

Henk, henk. "You owe me. Lie if ya get caught."

"She'll be okay. She's not loaded."

Margie's fierceness had suddenly dropped away, and she was just regular Margie again, even defending me. I realized there were many things I didn't have a clue about. Much to learn and the most engaging subjects were not taught in school. *For sure.*

The two cars pulled from the clearing together, stopped noses even on the pavement. The black-haired kid riding with Charlie jumped out and stood between the two cars, the headlights spotlighting him.

"Hold on. We're gonna jam," Ron said, eyeing the guy,

gunning the engine so that the car rocked and let out a sharp blast against the pavement. The kid dropped his hand. My head snapped back as Stroker screamed forward, the smell of scorching rubber smoking the night. I had just straightened up when Ron hit second, crushing me back against the seat again. Hard to tell it was a race; Charlie's car was not in sight.

Bellowing with henks, Ron let off on the gas as we crossed a yellow painted line on the road. Charlie shot past us. "Well, let him get some runnin' out of his system before he races tonight. Can't beat the man. Henk, henk, henk," Ron snorted, head thrust forward, peering after the taillights of Charlie's Chevy.

I hadn't peed my pants, but almost. "How fast were ya goin?" I yelped.

Margie's pink-tipped hands clutched the purse she held in her lap.

"Not even a hundred. Eighty-five's all. Got to be a little careful out here on the road." He nudged Margie's arm. "C'mon, honey."

"Is this where you're gonna race later? Are there lots of cars?"

"Sometimes. We move around though. Stay too long, some busybody'll call the cops."

"I want to come."

Margie's head shot around. "Liz! Just forget it. We're going home."

"We could sneak out."

"Maybe you can sneak out at your place, but you wouldn't get past Daddy."

"You better take it easy there, squirt. Margie's right." He leaned forward and looked at me. "Racing cars isn't like them horses you cavort around on."

No! It was definitely different. Cars went faster, were even more exciting, and you wouldn't have to worry about hurting a car like you would a horse or a man. Cars probably didn't feel pain. And they wouldn't start up and run away on their own. Cars could take you anywhere you wanted, and as fast as you wanted. *Now, I'll be in the driver's seat. Fantastic!*

"Anyway, it's a big guy deal." Margie snapped her head my direction, her long ponytail slapping his ear. "No girls. Huh, Ron?"

Obviously, something going on here that I'd have to ask Margie about when we got home. Just one of the things I'd have to ask her.

"Ohh, Margie," Ron groaned, the sound exploding from his nose. "Now, I didn't say that."

Chapter 21

IN 1999 ANNIE MAKES LINDA AN OFFER, WHILE IN 1958 SHE MEETS GABE

ARMITAGE HOUSE, MAY 16, 1999

I'd been up the road visiting Edward, Margie's dad, and was walking through the hayfield on my way back to the house. Sunshiny and bright after the rain, puddles lay like long jewels on the blacktop and the wind, a little brisk but not cold, carried the smell of the swollen river. In the beauty of the morning, my thoughts turned to Jim. Several days after he told me about the apartment manager coming to the jobsite, he'd called in a better mood. He said that she had wanted to talk to him about moving to another apartment and had been in a hurry to let the new renter know his answer. Since he was only there temporarily, she wanted him to move upstairs so an older woman with crippling arthritis could have his ground floor unit. She sounded rather frantic, but I could understand why she might have felt it was important. Maybe she was a nice person after all, not the desperate man hunter I'd imagined. But couldn't she have called? I hadn't said anything, just asked him if he'd agreed to move.

"At the end of the month," he said. "Maybe I can come then." He couldn't turn a sick old woman down but groused because he hated to change anything once he'd organized it to his specs.

"I hate Texas," he said. "I wish the damned job was over." I told him I was looking forward to him coming to Oregon. Thinking of his non reply, I had looked up and noticed my mother at the ranch house mailbox in her gardening clothes and muddy boots. She saw me and waved energetically. *Maybe she had something to say?* Earlier, I had hoped she would have something to offer but as the days had drawn on there had been nothing. She moved into the middle of the lane waiting for me.

I would be upbeat and cheery. She liked that.

"Isn't it a gorgeous day? Nothing pretty as these fields in early summer. Wish I had a horse to ride." I looked down at Jack's old place. "I'd even ride one of Loren's mules if I could take the trail along the river."

"We have too darn much to do here to go anywhere. Pup is just about running himself into the ground with all of it."

I looked towards the untidy barn where her husband could usually be found, closeted with his alcohol. "Oh? What's he working on now?"

"Well, he's . . . he's been in the house waiting for a call from the man with the big mower. We have to have the fields cut. We got a notice from the county. It's a county ordinance, and if we don't have it cut by the fifteenth of June, they'll fine us and send someone out to do it. Then we'll have to pay the county again on top of the fine. We just can't keep the place up."

Two years earlier, before she and Pup were married and before they'd moved to the ranch with Mam, he'd done all the maintenance on my mother's beloved glass house. He'd built her a new deck and had lots of improvement plans to get more money out of the place when it sold. He'd mowed then. Handy Randy, awaiting her every whim. After they were married, he couldn't do a thing, poor man. He had lived such a hard life as a ranch hand. I'd figured that about the only work he'd done in twenty years was to lift a beer glass and chase rich widows around a dance floor.

"I think if I ask around one of the neighbors will swing by and do it. I don't have any trouble mowing the front and back myself."

"They aren't very neighborly," my mother said. "Pup already asked the new man at Johnson's. He wanted a hundred dollars. A hundred dollars? Pup said they were trying to rob him because he was a new owner."

Oh, he was the owner now? I'd dropped my head and prepared to get away.

"Look, Annie, we can't keep it up. It just makes me sick to see it go down and we can't do it. Pup can't do it. He's not getting any younger and neither am I. We just want to travel and have a good time." My mother tilted her head so she could look into my eyes. "In the time we have left," she said. "Besides"—she turned and looked over at the small field which had once been Granddad's splendid garden—"it will never be the way it was when Daddy was alive."

She reached out to hug me, her arm clinging to my shoulder, then released me, patting me as I turned to go. I still had my head down aiming to dash off, but instead turned to her. "Mother, we can work this out. *I* can take care of the place by charging more rent, and eventually we can buy it from you."

"Oh, Annie," she said, shaking her head, her mouth curled in a sad smile, eyes welling with something that looked like sympathy. "*You* could never afford it."

*

JUDITH CLAYTON VAN

SUMMER 1958, GABE

Hands on her hips, eyes like rabbit pellets, "No, Annie!" my grandmother growled. "You're coming and that's all there is to it." Glaring at my hair. "You're at the neighbor's too much. You've never seen this country before, and it'll be a good trip. It's up on the Columbia, and we'll pass through the town where Granddad grew up. He's looking forward to it."

The last thing on my list. Stuffed into the backseat, a drawn-out drive to the northeast part of Oregon so she could judge a county fair, under her thumb for the whole trip, the whole weekend, the endless drive back. No music on the radio, only news. No smoking. Might as well be in school, jail, any hateful place. Linda was off with Big John on some big boating holiday, so I was stuck. I didn't reply, just gave my grandmother back the look she was giving me.

"Now, don't give me that! If you wreck this trip for Daddy and me, you won't know what hit you." Then putting on her nice hat, a big fake smile, "Everybody from the rodeos will be there. You'll have fun seeing everyone."

She obviously had not realized that I had moved on from that ruined world. No more horses and cowboys for me. Finally, having almost reached the magical teens, I was now into cars and the men who raced them. Could I stand the trip if I had a long book? Several?

Raiding their bedroom bookcase, hiding place of books they didn't want me to see, I found three that appeared promising, *On the Road*, *The Razor's Edge*, and *Peyton Place*. *Peyton Place* was my first choice, as *Life* magazine said that Grace Metalious caused a scandal by writing it. *On the Road* was about a guy who drove across America, and according to the back of the book, shocked the country from coast to coast. I took *The Razor's Edge* because my father's name was written on the inside page. I gathered old comics from the back of my closet. I'd hide the books inside the comics, and so avoid detection if anyone cared to look, which I doubted they would.

The appointed day was warm, but not hot. A perfect Emerald Valley summer day, pale blue sky, high cotton candy clouds. I slung my new round suitcase in next to a wicker box full of Granddad's tomatoes. In it were a change of clothes, riding boots, and makeup—plenty of it. I was trying new makeup colors because the morning after Margie and I came home from our night out with Ron, I'd talked her mom into bleaching my hair silver and cutting it in a brush-up like Kim Novak's. Afterwards, Margie and I had ridden the horses to the drug store at the crossroads and charged a violet rinse to Mam's account. LaVetta said they made it for old ladies, but I didn't care. I was becoming good at signing Mam's name. Either she didn't look at the slips anymore, or I was signing her name so well, she couldn't tell the difference. I didn't care if she knew. I was determined to look just like Kim. Even Margie's dad said the lavender hair looked pretty with my green eyes. At home that Sunday night, Mam had stalked circles around me, so furious with the "cheap" color that she was gritting her teeth. When she closed in on me, I had no trouble convincing her that I did it myself. LaVetta saved from the wrath of Mam.

"At least it isn't hangin' in your eyes anymore" Mam sniffed as I slammed the trunk lid. A month had passed since the Sunday night hair episode. Still, she blasted me with it anytime she could fit it in.

I had stuffed the books in my purse and carried the comics conspicuously in my hand. Finally, off. Drifting through the wild Oregon morning, sound muffled by the hum of fat tires on asphalt, drone of conversation from the cut-out figures in the front seat, I opened *On the Road* and began to read. I concluded, about the time I came to "crotch-eared mean-ass" as a tag for one of the minor characters, that this was a book for further investigation. However, the main character seemed a goof, funny but not my hero, plus the make-out scenes were flat. I reached under the seat and exchanged Jack for Grace. Immediately bored with the town and the characters, I skimmed for the sexy parts, finally recognizing that approximately every 25 pages or less would reveal something to add to my prurient repertoire. I passed the morning in a delirium of libidinous fantasies, occasionally lifting my eyes to view the paler world blur by.

We stopped for lunch at a low-slung diner on the south side of the Columbia River Gorge just outside Cascade Locks. In the parking lot, we passed a red pickup with a bumper sticker that read, "Welcome to Oregon. Now go home." Here, it was hotter and windier, sweltering gusts tore around the corners of the building herding dust into whirlwinds on the flat land around the road. Settled in a clean booth, we ordered sandwiches.

"Roast beef with mayonnaise and tomato"—keeping my face in the menu—"and a root beer shake." No protest forthcoming, I looked up, "Make it thick, please."

Tapping her painted fingernail on the table, Mam appraised the dim room then almost as an afterthought, to me, "Now when we get there, you're going to have to take care of yourself because we'll be busy. Harry and Alice Henry are the fairground managers. They live on the grounds and that's where we're staying. With them. In their house. You'll probably get the couch."

"Kids?"

"No. Alice said there's a horse you can ride in the grand entry."

Granddad ate his sandwich, studying the map-printed place mat, and didn't look up. Like me, family road trips were not his favorite entertainment. I knew he would rather be home in his garden or sitting at the kitchen bar with the paper, the radio tuned to a ball game. I believed Mam had wheedled him into coming so she wouldn't have to drive. The evening before, he had stood among the lush squash plants in his Bermuda shorts and thin undershirt giving Aunt Virgie detailed instructions on how to water each row and exactly how to switch the sprinklers from the front of the garden to the back. When she walked back to their trailer in the nine o'clock light, he stood gazing after her for a moment then came in the house and wrote down the whole scheme on a piece of paper he tore from Mam's yellow pad. When he finished, he took the sheet out to the pump house and stuck it on the nail by the door. He came back cradling a basket of ripe tomatoes, and as the sun flared pink against the shining gold straw, he had stood at the kitchen door surveying his darkening, splendid garden. God! What would he think if he knew what I was reading, imagining? The thought shuddered my insides clear through. The sandwiches arrived, turning my thoughts from my private world. Mam put her spoon in my shake and took a couple of slurps.

After lunch, full and sloshing with sweet milkshake, I resolved, for Granddad's sake, to put away Grace and try W. Somerset Maugham although I couldn't be sure it wasn't just as titillating. Lying back in my pillowed bunk, next stop Granddad's childhood home, I opened the front page of the slim black book. There, written in ink, spanning two lines at the top of the first page were these words: Los Angeles 1945 Lt. Jeffrey Butler, Jr.

The same loopy script as the mouse-chewed letters I'd discovered as a kid pawing through the old boxes in Granddad's shop. Ignoring the wind roaring down the gorge, buffeting the Mercury wildly and causing Granddad to laugh, I began to read. The last thing I heard was Granddad's voice.

"If you think the wind's bad now, Momma, you should have travelled this road in a buggy. Now there was a thrill."

The next thing I sensed was the car slowing, but I couldn't pull my attention from the page. Larry, one of the main characters, was just telling his girlfriend that he didn't care about money, he only wanted to find the answers to the very questions I'd been wondering about since last year's classes in the stone church. Whether there was a God, why terrible (Larry called them evil) things happen, and if when you die, it's the end. I couldn't guess the answers, and now here he was talking about them in a book and maybe he'd know. *This was interesting. Why did they hide it with the sexy books?*

"Now, Annie, take your nose out of that book." She glanced back, as I slid it to the floor, toed it under the seat. "This is where Granddad grew up."

He was driving slowly down the main road skirting a small wind-beaten town, some long, falling down buildings along the river, a few here and there in better shape, then raw, newly constructed shacks with heavy yellow equipment parked everywhere. The town itself, a few streets over, all white and brown, looked like a movie set for a western with a few modern additions thrown in helter-skelter. At the town's center stood several ornate pillared brick and stone buildings, and a tall-spired church to the west. Yet the jumble was made magnificent by the roar and panorama of the river and the soaring presence of two snow-capped mountains glowing white in the distance.

"Wasco County seat, coming up." Granddad gestured at the rumpled but elaborate building on our right. "That's the courthouse. Whole place sure looks different since they built the dam."

"When were we here last, Daddy? '50? Doesn't look like they've done much . . . except the dam."

"Now, ahh, see there, Annie, that's the hotel." We were passing a brick building, green awnings shading dark plate glass windows, Columbia House spelled across them in gold letters. "Used to be a fancy billiard parlor back in there. When I was a little kid, we'd all come to town on Saturday, and I'd hang around and watch through the windows till mother sent Lucas to come and drag me off. Then he and I would go to Celilo Falls and visit with Chief Tommy and watch the men fishing from platforms that hung out over the falls. It was thrilling for us kids."

"Where'd you live, Granddad?"

"Can't show you, but it was right over there." He nodded toward the east.

"Let's look."

Mam, turned in her seat, penciled eyebrows drawn together in a warning frown. "It's gone, Annie. Flooded out last winter. What didn't wash away in '48 is gone now. Whole state darn near washed away. It swamped some of the older places, and they had to tear them down."

We were now pressing along a dusty, treed road. On a rise to the right perched a tall old-fashioned house surrounded by swaying trees and a white fence.

"That place up there"—Granddad nodded toward the hilltop—"that was the Warrens'. They were the rich folks in town. Owned the cannery there on the river. He died on the Titanic. Mrs. Warren was pulled out and saved. Kept me from wantin' to get on one of those big tubs."

"Hmphff." This from Mam, looking straight ahead, not deigning to acknowledge the Warren place.

I'd heard the story. Mam had been trying to talk Granddad into booking a cruise, colorful blue and pink brochures spread on the turquoise kitchen bar, she pointing out spectacular sites they could see and things to do together on their floating whirl. He didn't usually disagree, didn't then either, just said as though reminding her of an issue thoroughly settled, "Now, Mother, remember Mr. Warren's sea cruise."

Strange thinking of Granddad as a boy. A man with

another life before I came along. Too strange.

The car slowed, tires creaking against hot pavement, Granddad leaning over the wheel, gazing out at the quiet streets. "Sure has changed." His voice sounded so sad.

"Well, they had to do it, Daddy."

"Yep." Shaking his head slowly, generous mouth pressed in a thin line. "A whole world's lost. It was the biggest native trading center in the northwest, Annie. Tribes came from all around back then. Didn't see an Indian on the river today. Town won't have anything going for it now."

"Well, Daddy, it's all changing. Hard to take when they take more and more for the roads and drown places for dams. But, that's progress, and I don't like it any better'n you do. We can't stay the same, can we? Got to get along with it."

Starting on the second half of our trip that day in 1958, I didn't realize what he'd lost, so the conversation didn't mean much to me. Why would he miss the Indians? In the book I'd stayed up reading the night before, the Indians were murderous and pure evil. Mam always said they were verminy and slothful and she was glad to see the last of most of them. At least in the valley. Maybe Granddad's river Indians were different.

She turned to look at him, then picked up her legal pad, and dropped her head to her papers. Since she'd lost the race for Republican gubernatorial candidate (apparently half on account of having to chase after me, and the other half on account of my Frankenstein hair), she'd been more determined than ever that her job policing the fairs was done, and done right.

Adjusting her glasses, she muttered to Granddad, "I've got to get these forms finished before we get there. I'll stick on the fair board for now, but next year Bob's appointing me to head the State Centennial Commission, and that job will take some doing. Someone needs to bring the damn state back together, and so far he's not doing it. I just will not sit around and let it go to the dogs, because that's where it's headed—and fast."

Granddad being the State Highway Commissioner, all her crabbing during the campaign to convince valley farmers to accept the new roads, I thought of offering some quip of my own, but figured I wasn't near as good at it as she was, and I'd better hold fire. Best say nothing. Always best to say nothing. Unless it was yes, yess.

I settled down to *The Razor's Edge*.

Hours later, we parked under the trees in front of a white bungalow on a county fairground bigger but not as grand as ours. While Mam and Grandad milled around, giving hugs and handshakes and such, I headed off to scout the grounds and see the horse I was to ride in the Grand Entry the next day. I stuffed the book in my purse hoping to find a quiet place to sit and read the last fifty-odd pages. Suzanne, the artist, was recounting how she had come to know Larry, and was just going to describe what type of lover he was when we'd pulled into the yard and I'd had to put the book down. I left Mam and Granddad talking with skinny Alice and her hairy-nosed husband and walked down the road past long lines of parked cars and horse trailers toward the whitewashed barns.

It was six o'clock. The heat lay on me like a sack of heavy grain, far hotter here in the northeast part of the state than in the valley. Here the only scalding shade was near the trees huddled around the house. Eastern air was dry, the ground dry, the place made of dust, fine blowing powder that lodged in my hair and ears, turned my teeth gritty. Dust was a hazard for me. My nose was watering, threatening a monstrous sneeze attack, and my eyes were itching. Nasty signs.

Rounding the corner of the row of barns, I came upon a blue pump positioned over a long wooden tub of green water. The alley was a canyon of shade between the long barns. Hay bales were stacked against the barn wall, and with the ground around the trough sopping wet, the place was relatively dust free. Forget finding the horse. I burrowed for the green scarf in my purse, slipped it in the cool water, wrung it hard, and tied it around my head, bandit-like. I sat on the first row of bales, back to the wall, and began to read.

Larry was a generous and inspired lover. Isabel, the main girl, had just told the narrator that Sophie, of whom she was jealous, was a drunk and would sleep with any tough who asked her to. The narrator, who I thought more highly of with each page, replied that it didn't make her bad. He went further, saying that a lot of people get drunk and have rough sex (rough sex?), but he only considered it a bad habit, like chewing your lip. *Extraordinary thought!* He believed a bad person was one who "lies, cheats, and is unkind."

Lies? Lies . . . I wondered if it made a difference what a person lied about. The narrator most certainly would not fit in at the First Christian church—or the stone church. I was pretty sure of this. Contemplating the nature of my many lies, I looked up from the book.

Standing at the pump was a tall handsome young man holding the lead of a donkey who wore a pink sun hat. The small donkey stood pigeon-toed in the mud, sipping daintily from the tub. The fellow was examining me closely. As I looked up and our eyes met, he smiled. Warm hazel eyes full of light reminding me of the pond at Grandma Delaunay's where orange fish flashed brilliantly in the flickering greenish shade. Caught looking, he didn't care. His wide mouth curled into a grin, showing even white teeth, causing dimples to pop. *Wow!* His chestnut hair drifting over his forehead was long and curly around his face and nearly blond from the sun, his skin tanned a dark brown. His body was lean and hard looking, not huge shouldered, but more straight up and down like runners I'd seen at the college track with Granddad.

FASTER HORSES

✻

The next day in the watered-down arena, I sat astride Alice's tall gray gelding, holding the State flag pegged in the stirrup cup, the "Star-Spangled Banner" blaring above the fairgrounds. I smiled down at the clown as he stood saluting the flag, his other arm draped around Thelma, his donkey. Seeing him there in the arena, face white with grease paint, his big orange nose and sad painted mouth, it was hard to imagine that under the mask he was such a doll. The night before, I'd ambled back to the stalls with him to put Thelma to bed, and then in spite of the exhausting heat, we'd just kept strolling and talking. His voice was low and soft, and he called me Miss Jody. I guess I had lying on my mind, perhaps something even more outlawed, so I had lied about my name. I thought Jody had a nice cowgirl ring to it. I also told him I was seventeen. Later, standing with our backs to his dusty blue Cadillac, he held my hand.

"I'm wore down," he said, surveying his gritty jeans and boots. "We got in from Montana just before I saw ya there. Got to get my gear ready for the show. But, ahhh, you want to get together during the break tomorrow? Something to eat?" Long sweet look into my eyes, hard hand lightly holding mine. "I, ah, came with some people," I said. He glanced at me from under his forelock. The look, guileless and expectant, held a message I wasn't sure of, yet it seemed a plea. "But, I don't have to be with them."

The wide mouth curled again, transforming the regular planes of his face, casting them in a Renaissance effect—a picture in one of Joe's books of Michael the Archangel standing with his sword on his hip, grave and radiant. The resemblance, my recognition, both disconcerting.

"I'll pick ya up under the stands there by the announcer's gate. Wait on me a bit? Takes some doin' to get cleaned up after the bulls."

Mam had contended that all clowns were a little on the brainless side after constantly getting their heads beat on the inside of the barrel where they jumped to find protection from the charging, nasty tons of bull meat. But without the clowns the bull riding would be too dangerous for the cowboys. Besides playing the fool to make the audience laugh, the clowns were there to protect a fallen cowboy from the bull. That was their job. To prevent accidents like the one that had killed Bud. Bud dying with a horn stuck in his gut. After all this time, that horn was still stuck straight into my heart. Sometimes the bulls won. But, Gabe didn't seem to worry about any dangers. He was lighthearted, funning everything.

Arm still around Thelma, he kissed her on the cheek, looked up at me and winked. Then the national anthem ended, and I kicked the gray into the colorful whirl of horses and flags charging out of the arena.

After the show, I was waiting for Gabe under the grandstands. Earlier, I'd climbed into the high announcer's stand to get a better view of him spinning around the arena playing the bulls. He was fast, light-footed, vaulting and leaping past the humped beasts, over the barrel as if his feet were winged. I was more impressed than I'd been the night before, and that was saying something. A Cadillac pulled up by the back fence. He leaned across the seat, grinning, and opened the door. I had thought of Cadillacs as old men's cars, but it looked perfect with him driving.

"There ya are. Glad you came."

Was he kidding? He was glad I came? But still, I'd play it cool, and older, like Margie had with Ron.

"Where is there to go around here anyway?"

The landscape was a burnt-out yellow, a few dusty trees, no rivers but the wild Columbia many miles to the north. I was hoping for some quiet gentle place that might provoke a kiss. I scooted across the wide seat but not too close, anxious for him to clear out of the area before Mam or Alice caught me. Sitting beside him, so aware of his exotic maleness, trying not to stare at him, I wondered if Gabe was new to rodeo. I'd never seen or heard of him but didn't ask. My questions might give away my connection with rodeo, my famous mother, all of it. Too complicated. I'd say I'd come with cousins—my uncle was a weekend calf roper, not a full-time professional. The last was true.

"Well, let's just take a drive around a little," he said. "One of the fellas who drove the stock up here said there's a place not far. Supposed to be pretty good. Ya hungry?" He patted the seat next to him. "Sit over here?" The smile slow, the hazel eyes shy.

I pretended to consider for a moment then scooted closer, resting my hand on the seat between us. He reached out, covering my hand with his. The smile.

"You were really good," I said.

"Ahh. Thanks. It's a lot of fun to do."

"How long have you been clowning?"

"Bet you're wondering why anybody'd be starting in on such a miserable job?"

"Well, it's not like a normal job, is it?" His laughter was light and throaty; trailing off into ha, ha's at the end, starting again. It was catching.

"I've been working with Mac Ross. He's an old friend from my hometown. He's clowned for, ahh, since I was a kid. He got hurt here last spring. I've been partnering with Dusty this summer. First summer without Mac, but I'm gonna stick at it."

Mac had been hurt? In New York I had realized how nice he was not only to Jeannie but to everybody and how much she liked him. After the New York rodeo, he and Jeannie, daughter of brandy-slurping Margo, had been married. At Christmas that year, Linda had received a card showing a snow-covered ranch somewhere in Idaho. But this was another connection I'd keep to myself. Seemed Gabe might have started clowning right after Linda quit rodeo. He wouldn't know her—but he could know of her, the professional rodeo world was not that big.

We pulled out of the fairground gates onto a gray slash of highway that appeared to travel straight forever. The Cadillac was quieter than the Mercury and smoother than Stroker. It seemed to float down the road, a self-contained world. There was only the warm smell of him, his leather gear, radio turned low, gospel singers and fiddle music. I moved closer. The road that I thought stretched forever now disappeared at the top of a low-rising hill, then rolled into a shallow valley. The golden yellow ground was utterly bare except for short, bleached grass. There was nothing but the rolling ground. Nothing on any of the multiple horizons. No houses, fences, cars, nothing. We were in a strange, naked world alone. I was mostly interested in exploring Gabe's effect on my interior world, in his smell, the warmth where our bodies touched. I didn't want him to realize his effect on me and kept my eyes trained on the land, taking it in like food. We didn't speak, just drifted peaceably through the alien landscape. After a while, it began to seem we'd driven a long way, and still no sign of a diner. At the same instant, we turned to look at each other and laughed. "You thinkin' what I'm thinkin'?"

"If you're thinking I'm thinkin' we're lost."

"Nah, Miss J. Don't think so. Let's try a little further, then if we don't come on it, we'll backtrack." He tromped the accelerator and the car surged up the hill. "I'm sure he said go left. Not like there's any landmarks. I'll bet it's right . . . over this hill . . ."

We saw more hills, nothing between. The heavy car, now moving fast, took the hills like a roller coaster.

"I'll bet you a dollar, it's right over the next hill."

I owed him twenty dollars by the time the Cadillac gained the top of another of the endless hills, and there in a depression beside the highway stood a roadhouse-café. A blazing white sign with red-painted letters announced the Moro Café and Dancing. Behind the building, a red water tank stood against the pale sky. The sun blazed off the noses of a row of cars and trucks in front of the place. *Where had they all come from?*

We were still laughing, arms around each other's waists, as we entered the diner.

Inside it was cool and dark after the brilliant yellow world. To our left a long counter, and across the aisle, red booths lined the wall. In an alcove a round-topped jukebox, and behind it more booths leading to the shadowy bar and dance floor. Bustle of talk, "Tennessee Waltz" playing on the jukebox, people glancing up from their food, we slid into the booth behind the jukebox, backs to the lunch crowd. We lifted plastic-covered menus from the stand attached to the table, looked them up and down. Nothing sounded good. I was too nervous to eat.

A plan had been forming in my mind since I'd watched Gabe working the bulls that afternoon. He was definitely the one. The one I wanted to have sex with for the first time. He was the nicest young man I'd ever encountered. Real cowboys, at least many I'd known who were raised on western ranches, are kind and polite to women. They know about life at its most elemental level but have a fresh innocence that is remarkably sweet. They go about their business with solemn gentle smiles, not conflicted about the life they lead. I guessed the world I'd decided to leave was more deeply ingrained than I wanted to admit.

"I'm starving," he said, flipping the menu back in its holder. "What looks good?"

I just smiled and moved closer when the waitress

appeared. Aproned, tall, bony, and flat, her pin-curled hair was bound with a cotton kerchief, the ends knotted at the front of her head, turban style. Large silver hoops dangled from her ears.

"What'll it be?" she demanded, standing flat-footed, pencil poised over the small pad that she held close to her chest.

After we'd ordered, steak sandwich for him, French fries and a milkshake for me, I excused myself. "Restroom," I said.

Gabe scooted out and stood beaming at me as I swung out of the booth and began the walk down the long aisle. I didn't really have to use the bathroom, only wanted to be alone, to reapply my makeup and refine the plan. I raised my head looking for the Ladies sign and received a staggering jolt. Facing me, two booths ahead, sat Granddad resplendent in his dark green Mounted Sheriff's Posse uniform, silver star on his chest, the uniform Mam had insisted he wear when escorting her on rounds of the fair. Head bent, he was taking a bite out of a hamburger, a highball sitting beside his plate.

Now I do have to pee! What if she was in the bathroom? Had he seen me? Should I just keep walking? Pretend I didn't see him?

He looked up then directly into my eyes. No surprise there. He'd already seen us. *Shit!* Now what? No food across from him, only in front of him. Maybe I wouldn't be crucified just yet.

"Hi, Granddad. I'll be right back." Conspicuously looking for the bathroom door. "Gotta find the bathroom."

He smiled slowly, nodded. Evaluating his gesture now, I couldn't say it was a smile. It was more a forced movement of his face, nothing reaching his eyes. I hurried toward the restrooms, thinking *maybe now I'd have to throw up, instead of pee.* Mam would kill me. In the bathroom, my stomach hollow with fear over being caught and excitement over my plans for Gabe, I examined myself in the mirror, concentrating on how I looked, how I could look better, not on the situation at hand and how things looked to Granddad. I used my new lavender eye pencil, and the pale pink lipstick I had also charged to Mam's account. Tugging my lower eyelid, holding it there, I was careful not to apply the color as darkly as I would have liked since Granddad would have to be faced. Now. Eyes satisfactorily enhanced, I turned from the mirror, sucked in my stomach, and prepared to bluff my way back into the good graces of my jailers.

Head up, walking resolutely out the door. *Jailers! Shame on you, Annie, Liz, Jody, whatever your name is, Butler. This is Granddad who used to sing "Big Rock Candy Mountain" for you as many times as you wanted, went back through the tunnel twice so you could hear him honk the horn, didn't whale you when you went joyriding and tore off the barn door. It was Granddad.* I didn't want to lie to him. It wouldn't make me proud, but I would if I had to.

Slowly, I approached the booth. On his plate, pushed to the edge of the table, were the substantial remains of the hamburger. He was pushing his drink back and forth on the table, making designs in the water rings left by his sweating glass. I screwed my mouth into a grin, and stopped.

"Done already?" Intently observing his plate. "I came with a kid I know." When I looked at him, he nodded, reached out, and took the check from beside the plate. "Some other kids were coming but I bet they turned around. We almost did." His only response was to reach for his wallet. I kept on. "It's a long way. We thought we were lost."

He set some bills on the check, slipped another dollar under the plate. I backed toward the door as he rose from the booth and stood contemplating me. He dropped his eyes to the gray Stetson he held before him, working the rim with knotted fingers, the diamond in his big masonic ring winking.

"Need a ride? I'm headed back." His voice neutral, level. I

stared at a spot just off his right ear.

"Oh, no... Thanks." Me, sounding like bird noises.

"Well," he said, placing his hat on his head. "See ya at the house." No smile.

He walked past me and up the aisle, stopped a moment at the door looking at the rear of Gabe's head, then turned, and pushed through the door without a backward glance.

Oh, shit. Oh, double deep shit. I lagged behind, stomach cavorting like a furious wild animal was loose inside it. It would have been better if he'd said something. Even if he'd said, "Get in the car right now. We're leaving." Not that I would have, but it would have been something. Now I didn't know what to expect.

When I approached the booth, Gabe's eyebrows drew together for a moment, then he rose, and grinned. "Thought maybe you'd hightailed it," he said, then settled in and went back to work on the steak. I eyed the soggy fries as I slid in beside him. Our lunch conversation, what I remember of it, was effortless. We sat for at least another hour, feeding the jukebox, Gabe doing most of the talking. He told me about his folk's big cattle ranch in Idaho, the names of his seven brothers and sisters, his theory of donkey training—they responded best when worked like big dogs, they were more dog-like than horse-like—how Thelma didn't like to wear the hats his mom had made for her. Reluctantly, we rose and wandered back into the blazing sun. On the way back, Gabe pushed the Caddy over the yellow hills, laughing at the dips and climbs.

At the Fairgrounds, he eased the big car down the crowded alley, weaving among the trailers and horse traffic, the cheerful spectators heading for the stands in a churn of dust. At the barn, as I turned to close the car door, he leaned across the seat, and looked up at me. "Meet me after the show? Rodeo dance tonight."

I hesitated. *Could I stay on the loose until then? If Granddad had told Mam, forget it.*

"Ya like to dance?"

"Ahh, No. Yes. I mean, yes! I like to dance. I'll wait . . . behind the bull pens." It worked best as a hiding place and none of them ever thought to come looking because it was not only loud but gag inducing from the shit stench of angry bulls.

Gabe left to check on Thelma and I trudged up the dusty road toward Alice's house; best to take my medicine now.

I found the house dim, cool, and empty. With the green curtains drawn to keep out the heat, it was cool and fragrant inside, even better, the place was mine for the moment. Inside the fridge was a jumble of food, part of a pot roast, what appeared to be a strawberry pie covered with foil, and a fat pitcher of red Kool-Aid. At the sink, I poured myself a tall glass from the pitcher, stood drinking it, taking in the kitchen. A note was propped against the salt-and-pepper shakers in the middle of the kitchen table.

>*Annie, Meet us at the Daughters of the Nile food tent at six.*
>
>*Mam*

She didn't know. At least not when she wrote the note. I carried my Kool-Aid to the living room, fished the book from my purse, kicked off my boots and flopped on Alice's doilied sofa.

*

My eyes opened to sounds of scavenging in the kitchen. Through the open door, I could see hairy nose moving about. I slipped from the couch, grabbed my purse, and beat it into the bathroom where I leisurely scrubbed my armpits, rummaged in the medicine cabinet for deodorant, washed my face, and proceeded to execute a perfectly conceived and artistically polished makeup job. Tonight I was Kim in cowboy boots.

I escaped the house when hairy nose finally had to knock and ask to use the bathroom. Outside, I skulked behind the barns, grabbed a corn dog from a vendor on the edge of the carnival, and slipped in behind the stock pens as the grand entry ended. I found a corner with a good view of the arena, out of the way of the cowboys rushing on their various errands, and settled down to watch the show.

Gabe spotted me and swooped by several times, his lithe figure silhouetted against the evening sun blazing on the arena. I was relieved to be free of my dusty, fly-ridden hiding place as the last bull snorted out of the gates and stood banging his horns on the pen across the alley. I rose, slapped the dust off my butt, checked my mirror for probably the twentieth time, and prepared to meet Gabe.

Two hours later, we were still in Gabe and his partner Dusty's motel room off the main highway, marked by a blue neon swimming pool with a flashing pink girl endlessly diving into it. I sat in the only chair balancing my beer on its arm, feeling very mature. Taking in the tacky pine-paneled motel room, similar to the many rooms I'd stayed in with Linda, it occurred to me that tonight I was taking Linda's place. She was always the woman in the scene, I the kid looking on. Now I was the woman. That was some progress on my quest.

The clowns were drinking beers, taking off their grease paint and reliving the show. Dusty, dressed as an old man clown, bum-like with an ancient beat-up hat, long striped socks and huge orange floppy boots, was standing at the sink in the bathroom piling cold cream on his face to erase the white paint. His contract for this show was to stand in for Mac Ross as lead bullfighter. Gabe was the comic and barrel man, in training to be the bullfighter. It was obvious from watching Gabe perform that he was already a great clown and would be a champion bullfighter. I was sure he'd be famous. I saw us standing arm and arm, me looking more glamorous than Kim or Liz, having our pictures taken for *Look* magazine. I could picture the headlines: "Young Rodeo Royals Marry."

"Get your tardy bones outta there and let me in the shower, Dust. Dance'll be half over."

"C'mon in, I ain't shy." Dusty leaned over, ripped a trail of toilet paper from the roll and began to scrape it up his face, leaving a wide swath of clean skin, punctuated by little bits of paper pinned to his whiskers.

Gabe smiled, shrugged, and rose from the bed. "Won't take me but a minute more. I'll get showered."

*

The long ramp leading to the wooden dance hall seemed to bounce as we approached the open doors. Outside, cars were jammed every which way in the dark field around the hall, many with all the doors open, couples sitting in the front seats drinking from paper-wrapped bottles, some standing around the cars talking. Inside, country swing, fiddles blazing high and sweet, dancers two-stepping to the thumping bass, singers belting, "Take me back to Tulsa."

Gabe, hand on the small of my back, swung me onto the dance floor. I was aware of the picture we made as we twirled around the floor, both of us wearing tight jeans, leather belts, and tight western shirts, his white with a red pin stripe and pearl snap buttons, mine pink with white snaps and white piping at cuffs and collar. As we whirled across the floor, I glimpsed people standing at the edge of the dance floor following us with their eyes, smiling, rather idiotically I thought. We danced well together, and though he was at least a foot taller, all our bumps and hollows fit. My head rested dreamily over his heart, his palm warm on my back, our hands firmly joined. He wasn't touching me in any way improperly or suggestively, yet it seemed that where his body contacted mine a new world appeared, not a tangible outward world, more a new inner space of possibility. That point of contact created the possibility of complete transformation.

My eyes opened instinctively, and I found myself looking into Mam's eyes. She and Granddad, arm and arm with Alice and hairy nose, stood at the rail on the edge of the dance floor. My eyebrows shot to their limit, but in that split second of amazement, I had the presence of mind to wave—with unrestrained enthusiasm. Gabe looked over and waved too.

"You know them?" Then pulling me toward the rail, "Wanta stop?"

Too late. All four of them piled onto the floor as the band counted off the next tune, "one, and a two," a slower two-step this time, the singer almost yodeling "Half as much," the pedal steel trading licks with the stand-up bass. Mam, with absolute focus, had engineered her way across the floor and was almost on us. I must have telegraphed my foreboding; Gabe looked down, a question in his lively eyes.

He seemed about to speak when Mam crowed, "Well, it's good to see that all those lessons went for something." The pedal steel interrupted but not for long enough. "Some dancing there, kid. Now, who's your friend?" First, the ingratiating political smile then recognition in her penetrating eyes. "Why, you're the clown."

"Gabe Rosser, mam." Gabe tipped his head, turned me under his arm, and pulled me back to him in one easy motion. She started to say more, but Granddad steered her away, Mam still peering over Granddad's shoulder at us. Gabe's back to her, she raised her eyebrows and mouthed, "He's nice."

Huh? I could barely encompass my magical escape from discovery—and she thought he was nice?

I cuddled closer to Gabe, using his chest as a shield. "My

aunt and uncle. The people I came with."

"She's some kind of official or something isn't she? She was with the producers this afternoon before the show. They were all up in the rodeo office when I went to get the lineup for the bull riding."

"Was Gran . . . uhh, my uncle with her?"

The tune ended, and we swung around to face the band.

"Yeah, both of 'em. Nice folks." Still holding my hand, he swung it gently back and forth. "I'm 'bout cooked. Wanna take a break?"

We moved together through the sweating crowd to the front doors, me not looking back. If they were watching me, I didn't want to know.

We walked through the field to the Cadillac, passing other couples seeking relief from the smoke and heat inside. We settled close together sharing a cigarette, drinking the beers he'd brought, shy with each other but working up to the kisses, stage one of my plan. Gabe, his arm around me, sank back against the seat, hoisted his legs into the notch between the open door and the frame of the Cadillac.

"Cowboy's hammock," he said. "I spend so much time in this car it's like a home to me."

I would have had to be a contortionist to get him to kiss me now. I took a pull off the beer, reached in his pocket for another cigarette. We drifted there in silence, me smoking, he looking up at the stars. As I reached to stub the cigarette in the ashtray, he thumped his feet to the ground, turned, and kissed me. I believe that he just aimed to give me a friendly smack, but I was ready. Pressing close, I kissed him warmly and thoroughly. After the briefest of hesitations, he reciprocated, finally pulling back with a sigh. "OooWee," he breathed.

He took me by the hand, and we started back to the dance hall. "I wisht I stayed in a place a little more. Now, where is it you live? We may have a rodeo there this summer."

"Uh, in Emerald City. The rodeo's over. Were you there?" *If he asked me for my number, I'd have to figure out what to tell him. No one would call me to the phone if he asked for Jody. Would I tell him I was Liz? Or Annie? Good question,* I thought. Then shied from it.

"Nah, not this year. Denver was the same weekend. Money's better there. Rodeo's bigger."

"I'm glad you're here."

He threw his arm around my shoulders and hugged me to him, almost lifting me off my feet.

The band had just come back from break and was playing with renewed energy, the two fiddlers standing at the edge of the stage, hands flying over the instruments, feet drumming the beat. The floor was a whirl of color and styles. There were ranchers and their wives, the men wearing western slacks or hard new jeans, the women gliding about in cotton dresses with flared skirts. Professional cowboys and their girls, mostly in shirts and tight jeans, townspeople checking out the rodeo people, every Jaycee in the county along with their wives and kids, and all of them seemed to be on the dance floor. Mam and Alice hovered at the end of the hall in animated conversation with three women dressed in colorful square dance skirts, their flounced crinolines quivering in the air, currents swirling across the board floor. I didn't see Granddad or Alice's husband.

"Now this is my favorite, here," Gabe said as the band paused then struck the first notes of "You Are My Sunshine."

"I like the old ones."

Off we went stepping and sliding, Gabe's handsome face lit with perfect good humor. Lifting my head from his shoulder, looking up at him, I wondered what he'd think if he knew what a liar I was. He squeezed my hand and led me in an intricate open step, our boots clocking heel and toe, heel and toe, then swung me around and walked me backward through the dancers, twirling as we went. The best dancer ever. I wondered how he'd learned to be so good—certainly not like me, with schoolkids in the basement of the Knights of Columbus Hall. I was jealous thinking of other girls—no, that'd be women—he'd danced with. We danced almost every dance, only missing half a number when we went to the bathroom and slurped water from the warm fountain on the porch.

The dance was near its end when Mam appeared on the dance floor and tapped me on the shoulder.

"We're going back to the house." Hair damp at the edges, face flushed, she was in one of her jolly moods, the kind that momentarily caused me to forget the others.

Gabe and I halted, still holding each other. She reached up and tucked an escaping red curl into its nest.

"You two sure can dance, now, that's the truth." She turned, spotted Granddad at the edge of the crowd, and raised her hand. "Daddy wants to go. Just come on in but be quiet." Then to Gabe, turning on the high beams, "Enjoyed your show. If you get to Emerald City, you come out to the Fairgrounds and look us up."

A new tune had begun, and I was dying to cut the conversation short. "Let's dance this one, Gabe, it's almost over."

"Well, thanks, Mam. It's swell to meet you." He dropped my hand and reached to take hers.

Leaning into him, she shook it strongly. "You go on now and have fun." She turned and started off across the floor, then swung back to me. "Don't be too late."

※

Much later, back in the Cadillac, sitting close, me nestled against his long side, he was taking to the kissing more readily. His mouth was so warm and giving, his arms around me so protective, it felt like love. I loved him with a pure intensity maybe aided by my fantasy of our future together, and for the first time in my almost adult life, I voluntarily gave myself over to a man. I focused my whole self, all my desires, onto the flesh where our lips met. I reached for his hand and placed it on my breast to join our bodies and spirits. As the kisses grew lingering and erotic, all of me was concentrated in my senses. I ran a hand slowly back and forth up his hard leg, creeping higher with each caress, finally coming to rest. He moaned and shifted. As though I'd always known how, I ran my hand the length of him, slowly moving lower. Again, he groaned, and leaning back slowly, uncoupled from our embrace.

He was looking down on me, a dark outline against the window opened on the silver night.

"We better slow it down here, Miss J."

Dragging myself up to the world of speech. "Don't you want to? I want to."

"I want to, all right." I moved close to him, pinning him against the door. He hugged me to him, and grazed my mouth with his lips. "But you're a girl yet." When I started to protest, he touched my lips with his fingers. "And I've made a promise that the first woman I'm with will be my wife."

"But, I want *you* to be the first one . . . you know . . ."

He hugged me harder. "You're too young to give yourself away to an ol' boy like me. Give it some time, and don't be thinking you have to hurry it up. You'll know soon enough. And me, I'm twenty-three but I don't plan on marryin' yet. I got Thelma, and this old car, but don't have much built up. No place or nothin'. Gonna be awhile 'fore I'm fixed."

"But you like me?"

"Oh, honey." He dropped his head down close; put his warm mouth near my ear. "I like you. I surely do like you."

We kissed again. This time, he directed our course, curbing it when I forgot. We drowsed and kissed, and talked.

He telling me his dreams of building a ranch, having lots of children, raising and training little Thelmas for new clowns. "Gotta have a gimmick on this deal to make yourself a place. I seen this lovely little spot last time I drove through Utah. It's around Kanab, where Mac's ranch is. Lots of trees, grass belly high, and good water. That's where I'm gonna look."

As night turned toward cool morning and the crickets sang in the fields, we kissed without caring what came of it. Sometime before sunrise, I roused myself and we parted.

"See you at the barn in the morning?" he asked.

In love, I floated toward the bungalow under the trees. The first sunlight hit the edge of the porch step as I hesitated before the screen door. I couldn't bear to be with Mam and Granddad, anyone but Gabe, not even to talk to. It would break my new world. I turned and walked to the orange and white Mercury parked under the tree. I stretched out on the back seat and passed into the only world where I felt really at home.

*

"Well, here she is, Daddy." Bumping and jostling, slamming of doors. It seemed I'd slept for only a moment. Mam had jerked the seat back and was shoving pillows in on top of me. I moaned and covered my head with the pillows, hoping they'd go away. "Granddad thought you'd run off with that clown." Sounded like she was the one who thought so.

"It was too hot in there," I mumphed from under the pillows.

"C'mon now, you better git in there and use the bathroom. You already missed breakfast. We're ready to go."

More racket as Granddad slung the suitcases into the trunk. In the steamy bathroom, I delayed as long as possible, even considered climbing out the little window and hightailing it to the barn to find Gabe, but there were too many people nearby. If I were caught, if I embarrassed Mam in front of outsiders, my life wouldn't be worth a wet whistle. So before I was really awake, we were on the road and I was mourning Gabe, wondering if I'd ever see him again. As we swept down the long road out of the fairgrounds, I looked out the back window hoping to see Gabe's car, but there were only the quiet morning barns, a few people carrying feed for their horses. Turning around, slumping into the seat, I saw Granddad watching me in the rearview mirror. He glanced away, and I knew he hadn't told her. He hadn't told her even when he suspected I'd stayed out all night. I wondered if he'd ever mention my outing. I knew I wouldn't. I tried escaping into sleep but couldn't. I fished *The Razor's Edge* from my purse and began to read.

I had finished the book and was staring out at the yellow fields slipping by. I didn't think the book answered the really big questions, but I wasn't sure. At the end of the book, everyone got what they wanted. The guy telling the story said he figured that because everyone got what they wanted, it was a success story, and that people liked success stories. Isabel, the fly in the ointment of the story, gained a good social life, a husband, and money. But she didn't have love, because she loved Larry. Sophie, the one Larry loved, the one who turned to drinking and rough sex because of a tragedy in her life, ended up floating in a French harbor with her throat cut. Larry, the hero, gave away all his money and went to be a mechanic, and hoped later to become a taxi driver in New York City. He wanted his mind free to study the big questions. He didn't want the responsibility of owning things. From my young experience of New York taxi drivers, I figured Larry didn't know what he'd signed up for. I took the book's message to be that even if it didn't sound so good to others, people should get what they really want, and this would make them happy. Following that reasoning, I decided that to be happy,

I'd have to know what I wanted. I didn't have to think long or commit the list to writing. It wasn't hard. I wanted my own family. A handsome and kind husband, a happy marriage, some kids, lots of horses and dogs, and for all of us to live together at the house on Armitage Road. This would make me happy. In light of recent events, I judged I'd need an older man to get my mission rolling. It didn't occur to me then that I should be older too.

Chapter 22

WHAT'S WRONG NOW?

ARMITAGE ROAD, 1958

We turned down the lane leading to the ranch at 6:30 that evening. Unbending myself out of the car, I became acutely aware, maybe because my encounter with love had heightened all my senses, how perfect the ranch was. After the initial panic at leaving my first house and world, I'd quickly grown to love the wide valley, the cozy woods by the river, the green water, the stretches of yellow fields to the west and mountains all around. It had enchanted me from almost the first day I'd seen it, but I had never felt so strongly that it was my right place in the world. Standing by the car, I took a deep breath. The place, soft and alive, was not outside me, but effortlessly part of me, every sight pleasing. I ran inside, changed into shorts and a top, slipped through the front door, and flew barefoot down the warm road to tell Margie of my new love.

LaVetta's roses, flourishing under the kitchen window, were tall and bright, their fragrance thick in the late afternoon. I barreled up to the door, hit the latch and jolted to a hard stop. I pressed the latch thinking it jammed. Pressed again. The door seemed to be stuck. I pounded on it. Nothing.

I hollered, "MARGIEEEE."

The garage doors were closed, which meant they were home. I abandoned the front door, and raced around the house looking in the windows, but all were draped and the drapes drawn. I scurried through the south gate and scanned the side yard which was empty of clues. Back at the front door, I stood tiptoe on the rocks before the roses, jumping to peer through the kitchen window. I was nearly sure I glimpsed LaVetta at the kitchen booth, but couldn't be positive—maybe it was Edward. I pounded with all my strength, striking the door with both hands. I raised my foot to kick it, thinking I'd give it one more try, and if no one answered I'd have to run to Grandma Delaunay's and have her come. Something was wrong.

The door cracked open half an inch.

"Annie, go home." A strained croak. "You can't come in." It was LaVetta, eyes red, handkerchief to her nose.

"But, I have to see Margie. What's wrong?"

"Nothing. You just need to go home. You can't be here all the time."

". . . but . . . why? Why can't I? Did I do something? Can Margie come out then?"

"ANNIE," she raised her voice to me, as Mam often did, but the strident caw was devastating coming from my gentle friend, my safe person. I dropped back from the doorway, tears imminent, throat full of strangled words. The door closed. The bolt rasped as she slammed it tight.

I stood staring into the big friendly roses, crying in the face of their kind beauty.

*

Two weeks had passed and there was no word from Margie, and there had been no sign of activity at the Delaunay's. It was

Friday night. Cable's, the drive-in beneath the bridge, was full of freshly washed gleaming cars. Music wailed over the big parking lot from KEX, the Portland rock and roll station to which nearly every car radio was tuned. The saxophone was trilling behind the Coasters, rocking "Young Blood." I watched each brilliant car as they slowly cruised the brightly lit block, their occupants yearning for excitement, making sure they were seen. I was looking for Stroker.

I had blackmailed Freddie, the skinny kid who worked as a handyman for Grandad at the bank and sometimes at the ranch. All he cared about were cars. He lived with his mother, the janitor at the bank, and spent every penny he made on his car, a stock maroon and white '56 Chevy. One day when he was working at the ranch and I was in the barn loft where I had stashed a carton of cigarettes, I'd noticed him filling his gas tank from the big tank behind the barn. I wasn't sure this was taboo, but from the slinky set of his back, his quick glances toward the house, I figured it must be. I hadn't said anything then. I remembered it when figuring out how to get to town without having to steal Mam's car.

"Come and pick me up on Friday night at 10:00. I'll be on the side of the road up at the junction where Armitage hits County Farm."

"Pick you up like a flattened toad. In your dreams, kiddo."

"I'll tell Granddad you're stealing gas."

"What in the hell do you want? Marshall'll kill me if he knew I was taking you to town."

"All you have to do is give me a ride to the drive in. I'm supposed to meet somebody. My girlfriend had a big fight with her boyfriend, and I gotta find him. No one will know you took me."

"No dice. I'll lose my job."

"Think about it this way, if you take me, you'll still have a job because I won't tell about the gas, and I won't tell if you do it again. You drag, right?"

FASTER HORSES

❋

I thought I looked cool. I was dressed all in black, tight pedal pushers, silk V-necked blouse, my bleached hair neon violet under the drive-in lights. My beatnik phase. Like my models in *Look* magazine, I was always wearing black, into poetry, smoking, drinking coffee, and of course any booze I could find. Freddie didn't seem impressed. He scowled as he watched me check the cars.

"You're looking for Ron Walker? What if he doesn't come here first?"

"Then you'll have to take me out to the drags."

"I ain't takin' you out there with me! He drew his lips back from his pointy teeth as though he smelled something that caused him pain. "Forget you. I ain't no baby driver."

"I'll tell Mam and Granddad you brought me down here and left me." He scowled more furiously. *Not convinced,* I thought. "I'll call the police. When they take me home in the police car, they'll tell Granddad *you* left me downtown."

He wasn't smelling something bad, he was snarling. He jerked his head toward the street. "Well, he better get here 'cause I don't care. I'm not taking you out there."

"Let's get Cokes! You got any money?"

❋

We lurched down the dark road that led to the barricaded freeway, me wondering if Freddie wasn't being rougher and driving faster than called for. Half a mile to the east, the river snaked around the bluff. Behind it the dark humps of the Armitage Hills rose like a mythical dragon, crouched, head resting on its front feet. Looking out at the familiar knobbed ridge, I calculated that we weren't a mile from the ranch. We'd missed Ron at Cable's, and now were lined up with many glistening cars all crawling toward the unopened portion of the new important road they were calling a freeway and sometimes an interstate. A new super-duper highway that Granddad called a boon to the state. Mam said the state had just appropriated a strip of land down the back of the big pasture where Grandad had planned to keep the new cows and he hadn't bargained for that. Windows rolled down on the thick September night, I inhaled the clean barky smell of cottonwoods and fresh grass, mixed with fumes from the idling cars, the clean new car smell of Freddie's Chevy—new smells to replace the stinking Brahmas, the steaming manure and sawdust reek of my childhood dramas.

At the end of each new freeway section, every twenty miles or so, sprawled a construction staging area for work trucks and heavy equipment. Bustling work sites during the week, they were empty on weekends and each big flat yard led directly onto the newest section of freeway. A perfect drag strip, the new freeway stretched flat and straight for fifty miles north. Bulky cement barricades blocked the entrances, but they were nothing for twenty or thirty impatient young guys to move, and then to move back so the cops couldn't catch them before they fishtailed off the strip at the next construction yard twenty miles north. They called the drags the Midnight Nationals, but they really started at eleven when the shift changed at the police station.

"There he is. There he is. Stop! I'm gettin' out."

"Just shut up." He looked over, glaring like I had assaulted him. "He don't even know you're here. You think he's gonna let you anywhere near that car a his, you're nuts."

"Stop here!" I opened the door and started across the dusty yard toward Stroker. There was no moon that I could see, no stars. The large space was illuminated by the headlights of the idling cars, the perimeter cast in profound shadow. Ron, holding a fat red crayon and a big tablet, stood at the end of the lot, just within the circle of light. Stroker was parked directly behind him, headlights on high beam outlining his figure. As each car approached, he slashed a large number on the paper, slapped it under the windshield wipers, then gestured each car to its place according to racing classification. Just behind him, a tall red-headed woman carved the drivers' names and numbers on a yellow legal pad pressing the pencil into the paper so that it made a dent I could see even in the dim light. The red hair seemed familiar, but I couldn't place her. At my approach, she looked up from the pad, huge brown eyes flicking over me like a sharp tongue. I smiled, my most ingratiating, 'I want to be your friend' smile. Grin pasted to my face like I had something to gain by it, I scooted by her long leg and sidled up to Ron.

Standing next to him, I noticed that I came to just above his belt buckle. He slapped the number under the wipers, gesturing a white '57 Chevy with louvered hood and silver-paneled fins toward the line. The guy in the car was cute. Gleaming curly black hair combed straight back, friendly brilliant blue eyes, high round cheekbones. Kind of exotic. And the car—well, it was day and Stroker was night—it wasn't Stoker, but it was fine. If I wasn't already set on Ron, maybe I'd see about him.

Blank-faced, Ron gazed down at me, dark brows drawn together. Then, squinting, he snorted. "Henk! On your horse, amigo! What you doin' out here, squirt?"

"I have to talk to you." I lifted my index finger, wagging it toward me. With a deepening frown, black eyes inquisitive, he cocked an ear in my direction. "Ahh, about Margie."

I didn't imagine it. The corner of his mouth quivered, and he flinched like a spooky horse.

"Well, how the hell did you get here?"

"I came with a guy, but he left. Can you take me home? . . . Please?"

A scarlet '58 Pontiac with long flat fins ripped in front of us. Ron hastily scratched the number on the pad, flipped the wipers up and secured the paper. With one knuckle, he knocked lightly on the car's side panel. It slipped away, taillights glowing neon.

"Can't talk to ya now, kid." He raised his arm and motioned the next car forward. "You go back there with Red."

"But you'll take me home, right? I can't walk it."

*

I watched the races perched on the hood of a car next to Red, who I'd finally remembered from the drive-in.

"I'll get ya home, but you stay with Red. Don't go off." Ron had winked at us, his dark eyes glittering in the headlights, then turned, and cleats ringing down the new pavement, hurried to his place at the starting line.

Red sat on a blanket thrown over the hood, her knees drawn up, pad resting on her long thighs, flashlight trained on the pad, recording racing times that a series of guys holding stopwatches brought her. After about five races, my head began to swell from the dust and gas fumes. Red didn't have much use for me to begin with, but when I started to sneeze, she turned to glare at me with each eruption.

"Chhh! Ah, chhh!" The smell of thick exhaust, the dust, and Red's head-banging Hypnotique all contributed. "I, I've ahhh, got to go find something to blow my nose with."

She was erasing furiously, fiery stands of hair bouncing, glaring at the page, wiping my little outbursts from her sheet with the back of her hand like it was me she was eliminating. I slid carefully off the car and drifted over to another group where an older guy with a sandy crew cut handed me a beer though I hadn't asked. I recognized him from the first time I'd been with Ron and Margie at the drive-in. His dark and curvy girlfriend rummaged in the glove box until she found a tissue.

"Dust's bad tonight, isn't it? Won't get better until the wind quits. I'm Sunny"—she nodded to her boyfriend, now turned to watch two '56 Chevys peel from the starting line—"and that's Duane."

Her smile was Nude Pink and genuine, and I was glad to be away from Red who not only stank of perfume but was grouchy as a witch in water. I leaned against Duane's car, sipped my beer and tried to calm my troublesome membranes. The cold beer helped. I tipped my head back and glurged.

"Unhh, Duane," I said when he turned back to us, "could I get another?" I hoped the beer would numb my nerves and clear my head so I could complete my plan. The alcohol did help calm my membranes; it lulled them and eased my itching eyes.

The tips of the grass glowed silver in the headlights, the meadow shrouded beneath a close indigo sky, the blue-black horizon fogged with gray exhaust punctuated by flashing crimson taillights, and all around the roaring rap of glass packs rent the layered night. And people my own age (well, I was almost their age) were running the show. Before, it had always been adults: Mam, Granddad, Linda, Uncle Jack, all the rest, and all in charge. Now, although standing apart, an observer, I felt more a part of the world than I had since I lost Bud. I'd probably never see Gabe again either. My throat constricted and sudden tears sprang to my eyes. If Bud had lived I could have lived in my old world and everything would have been different. It would have. I swiped my hand across my eyes, then dabbed them carefully with the tissue smushed in my hand. Wouldn't do to smear the tons of mascara I'd earlier so deliberately applied. Damn! This was no time to cry about Bud, about anything that had happened before. I'd been a baby then. I was no longer baby or child. I started around the semicircle of parked cars at the rear of the races, pausing to beg a smoke, a beer, listen in on the chatter. No one paid much attention, and when someone did notice me, they smiled, accepting me like I had a right to be there.

I was on my fourth beer, had worked my way to the far right of the semicircle, and was leaning against the wire construction fence when I sensed a change in the crowd. It started as several of the guys, their cars bunched in one area of the lot, began to look back toward the construction access road. The head turning seemed to ripple inward through the crowd, accelerating as people stooped to gather blankets, beers, and stray clothes. I ripped through the crowd of cars toward Stroker and arrived slightly out of breath at the same moment Ron did. Loping along beside him was the dark-haired handsome boy I'd seen earlier driving the white '57. Ron charged past me, leaned into Stroker and began tapping the horn. Three short blasts, three long, three short.

"Git in, kid." He grabbed my arm and shoved me across the seat to the passenger side. "Billy, you take Red. We'll meet at Risher's." As the last horn blast faded, the cars doused their lights and the field went dark. Down the freeway, I saw receding taillights sail into darkness. Ron turned the key on Stroker. "Hold on, kid. Cops only caught me once. That was the last time . . ."

He eased Stroker onto the new freeway and stomped the gas. In the side-view mirror, just before my head snapped back, I'd seen the white '57 leaping up behind us trailing two long lines of cars. Hitting the freeway in pairs, the drivers punched the gas.

"Henk, henk, henk," Ron snorted, leaning into the steering wheel like it would help him see into the darkness. The speedometer needle drove straight past eighty, my eyes widening as the red sword cut around the numbers. I felt no fear. My fingers crawled up the front of the silk shirt and I unfastened the first three buttons. My breasts couldn't match

Margie's or Red's, but it couldn't hurt to flaunt a bit of what I did possess. Now the headlights of the last pair of race cars snapped into view behind us.

"Henk, henk . . . better step on it, nobody's gonna crawl up our ass, baby."

I didn't know if the strange noises were laughter or commentary of some foreign sort, but I didn't find the sounds offensive as Margie had. I decided to make it simple and take it as laughter. Was he calling me or the car baby? Surely not the car, as I imagined Stroker must be male. I sat back fishing in my purse for a cigarette as I felt the car slow slightly, the needle dropping from ninety back to eighty-five. Careful not to get in Ron's way, I punched the lighter on the dash and waiting for it to pop, studied him. Don't think I wasn't aware of the road, I was. But, there was nothing to see except the two paths of light ahead of us, all else was hidden in the night. Stroker's interior became a safe bubble, a gleaming glass shield. I liked the speed. It calmed me—my life was out of my hands—and I didn't care. Whatever would be, would be. Like the song.

Ron glanced over when I reached for the lighter and smiled, a tight slice of lip turning up at the corner.

"Not fast enough for ya?" His eyes snapped back to the road, and I noticed in the dim light of the dash what looked to be a thin sheen of sweat on his high forehead.

"I like it."

*

We didn't go to Risher's. After halting at the barricades, we waited while the boys ahead opened them wide to let the stream of cars through. Stroker bounced off the freeway and ran the back roads home. In town, Ron stopped at the Glendale store to pick up a case of beer. When he came back to the car,

I convinced him to drive to the river beach off McGowan Creek Road.

"I really have to talk to you. I just feel so, so . . ." I'd dropped my head and brought my fist to my watery eyes. They were still a little itchy, but he hadn't been present for the epic sneeze attack, so he could assume that I was in the grip of some intense emotion—or not. He was still charged with energy over his escape, his finger tapping the wheel as he drove. I knew he wanted to go to Risher's and talk to "his guys," but I thought my presence, the open neckline of my blouse, had created some curiosity. I'd noticed him darting longer and longer looks my way, and on the dark ride back to town, I'd made the view available by leaning over to light cigarette after cigarette, leaning closer, then scooting closer with each cigarette.

By the time he turned Stroker on the road toward McGowan Creek, I was sitting beside him. He cast a quizzical look my way, whereupon I smiled brilliantly and brought my far arm into my bosom to pop my cleavage a little further into view. His tanned arm was almost touching mine, my shoulder even with the cuts of muscle defining his biceps, a close faint scent in my nose that might have been Old Spice. This mellow fragrance did not excite my membranes as had Red's violent odor. Bringing my eyes to his face, thinking of my next move, I noticed that he had once suffered from acne, but the scars were not gory purple or red, only tight smooth pocks that marked a faint trail around his hard cheekbones.

"How did you get to be King of the Races? You really run the whole thing, don't you?"

"Ahh, henk! Me and Duane. We started The Klan and it just kind of kept on goin' under its own steam." And then he surprised me by making a sound I recognized as a regular chuckle, a sound that originated in his throat and didn't croak out his long nose but rumbled warmly in his throat. "King of the Races. You're funny, squirt."

But he liked it.

I watched Ron driving along, cigarette clamped in the side of his mouth, windows down, balmy wind playing at the edges of his hair, and thought about my plan. After giving some thought to the circumstances in which I'd found myself with Joe, with Rudy, and then Gabe, and no encounter turning out as I'd hoped, I had determined to follow what I now thought of as my Samson and Delilah plan. I'd taken the scheme from Starlight movie classics. The Bible story was properly told even at the First Christian Church, and Delilah was a famous seductress, so I figured I'd do what she did. Basically, the idea was to talk very softly, tease, flatter and bug him continuously, put myself in his way, and ask questions so he'd talk about himself and give away his secrets. My lesson: if she did this, a woman could have power over a man and do whatever she liked with him. And I didn't want to ruin him as Delilah tried to do to Samson. I just wanted a boyfriend. I didn't care if he was used. And, from what Margie had said, she was through with him anyway.

As we swept past the dark trees crowding close to the road, I imagined my strategy, my moves, lined up on the dashboard before me. Men liked to be flattered. How could I flatter him?

At the end of McGowan Creek Road is another road, really a trail up the mountain, that thirty years before had been a logging road. On our horses, Margie and I could climb it to the bluff-top and look across the whole valley, but Stroker was slung too low to make the trip. Ron carefully turned Stroker around in the needle-padded road, his head hanging out the window to see in the dark, and backed up the narrow trail, hiding Stroker's tail beneath the tall trees. He set the brake and bounced from the car. I heard and felt the spring and thunk of the trunk lid. He plunked a six-pack on the floor of the car and slid into the seat, leaving the door open on the warm fir-scented night. He flipped the caps off two bottles, handed me one, and took a long drink. I'd drawn my feet under me and was almost leaning against his arm.

"Stroker is the most beautiful car I've ever seen. I'll bet it's the fastest too, isn't it?

He opened one long black eye and looked down on me. He lowered his almost empty beer and grinned. "Where'd you hear that? Did someone say that?"

I could tell by the way he cocked his head to listen that he was interested. "No. I just think so. Am I right?" I rummaged in my purse for another cigarette. Ron reached behind his feet for another beer. "Where'd you get Stroker? Can we turn on the radio?"

"Look, Sq . . . uhh, Liz . . ."

"Okay, forget the radio. Tell me about Stroker." I lifted my hand and patted the steering wheel with my fingertips.

While Ron gave me the lowdown on Stroker, almost from the day the metal was made in the foundry, then told about being an Engineman E-6 in the Navy where he learned everything about engines, I practiced Delilah poses. Soft smile, gazing into his eyes, occasionally touching him instead of the car, brushing slowly against his leg or arm. Delilah probably didn't smoke, but here I deviated from the script, imitating my late-night movie heroines Dietrich and Bette Davis, eyelashes fluttering through clouds of smoke.

After finishing his tale and a fourth beer, Ron sighed and turned to me, thin lips drawn inward as though hesitant to proceed. "Now what's this about Margie? I have to get you home."

"I don't have to get home. I can stay as long as I want."

"You said it was important. Did Margie tell you something to tell me?"

"Uhh, haven't you talked to her?"

He dropped his hand and went for another beer.

"Me too?"

He reared back a little and focused on me. "You look okay," he said. "I don't want ya gettin' drunk on me, now."

"Yeah, I'm gonna be very drunk on two beers." I smiled up at him, my perkiest 'I'm fine' grin, thinking of the beers at the drags which were making me feel the need to pee.

"You're cute, kid. I'm not kiddin' though." He popped the caps on fresh beers, and handed mine across.

"So, uhh, you haven't talked to Margie?" I asked. "Since when?"

Another big sigh, head turned down to me, eyes sad. "Awhile now. Maybe a month," he said.

"Didn't you go over there?"

"No one came to the door. I unhh, called. LaVetta said Margie didn't want to talk." He was still looking down on me, dark eyes intent, fine lips taut.

"So, uhh . . . that's okay?" I leaned closer, so that my shoulder was nested right under his armpit. "If you were my boyfriend, I'd never do that."

"I don't know. Thought I'd give her awhile and see. Where . . ."

I had scooted across the seat to my side and was opening the door. Even though I thought we'd had a good moment going, I couldn't wait any longer.

Pressing my arms tight, squeezing both breasts upward, I leaned over to place my bottle on the floor of the car.

"I'll be right back," I said and waited a moment longer than necessary, knowing his eyes were on me. I hoped he was getting the picture.

I thought that relieving myself would also ease the tremendous pressure I'd been feeling in that region, but it only helped a little. Walking back to the car through the dark trees, I was conscious of the ache, and of my nipples, hard as winter berries, pressing the silk of my blouse. As I stumbled out of the brush, Ron was at the rear of the car again. He slammed the trunk and walked toward me, brushing at his khakis, a new six-pack dangling from his hand. He offered an open beer and stood beside the car door looking down at me, his mouth tensed in what seemed to be a smile. I slowly moved around him and lowered myself into the driver's seat, sipping my beer and wondering what to do next. When Ron leaned over to set the six-pack on the floor, I kissed him.

He started a little slow, but the kiss was like turning the key on a big, hot engine. What I didn't recognize then was that with the same key I had started my own engine, an engine that was just as big and just as hot.

*

It appeared to be about four in the morning, still dark but becoming transparent toward the east, the dragon-back ridge of the Armitage hills barely visible when Uncle Jack's log truck came booming down the road. I had parked on the verge at the junction above Margie's and the big empty log truck passed so close that Stroker quivered. I hadn't given Jack a thought when I'd parked the car. I'd only had one thing on my mind the night before, and it hadn't been my uncle. I remembered Mam saying timber was down this year, and he was hauling seven days a week, up at three, out early to get three loads a day because he was saving to buy a boat. I knew he wanted a new boat to impress the gorgeous Dr. Karla, a professor at the university and the wife of Bill, one of Linda and Jack's high-toned lake buddies. He thought no one knew, but he had such an obvious crush on her that even I, who didn't want to know anything about him, could tell.

I pictured him at the dark morning window of the trailer, staring out, pug dog scowl on his face. But there was no way he could know it was me in the car. Was there? He'd think it was Margie, "The Tramp." Ron was still asleep, dark head canted to one side, the tip of his widow's peak resting against the passenger window, mouth hanging open, snoring gently.

With a yell that must have startled the wildlife on McGowan Creek as much as it did me, he had gone limp and then to sleep after he'd finished his part of the sex thing. I had struggled out from under him and rearranged my clothes. Sitting in the dark with the windows down, I drank another beer, replaying the physical events, glad to finally know how it all worked, and waited for Ron to wake up. When it didn't appear that he'd come to, I gathered the six-packs of empties, went around back, placed them in the case and closed the trunk. The window down, I looked out on the dark forest, a few stars winking though the branches, and to the accompaniment of chirping crickets, smoked another couple of cigarettes, wondering if that was all there was to sex.

Checking the feel of my body, I found it didn't hurt like I'd thought it might. Although he had felt good inside me, I decided there was probably more to it. The squirting and the sliming had been unexpected and rather messy, but that seemed to be the best part for him—or the worst part. I'd have to ask him about the yelling. But yelling probably meant it was okay. Horses screamed like women when they bred. I'd wait and see what happened next time. I turned the key and after one false start realized Stroker worked the same as the hay truck Granddad had taught me to drive. Same floor shifts and all. I had no problem driving the growling car through the dark back roads toward home. Testing the feel of my new body, I was a little woozy from the beer, but realized I'd completed step one of my plan. Now, I was a woman.

But even a woman who breaks the rules should try to get back into the house without being discovered. No need to ask for trouble. Eyeing the silent ranch house through a mist of dew, I shook Ron's bony shoulder. "Ron, wake up. Ron!"

He moaned.

"Ron. Wake up and go home. Everybody's gonna be up." Shake, shake, shake; the money in his pockets clinked.

One sleep-caked brown eye slit on the dawn.

"You've got to go. It's almost light."

He struggled away from the window, hands scrubbing his face, kneading his long bony muzzle. "Oh, Sally," he moaned through his nose. He looked over at me in the driver's seat, glanced out the window, reached up and with his arm wiped the condensation from it, revealing the long field north of Margie's where we'd been riding the first time I'd seen him.

"Kid . . ." Frowning, he looked out at me from under a crooked brow, peering down his long nose as if concentrating on some serious issue. I giggled and slid close, burrowing against him and kissing his neck. His arm came around my shoulders. "Oh, kid, you best . . . Now, nothing happened up there . . . Right? Nothing happened."

"No. Something happened." I kissed his cold, compressed lips. In a moment, they softened and he kissed me back, but not with the eager heat of the night before.

"Oh, God," he groaned, rubbing at his head with one hand, the other arm still around me. "I've got to go. Don't say anything about this . . . until . . . Ahh, God . . ."

"What's wrong? Didn't you like it?"

"No, ahh, oh God . . . I gotta go."

"Where will you be?" He withdrew his arm. I reached to touch his face, but he caught my hand with his and held it off, pressure building between our palms until I moved both, bringing our hands to rest over my heart.

"Kid, this ahh . . . well, this isn't ahhh . . . a good idea." His words came squeaking out like tiny mouth farts. "You're ahh . . . how old are you?"

"What difference does *that* make?" *How old does he want me to be?* "Look, I gotta go. I'll see you next Saturday." He opened his mouth, but I talked over the top of him. "I'll be there. You don't have to come get me."

I closed the door, whirled and ran down the chilly road toward the ranch house. I turned and looked back through the early mist to see Stroker still parked on the side of the ditch, a dark blue wedge crouched on the yellow morning grass. I waved, jumped the ditch and kept close to the hedge. I'd dodge behind the laurel, skin through the hole in the hedge, and slip across the side yard under Granddad's magnolia tree. Using the hydrangeas as cover, I'd creep in the back door, fingers crossed that Granddad wasn't already up and eating cereal at the breakfast bar. If he was, he'd hear me.

As a line of sunlight appeared over the barn, no one heard me crack the back door and slip into the heavily draped den that led to my red and black bedroom. In the bedroom, I shucked my smoke-smudged shirt and pants and hid them in a deep closet recess, occasioning a trickier problem. I stood in the doorway looking owlishly around the dim room for a champion hiding place and finally sandwiched my slimed underwear between the mattress and the box springs so Mam wouldn't unearth them while I slept. My mouth was parched and foul as a gutted and dried goat's stomach, but I couldn't risk turning on the water and waking the patrol. I drifted onto my old bed expecting to savor my new state, but I was asleep in moments.

Chapter 23

BIG RED MAKES A MISTAKE AND ANNIE ESCAPES WITH BILLY

MCGOWAN CREEK MEADOW, 1958

"Mam, c'mon," I'd begged. "I'll be home in time. I promise." I had asked to stay overnight with my new friend Sunny, but I really wanted to be with Ron for a whole night and after his earlier call thought maybe tonight could be the night.

"You ARE NOT going anywhere. You're going with us in the morning, and that's the end of it." Mam had said, with her 'don't-give-me-any-shit' look. I had to sleep at home, and had go to the family reunion the next day. Had to.

It was Friday, September 19, 1958. I was thirteen years old, and it was 9:30 p.m. according to the clock radio in my black and red bedroom. Listening to The Champs' horn player wailing on "Tequila," I was grooming myself to go out while appearing, to the casual observer, to be doing absolutely nothing. Now I had to wait until my grandparents were in bed to sneak out, and then I'd have to sneak back in. A drag.

Upon Mam's ultimatum I had switched plans and rushed to the phone to call Freddie. "You have to drive by every half hour until I show up. I don't know what time they'll go to sleep." I answered his snarly protests, "If you do this tonight, you won't have to do it again." I lied.

An hour later, Fearful Freddie dropped me at the edge of the lot and wouldn't let me ride into the enclosure with him. He said he didn't want anyone to see us together. I thought I looked good in Linda's new black silk blouse and my favorite skintight black pedal pushers, and didn't understand his problem. I watched his '56 slither across the grass to the knot of cars at the freeway entrance.

Walking through the long grass toward the cars, attempting to track gracefully, if anyone—Ron for instance—was looking, I wondered what Ron had in mind. He had called me to make sure I'd be at the drags that night. He'd never called before, so my imagination had us, well, maybe not running away together just yet, but for sure it was something exciting.

Ron was huddled with the cute white '57 guy, and Big Red. They stood in the blare of Stroker's lights, their heads circled with neon haloes.

"Hey," Ron said as I stepped into the glare. "You're a little late, Miss Lizzie. You wait until we're done. Wait over there with Billy."

Oh, it was Billy? The white '57 was Billy. Okay. Up close Billy was even more handsome than he'd appeared when I'd seen him in his white and silver Chevy the first night at the drags. At closer range, I noted shiny black hair waving back from a curly widow's peak that pointed down to two cobalt blue eyes and further to lips of a curve, depth and hue to jolt me from my lull. Such white teeth. *Spectacular.*

"Hi," I said. His hair was blacker than anything. Skin not tan—more dark cream. The curve of his cheek jutted from his temple, dropped straight and curled into the corner of his mouth . . . *Man, that is the prettiest mouth I've ever seen. He's really . . .*

"Hey." A smile played on Billy's red lips. He looked down at Stroker, revealing the side of his muscled neck, and patted the hood. *He's shy. . . I thought. A shy boy.*

"Later," Ron said, starting toward the racers. He turned back. "Don't sign up any more, Red," he called. "We got nine pairs left." Seeing me edging away, he barked, "Liz, you stay around." He glanced at Red, then moved toward the start line, head hung like a dog in trouble.

Sometime later, the last pair of racers preparing to smoke down the dark freeway, I stood on the exposed roots of a big maple tree that gave me a foot above my usual five feet, watching Ron at the starting line. Duane and Sunny were parked just behind Stroker, and I began to edge their way.

"They're gonna be done here pretty soon," Duane hollered over the scream of tires and the blast of pipes. "You going to the river?" He handed me a beer.

"What?"

"Well, we're going. There's gonna be a band. They've got a truck generator to run the amps, so they can play until their juice runs out."

Sunny stood next to Duane, brushing her long hair, her perfect figure outlined in the car's interior light. "Supposed to be good. They're Josie's kid brothers—Mike and Jess. They're Mexican or something. Jess is a wild kid, but he can really sing. They've been playing at bars, but they're just getting started, so they said they'd do it. Good, huh?"

"Yeah. I'll see what Ron wants to do." I was ready for anything because I'd taken some of Linda's dexies to stay awake and keep the beer from kicking my butt. Thing is, dexies can kick your butt too, but I didn't find out how until sometime later.

"Oh, he and Red are going. We're supposed to meet up . . ." Sunny broke off, then waved and stooped to gather her things from beside the car.

"Oh. Uhh, okay. See ya," I said. I set the empty in the crotch of a tree. There at the edge of the dark field with the drag cars rumbling around me, clouds of dust filming the scene, Duane started his car, and the radio came on blasting, "Lonely Teardrops..."

The syncopated music, Jackie's pleading voice accompanied me as I crossed the flattened grass. When I approached Stroker, Ron and Red were engaged in close, tense conversation. Their heads were poked inside Stroker facing each other from opposite doors, their behinds hanging out, their busy hands shuffling papers on which the various cars' racing times were written. I walked up on Ron from behind. Red's head jerked up and she glared past Ron at me.

"Hi," I said, sliding my hand down his thigh, feeling the immediate quiver beneath his skin. I knew he didn't want me to touch him when people were around, but I figured she couldn't see well enough in the dark to make an accusation stick.

"Hey, Liz. Where'd you get to?" He backed toward me. I stood my ground, causing him to brush against me and turn so that we touched all the way down. I moved my hand to his waist and felt the hard flash of him on my front.

"Okay," Red said, busting around the side of the car. Ron and I stepped apart. "Here's the deal. Now, I'm getting Billy and when I get back, we're going. Right? Ron?"

Ron grinned. "Henk! Henk! Whee." He touched a finger to his tongue, then held it out to Red as she stomped away. "Ssssss!!"

Ron swung back to me, the silly grin still on his face. "Uh, Liz, uhhh, well, I brought Billy along... ahhh, for you. He's..."

"What does that mean?" I took his hand. He didn't pull away but wouldn't look at me either. He finally glanced at me, but immediately cast his eyes down.

"Look, uhh, we can't... You know, kid... I told you."

"Why?" Our woven hands were warm.

"Ohh," this in the form of a low groan. The drowning look in his dark eyes said he'd do anything rather than have to talk about it. Finally, he ran a hand up the side of his face, and muttered, "Red said she'd say something if you kept coming around."

"Say something?"

"Liz . . . you're thirteen. Do you know what that means?"

"Duh!"

"No . . . Do you know what it means for me?"

At this moment Red came charging back through the cars, hair flying like strands of fire in the dim light, Billy loping beside her. "Okay. We're ready." She came to Ron and threw her cigarette on the ground, stabbing it out with the nervous toe of her flats. "Liz, you go with Billy." A command.

"Uhh, no." This said looking right into her mingy brown eyes. "We're talking." I started edging Ron toward the car, gently until he got with it and began to move. "He's giving me a ride to the river." I skipped around the car and darted inside.

Faced with us both in the car, Red's pouty mouth clamped down, she slammed a hand to her hip in frustration, then stepping to Ron's side of the car she leaned down and whispered to him. Her eyes closed, sibilant message seeming to bore into his head, she lingered. Finally, jerking away still hissing and with an outraged glare, she turned and charged off in the direction of Billy's car.

I snapped on the radio, the announcer saying "and now number 40 and rising, Eddie Cochran and 'C'mon Everybody,'" then the loud twang of the base.

"Let's get out of here, before they follow us." I turned to look out the back window. Red was striding ahead, her long legs pumping furiously. Billy walked a little behind her, keys in hand.

"Henk henk! Be sure they'll follow us." Ron looked over

and smiled at me, a jaunty thin-lipped line. "Last race of the season. Big party, kid." The hollows beneath his cheeks were dark caves that narrowed his face.

We bumped out of the meadow, threading our way through people hustling to their cars. I rolled up the window when we hit the pavement. Ron didn't gun it flat out, but hit the gas hard enough and Stroker, let loose, ran squealing down the dark road. Red and Billy didn't show up in the rear view. At the junction heading to the river Ron turned the other way, jammed down a side road, then pulled over and shut the lights.

I scooted close, and placed my hand on the depression just above his ribs. Ron, hands folded loosely on the top of the steering wheel, looked at me and I knew that no matter what he said, he wanted to kiss me.

At my touch he said, "Now, Liz. I mean it." A tense, controlled whispering.

I kissed him. I kissed him and unbuttoned my blouse. I kissed him and guided his hand to the rising tip of my breast. If he were a roping horse, he'd always be breaking the barrier. Coiled, ready . . . And now that I knew how to start him, I liked it. And I liked him.

"NO! Now, I don't know how to say this any other way." He still had his arm around me, and an erection that caused the zipper in his khakis to stand straight up in his lap. He rolled my nipple between his fingers, then leaned down. When his head rose, he kissed me on the mouth, then began buttoning my blouse. "Really. Git straightened up, now. We've got to get over there, Liz." I didn't move, just sat and stared up at him. "Liz, we won't do this anymore."

"Why?" Both my hands on his chest.

He moved a shoulder, slowly, like he was testing it after an injury—same pained look on his face that I'd seen on cowboys who blew their ride, got hurt, didn't score.

"It's not . . . I'm too old . . ." His voice was low, the tension in his throat causing the sound to be pinched.

"I don't care." I arched my body closer. The warm lump in his khakis had not diminished.

"Liz, they could arrest me. I'm twenty-six years old. I'm over twice your age. If Red tells anybody, it would be . . . really bad, for me. They'd arrest me."

"Look, nobody knows. I don't know what you're so worried about if I don't tell anybody."

"Red knows."

"You told her?"

"God no!" Even in the dim light he looked so horrified, eyebrows shooting to the top of his head, that I almost laughed. But I was getting the idea that he was serious.

"Then how could she know? Was she looking in the window? Did you tell someone?"

Eyelids drooping, he shook his head, dark hair falling over his eyes. "Liz, uhh, you know I was with Red before. We were . . . ya know." He hesitated and took a deep breath through his nose. "Then I haven't been around . . . for the last couple of weekends, and she, uhhh, saw me with you, and that pretty well told the story for her. See?"

"She's guessing. Would you rather have her than me?"

"Ahhh, god dammit!" He hadn't moved, just a big eruption of sound. "I shoulda never let this get started. Now, it doesn't matter what you do, or don't do. It doesn't mean I don't like you better than Red, or anything in the dammed world." He was leaning toward me in the dark car, our faces inches apart. The planes of his jaw, always sharp, now stood out like exposed bones above a quivering mouth. "Fer Chrissakes, I've got a sister a year oldern' you."

I could have cared less, but it was obvious that he thought the sky was falling. *Shit!* "Well, if it's that big a deal, then fine. What do you want?"

"Billy. Billy's eighteen. I've been helping him with his car and he's around all the time. He's got a mill job, a little money. Go out with him. We'll all go around together, double date, go bowling or something, so Red—err anybody, can see for themselves . . . And Billy don't have a girl. . ."

"What did you tell her about me?"

"No, really, it'll work out." He patted me, and I think he forgot his new rules for a moment because his hand smoothed across the inside of my leg, then remembering, he patted it more briskly. "I told her you were worried about Margie because no one had seen her. Red knew you were with us a lot . . ." He paused, and reached into his shirt pocket for a cigarette. "I told Red you thought you could get Margie and me back together."

Reason enough for Red to be pissed—even if she didn't know what Ron and I were up to. I took the cigarette from him, lit it, took a long drag, and handed it back. "And you want to double date? What'd you say to Billy?"

"That you're smart. Fun. I told him he'd like you if he got to know you." He must have read my real question. "You mean did I tell him about this?" He stuck the cigarette in the ashtray, tilted my head up and kissed me in detail, his tongue giving me a small sample of what we weren't doing anymore. He withdrew his mouth from mine and whispered against my ear. "I'll never tell, honey."

"So, you can just quit?" I breathed back. For the last several weeks, even after bathing I was still wet from him— from the thought of him.

"We'll just quit." He held me close in the curve of his side, hands straying down my body, then sighing turned to face ahead. "But I'll be around, kid. I'll be around." He turned the key and started the engine.

With perhaps some conflicting ideas about Ron's new policy regarding me, we headed down a tractor road leading to Jacobson's meadow and straight for Billy's white '57. Ron pulled in and parked beside it in the soft grass, joining the wide circle of parked cars, noses pointed to the flatbed truck which bloomed with wires, microphones and musicians.

*

It was about 4:30 in the morning. The band, set up on the back of the truck, was laying down a pounding rockabilly beat that made the truck bounce slightly on its springs. They were driving "Great Balls of Fire" to the wall, no mean feat after Jerry Lee. I'd danced with Billy for the last three or four fast dances. Who would have thought he'd be a dancer? He twirled, and checking me with his thumb, threw me out, and brought me back right on the beat. A loose, wild dancer. The band's drummer, some kid they called Gopher, wasn't much for talking or for looking at but was dead on with his sticks. Someone had brought bottles of Jack Daniel's that were slowly moving through the crowd, and there was enough beer to float us into town, should the river run dry.

"Hey, I gotta wait one out, Billy." I was laughing at the 'who-you?' look on his face. Flushed, my lavender hair curling damply in my face, I lifted the front of my blouse and used it as a fan. "Can you find us a beer? "

Billy grinned—his mouth some heavy, juicy piece of art—and took off. He was easy. I stood just below the corner of the stage, resting against the fender of the truck cab, still flapping my blouse at my face. Jess, the lead singer, a good-looking kid who did appear to be Mexican or black, or maybe both and with a big black man's voice, jumped up and down, brought his guitar almost to the truck bed and slammed his strings as the drummer laid down a final riff on his big drum. The dancers stopped dancing and swung around to clap.

Ron walked through the crowd toward me. "Looks like

you're havin' a good time . . ." His walk was a little more swinging that usual, his gait not quite sure. He stopped in front of me, grinning. "I shoulda known you'd dance like that."

"I could dance with you." I leaned off the fender, fingers laced in front of me, and stepped close. I stared down at the top of his dusty wing tips, waiting. His arm came around my waist and he pulled me to him. "Let's forget what I said before . . . once," he said. The band began playing "Dream . . ."

"Let's dance." I reached for his hand. His body smelled and felt like it did before sex, sweaty, and smoky, fixed with suppressed eagerness. As he walked close beside me, I knew he wanted to cup my breast in his palm, suck until he began to moan, and hiking my bottom in his other hand, enter me. When we first started, he couldn't wait, but would explode with my hand on him. Thus my wondering if that was all there was to sex. I'd watched horses, but did their method apply exactly to people? I had been very happy to find out there was more to it. The Saturday night before, I'd made Ron wait for me. I thought he wouldn't like to, or wouldn't be able to, but he stopped and guided me with his hand showing me how to slow him down. He liked it so much he had me slow him again and again, but finally I'd held him to me until he was bucking to get away. Capturing his hips tight with my riding legs, I held him. When I came, it excited him so much he did too, hollering loud enough to scare the mice in the field.

We were walking slowly toward the dancers who were now thinning a bit, the rest quietly clinging together.

"Ron!" A bird-like screech from behind. Ron came to a full stop, grimaced and sighed.

I turned to face Red. "We're just gonna dance." I said. "You wanna dance? I'll dance with Billy."

Red was puffing out like a mad mare, breast rising toward me, red mane waving in the breeze off the river. "Just get away from him," she hissed, lifting a shoulder toward me.

I looked up to see Billy at her side, gawking, plainly uneasy. My experience with pissed off mares warned, stay away from teeth and feet, but before I could move, she came after me. Her hand shot out, clawing my shirt, hooking her fingers in the buttonholes, and ripping. In that moment my eye surveyed the perimeter, scanning the feet of the crowd when her other hand slashed into my hair. My strongest parts are my arms and legs from riding, and how many times had I seen Granddad's demonstration of offensive blocking stances? I crouched, head down, arms and shoulders tensed, then driving with my legs, charged.

When I hit her soft center, I knew she couldn't whip me. She was bigger and taller, but she was delicate, no athlete. I grabbed the flesh of her waist and ran right over the top of her. As she tripped and fell, I curled into a ball and rolled. I bounced up as she staggered to her feet trying to kick off a shoe that had slipped part way off and was hanging from her toes. Walking away, catching my breath, I glanced down. I had been unaware of the gaping tear, my exposed breasts, the long red streak slicing from breastbone to belly left by her nails. Some instinct made me turn back just as she came again. I had a perfect shot. I drew back, cocked my fist behind my shoulder, and was ready to let fly when from behind, I was lifted off my feet and whirled around.

"Liz, don't." Harsh breath in my ear. "Don't do anything." His arms were wrapped clear around me holding me off the ground. Tearing around Ron, Red launched herself. Clutched in his arms, I was like a wart on a toad's nose.

"You slut," she howled. "You think you got somethin'? They don't want . . . they . . . they just screw you! Whore."

The last came out of her in a sound approximating a movie monster screaming, DIE!! A guttural shriek as she charged a third time, lips wrinkled back over her mare's teeth.

Bracing against Ron, I whispered, "Hold on," or maybe

only thought it. I jerked my knees to my chin, sprang out with my heels and kicked the crap out of her chin. Of course I remembered what happened when I thumped Rudy in the side of the head—but I'd been wearing boots that night. As it was, my kick only bloodied and stunned her.

"Ah, shit, kid . . . Get out of here." Ron set me down like I was suddenly too heavy to hold. "Get Billy, and get out."

He looked at me, and for brief a moment I thought I saw something—inquiry? longing?—abruptly replaced with what may have been surprise, but he didn't speak, only shook his head, and swung around to help Red.

I backed through the crowd of onlookers, watching the smooth curve of Ron's back as he hoisted Red to her feet.

Chapter 24

ANNIE ATTENDS THE ANCESTRAL REUNION IN THE DAPPLED SHADE

WOODWARD CREEK, OREGON, SATURDAY, SEPTEMBER 20, 1958

The September sun flickering through the trees played over the backseat and my dehydrated form, tormenting me and making me feel sicker than I already was. The slight swaying of the car incited my stomach to further flip flops. My mouth felt like the barn cats had been at it, and my head pounded like the side of the stall when Lady kicked it. Mam and Granddad's voices drifted on the flickering shadows, seeming to float on the light, the sound coming in spurts, sometimes audible, sometimes a murmur. Mam, who was at her most humane when someone was sick, had almost relented, and not forced me to go. Of course, there was no question of her staying home with me. Since she'd lost again in the primary race for Governor, she'd thrown herself passionately into campaigning for the handsome and charming Mark Hatfield, and today she had to ensure that the entire family was in line to vote for him. I'd only thrown up once, so this finally made the decision. I would go with them to the reunion, and if I began to feel worse, or embarrassed her by throwing up on someone, Granddad would drive me home. I eased slowly onto my back, giving up hope of sleep, and through the window of the Mercury watched the trees flow by.

The night before, Billy had snagged a six-pack from Stroker as we'd escaped Red's screaming curses. We'd driven up McKenzie View to the bluff overlooking the river where he parked, then brought me an old sweatshirt from the trunk to wear over my ruined blouse. It smelled of oil, and boy. It smelled good. The interior of Billy's car was plusher and prettier than Stroker's. Where Stroker's interior was dark blue and gray, no floor mats, no chrome, Billy's '57 was loaded with chromed knobs and buttons, sumptuous red carpeting, plush red seats trimmed with white leather, the headliner and door panels also brilliant white. And not a mark on it. I'd slugged down two to each of Billy's beers, but he was sweet and didn't protest when I took the last one from him and drank it half down in a gulp.

He hadn't said anything about the scene we'd left, but then he laughed a little. "Never saw anything like that Red. You say somethin' to get her goin' like that?"

"No . . ." I shrugged, charmingly I hoped. "I wanted Margie and Ron to get back together, and she knows it."

He raised an eyebrow. "Ahh, she sure was mad. Red and them are Catholics, ya know. The Mexicans, they got their religion. They got a way of thinking about how things has to be, and she wants to get married."

"It's my fault. Ron and Margie used to take me with them. When they quit going together, well . . . I didn't want to stay home all the time, so I thought . . . you know, if I could get them back together . . . Mam always let me go with Margie."

"Ahhh . . ." he hesitated, lowering his cornflower blue eyes and looking directly into mine. "Do you think they'd let you go . . . with me?"

I scooted close to him. "If they won't, I'll come anyway."

His mouth drew into a lazy smile. "You don't want to be getting in trouble. You should mind your folks."

Oh boy, if he only knew. "I'll ask 'em, Billy."

At about 5:30 that morning, hoping that Uncle Jack wasn't watching out his window, I'd snuck home through the back hedge, and revved by the beer and excitement quietly extracted the bottle of scotch from the mudroom cupboard. I sat in the open doorway slugging off the bottle, my gaze tracing the gray-green herb garden, the emerging outline of brilliant orange nasturtiums under the magnolias, my senses taking over, dissolving all thought in the color, forms and earthy smells of the garden until the sun rose fully over the barn and I went in.

*

Granddad stopped at the junction, then we climbed the hill where at the top, all the relatives who would not be attending the reunion were buried in the pioneer cemetery. At the old home place where the Woodward family reunion had been held for the past eighty years, we rolled over the wooden bridge and bumped into the tree-shaded field where cars were parked every which way. Inquisitive, laughing people lugging steaming casseroles, tubs of sweet sodas, screaming kids batting balls around the clearing, squishing hugs from stale smelling old people—relatives whose names I could never remember. And the best of them Reeepublicans, because according to Mam her relatives were smarter than most. Here and there among the tree shadows, old women walked together wearing ancient sunbonnets after the fashion of their pioneer ancestors. *Maybe they'd saved their parents' bonnets. Jeez. Who could hold onto a bonnet that long? Who'd want to?* I trudged along beside Mam, who carried a large pot of fried chicken in one arm, a loaded bag full of plates, napkins, and cups in the other. We were plowing through the slew of greetings toward a stand of oaks where plank tables stood already cluttered with food. I carried nothing and didn't care; remaining upright was enough. Granddad came behind us lugging camp stools so no old people would have to stand or sit on the ground. I'd been coming to these family powwows since I could remember, and only liked them for the food. Now the thought of eating was so noxious, I had no use for any of it.

Yap, yap, yammer and yap. I'd already heard it all. Blah, blah, de blah . . . this family could tackle anything. Saw down whole mountains of trees, mill them into barn boards, walk logs in the mill ponds their boots blooming with spikes, be millionaires, timber bosses, ranchers and horse-breeders, religious fanatics, politicians—stars. They were True Oregonians; they could manage. Blah, de blah, de blah. Through slitted eyes I took in the knot of people writhing beneath the oaks. As a family, their main traits seemed to be drive like a hooting train carrying overweight, wheels on fire, hurtling from the mountain to plow you down, a hilarious sense of the obvious, and a wit that mauled like an axe more than sliced like a razor. Uncle Blue and Aunt Twittie were settling their dishes, bustling around the food table to hug a frail older woman who wore my grandmother's face, only thinner. One of her sisters, aunts? She'd had nine brothers and sisters, too many to remember.

In terms of extremis, life with this family was a slow brutal punishment to death. Total transformation only, would do. Because surely my crimes, both of commission and omission, were so grossly and unacceptably human that I must die for them. I was widely known among them for being a hard case and they didn't know the half of it. At thirteen I considered all this, shrugged, and concluded, *Oh, well.*

Aunt Alice, her brown hair down and shining, trundled up from the opposite field carrying what I knew were made from scratch lemon meringue pies. The best pies at the whole reunion. The pies were why I not only remembered her but had a special affection for her. The story went that she'd had a first marriage no one would discuss, then a bad accident when she almost died. But how had that accident occurred? There was some speculation. That's how she came by the deep scars on her body, and then Great Uncle Joe who owned the sawmill at Redmond married her anyway. And even though the family was vaguely disapproving of her previous marriage, she was a champion pie maker, funny, and had given the family a big, beautiful Woodward boy. She'd done her job.

I didn't like it, but as ever, couldn't help being drawn into Mam's tales. In Mam's company each person appeared as a walking story, stories she liked to tell over and over. And yet— the ones she didn't tell but only hinted at were most intriguing. What did Great Aunt Lilly do? Why did her daughter hate her and refuse to come to the reunion? Why did Lilly's husband deserve a medal for staying with her? They all knew but wouldn't tell me. Why did Cousin Valerie run off with the mayor if Cousin Hank was richer than God? These were mysteries that still intrigued me. I wondered if any of the elderly could really have done anything dreadful. After all, here they were at the reunion. Surely family retribution wouldn't allow relatives into the sacred grove if they were truly sinners. I was only here because no one knew. I glanced around the swirling tangle of relatives inwardly shuddering— if they knew—they'd . . . What? This stopped me for a moment. Surely—they wouldn't kill me. My stomach again flopped not only at this lurid projection, but at the smells, movement, and babble of the herd.

Just then Blue—coming from hugging on an old man sitting on a camp stool—clapped me on the shoulder. "Hey, kiddo. How you doin'? You still after them ponies?"

"Ah, hi, Uncle Blue." I gave him the best smile I could and suffered his squeeze crushed up against his hard round belly, blinking up into his happy blue eyes.

At least Linda wasn't here being miss goody girl. She was going to the lake with number three, but they were coming here first. Uncle Jack and Virgie were late too. Maybe they wouldn't come at all. I didn't want to think of Uncle Jack—of what he could have seen recently, maybe even last night. Of what he might know. Blue released me and turned enthusiastically to accost another victim. As Mam and Granddad stepped off through the rustling trees to pat and hug, to bump and nuzzle with the long lost, I made my way across the field toward the creek that branched from the river and skirted the homestead property.

The grass was high and white in the Indian summer noon, the air soft and full of the kindly smells of water, earth and stone as I distanced myself from the relatives and eased to the water's edge. The grassy creek bank sloped to flat rocks that dissolved into sand and silt in the cold burbling waters. I sat tentatively on one of the larger rocks, kicked off my tennis shoes, and slipped my feet into the icy creek. The shock roiled my stomach and caused a bolt of ice to pierce the root of my right eye. Arghh! At dawn the whiskey had been so good going down, and was now so *not* good threatening to return. Elbows on my knees, I propped my sweaty head in my hands. I let my mind drift with the sound of the river merging with the creek upstream, a gentle roar soothing as spring rain on the ranch house roof. Through the flickering trees across the creek, I glimpsed the island shimmering between the creek and river. The land was part of everyone's story. Sitting alone, gazing over the water, I hadn't escaped Mam or any of them. I could hear her voice. Another reunion when I was small.

"See that island?' she'd said, pointing to a long tree-fringed mound between the creek and river. "And this is where I lived when I was your age. She moved her finger north where the creek broke away from the river. "Our house was on this side," where I now sat with a head-knocking hangover, "but the farmland and big pastures were on the island."

The first time she'd told me about it I pictured the spot on the elevated center of the island where the big drying house had stood. I imagined a beautiful warm May day, the family moving from the main house to the island where they camped in the drying house and planted the spring garden. I saw Mam's mother and father, her middle sister Daisy, moving back and forth from the fields to the weathered board house, hoeing and weeding the ground for several warm days. In the evenings, my great grandfather would have been fishing, his plump, aproned wife frying the catch over the campfires. Later he'd play his fiddle and they'd sing until the mosquitoes drove them inside.

The way Mam told it, the family had finished the spring work and were packing the wagon, planning to cross for home the next morning. In the night a hard rain sent Woodward Creek and the McKenzie pouring over their banks. The next morning, Mam said the family stood at the door of the drying house in the dripping dawn, clothes smelling of wood smoke, sleepy eyes surveying the rushing brown river from their piece of dry ground, lamenting the flood that had already erased half their careful work in the gardens. According to Mam, there was no bridge, and by then the ford was too deep for the wagon, horses, and Mam's pregnant mother to cross. They decided to settle in and wait it out. I heard Mam's laughter, "Guess I got off schedule somehow 'cause I turned up early. Daisy said that Dad dashed around all that night with his boot strings dragging because he didn't have time to lace them. "No fuss about it," she'd said, "when the river went down, they climbed aboard the wagon and went home—with one extra—me!"

I wished it was me who had been born then. Then I'd be Mam. I'd have a real mother and father. I'd be Mam, but I wouldn't have some grandkid I didn't want to raise. I would have a son and a daughter but the daughter would not tear all over the country with a rodeo, and my son would be a kind and happy person who minded his own business. I'd be Jack's mother and could give him a good smack when he needed it. At that moment, I was quite sure that it would have been better to be anyone but me. I rubbed little circles at my temple, wishing my headache away. The slices Red's fingernails had carved down my chest stung like the main drag in a fire ant parade. Recently, I'd been thinking that the more I was with Ron and away from my family, the more it seemed possible to like being me. Considering last night, I wasn't so sure.

After sunning my feet in the warm sand, I dipped them into the icy water and it was no longer so shocking. My stomach was giving hints that it might return to almost normal, but a foul and heavy haze lurked in the center of my head. I pictured its interior, a putrid yellow green at the center, fading to black as it carried to the edges, then a brilliant line of nervy scarlet connecting me to the outside world.

A yellow twig floated downstream on the current. "A log on the 100-mile drive in 1908," Mam's voice chirped. I couldn't even get away from her when I was away from her. That tale had been about the dangerous river drives and why Granddad would fire any logger who drank during the drive.

Okay, so my great grandparents weren't drinkers. But were they all so proper? I had never smelled them or looked into their eyes, so how could I know them? They were only visions imposed on my mind through my grandmother's busy mouth. If my great grandparents were looking down on the reunion and could see into people, as I now supposed God could, then if they saw into me, they'd be as sick to their stomachs as I was. Both of them, because Mam said they always did everything together. Even died on the same day. Was that really sweet and spiritual, or twisted and weird?

I'd just sent the perfect skipper bombing across the creek when I heard the dinner bell kick off with a head-cracking clang. That would be Uncle Shorty, Mam's older brother. He was the self-appointed dinner bell whacker. I rose, taking care not to upset my head, and bare feet scuffing the warm dirt, started back toward the tables under the oaks. Johnnie and Sherd's kids tossed bats and mitts on an old horse blanket, in use as a temporary catcher's plate, and came galloping from the opposite field. Granddad, always the coach, his favorite fedora pushed back on his head, walked beside Butch, the biggest kid and best hitter, demonstrating a ball grip. I knew he was talking to Butch in the quiet, kind way in which he always met things. I eyed the loud boys. The year before, I'd been running with them; now they looked like scruffy little kids.

"Feelin' better, Punkin'? Granddad said as I approached.

"Yeah, kinda." I smiled my best 'I'm really a good kid' smile. Mam had probably told him it was about my period. She seemed to think my recent period was a big deal. The way she said it, kind of pursed in the mouth and facing away from me, "Now that you have your period"—fill in the blank—"who knows what might happen; there is woe; yes, I know the pain," and all that. Truth was, I never even knew I was having a period, until I did. It was no problem, just an inconvenience like having to get dressed before going outside.

These relative women with their boobs and perms, their bossy ways, seemed to run the whole show. Some were soft, and some, like Mam, were not, but at these events they were always in my face just like Aunt Elsie there by the food table. Standing covertly watching the feast preparations, trembling on the balls of her tiny feet waiting to step in at any catastrophe of spilled food or bruised feelings, to plunge in and right the entire production, this was her mission in life. That, and introducing everyone to her Jesus. She always said the prayer before dinner, and sometimes her brothers made faces over her head while she was doing it. So did Mam. If anyone found me a sinner, Aunt Elsie would be the one to do it. She was cute though, and I liked her, but her clean world scared me. She hurried toward me on little feet. The same feet as Mam, but even smaller and cuter; the two were rivals, in style and for top family woman of their generation. It burned Mam that Aunt E was proud to be the younger of them. Mam of course was the one with better sense.

"Oh, Annie, now, the Lord has certainly blessed you this year, dear," Aunt Elsie trilled.

She delivered this appraisal looking me up and down with penetrating hazel eyes, a very sweet smile on her clean pink lips. Her blouse was feminine with white ruffles framing her creamy, non-freckled face, her bright red hair waving into a soft twist at the back. A little plump, but smartly turned out in pumps and matching purse, trim linen duster—nothing out of place but the merry inquisitive sparkle in her eyes.

"Now, Jewel, Jewel," she turned to find her daughter, cousin Jewel. Jewel, as Jewel In The Crown, was the tall one, the perfect one, the one with the stiffest crinolines and the highest grades. She was a soprano, and a piano player, she was the perfect cousin. To me, just another strange adult.

Grasping Jewel by the hand, Aunt E hurried her to me and presented her for my inspection. *Just too wonderful for words.*

"Well, Cousin Annie. Aren't you looking well? Isn't this a pleasant day?" Jewel clasped her hands at her waist and waited for me to answer.

The bell clanged again, rending my fog.

"Shhshh! Shsshh! Uncle Shorty's going to speak." Uncle Shorty was the one with ALL the money. "Sshhh!" *Oh, and who's Mr. Proper, scowling at me from the edge of the crowd?*

Uncle Jack had finally arrived. *Was that look because he knew something or was this just one of his bad-to-worse days? Could he know that I had seen him mooning over the dentist's wife and trying to kiss her after the BBQ at the lake? Had he seen me last night? I'd have to keep an eye out.* I never knew when or where he'd try to nail me nor the weapon he'd use to pound it.

Shorty stood in shirt sleeves and suspenders under the oaks in the middle of the circled kin. He wasn't called Shorty in an ironic sense; he was shorter than most of the Woodward men and a little stout but always strong looking and in charge, his laughing eyes calculating, his memory long. "Let's all come on into the center now. Sister Elsie will do some praying. Come on here, you kids. Let's get started now so we can eat!"

Aunt E, smiling and looking very prim, nodded to her redheaded girls who began a hymn to the Lord, the tune of which I can't remember. The sisters could sing, and after six full verses they transitioned smoothly into the blessing—Aunt E's kick in the ribs. She gained speed like a newly broke wild pony who breaks the rope and runs away. She ran on . . . and on. Head down, eyes cast down, hands clasped in front of her. "Lord bless, more, more, and we thank him, and we just love and appreciate him . . . more, more, and he guides us, and we are nothing without his blood. Jesus, we plead the blood over the family and . . . more, more, more . . . And especially cleanse us, Lord, cleanse us, Jesus, cleanse all those here today of the evils of alcohol and tobacco, and bad language and . . ."

Shorty's hand shot in the air, "Thank you, sister." Then, louder, "Thank you. Amen, folks. Amen." Still holding up his hand like a benediction.

Aunt E looked up, lashes rising a tiny bit at a time rather uncertainly, smiled slightly and nodded her head to Shorty as if to say, 'Yes, brother, I'm done, but I got that part in. I got it in because the Lord wanted it.' A slight sweet smile. It was well known that Aunt Elsie thought our side of the family, namely Mam, was largely responsible for her brothers', especially Shorty's and Eli's, bad habits, and she always made a point of it when the families were together. For years, she'd been highly upset with Mam for letting the boys get away with blue murder. Furthermore, she said Mam's indulgent attitude toward them had beguiled them down the path of the demon booze. These charges referred to Mam's habit of inviting them to sleep off their wild nights on the town in Jack's basement room at the house on the hill. Mam had said she figured this was better than them ending up in the ditch or worse, having to face her sister, Great Aunt Flora, their bodies reeking of alcohol. Aunt E pronounced behaviors both on Mam's part (she should know better) and the boys' (wild kids) shameful, shrugged deeply, and asked anyone who would listen, "What can I do given the family history?"

Well, she could talk, she could mention Jesus with every breath, and she could surely make me feel like I was going to burn if I couldn't live up to her fair and lovely Jesus. Still, I liked her. She was funny even though she didn't always mean to be, and she seemed to like me. Granddad said that where Aunt Elsie made her mistake was broadcasting on the evils of alcohol.

"No one," he said, "can understand and expound on the comprehensive evils of drink—doesn't matter that her dad took too much too often—unless one has drunk, and usually far too much." I guessed that meant he didn't think she knew what she was talking about.

Flurrying about, radiating goodness, Aunt E crossed to their table. "Annie, you come and sit with us if you'd like. We've been doing some interesting work that you might like to hear about."

At their table, she whipped out a flowered cloth, and spread it over the wooden planks.

Her interesting work would be church stuff, but even that was better than having to sit with Jack. He and Virgie and the kid were slipping into the bench across from Mam and Granddad. Granddad liked the kid, but I was still jealous. I didn't want to be, but she seemed to have the better deal. With all that blonde hair and big brown lost doggy eyes, she was cuter than me, even if I was older, and the real grandchild. *Oh shit, Aunt E's Jesus would surely strike me down if I didn't quit that kind of thinking. Right now. Hah!*

I slurped water from the red cooler wishing it were beer and watched the relatives swirl around the food like worms on a cadaver, leaving nothing but clean-picked bones and a litter-strewn empty table. I sat through dinner gingerly, at the end of the bench, trying to pay attention to Aunt E's description of the terrible plight of the Indians on a reservation in Arizona while the flies dive-bombed our plates, and I tried to ignore my pounding head and aching chest. I glanced up to see Uncle Jack glowering my way and ducked my head attentively toward Aunt E.

"We're collecting clothes and money for them. Why you just cannot imagine how bad they have it. Did you know they have TB down there? We're sending missionaries to build a church house."

"Wouldn't it be better to build them a hospital?"

Aunt E's husband, George, his bushy white head nodding, smiled my way.

"Oh, Annie, now remember," Aunt E beamed with real concern. "Jesus is the one who heals. If we give them Jesus, they'll have what they need."

"But the church does send medicine," George said, wiping his mouth, waving his napkin at the blue flies, then placing it on his empty plate. "We can't find doctors who want to practice on the reservations—yet. We're working on it though. We've raised plenty so far."

If you feed a dog, they'll quit hunting. This was Mam's take on helping the down and outers. Yet, faced with some poor sick individual, she'd be all over them with kindness, like the flies on the dessert table. Hard as nails one minute, soupy with charity the next.

"Well now," Aunt E said loudly, standing and beginning to clear away the plates, "we thought we'd get around and sing together."

The party crowd sitting behind her sagged noticeably. I figured they probably had a bottle out in their truck and wanted to get back to it. When Blue noticed me watching them, he said, "They're taking bets on the Oregon State game next week. Oregon lost to Idaho yesterday."

I sidled toward the one remaining piece of lemon meringue pie then moved to the base of a big oak and sat eating the pie and thinking about Ron. Billy was more handsome, but Ron was the one I wanted. The background music to my romance was the Cardinals singing about being as close as two things could be, what they called a doo wop song, and I couldn't get it to stop; that dip and slide, the feeling that I was honey, and he was the bee. That's how close I felt to Ron. Somehow, we were weird in the same way. But, after last night, I didn't believe he liked me at all, and I also did not believe what he said about me being too young. I obviously hadn't been too young when we started. And it was also obvious he liked sex with me, so Red must be better at it. *He shoved me off on Billy because of Red. He likes Red better. Fine. I'll like Billy better. Billy is more handsome. Much better looking than Ron. I just don't know him very well. When I get to know Billy better, we'll be as close as Ron and I, and then I'll forget Ron . . .*

"ANNIEEEE."

I jumped up and tossed my plate at the foot of the tree. She barreled around the trunk still screaming my name just as I was fixing to run.

"Oh, there you are." Her long red hair pulled back and fastened with a barrette at the base of her neck, she wore my favorite black blouse tucked into white shorts. "Mam said you were having some troubles. Did you start your period?"

"No. I just didn't want to come. You took your time."

"John had to get the boat ready. She gestured toward the field where the cars were parked. Hard to miss. The boat stuck up behind the pink Chrysler like a giant golden banana. "We thought you might like to go to the lake when we're done but I guess if you're sick . . . .."

"I'm gonna go home and ride." Even if I had wanted to go to the lake, my lacerated chest would tell a story I wasn't about to share.

"Now . . . if you're having your period."

"I am *not* having my period." I growled this through my teeth. *Was she deaf?*

"But if you are, maybe you shouldn't ride."

"But I'm NOT. Can't *anybody* hear?"

"Now, don't raise your voice. There's no reason for you to raise your voice."

*

We were standing in a big, ragged circle, Aunt E intending to lead us in song. In the shifting shade, the relatives looked like they had some weird splotching disease. Outside the circle, the September sun had turned the scorching afternoon a dazzling white. Uncle George handed me a songbook and patted me on the shoulder, a wide-open grin on his big face. *Oh, jeez, did they all have to be sooo nice?* I glanced down at the paper to avoid the smirks on Mam's and Linda's faces. *Church songs of course.*

"Let's turn to number six, 'Where Could I Go But To The

Lord,'" Aunt E said, and they launched into a four part harmony. A better mimic than singer, I was able to adjust my wavering soprano to hers. She turned her head sharply towards me, smiled and lifted her sandy eyebrows, I assumed in encouragement, and we sang along together, vowels flattened, voices raised, until the song's end where she left me in the dust with the final high notes.

In the pause before a new song, encouraged by my small singing success, I blurted, "Let's sing 'Michael, Row the Boat Ashore.'"

"Well, now . . ." she paused, eyes on the printed sheet. "I don't see that one." She frowned slightly.

"Oh, you know, it's on the radio. It's a folk song."

A small curl of smile that did not reach her eyes. "Oh, Annie. The radio? Why, we don't listen to radio music." Her voice was not accusing, more pitying.

"It's like this . . ." and I began to sing. Now she was frowning, her clear brow contracting into a rumple of disapproval, her hazel eyes narrowing on me. I glanced up to see Shorty looking on with a big grin on his face.

"That is not the kind of thing we'll want to sing or listen to, Annie, and it would be better if you didn't either."

"But, Aunt Elsie . . ."

"Turn to the last page." She reached out and flipped my book over, then humming a note, she began, bright eyes holding mine. "Drifting Too Far From The Shore." She sang the whole song right to me, the two Js piping along. Face flaming, head pounding again, I cast my eyes on the page and pretended to sing. As we blundered through the second chorus, I looked up to see her smiling mouth, still singing to me. I wished that like some of the other elderly, she had a long whisker, so I could pull it. "Come to Jesus today," she warbled. "Let him show you the way. You're drifting too far from the shore."

Later, finally walking down the path toward the car, I heard footsteps coming up behind me when Uncle Jack was at my side, his head dropped even with mine: "You think you got away with something last night? Well, you didn't. I saw you, and I'm gonna tell them." His big face was close to mine, his whiskers red and sharp looking, thick lips darkened by his foul-smelling chewing tobacco.

"I'll tell Mam and Virgie I saw you at the back of the boathouse with your hand up Mrs. McCarthy's dress. I can prove it too." *I couldn't but how would he know?*

His head jerked around when Linda hollered: "Jack! Mam says to come talk to Blue about helping with the Logging Convention before you leave."

He looked down at me, his face redder even than usual, his eyes huge behind his glasses. "That's a damn lie and you know it! You say one word, and you won't know what hit you."

*

"Well, I guess you'll listen to me from now on." Mam sat in the front seat knitting, stabbing the needles through the yarn as if it were her offending, more petite, and richer niece. Granddad, driving us home, was smoking. "She's nutty as a fruitcake, Annie." She looked at Granddad. "How George can put up with that is more than I'll ever know."

"So, she doesn't listen to the radio because of her church?"

"And she doesn't read books because of the church. And she doesn't go to dances or movies because of the church, and she doesn't wear lipstick. Gawd knows what else doesn't she do because of the church. Humph," Mam snorted.

Granddad turned his head toward her, "Now, Mother . . ." He looked at me in the rearview.

"Well, Daddy, I just do *not* know what to do with her. She gave that big diamond ring George bought her to the church.

I can't believe it. She's just driving her family crazy with it. You ought to hear . . ."

"What kind of church is it? Is it like LaVetta's?"

"Oh, for Gawd's sake, Annie. It's some snake-charmer tent church where they moan and flail in the dirt looking for their bleedin' Jesus. How any relative of mine got into such a mess is beyond me, and now look! Her whole family's just a mess except the boys, and don't you believe it doesn't have its effect on them."

"If your family didn't go to that church, why did your sister?"

"Lookit errr, Annie." He was going to call me Punkin' again, but apparently decided not to. "Not everyone believes the same way. Now, Mother"—and he tipped his head to Mam—"and I believe another way than Grandma and Aunt Elsie's side of the family, and that's just it."

"What?"

Mam's needles stopped clicking and they both turned their heads to look at me.

"What way?"

"Annie, that's the thing about it. All of us can believe what we want." He looked sharply at Mam, who set her knitting aside. She twisted fully to face me, wearing her 'get-to-business' face, her cheeks pink from the day.

She launched with an exasperated sigh. "The Woodwards are too smart to buy into some church scheme. William—now, he was my great, great, great grandfather—came from England on a ship indentured to a preacher in Boston. That means he had to work for this preacher until he paid off his trip. Elsie still has a letter from William to his wife, telling of four-hour sermons preaching hellfire and damnation that he had to sit through twice a week. William was a Christian, but he'd just crossed the ocean to get away from that kind of religious craziness that Mom and Elsie are messed up with."

She looked meaningfully at Granddad, who kept his eyes on the road. "William had paid hard-earned gold to get to this country, and he wasn't going to be bound by the same hysterical maniacs who were killing their countrymen over religion. He hightailed it."

"He left?" *This was interesting.* "So, he was an outlaw? "Where did he go?"

"Oh, Connecticut, a little before he should have, but no one followed him. My dad figured William didn't hold with that kind of hard religion. Neither did his brothers who came over later. They were believers, but they believed in God, not church. That's what the Woodwards have always believed. And that's what Daddy and I believe."

The hush of tires rolling along the road filled the car, punctuated by Mam's clicking needles and the chomping of her gum. I had just finished reading *Exodus* and had been thrilled by the intense fight the Jews had been willing to put up to live and believe as they chose. And there was Mr. Melnyk standing on the deck of the boat in the cutting wind. He'd called Mam a criminal for telling me what to think. Too much for one day.

"Well, I don't get it. If there's only one God, what difference does it make which church you go to?"

Grandad glanced into the mirror and winked. "That's it, kiddo."

As Mam turned to face the front, I said, "What would you say if I told you I saw Uncle Jack behind his truck kissing Eddie's wife?"

Chapter 25

ANNIE AND BILLY CALL ON A NATURAL BEAUTY

SPRINGDALE, OREGON, APRIL 1959

That fall, I had spent time working my way back into the Delaunay's' good graces. At first when I called, LaVetta wouldn't let me talk to Margie, but I had finally worn her down. Nearly every day that September, I would ride Lady down the road to the cottage under the trees, drop the reins, and leave her grazing in front of the roses. While Lady rummaged in the yard, I'd knock on the door until someone peered out the window and told me to go away. I called every single day. Often after school, I'd call then walk down the road and help Grandma Delaunay in her front garden. I kept a sharp eye out and if anyone ventured from the cottage across the road, I'd make a point of hollering, "Hi, I made it."

One day, Grandma stood in the side garden with her flesh-colored stockings rolled around her ankles, holding a basket and peering at the cottage across the road. I was pulling up carrots and handing them to her.

"She's living over there like a hermit, now, and it's just got to stop." She brushed dirt from the carrots with fleshy knobbed fingers. "Annie, you go over there and cheer Margie up."

When Margie's grandma humped into her house, I walked down the rock path between the big maples, crossed the road and stood looking at the kitchen window where I could see LaVetta at the sink. I waved.

By November of 1958, I was back, and Margie's stomach was poking out. Pregnant! Margie wasn't showing too much by then, but LaVetta had a nervous breakdown, stopped going to church, and weighed about two pounds.

"That woman is too wound up for her own good," Grandma had remarked one afternoon as we were strolling through the filbert orchard behind the house, checking to see if the nuts were ready. "Why, you'd think no one in the world ever had a baby." Grandma wasn't a big one for smiling, but she'd smiled down at me then, and it occurred to me that she'd wouldn't be at all upset at having a baby around. She added another ripe nut to her apron pocket then brushed her hands and turned toward the house.

*

I remember the winter of 1959 as a blur of cruising and making out with Billy. But only making out. He was a shy boy but a good kisser. It wasn't because I hadn't tried that we had not gone further. We'd get so far, then he'd give me a hard hug, and say, "time to go now," . . . even if it wasn't. I didn't know why he was so polite, so good, until that spring, around my fourteenth birthday. It was a sharp sunny day in April after what seemed like weeks of rain, and everything smelled of grass and lilacs. Billy didn't like to drive the car in the rain because it dirtied the gleaming white undercarriage, so we hadn't been out for a couple of weeks. When he called that morning to ask if I wanted to go for a ride, I'd said sure.

"Wear something kinda' nice," he said. "We're going visiting."

I had a new blue and white striped seersucker outfit, a tuck-in shirt, straight skirt, and a white sweater to go with my gleaming white Keds. The lavender had washed out of my hair, leaving it pale and white as milk. It was long, waving past my shoulders, and LaVetta had just trimmed the back straight across like Candice Bergen's.

That day as Billy and I drove by the Delaunay cottage, Edward was out in the front digging in the rose beds. I had Billy honk, and we both waved. Edward looked up, but we passed the house before I could see if he waved back.

"How's Ron?" I asked. Billy had stopped at the crossroads and was listening to the car's idle, revving it, then listening again. The October before when Ron had found out that Margie was pregnant and didn't want anything to do with him, he'd gone into a slump.

"Pretty good. He's been takin' it kinda' easy here lately. Nothing much goin' on 'til May, when we can race," Billy said. "He put new heads on Stroker . . . been working on that for a while. He's driving his dad's truck, so he's sticking close."

"Oh. Well, we should go to the show or something. Ask him to come. Does he have a new girlfriend yet?"

"Nope. He's still pretty mad about everything."

I had been satisfied to hear from Billy that Ron and Red had split up, and Red had left town. As far as I was concerned, she couldn't go far enough.

"Do you like this?" I said, lifting the collar of my new shirt. He hadn't said anything about my outfit. "Where are we going?"

He was turning down the Old Coburg Bridge Road toward Springdale. He drove on, not replying, lighting a cigarette, keeping his eye on the road, heading toward the river. At the intersection leading to the bridge there was a barrier and signs with lots of big earthmovers parked in a vacant lot. We turned and took the old road that ran along the river.

"C'mon, Billy. Where are we going? What's all that equipment parked out here for?"

He patted my leg lightly. "Dad told me they're building a ramp onto the new freeway. Damned if I know why they need it here though. And you look pretty as always. I like that kind of skirt. Makes you look taller than the fluffy ones."

Was that a compliment, or what? I frowned into my lap. Maybe he was teasing because I thought I looked really good. He'd said this was a special date, so I'd taken extra care that I was turned out as they'd taught me in the department store charm school Mam had made me attend that fall. I had liked the class because they had given all of us makeup cases and I'd had my picture in the paper, modeling a very tight skirt. "The freeway doesn't even come out here, anyway."

I looked up to see him grinning down at me. "It will before you know it. It's supposed to be open in five years or so." *Oh, boy, that red, red, mouth.* He could do anything, and it'd be all right with me. His black lashes swept over a brilliant blue eye when he winked. "You look perfect, Lizzy."

We were in a part of Springdale, the mill town across the river, that Mam said was like all lumber towns—rough and rowdy. The road ran directly beside the river, a swath of deep green on the water side, a steep, treed hill on the other. Soon, we turned up the hill. And then a long, steep driveway, where we pulled into a parking spot in front of a white house with large windows overlooking the wide river. The house had the best view of the valley I'd seen, except maybe from Jo's house across the river. The mountains to the east were clear blue, the river before us glittering green in the sunshine, the town spread below softened by distance. You couldn't see the poverty, the run-down shacks of the old mill town from up here.

"Now, we won't smoke."

"Okay, Billy. Where are we?"

"You'll see." He was grinning again, stabbing out his cigarette in the ashtray. He moved the mirror (something he'd told me never to do), adjusted it just so, took a comb out of his back pocket and carefully tamed his curly hair into smooth black waves.

Inside, the house was full of light. The colors softened almost to fading, all cream, rose, and whisper green, the silvered spring light falling in washes across the living room floor. Before the window in a blue velvet chair sat a pale, erect, and beautiful woman.

"Ah, Billy, dear." She did not rise as we entered the room.

"Mama." He crossed the room and kissed her cheek. For that moment it was as though they were alone. I stood in the doorway surveying the room. It wasn't as big as it first appeared, but everything in it was perfect, a perfect setting for the woman. All feminine, full of light and mellow shadows, clean, and in absolute order. A Selznick movie set. Billy stepped back, and turned to me. "Ahh, Mama, this is Liz. Liz Butler."

Her hand, still holding his, was thin and pale, her middle finger almost an inch longer than the others. She wore a soft white blouse, tucked into a dark skirt that completely covered her legs and feet. Long black hair, silvered around her face, was swept back and trapped in a heavy black net. Her skin was milk white and smooth. The dark blue eyes were not as keen as Billy's but somehow softer and a shade lighter. The smile as I approached her was warm, but reserved. Or was it vague?

"Why, Liz. Billy has told me so much about you." She gestured me to an armless chair facing her but slightly distant. She patted a chair next to her indicating that Billy sit there. Then as if recalling something she'd lost, "Oh, darling, would you see to the tea?"

She looked in my direction, smiled again. Wan effort, I thought. Definitely from the south, somewhere deep and humid, maybe Louisiana, places I associated with television and black children walking into white schools. The drawl had not originated in Oregon. Billy turned and moved through a white-painted, much-polished swinging door, and we were alone. We stared at each other, me sitting with my back straight, ankles properly crossed. *Jeez, if she knew what I thought about when Billy and I were alone together, she'd probably croak.* She didn't look like she could take much of anything.

"Please call me Lillian, dear. I hear from Billy that you like to ride and have a lovely black and white horse. Tell me about your horse, will you?"

"Oh. Thanks, ah, thank you. Mizz . . . Lillian. Ahhh, she's . . ." What could I tell this woman about Lady? She didn't seem the type to bother distinguishing horse from dog. "Well, she was my mother's horse. But now I ride her." Best not to tell her about the rodeos.

There was a muffled bang as Billy pushed through the swinging door carrying a cloth-draped tray and arranged upon it an elegant tea service with three china teacups, a green teapot, matching sugar and creamer, and three white lace-edged napkins.

"Yes, Billy told me your mother was a rodeo rider." The words were foreign on her tongue.

Billy set the tray on the table between their chairs, then stood back surveying it.

"Is that it, Mama?"

"Thank you, dear." She reached for the teapot, then hesitated. "Perhaps you don't take tea, Liz?"

"Oh, no, we have tea. I like tea."

"Sugar, then?"

"No. Ahh, no sugar, thanks. No cream either."

She poured carefully and held the cup out to me. I rose, accepted the cup, and clinging to the fragile saucer, cautiously retreated to my chair, the cup brimming with steaming, quaking liquid. There was no table on which to place the saucer, so I held it in my hand, not drinking. Inch by inch, sluicing only a bit over the cup's rim, I lowered it to my bare knees, where it sat, burning.

"You sure have a pretty view." I'd play Mam pretending to have manners. Talk about whatever came to mind, as long as the subject had no substance and flattered the target. Lillian turned and gazed out the window, her eyes passing over the town, the river, coming back to rest on Billy. Set against the window, her profile was severe yet softened by the fullness of her lips and the slight droop of a winged eyebrow. Her faintly slanted eyes were like lapis stones set above prominent cheekbones, the longish perfectly straight nose with finely cut nostrils led the eye to an elegantly shaped mouth, a finer version of Billy's more succulent one. All this glory was set on a slender white neck swathed in a frothy scarf that made her neck seem even longer. No makeup. A natural beauty.

"Yes. I like it here." There was a note of something like regret in her voice. She was saying she liked it, but that's not what she said. It made me wonder about Billy's dad. I'd met him once briefly at a garage in Springdale. A wiry man, who, when I'd seen him, had been wearing oily overalls. A grease-smudged face and thinning gray hair combed back from a high forehead, but most distinct was a high, nasally laugh. He'd reminded me a little of Ron. "Billy, did you happen to see that list in the kitchen, dear? If you could just stop by the market for me later . . ."

She looked at me, shoulders raised, eyebrows elevated in what might have been a look of apology. "Billy's so good to help me. He's just the best boy in the world."

"And you're the best, Mama," he said.

Chapter 26

IN 1959, A CONSEQUENCE OF ANNIE'S MISCONDUCT BRINGS UNCLE JACK TO THE RESCUE, WHILE IN 1999, ANNIE MAKES A FATEFUL DECISION

CHAPMAN RANCH, ARMITAGE ROAD, MAY 1959

The next Saturday, Billy and I cruised through the sunshine to the do-it-yourself car wash on River Road with the radio blaring "What a Difference a Day Makes," Dinah singing. We spent the afternoon listening to the radio, washing, polishing and vacuuming his '57. It was my job to scrub the wheel wells with Brillo pads. I tried to stay clean and not get soap in my hair, but it was useless. My white blouse was black spotted, the sunburned ends of my hair slimed in suds when I finished. We sat on a short concrete wall and drank Cokes while the sun dried the car and us. On the radio the Cardinals were singing, about crying from loneliness-doo-wop-declaring their open and undying love.

Next step, detailing. I held up a newspaper shield while Billy squatted beside me and resprayed the wheel wells white. The searing smell of paint flew directly up my nose, making my head spin, but he kept shaking and spraying, shaking and spraying until a perfectly smooth and sparkling coat of white framed his wheels. The song ended, "close as two is to three," and I thought of Ron but as Billy sprayed and shook the can, I watched his sinewy arm, the delicate ropy muscles shifting beneath gold skin, the white T-shirt pulling over his wide-boned shoulders and wanted to run my hand down his back.

I wanted to be close with Billy like I had been with Ron, but Billy sure wasn't Ron. When things got barely warm, Billy would say, "Why, Liz, now, you want to be careful." Like there was something hidden to be careful of. The more I tried not to think of what it might be, the more I was sure it was some new intriguing sexual situation that could potentially occur between us. But what?

Finally finished, we placed the blanket from the trunk on the front seat and sat with the doors open talking about nothing, waiting for the wheel wells to dry.

"Good to get her cleaned up now. Only a few weeks 'til we can start racing. Some car club guys asked us to help build their engine, so me and Ron's gonna be over at their garage working on it."

"Is that where Ron took Stroker?"

"Yeah. It's almost finished." Billy looked down at his cigarette, long lashes veiling his eyes. "We'll be taking it to the drags in Woodburn this year, besides the midnight runs. He's got the money."

What he didn't say was—I wish I did. But it was loud as if he had spoken. *Why didn't he have money? They worked together at the mill.*

When Billy figured the wheel wells were dry enough, he reached into the glove box and took out a longish box. Inside was a new chrome gear shift rod with The Klan logo stamped on it. He unscrewed the round chrome knob on the old shifter and handed it to me to hold. He affixed the new rod which did add a very special finish to our efforts. We admired it together, shook out the blanket, stored it in the truck, then cruised slowly home.

Billy and I drove up to the ranch around five that evening. I had snapped off the radio when the news came on. Everything was silent save the crunch of sparkling clean whitewalls on gravel. No one at home. I was to feed the horses because Mam and Granddad had to wear their dress clothes and preside at a Masonic doing and then go on to a second event, a big political party for Hatfield (again). Mam said he was an Eisenhower Republican, a man and handsome to boot, and as such he had to win the election. They'd be back late. I'd tell Billy I needed him to help feed the horses, then promise food to lure him into the house.

We were sitting in the front living room in Granddad's big leather chair. Me on Billy's lap, things heating up. I slid his hand inside my blouse and hiked my skirt so the material wouldn't be between us. He was hard under me, his mouth wet and open, my hair falling over us, veiling the light, curtaining a moist, tumescent world. I thought we were finally getting somewhere. I moved my bottom, gently rocking, lost in sensation and anticipation. His open mouth enclosing mine seemed to ooze water and he suddenly relaxed under me like a racehorse who has reached his limits and gives up the race.

He pulled back, patted me, and looked at his watch. "I gotta get. Got to be someplace."

Too dazed to register this pronouncement, I simply sat in his lap looking into his eyes, trying to read them. "Ah, git up now, Liz."

"Billy, what's wrong? Why do you always stop?"

"Now, Liz, I uhh, I just . . . I really gotta get back." He began to stand, bracing me so that I didn't fall. At the door when I tried to lean into him, he only held me for a moment before he turned, pushed the screen door open and skipped down the steps two at a time.

"Well, call me," I said more to myself than to his back.

I staggered back to the big warm chair, slid into it, and watched out the window as Billy's beautiful car shot down the drive. I heard it growl onto the road. I sat.

So enmeshed in my own gloomy web of plots and counterplots, motivations and psychological sussings, I didn't immediately register the vehicle in the driveway. *Could he have come back? Oh, murder! Uncle Jack. All of 'em, and the dog, piling out of Aunt Virgie's Chevrolet.* Uncle Jack led the herd, charging up the front walk like a rutting bull. With a boom of the heavy door hitting the wall, he entered the house. He stood plaid shirted, red suspendered, towering in the arch between the entry hall and living room surveying the big room, arms hanging straight at his sides.

"Virgie," he roared, "go down and see if there's any more of 'em."

She turned and disappeared through the kitchen.

"What's goin' on?"

"That's just what I'm here to find out." He glowered there, stolid as a stump of the old growth timber he hauled every day on his truck. A cross between a frustrated bull in heat and a 1000-year-old tree stump—he stood firm, snorting into the room.

"Okay, git up, and git your stuff. You're going to your mother's."

"I'm not going anywhere. I'm feeding, and I'm staying here."

"You had someone here. You're going to your mother's, and right now. Git up."

Virgie, holding her darling golden-haired child, appeared in the hallway behind him, face sober, eyes wide. She shook her head at me. Was it in condemnation, or was she trying to tell me something?

"You can't come around here and tell me what to do. You're not my boss."

He stepped into the room. "You treat the folks like they was nothin' to you, and you're not gonna do it anymore. You're also a damned liar." He delivered his message with utter assurance. "They told you. They said you couldn't have anybody here. And yewww had 'em here anyways. Now, git your stuff."

"I didn't know anybody peed in Granddad's boot that time . . . it wasn't my fault. Billy just brought me home. Do you see anybody here? Do you see any big party? Besides, I'm not the one sneaking around trying to kiss people's wives. Just leave me alone."

He took another step. I was sitting with my knees drawn up in the big chair. I'd been letting it cuddle me while trying to understand Billy's ways and was in no mood for Jack.

"Why don't you just keep your nose out of everybody's business? Go home and look out your window some more or I'll tell them what else I saw."

"You *will* do what I say, by gawd." Behind him Aunt Virgie took a step back and shook her head frantically.

"You can't scare me like you scare them. Not anymore . . . Bully-boy!" I'd delivered my message with utter assurance to match his.

He leapt forward.

Suddenly wound up, I uncoiled from the chair, like the back leg of a horse that springs to nail you. He tried to grab my feet but missed, catching me by an arm and side where his meaty claws dug into my flesh like thick knives. No sharp strikes, this was a mauling. I had thrown my arms overhead to defend myself when he drove me into the floor, rolling on top of me, banging my head on the thickly carpeted floor, nearly taking my wind. I powered my feet into his fat belly, struggling silently, landing sharp blows, and gouging with my nails.

With a grunt, he pried me onto my back, preparing to

straddle me, going for my arms to pin them over my head. I bucked and using my muscled riding legs brought my knees up sharply, turned under him and squeezed out between his meaty thighs. Scrambling to my feet directly behind him, I took aim between the red suspenders and landed a stunning barefoot blow somewhere between his back and a slab of blue-jeaned butt. With a bawl, he turned and threw himself on me, this time whaling fists to my head and shoulders. Ducking blows, I streaked to the other side of the big room, aiming to slip between the sofa and wall, use the upholstery as a shield. I became aware of the dog barking and Aunt Virgie's piercing screams as he blundered toward me, a grimace dragging at his heavy features. I was panting, wondering how far he'd really carry this thing. *Why doesn't Virgie do something? What grown-up is supposed to behave like this?*

About that time, Uncle Jack seemed to notice the screaming, and chanced a look in his wife's direction. Leaping past him, I tore through the entry hall leaving bug-eyed looks on the faces of Virgie and her charming child. I hit the back door, sprinted behind the hedge, through the barn, and was halfway to Grandma Delaunay's place, before I heard the car start. It was more or less understood that Grandma Delaunay's orchards were off limits to outsiders, but Grandma and I were friends.

As usual at that time of the evening, she was crocheting in the upstairs bedroom when I skidded onto the porch and tapped my special rat-a-tat-tat at the back door just out of politeness. She was going deaf, and I didn't want to scare her.

"That you, Annie? Up here."

"Can I use the phone?" I hollered up the stairs.

"Hey?"

I climbed the first two steps. "Phone," I screamed.

"Come up when you're done." She was used to me stopping in, but less since I'd found men and cars.

I could have called Linda at her fancy cocktail party, made her come to the ranch to witness the carnage her brother had inflicted on me, but instead I called information for the number of the cab company. "Pick me up at the corner of Armitage Road and County Farm," I said. *I'd just go on over there and let them see the damage firsthand.*

*

The whiskered cabdriver hesitated, looking me over through dust-splattered glass before rolling down his window halfway. "Now what's all this?"

"I'm going to 20225 Timberline, over by South. My mother's paying." My stomach was threatening to burst out of my body, my head to pop with adrenalin.

"Well, git in," he finally said.

I sat on the edge of the seat inspecting my beat-up and bloody bare feet and thought about what I'd tell Linda. I was pretty excited, but I didn't know if I was mad, scared, or what. A sense of the pains in my neck and shoulders began to alert me to the physical world again, to let me back into my body. I'd stayed in my body through the fighting, but the moment it was over and I was running away, I was outside of myself peering down on events. I thought about this as the cabdriver made his way through town. Was this what happened to people when they died in fights or war? They probably just kept on doing the best they could to survive up to the very end when they either walked toward death, lay down and let it come or turned and ran so fast that maybe a few managed to outrun it. I was cold, trembling, and sweating at the same time. My head, arms and legs reverberated with dull, heavy thuds, his fists still broadcasting blows, my flesh ringing with them, like big bells sounding, imprinting at an atomic level. By the time I arrived barefoot and disheveled at the foot of the sloping driveway, at the top of which stood a magnificent many-windowed modern house, I was a wreck.

I knocked, asked for Linda and when she finally emerged, flawlessly made-up face peering from the other side of the door, saying, "Who? Who wants me?" I launched into my tale.

"I wasn't doing anything . . ." I bellowed. "I was sitting in the living room chair."

Soon onlookers appeared from inside. All Big John and Linda's buddies from the lake, the high-toned clever crowd, slouched over their cocktail glasses. Someone paid the cab-driver. By this time, my white hair was blowing wild and black tears coursed down my grubby cheeks. Through gritted teeth, I gave them the whole fight, the blow-by-blow lowdown. The crowd looked on with strict attention, the lady of the house ahhing at climax points in the tale. The dentist's wife, raising her eyebrows, knocked back her drink. In unison, the men stepped back when I demonstrated how I had escaped Jack's hold.

"I was barefoot," I wailed, "how is that an even fight?"

Later, Big John told me I'd made quite a deep impression on their gang as my drama unfolded in sobbing scenes of recreated battle. I had given little thought to my audience or the outcome of my dramatic presentation, I was just getting Mam's honey boy back in the first and most direct way I could think of. Linda was furious as Big John bundled me into the car, but I couldn't tell if she was mad that I'd interrupted the party or mad at her brother.

Wish I could remember the exact date of that Saturday. I'd review my horoscope to pinpoint which planets caused the moil, then if the same planetary wild horse race ever formed again, I could stay in bed that day. And Billy? Billy never called again—which was definitely an ending but not the end of our story.

ARMITAGE HOUSE, MAY 21, 1999

I had wandered around the house, from window to window, following the light as the sun moved further into the front yard. I hadn't been proud of it, but several days after our last encounter, as mourners were leaving Loren Johnson's packed funeral, as friends and neighbors made their way down the mortuary aisle, I'd hung my head and stared at my hands so I wouldn't have to look at my mother. When I had arrived, she was already seated at the back, and although there was space near her, I had continued down the aisle, past the Calefs and Osbornes, and slid in next to Edward and some of the Lawrence cousins, all dressed in their good suits and looking uncomfortable in the heat.

It had felt peculiar to be attending Loren's funeral. A smallish, wiry man, he had been a newcomer to our part of the valley. After Jack died he'd bought the acreage from Virgie, and he had seemed old even then. The retired owner of an electric company, his passion was hunting big game, elk, moose, and bear, packing his gear on mule teams. Mam said the family must have come from the west side because she'd never heard of them. During the next twenty years, he had never seemed to grow any older and we had never quite become used to them (and their confounded mules) living on what Mam and I had considered our property. But finally, we'd had to accept them and forgive them (for everything but the pink plastic flamingos looming among Virgie's peonies). Then, when he was only 79, while backing out of the drive, he'd dropped dead. The car had drifted into the ditch, back wheels and trunk sunk in the blackberry hedge, and sat there running until his son found him.

During the service, I could feel my mother's eyes on me

and had wanted to turn and look back, but I didn't. I felt so hardened because earlier that morning I'd looked at several properties trying to find land where if the worst came, I could move the house. I had learned that property in our area was worth too much to sell piecemeal for house lots, and what was available, my mother was right, I could not afford. The real estate person reported that other city and county land use laws had made it so only the rich, or the very lucky, could finance a development then carry through on the lengthy process of approvals for new building sites, and this had driven lot prices way up. Not only that, but the county had passed a new law declaring that big lots could be divided into much smaller parcels than previously so all the medium to large old places were not selling. Their owners were waiting for the new law to take effect. It would mean even more money.

Arriving home from the funeral, I had pulled up and parked under my tree. I considered walking to the river but felt exhausted with emotion and the energy outflow of trying to figure out what to do. I certainly could not pay the jacked-up land price then pay more to move the 100-plus-year-old house, then add the costs to practically rebuild it and have it set on a new foundation. I had thought of applying to someone for a loan, but who would lend to a graduate student who already had no money, and because I didn't have the title, no collateral? No one. Maybe I could find land farther out, but transport would also be too costly, the journey too risky for a house so big, so old, so a part of its place on Armitage Road. I didn't think we'd live through it.

I had a lot of fight in me, a lot of pain and sadness too, but there was nowhere to assign it—finally it all turned back to me. I was alone, and mourned that I felt a coward, not strong enough to take them all on. I couldn't do it alone. I had no significant savings. No proof of ownership either as I had trusted Linda to keep the records. I had no support. Not Elsie who was sympathetic to Linda's plight, nor Mel who was working out of the country. Not even Jim.

He'd said, "Getting into a mess like this is like walking into an exploding grenade. It's your family. I'm out."

Why couldn't any of them see that it was the sheer beauty of the land that made the Armitage place so valuable? Why did they only speak of it in terms of troubles and money?

I sat in the living room chair looking into the sunset trying not to think. As the sun hit the porch step, the phone rang. I didn't want to talk to anyone. Anyone except a former renter then a law student, now a lawyer. But I wasn't ready for that either. Talking to a lawyer would make things feel too real, like something was truly happening. I let it ring, suddenly thinking of the night earlier that spring when they had called to tell Jim his brother was dead. I opened the side window looking out on the filbert orchard and took a deep breath. It was painful. And had grown even more painful at the thought of the amount of work that might have to be done in the space of three months. I felt for Jim, with his brother just dead and this happening. The ringing had continued. I pushed myself from the window and the past, trying to put my thoughts in some order. After considering what the real estate person said, I supposed if the worst did happen, I'd look for a house to rent or try to buy. A place to transport the furniture—and my life. It was the practical thing to do, but on even touching the idea of leaving, it had felt like a terrifying weapon had been thrust into me, paining not only my body but my soul.

Moving to the front door, I stepped onto the porch and stood looking over the small field toward the ranch house next door. Standing there as I had so many times, on good days and other days of sadness and trouble, I felt a rising of hope to see the ranch solid as always, so plain and lovely, so unchanging. And The Armitage House had seen a lot of change in its one hundred and fifty years but had weathered everything. It was stable; its history only added to its goodness. It was forever. Linda could not do this. She was my mother after all, and in some deep part of me I not only instinctively felt bound to trust her but consciously chose trust to replace my fears. I believed that when it came to acting my mother would not betray me—or herself.

The phone rang again, and I answered it.

PREVIEW OF

Younger Women

BOOK TWO OF THE OREGON SERIES

EMERALD CITY, OREGON JUNE 1, 1999

So much for intuition or knowing. If I had even a tiny clue of what would come about from the morning visit, I would have been miles away rather than walking up the broad steps of the stone building in downtown Emerald City. There, according to my mother, Linda, we would find the office of the man who would help us "solve everything."

"Annie?" she'd said earlier that week when I had finally decided to pick up the phone. "Annie? Oh, there you are! I just had the best talk with an old friend of your grandad, and I am just so excited. He is the attorney Granddad used at the bank and they were friends for years. He said he thought he could help us straighten out the situation with the place. We have an appointment Tuesday morning at 10:00."

I had trusted my grandfather and despite her bewildering behavior and horrible husband, I had made a recent decision to trust my mother. "I'll drive," I said and set the phone on its cradle.

We were about halfway to town when I noticed that she carried nothing but one of her smaller purses. "You have Grandad's will with you? Right?"

"Oh," she said exhaling loudly. "I can't believe I forgot to get it. It's at the bank but William has a copy." She looked at her watch.

William?

"We'll be late if we have to go back."

The office was wide and light with windows of billowing trees along the back wall, the side walls hung with certificates, awards, and framed photographs. A thin, dark-haired man rose from behind a curved desk and, smoothing his tie, held out a hand. He helped my mother to a chair on the left, patting the shoulder of her black watch coat. Her "good" casual look. She looked up at him and smiled her best smile. Moving to me, taking my hand, murmuring, "William Stevens. Please call me William," he indicated a chair on his right, guided me to it then sat behind his desk. He wasn't as old as Granddad had been. He was more my mother's age, maybe older, but it was hard to tell. The suit fit perfectly but didn't do much to set off features which seemed totally unremarkable and, in their plainness, showed little of his character, yet my impression was one of contained energy. The curve of his lips said he was friendly but his eyes, which considered me, were a luminous hazel, cold and sharply focused.

"I was a real fan of your grandfather," he said with a smile that seemed painful. "Coach Chapman was the best. I ran in school then went to Oregon to have him coach me. We found out I wasn't good for much besides the 200-yard dash and Oregon already had Mack Robinson then. Your granddad helped me anyway. He helped me figure out how to make the best of the strong qualities I did have. He's the reason I went to law school and the first to trust me with a case." His long hands were folded on the desk, a gold signet ring staring at me. "I've done a little research into this, and we'll clear it all up. We want to do the best for you and the family. It's all about family, isn't it?"

"I want to make sure his will is honored." I said. "He wanted the kids and I to have the house and the three acres that go with it."

"Yes. It's here," he said gesturing to a stack of papers on the desk. "I know you wouldn't ever want to stand in the way of what's best for you all." He didn't wait for me to reply but rambled on. "I hear that you are a great reader. I am too. Who is your favorite author?"

Who's my favorite author? Isn't he odd? "Faulkner. Faulkner's the best writer I've read. The Snopes Trilogy. Or Pasternak. Have you read *Dr. Zhivago*?"

He looked at me fully, a probing stare, then smiled over at my mother. "Faulkner! Well, there's a family for you all right." My mother chuckled, although I didn't think she'd ever read the books. He said, "I read Faulkner in college. Rough stuff then." Smiling still, "I'm more into James Bond these days."

"Now let's get this county paperwork in order," he said, opening a file. "It will help you right now by giving you a bigger tax refund because the estate will assume the tax burden for both properties. In the future if your mother does decide to sell the property, joining them will make it much more valuable to you both. I've had years of experience with these situations. This is the best plan.

If? "So, you mean she hasn't sold it?" I was tempted to look at my mother but didn't.

"She has not," he said, opening the folder in front of him. From the side of my eye, I glimpsed my mother looking at her watch.

I sensed my whole body relaxing and felt as if I might elevate from my chair and keep on rising up and out of the room.

"This just makes good sense," he said, pushing the papers across the desk toward me. "I know what family means to you. You're a good girl. You'd never want to sue your mother."

Acknowledgements

My thanks to:

Bill McEldowney who encouraged me to aim high.

Kris Daines and Jill Richards Young, who have continually believed in the Oregon series, read countless drafts, asked the right questions, shared many pots of soup and much laughter.

Jan Kelly, author, kind friend, and reader, not only for her unwavering encouragement and faith in the project but for generously sharing her insights on writing, publishing, and publicity (and sunny afternoons of research).

Bernadette Murphy, author of *Harley and Me*, who inspired me with her courage and will.

Mentors and friends, Alberto Rios, Ron Carlson, Melissa Pritchard, and Jay Boyer who saw *Faster Horses* when it was an ungainly colt with legs that wouldn't quite support it.

To Trish Murphy, dear friend, and poet, without whose friendship and support this book would not have been written.

About the Author

Judith Clayton Van was born into a family of early Oregon pioneers, grew up on a Willamette Valley horse ranch, attended the University of Oregon, and later became involved with the music industry which led to owning night clubs, booking bands, and promoting concerts. She completed a BFA in Painting, then an MFA in Creative Writing at Arizona State University. From 1989 to 2011, she served ASU as an Instructor of English, Director of Harry Wood Gallery, Fiction Editor of Hayden's Ferry Review, and Art Editor for Superstition Review. She also performed for, taught, and mentored creative writing students for fifteen years as a juried literary artist with the Arizona Commission on the Arts. Judith lives in Oregon with her partner, Bill, where they keep a garden.

About Atmosphere Press

Atmosphere Press is an independent, full-service publisher for excellent books in all genres and for all audiences. Learn more about what we do at atmospherepress.com.

We encourage you to check out some of Atmosphere's latest releases, which are available at Amazon.com and via order from your local bookstore:

Staged, a novel by Elsie G. Beya

A Grip of Trees, a novel by Philip Erfan

DEAD LEGENDS: On the Heels of the Earl: A Randal Murphy Mystery, by G. R. Miller

Yellow on Blonde, a novel by Stephen M. King

A Gathering of Broken Mirrors: Memories of New York Survivors, a novel by Anthony E. Shaw

Hey, White Girl, a novel by Judith Bice

Moratorium, a novel by Gary Percesepe

Telling Shadows, a novel by Deborah Partington

CPSIA information can be obtained
at www.ICGtesting.com
Printed in the USA
BVHW081545210622
640292BV00003B/436